A GOOD MAN GONE

Mercy Watts Mysteries Book One

A.W. HARTOIN

ALSO BY A.W. HARTOIN

Afterlife Issues

Dead Companions (Afterlife Issues Book One)

A Trunk, a Canoe, and all the Barbecue (Afterlife Issues Book Two)

Old Friends and Fedoras (Afterlife Issues Book Three)

Mercy Watts Mysteries

Novels

A Good Man Gone (Mercy Watts Mysteries Book One)

Diver Down (A Mercy Watts Mystery Book Two)

Double Black Diamond (Mercy Watts Mysteries Book Three)

Drop Dead Red (Mercy Watts Mysteries Book Four)

In the Worst Way (Mercy Watts Mysteries Book Five)

The Wife of Riley (Mercy Watts Mysteries Book Six)

My Bad Grandad (Mercy Watts Mysteries Book Seven)

Brain Trust (Mercy Watts Mysteries Book Eight)

Down and Dirty (Mercy Watts Mysteries Book Nine)

Small Time Crime (Mercy Watts Mysteries Book Ten)

Bottle Blonde (Mercy Watts Mysteries Book Eleven)

Mean Evergreen (Mercy Watts Mysteries Book Twelve)

Silver Bells at Hotel Hell (Mercy Watts Mysteries Book Thirteen)

Short stories

Coke with a Twist

Touch and Go

Nowhere Fast

Dry Spell

A Sin and a Shame

For Mark
He is my North, my South, my East, my West.

CHAPTER ONE

I crouched on the edge of my parents' bed, my toes gripping the side board until I stood and let fly. I fell, eyes closed, into the marshmallow fluff of what my mother called The Oasis. I lay face down, sinking into the double layers of down, smelling Mom's perfume and feeling the stress flow out of me. Heaven. It didn't get any better. Well, maybe a mouth full of dark chocolate would've upped the ante, but it was pretty much bliss, especially after my last two weeks.

I'd just finished a double shift in St. James's emergency room, at time-and-a-half, thank you very much. Two and a half weeks in any ER was way too much. I was sick to death of drunk-driving accidents and ear infections. Lucky for me, I didn't have to go back. I worked PRN, which meant I worked through an agency and filled in when somebody was short a nurse. I didn't love being a nurse, but I liked it. Which was something I couldn't quite explain. People thought nursing was warm and fuzzy, helping people, curing the ill, all that crap. For me, it meant getting vomited on or felt up at least once a week. I seemed to bring it out in people, the worst, I mean. I walked into the room and people did what they quickly wished they hadn't. But still I liked nursing, and I was good at it. There's a lot to be said for being good at something and, occasionally, people were grateful. Plus, I set my own hours. That was the part that my dad loved. I could set my schedule to suit him. It was enough to make me consider a permanent position.

That morning I went to my parent's house instead of my apartment. I promised to check their messages, water plants, feed the cats, file and straighten out any messes that cropped up. They were on a cruise, their first real vacation in years. Usually, they combined vacations with work. Dad was a retired St. Louis police detective turned private investigator and Mom was his assistant, if you go by titles. In reality, she was more of a partner and even nosier than Dad.

Instead of listening to Dad's messages or feeding Mom's evil Siamese, I went to bed. Sleep, beautiful sleep—I never got enough. Plus, the opportunity to snooze in my parents' bed didn't come up very often. I loved their bed. It was an 1850s plantation cannonball bed with the best quality down and bedding. Anything less than a five-hundred-thread count was a sin in Mom's estimation. My mother knew how to make a bed.

I slept like I was sedated until noon, when the phone rang. Coming to took awhile, and I had a lovely floaty feeling in my stomach. I tried to ignore the ringing, but it was Mom's landline. Dad still insisted on having landlines but not one of those old-school answering machines, so it just kept ringing. Another good sleep ruined by reality. I hated that. Reality pissed me off, especially reality in my parents' bed. Getting a call there was twice as irritating as anywhere else.

"Hello," I said, sounding as grumpy as possible. You never knew, maybe they'd have a heart and hang up.

"Carolina?"

"No, it's Mercy," I said.

It was a woman, her voice distant and strange, yet familiar. She said nothing else for a moment, and the pleasant feeling in my stomach melted away. The background noise was familiar, too. I'd been a part of it only a few hours earlier. Whoever she was, she was in an ER.

"Can I help you?" I said.

"It's Sharon."

Sharon, Sharon. I probably knew half a dozen Sharons. I couldn't place this one.

"Okay. Sharon who?"

"Sharon Flouder, your mother's best friend."

That's why I couldn't place her. I'd called her Dixie from the moment I could talk, like Gavin, her husband, did. Some people insisted on calling her Sharon. She looked more like a Dixie to me.

"What's wrong?" I asked.

"Is Carolina there? Or Tommy?"

"No, they're on that cruise."

"Oh, God." She started to cry in short, tight bursts.

"What's wrong?"

"Gavin's dead." She said it slowly, in a kind of rhythm between her sobs.

An electric chill went through me. Gavin dead at fifty-five. That couldn't be right. "What happened? Where are you?"

She didn't answer.

"Dixie, please," I said. "Where are you?"

She continued to cry, but I could hear her pulling it together. From the sound of her voice, it took quite a bit of effort.

"St. James's," she said after a moment.

"I'll be right there."

I burrowed out from under the duvet and brushed the hair out of my eyes. I'd forgotten to pull the shades and light streamed in through Mom's gauzy curtains. They billowed up as the air conditioner kicked on and floated in the air, lazy and beautiful. It was silent other than the machinery and I was sleep-drunk and confused. It couldn't be real. Dixie did not just tell me Gavin was dead. He couldn't be dead. Plenty of people die, just not my people. I rubbed my eyes and looked at the phone sitting on the bedside table. It gave no clue whether or not I'd just been speaking into it.

I flopped back onto Mom's pillows, grabbed the phone and dialed St. James ER. I closed my eyes and listened to the ringing, imagining the clerks and nurses yelling at each other to pick up the phone.

On the sixth ring, someone did. "St. James ER. May I help you?"

"This is Mercy Watts. I need to know if you have a patient there."

"Hey Mercy, it's Evelyn. Who's the patient?"

"Gavin Flouder."

"Yeah, we got him," she said.

"Is he dead?" I asked, squeezing my eyes tighter.

"Yep. He wasn't one of yours, was he?"

"No, he's a family friend. Thanks, Evelyn." I hung up and let out a whoosh of breath. It was real. I opened my eyes and looked around my parents' room. I said it was my parents' room, but it was Mom's. It had her woven into its very fabric, its wood, its paint. Her Lalique perfume bottles glimmered in the light on her dressing table and I could smell their scent even at my distance. I lay there on The Oasis, the altar of the sacred bedroom, and wished she was there looking at her precious things and, damn it, answering her own phone.

But, of course, Mom wasn't there. Mothers are like cops, never around when you need one. So I slid out of The Oasis and landed painfully on my heels. The bed was four feet high. Dad built a step for Mom, so she could get into it.

I leaned against the bed and rubbed my bare ankles. Crap. No decent clothes. The ratty T-shirt and the scrubs I'd worn home were lying in a pile and covered with unknown substances. I'd have to borrow something from Mom. She wouldn't like that, but under the circumstances, how could she complain?

I straightened up and trotted across the glossy wood floor dotted with various Oriental rugs to the wardrobe. It was an enormous beast, ten feet by six, and at that time of year, it held Mom's summer clothes. I turned the large brass key and the right door swung open without a sound. That used to creep me out when I was a kid. My best friend Ellen and I spent rainy days crawling around in its depths, waiting for magic to happen. Dad told me Grandma George shipped it over from England and it was *the* wardrobe from *The Lion, the Witch and the Wardrobe*. I didn't notice till I was ten that my parents' bedroom furniture matched. All five pieces were the same dark walnut with delicate carvings of birds. I guess I was a dense kid, but I never thought about it. Lord knew nothing else in our house matched, not even the dining room chairs. How was I to know it was a family suite passed down five generations?

The wardrobe glowed with a rainbow of colors. They were so

Mom. To the far left, I found a pair of black shorts and a crisp white linen shirt. They were only one size too big. I'd seen my future, and it wasn't half bad. I pulled them off their hangers and reached to close the door. At the last second, I stopped and shoved my arm between Mom's sundresses. I strained until my fingertips touched the unfinished wood at the back. Oh well, better luck next time.

I dressed, gargled with Dad's industrial-strength mouthwash, and ran down the stairs to the first floor.

The Siamese weren't there yowling at me, threatening to shred my ankles, so I ignored their bowls, and went for the espresso machine. Super-automatic is the way to go. Even I could handle pressing a button.

I found my nursing shoes in the butler's pantry. They looked worse than my scrubs. Oh well, nobody ever looked at my feet, anyway. While I put on my shoes, the smell of espresso filled the kitchen and the promise of caffeine awakened the rest of my brain. I tossed back a double, shuddered, and rinsed out my mouth.

Gavin was dead. He really was dead. I considered calling Ellen for moral support, but she'd just cry, so no more delays. Just suck it up and go.

I walked past my truck and got in Dad's baby, a brand-new Chrysler 300S. If I had to go deal with death, at least I could do it in luxury. It took me five minutes to pull it out of the garage into the alley. If I damaged his car the phrase "hell to pay" wouldn't cover Dad's reaction. Driving Dad's car, wearing Mom's clothes, it was bad enough to almost feel good. If I could've gotten Dixie's voice out of my head, I might've smiled. I couldn't, so I concentrated on not getting a ticket on the way to the hospital.

St. James is the biggest hospital complex in St. Louis and the parking's a pain. Spaces near the ER are at a premium, so I parked illegally next to the never-ending construction on the doctor's building.

"Hey Al, check out this rack," a voice yelled from the construction area.

I locked my door and ignored the voice.

"Come on, baby, let those titties bounce," said a second voice.

Great. Construction workers. They were one of those stereotypes that were a stereotype for a reason.

"Drop dead, troglodyte," I said.

"Nice. Sassy and stacked."

I slung my purse over my shoulder and flashed them the bird.

"She's wet for me, Al. Holy shit, look at that ass," said the first voice.

I walked away from the construction, trying not to bounce, and into the ambulance bay. Once into the ER, I looked for someone I knew. I saw the charge nurse jogging down the hall from the direction of the lab.

"Hey Claire. You got a Gavin Flouder in here?" I asked.

"Thank God you're back. I had three sick calls. Can you believe that? Hurry up and change. We've got two MVAs coming in," Claire said. She wasn't much of a listener, but a damn good nurse. Maybe she loved it. She never seemed to go home.

"I'm not here to work. I'm looking for Gavin Flouder, a family friend. His wife called and said he was here."

Claire pursed her lips and put her hands on her hips. She glared at me through thick glasses and said, "What's he in for?"

"Uh, I don't know. She said he was dead."

"Old white guy?"

"Yeah."

"He's in six. MI." With that she did an about face, jogged to the desk, picked up a phone and yelled into it.

A myocardial infarction. Gavin's heart stopped. I stood in the hall and absorbed the information. I expected a car accident or a fall off the roof. Gavin was putting the roof on the cabin he'd built for Dixie. He'd worked on that sucker for at least ten years. Until recently, he was too fat and out of shape to get much done. Dad said they'd both be dead before he finished. Now he was halfway to being right.

I walked toward Room 6, my stomach tightening with every step. I flashed back over the last two weeks. How many people had I seen die? Probably three or four. It'd been bloody, but I couldn't remember much about it. Those people faded into a jumble of patients and rooms in the back of my mind. I forgot them easily and any pain I felt at their deaths wouldn't be felt again. Room 6 wouldn't be like that. I'd remember it and Gavin lying in there forever. I didn't want the memory, but it was unavoidable. Dad would say it was my duty to go in there and get that memory. He'd be right because Gavin was like family and you don't let family down. No matter what it cost you.

I walked to Room 6 and stood outside with my fingers pressed against the cold metal of the swinging door. I didn't decide to go in, but before I knew it, I'd pushed the door open and walked inside. The floor was littered with the paper smocks the staff used while treating Gavin. Thankfully, there was no blood. I guess there wasn't a point in cracking his chest. His body, when I was able to look at it, was covered in a white sheet with the words St. James Mercy Medical Center printed in blue on it. I'd never noticed how many times they printed it on the sheets. Apparently, they worried about theft, as if people were eager to steal hospital sheets. Then again, maybe they were. People steal some crazy shit from hospitals.

I walked up to Gavin's gurney and picked up the chart lying across his legs. It was Gavin, and Claire was right. MI. He was dead before he got there, but they'd made a good effort, anyway. I felt proud of the staff for trying. How many times did I see staff give up before even assessing the patient? Too many to count and I'd been in their number more than I cared to remember. Now Gavin was on the table and someone tried. I noted the doc's signature. Robert Guest. I didn't know him, but I'd seen him around. He worked traumas, and I was a temp, so I did all the crap the regular staff didn't want.

I reached up and brushed the tears off my cheeks. I don't know when they started. The front of my shirt was damp, and I wanted my father, my mother, and Gavin most of all. His body didn't look right under the sheet. It was too small, diminished from the man he'd been in life. Gavin, in my mind, would always have a potbelly. He was a big man. For a moment, I imagined it wasn't him. That there was a mix-up, and he sat upstairs on the ward, eating pudding and rubbing his stomach fondly.

"Mercy."

I jumped and turned to see Dixie standing in the doorway, her dark hair curled in soft waves around her pretty face. Her clothes looked like she was headed to a nice lunch with Mom. It was Dixie as she normally was, except that she held a cup of coffee, and it shook like we were having an earthquake. Coffee slopped over her fingers and dripped onto the floor. I put my arms around her. Neither of us said a thing. I felt the coffee's wet warmth spread onto my back.

She pulled away, looked at the cup, and said, "I'm sorry. I got you all wet."

"Don't worry about it."

"You came." She said it like there was a possibility I wouldn't.

"Of course I did. Can I call anyone else for you?"

"Not now." She smoothed her hair with her right hand. Her left continued to shake. I took the cup from her and tossed it into the trash. A nurse I didn't know walked in and gave us the once-over. We must've looked like we had it together because she said, "We need the room. I'm sorry. I'm going to have to have Mr..."

"Flouder," I said.

"Yes, sorry. Mr. Flouder transported to the morgue."

Dixie covered her eyes at the word morgue.

"Fine. Is Guest around? I'd like to speak to him, if I could."

"He's with another patient. It could be a while."

"I'll wait. Do you have the paperwork?" I put my arm around Dixie.

"Yeah, it'll be at the desk when you're ready."

"Right." I took Dixie's arm and walked her out of Room 6. We kept going until we left the ER and entered the main body of the hospital. People hurried by, not giving us a second glance. They seemed happy compared to the way I felt, but they couldn't be. Hospitals weren't filled with happy people, unless you counted obstetrics. It was a different world up there.

We sat down on a fat sofa across from the information desk. I looked at Dixie and she at me. I marveled at how normal she looked. Aside from her red eyes, she looked like the same old Dixie I'd known forever. She was dressed in a silk blouse and pants set. The burgundy color set off her pale skin and dark eyes. There was a certain air about her that spoke of 1940s movie stars and elegance. It didn't matter if she achieved it with makeup and scalpels. I looked at her and thought of Gavin lying on the cold table in Room 6. It seemed no more likely

Gavin could've left Dixie than he should've married her in the first place.

Gavin was big, gruff, with hair everywhere but the top of his head. His language made men blush and if I ever saw him in a clean shirt, one without drips of ketchup, grease or ink stains, I don't know when that was. Somehow, he and Dixie fit perfectly. How was a mystery to me, and I'm not the only one who was puzzled about it. Dixie was the woman other women aspire to be. She sat beside me looking perfect, as she always did, and I wondered what it would be like to be elegant and serene. Sure, I stopped traffic, but next to Dixie I was showy and garish. I wanted to be classy like her. With a look like mine, it wasn't going to happen.

"Do you want to tell me what happened?" I said.

"Sweetie, I don't know. I went out for my walk this morning and he was fine. When I came back, he was passed out in his office. When the EMTs got there, they said his heart was beating, but then it just stopped."

"I thought he had everything under control?"

Dixie clasped her shaking hands together. "He did. I thought he did. We did every single thing Dr. Kahn told us to do. The diet, exercise, medication, everything. You saw him. He lost forty pounds. His last checkup was wonderful. They lowered his meds. He was doing so well."

"When was that?" I asked.

"Oh, I don't know." Dixie pulled her iPhone out of her bag and punched a few buttons. "Three weeks ago on Friday."

"And everything was good? Did they do an echo? A stress test?"

"They did the full series. Dr. Kahn was very pleased, especially with the weight loss."

"We'll figure it out," I said.

"Will we?" she said, brushing a fresh tear off her face.

"Definitely. I'll take care of it. Do you want to go home now?"

"Home? What for?"

"Well, you could lie down for a while or something." I really didn't know what to do. Dixie waited for me to decide, to tell her what was next, and I hadn't a clue. I'd comforted people plenty of times before, but it was a short-lived operation. The bad news was broken, backs patted, calls made, coffee given, and they went on their way. I'd no idea what happened after they left the hospital. It wasn't my business to know. Mom should've been there. She'd know what to say, what funeral home to call, everything. But Mom was incommunicado, and I was on my own.

"Can I get you something, coffee or tea?" I sounded lame, even to myself.

"Tea," she said.

I think she wanted to give me something to do, or maybe she wanted to be alone. I went to the staff lounge and rooted through the cabinets till I came up with some chamomile and lemon zest. I didn't know which Dixie would want. I made the chamomile because that's what Dad drinks after a bad day.

I returned, measuring my strides, not anxious to get back. A group of nuns crossed my path, and I felt the warmth of the tea comforting me through the cup as I waited. Hot drinks did it for me. Whether it was a hot chocolate, mulled wine, or one of Dad's yummy hot toddies, I felt better the moment the cup hit my hands. Then a feather-light touch on my shoulder brought me out of my revelry.

"Mercy?"

I looked up into the ancient face of Sister Francis. I wondered how long she'd been standing there. She touched my shoulder again and said, "Are you alright, dear?"

I choked on the word yes. My throat was too hot and tight for words. I wished she hadn't asked. Her asking made me feel worse.

"Come sit down with me," she said.

I shook my head and said, "No." It came out more like a croak, but Sister understood.

"Please, dear. You don't look well." She took me by the elbow and guided me to the waiting room. She was strong for the world's oldest nun. I made the punch for her ninety-fourth birthday party last year. She was also the tallest, maybe six two in bare feet. My great aunt Miriam once told me Sister Francis joined the order because she was too tall to get married. Aunt Miriam and Sister Francis weren't the best of friends.

Great Aunt Miriam. I don't know why I didn't think of her before. She would know what to do. Shit. I was stupid. It was her job. She was a Sister of Mercy, too.

"Aunt Miriam," I said.

Sister Francis started and said, "Miriam? Has something happened to Miriam?"

"No. Sorry. I just realized I need to talk to her. Do you know where she is today?"

Her face hardened, then she said, "I wouldn't know. I believe she has a cellular phone."

Sister Francis didn't believe in cell phones. She thought they made a person too self-important. She was probably right, but then again, Sister Francis didn't believe in microwaves either.

"Thanks, Sister. I have to go."

"What's wrong? What's happened?"

"Family friend died. I have to call Aunt Miriam."

I found Dixie and gave her the tea. "I'll be right back."

Dixie probably had her cell phone on her, but it didn't seem polite to ask. I, of course, had a dead cell phone. It spent at least fifty percent of the time dead. Long battery life, my ass. Lucky for me, none of the hospital volunteers were on duty at the information desk and I didn't have to explain using the phone. Those ladies in pink were surprisingly territorial about their phone. I'd been told off more than once.

I did have the little address book that Mom insisted I carry because technology can't be counted on. Why was she always right? I dialed Aunt Miriam's number and waited. Aunt Miriam was notorious for being unable to find the on button on her phone. Her service invariably picked up. Once I called back four times before she figured it out. Aunt Miriam isn't as old as Sister Francis, but she's getting up there.

"Hello." It was a miracle, only two tries.

"Aunt Miriam, it's Mercy. Are you busy?"

"It's Tuesday. You know I'm at the council meeting and they're waiting," she said.

I didn't know. Why would she assume I kept up with her schedule?

"This is important," I said.

"I'm sure it is." Aunt Miriam sniffed.

"Gavin Flouder died. I'm at the hospital with Dixie."

"I'll be right there." She hung up without ceremony, and my chest flooded with relief. Aunt Miriam would take over and I was off the hook.

CHAPTER TWO

Before I knew it, I was staring at Aunt Miriam's shoes instead of the stained bit of carpet I'd been eying. My eyes went up from her black gum-soled shoes, past her compression hose, her dove gray A-line skirt with matching sweater to her wrinkled, thin face crowned by her veil. For me, her face wore an expression of critical appraisal. When she looked at Dixie, it softened to gentle concern. I wouldn't get that expression unless critically injured. Aunt Miriam sat down between us, put her arms around Dixie and gathered her into her bony chest. Dixie took a huge breath and her body began to rock with the slow rhythm of grief.

"I need to speak to the doc," I whispered to Aunt Miriam. She nodded in reply and I left.

Dr. Guest sat in the lounge doing chart review and drinking a chocolate diet drink. From the look of him, he needed to forego the candy bar next to the drink.

"Excuse me, Dr. Guest?"

He looked up, sucked in his belly, and smoothed his comb-over.

"Yes, I'm Dr. Guest." Emphasis on the doctor.

"Hi, I'm Mercy Watts, a friend of Gavin Flouder. I need to talk to you about his case?"

"I'm afraid that wouldn't be appropriate. You know you look a lot like..."

"Yeah, I know," I said, crossing my arms.

He stared at me. I expected him to start rocking like a hypnotized cobra.

"So...Dr. Sanderson will vouch for me. I was PRN here last night." I flashed him my hospital badge and hooked it to my waistband.

He looked at my badge and smiled in recognition. "What do you want to know?"

"Are you sure it was an MI? He was following a regime and was on meds."

"That's why I'm sure. These things happen and all the drugs and all the workout plans in the world can't stop them."

Not exactly the reassurance one wants from a doctor. Maybe that explained the candy.

"I understand that, but his wife would feel better if she knew what went wrong. He was pretty young. Were his drug levels adequate?"

"They were, but we don't know to what extent his heart was already damaged."

"Will you recommend a full autopsy?"

"No. Cause of death is apparent."

"But they'll do one if the family makes the request, right?" I asked.

"Of course. What do you suspect?"

"Not a thing. I think his wife wants to know it was unavoidable. Do you think you could write her a script for Ativan? She's pretty freaked out."

Dr. Guest gave me an evaluating look, pulled out a prescription pad. "What's her name?"

"Sharon Flouder."

"I'm only giving you two doses. If she needs more, she'll have to go to her family doctor."

"Thanks. I appreciate it," I said.

"No problem. Have time for a cup of coffee?"

"Some other time. The wife's waiting. Thanks again."

The diagnosis was exactly what I expected to hear, but I didn't like it. Gavin did everything right, and he was still dead as hell. I wished he'd spent his last year eating Ho Ho's and lying around, instead of eating salads and working out. He would've been happier, even if Dixie wasn't.

I ran next door to the pharmacy, got Dixie's Ativan, collected Gavin's paperwork, and went back to the sofa. Dixie wasn't crying anymore. She sat with a dazed expression on her face, looking at her hands. I showed her where to sign the forms and asked her if she wanted an autopsy.

"I don't know." Dixie looked at me like she wasn't sure what I was asking.

"Why don't we leave it for now? I'll ask for a full chart review," I said.

Dixie nodded. I took care of the paperwork and review request. Then I went back to the sofa, feeling drained and very young. Maybe that's what it feels like when you lose someone for the first time. I went back to feeling like a child in a big world without a compass.

I dropped onto the seat next to Aunt Miriam and she said to Dixie, "Who would you like us to call?"

"I don't want to talk to anyone," said Dixie.

"We'll do it."

I hoped by 'we' she didn't mean me. Gavin and Dixie didn't have children, but they were very close to his brothers. I couldn't imagine telling them their little brother died. It'd be a nightmare. I'd have to tell Mom and Dad. That was bad enough.

Dixie gave Aunt Miriam her phone, and I edged away, hiding my hands under my butt, so Aunt Miriam wouldn't give it to me. Lame, but it was the only way I could think of to protect myself from that awful duty.

Aunt Miriam put the phone in her little grey purse and said, "I think it's time to go now, Mercy."

"Where are we going?"

"Home, naturally," she replied.

"I don't want to go home," said Dixie as she looked from Aunt Miriam to me and then back.

"Let's go to Mom and Dad's," I said. "Mom'll be pissed if I don't water the plants and feed the cats."

"That'll be fine," Dixie said.

Aunt Miriam gave me a rare smile, and we left. The traffic was vicious, and it took us forty-five minutes. The drive gave Dixie some time to collect herself, and her eyes were clearer when we got there. We sat Dixie down in Mom's enormous kitchen and Aunt Miriam put the kettle on. I went into the butler's pantry to find more tea and some hot cocoa for me.

Hmmm, Ghirardelli.

Nothing like chocolate for cold or heartbreak. I'd had enough of both to know. Mom served it up with little marshmallows and Dad with a splash of peppermint schnapps. Dad forbade me to tell Mom about the schnapps, but I suspect she knew.

Dixie, being a sensible woman, chose the Ghirardelli. I pulled out the prescription bottle and placed it on the table.

"What's that?" Aunt Miriam asked.

"Ativan. Dr. Guest gave me a script for Dixie in case she has trouble sleeping."

"You think I need Ativan?" Dixie looked at the prescription bottle like she'd never seen one before.

"No, but I thought you might want it. It was just a thought," I said.

Dixie looked into her mug and then at Aunt Miriam.

"Take some if you care to. Everyone needs help now and again," Aunt Miriam said.

I doubted very seriously that Aunt Miriam ever needed help of any kind. She never took so much as an aspirin. At least she didn't tell me what to do with my little pills. She would've if she felt it was a bad idea.

Dixie read the label and took two small white pills. While they dissolved into her system, I made sandwiches. Then we ate and talked about the weather, the Blues hockey team, and topics that didn't matter one bit. After an hour, Dixie's eyelids drooped, and I took her upstairs to The Oasis. I slipped her shoes off and tucked her in with a glass of water on the side table. She was asleep before I left the room.

Aunt Miriam was standing in the kitchen with her arms crossed when I got back.

"What?" I said.

"What did that doctor say?"

"Not much. Just that he didn't know how much heart damage Gavin had before he started taking care of himself."

"And?" Her fists went to her hips, not that they had much to rest on.

"And what? The man had a heart condition."

"He was doing extremely well. He nearly got a clean bill of health at his last checkup. Dixie is very concerned."

"What's she concerned about? It's over and done with now." I sat down and picked up my mug. What was Aunt Miriam trying to say? It wasn't my fault Gavin died. Hell, I wasn't even there.

"She's concerned that he didn't receive adequate care, and this could've been avoided. Now, what are you going to do about it?"

"Me?"

"Of course you. Your father isn't here." She sounded like she resented Dad's vacation. Maybe she did. She didn't take vacations outside of her retreats with the church ministry.

"Well, I guess I could look at the pathologist's report. That should clear a few things up. I'll call Mom and Dad."

"Yes, do that. I'll call Straatman Funeral Home. They're the best." Aunt Miriam's expression went all flinty and cold like a raptor. Straatman's were known for putting on a great memorial and, also and less flattering, predatory practices in the funeral biz. But they hadn't experienced Aunt Miriam yet. I almost felt sorry for the chiseling bastards.

"How long will Dixie sleep?" asked Aunt Miriam.

"Probably all night," I said.

Aunt Miriam stood, straightened her veil and tucked a few faded ginger hairs in. She gave me a hard look and left through the back door. I got up, made some more cocoa, and called Ellen. She cried and then had to go because her two-year-old, Sophie, found the house keys and was trying to escape out the back door. I liked to think that little blond devil took after me. Ellen was at her wit's end most of the time.

I settled in and turned on the TV. The news was on and, for some reason, I expected Gavin's death to be reported. Something like "Celebrated St. Louis police detective dies at age 55", but, of course, there was nothing like that. The talk was of our beautiful June weather and a couple of ghastly murders that I tuned out. Gavin was more than enough death to think about.

After a couple of fortifying cups of cocoa, I went upstairs to my father's office. His whole life was in his room, books, files, photo albums, and, most important, his desk. The desk was a veteran of his police career. He took the beast with him when he retired and, boy, was it ugly despite the coat of paint Mom insisted upon. Dad likes to say there's a dent for every case he worked on and he was a police detective for twenty years. The beast resembled a pale gray boulder with legs. The drawers didn't open anymore. Every once in a while, Dad enlisted my help to try and get them open. About once a year, he got it into his head that vital information is contained within them. We've never succeeded, so who knows?

I sank down into Dad's deluxe, black leather massage chair. I flipped the switch and let the magic fingers go to work on my butt. After a few minutes of sublime pleasure, I looked over the desktop. Mom had told me she left their travel itinerary on Dad's blotter. I called the number for the cruise line and got the runaround for a half hour. I lied and said it was a family emergency, but it didn't help much. But if I'd said Gavin wasn't a blood relative, they would've hung up. So much for customer service. After a few well-placed threats, I got a call put through. My parents didn't answer their phone or their page. My head was down on the blotter and I was about to start banging. They were probably sitting in a Jacuzzi tub sipping margaritas, looking at the Mediterranean sea. I hated to ruin it. Even so, they had to be told. The cruise was three weeks long, and they were five days out. By the time they got back, Gavin would be buried, and I'd never be forgiven. I left a message and went to check on Dixie.

I found her sleeping in the spoon position with a pillow. Her dark hair fanned out around her head and I saw some gray peeking out at the roots. I looked at the gray for a while. I'd never imagined Dixie to have any gray, although I knew she was older than Gavin. Her face was soft in sleep and without the animation of wakefulness; I could see wrinkles beneath the heavy powder she wore. I wanted to curl up behind her the way my mother did with me when I was hurting. Instead, I brushed a lock of hair off her cheek and went downstairs.

I got Dixie's address book out of her purse and called her doctor. I explained the situation, and he called in a prescription for Ativan for her. I could pick it up for her later, provided she needed it.

The phone rang as soon as I set it down.

"Hello," I said.

"Mercy, it's Mom. What's happened? Are the cats alright?"

"The cats are fine." Unfed, but fine. At least, I assumed so. I hadn't actually seen them, and I considered it the only good thing that happened that day. "I'm fine, by the way."

"Please, just tell me. I knew something would happen if we went away. What was I thinking?"

"It's Gavin, Mom. He died."

Mom didn't answer. I heard a slow release of breath and then nothing.

"Mom?"

"Mercy, it's Dad. What happened? Your mother is bleach white. Are you pregnant?"

"God, no. What made you say that?"

"Well, I always thought you'd hit us with that one at a bad time. Like when you set the Bleds' garage on fire when we went skiing."

"I was seven."

"You're due. Now what is it this time?"

"Gavin died."

Dad let his breath out like Mom and said, "What happened?"

"He had an MI, a heart attack, this morning."

"How's Dixie?"

"Sleeping upstairs," I said.

"Are you sure it was his heart?"

"He did have a heart condition, Dad."

"Did you talk to the doc?" Dad started to sound like an investigator, all business.

"Yeah, but he wasn't much help."

"Was he single?"

"What does that matter?" I needed cocoa with more than a splash of schnapps.

"You could've pulled out the charm, batted your eyelashes."

"I never bat my eyelashes."

"Fine, the equivalent then. Can we get back on point, please?"

"And what is the point, Dad?" Maybe I'd skip the cocoa altogether and go to straight schnapps.

"So the guy didn't know anything?" Dad asked.

"Not a thing. I'll check the final report as soon as it's finished," I said.

"Yeah, and see if you can get Simon on it."

"Simon who?" I asked.

"Simon Grace. The head pathologist at St. James."

"How do you know him?"

"How do I know every pathologist in the state? Think, Mercy," Dad said.

"One of your employees could talk to Grace. You know, one of the actual detectives," I said, without much hope.

Dad growled, very much like Aunt Miriam, though not quite as scary. "Are you saying you're unwilling to look into the suspicious death of a man you've known since birth? A man who took you camping, fixed your speeding tickets, picked you up drunk from frat parties, and employed you when you weren't qualified to do anything."

"Never mind. I'll pay Grace a visit," I said, my face in a hard flush.

"That's right, you will, and you'll be happy to do it."

"Absolutely, Dad. I'm on it."

"We'll fly home as soon as we pull into port."

"When's that?" I asked, trying not to sound desperate.

"Three days. And don't forget about the Smith file. You can take care of that while you wait for Gavin's report."

"The Smith file? Are you serious? Gavin just died, Dad."

Dad got quiet and then said in a low voice, "I know my friend is dead. No one, except Dixie, feels it more than me. But there's no point in sitting on your hands while you wait for that report. I want my money before that old fart drops. He'd do it just to spite me."

I rubbed my eyes and groaned. I'd forgotten about the Smith file the moment my parents passed through airport security. Dad was forever giving me assignments, none of which I wanted, but I did them slowly and with plenty of reminders. I thought I was free for the duration of their cruise. I should've known it wouldn't be that easy.

"If I must," I said.

"You must. Call me if anything develops?"

"Like what?" I said as I grabbed Dad's schnapps and added a generous amount to my mug.

"You know what I'm talking about. Call Chuck if you need help."

Chuck was a detective in the STLPD and my cousin by marriage. He was also the head of the sleazeball brigade. Calling him would never happen. "I don't need Chuck. I can handle anything."

"Be careful, Mercy," said Dad, more serious than I'd ever heard him. "I have a feeling."

I hung up without delving deeper into Dad's feeling. First, the Smith file and now this. Fantastic. I knew Dad's reputation well enough to know it wasn't a good thing. Like most good cops, Dad seemed to have an extra sense. He knew when things were about to get messy. I hated messy, unless it was my apartment. Then it was just fine.

CHAPTER THREE

The next day, I put on a red wrap dress and a pair of peep-toe stilettos. If I had to take care of Dad's problem, I wanted it over quickly. In my experience, slinky red dresses are good for that. And the Smith file wouldn't be easy. It was one of those pesky payment defaults Mom usually dealt with. Gerald Smith had hired my dad to find his first wife, Ursula, who divorced him about thirty seconds after he came back from WWII. Gerald's second wife died a year ago, and he needed a replacement. He thought finding Ursula was easier than recruiting a whole new woman, providing Ursula was still alive. She was, but not at all eager to reconnect with Gerald. She told Dad that if Gerald tried to contact her again, she'd have him shot.

That was six months ago. Gerald refused to pay because Ursula wanted to shoot him. He thought Dad must've put it to her wrong, and it was Dad's fault that he didn't have his replacement wife. He was hungry and his house was a disaster area. Gerald thought Dad should pony up for a housekeeper and cook, preferably Filipino.

I spent the morning driving around looking for Gerald, who despite his eighty-nine years was on the go from sunrise. I went to his house, his health club, the coffee shop he frequented, his chiropractor, his friend Ed's house, his favorite bar, and finally got a tip that the VFW was having a shindig at two.

Shindig was right. The Ballwin VFW's parking lot was full, and the street was parked up for two blocks. I took off my heels and stood on the hot pavement looking up at the beautiful brick mansion the VFW had destroyed with weird additions and a red, white, and blue paint job. I joined the queue of elderly walking to a side door. They were all men in various states of disintegration and wearing hats weighed down with medals, ribbons, and pins. Their skinny necks and sparse hair made them look like the buzzard from the Bugs Bunny cartoons, but they hobbled along, smiling and laughing. I remembered how long it'd been since I'd seen my grandpa. He was a Vietnam vet, and technically old, but it was hard to connect him with those weathered men. Grandpa Ace wouldn't be caught dead in a VFW. He preferred to forget.

"Hello, honey. Coming to see your grandpa?" asked one man with a hat so encased in medals that no fabric showed through.

"No, I'm afraid not. I'm looking for Gerald Smith. Do you know him?"

"I certainly do. He'll be here, rest assured. I'm Jed Avery and you are?"

"Mercy Watts. Pleased to meet you." I shook his large, rough hand and glanced into his faded blue eyes. Mr. Avery was one of the few moving without a cane or walker. I saw in his eyes the young man who still resided there.

We walked together, chitchatting about his grandchildren and various health problems, until we got to the double doors.

"That didn't take too long," said Mr. Avery.

I guess twenty minutes isn't too long if you've lived nearly a century. I was about to tear my hair out when we walked through the doors. A long table covered in a tattered tablecloth filled half the vestibule, and three veterans sat behind it selling tickets and bingo cards. When Mr. Avery and I got to the table, they all frowned. I knew my attire wasn't the best, but I expected to see Gerald at home or his bar. I thought getting money out of an old guy would be helped by a formfitting dress, not hindered.

"Hi Abner," said Mr. Avery. "How much?"

Abner squinted at me. "Five to get in and two per card."

"That's highway robbery. Five is way too high."

"It's all for the Christmas party this year. We're going to have a doozy," Abner said, still squinting.

"What about my friend here?" Mr. Avery patted my shoulder. "She's looking for Gerald Smith. Is he here?"

"He is, but he just went to the bathroom. He could be in there for an hour."

"I'll wait. Just need to speak to him for a moment. It's a business thing," I said.

"Don't matter. I can't let you in."

"I'll pay the five bucks. No problem," I said, opening my purse.

Abner looked at Mr. Avery, who shrugged.

"Can't do it. Not unless you're a member of the VFW. Are you?"

"No. I just need to speak to Mr. Smith. That's it."

"Can't let you in without a membership," said Abner.

The vestibule was crammed with old guys, and the smell of Aspercream was getting overwhelming. I breathed through my mouth. "Come on. It's just a couple of minutes. Can't you do something?"

"Come on, Abner. Don't be such a hard-ass," said Mr. Avery.

Abner coughed a deep, phlegmy cough that reminded me of Dad. I had to get in there or I'd spend hours tracking Gerald down again.

"Please, please. I'll make a donation," I said.

Abner squinted again. "One hundred bucks."

"I'll give you twenty-five," I said.

"Seventy-five," said Abner.

"Fifty."

"Done." Abner shook my hand and gave me a sheaf of papers.

"What's this?"

"Standard release form."

"Don't worry about it, honey," said Mr. Avery. "Abner's just our resident worrywart. You're not going to sue us if you slip and fall, are you?"

"Not a chance," I said.

"Then sign it and you can get on with the rest of your day," he said.

I slipped on my shoes, flipped to the last page of the release, signed, and made out a check for fifty bucks. What a pain in my ass. I didn't suppose there was a chance of getting Dad to reimburse me. He'd argue that I could've held out for less.

Mr. Avery paid for his ticket and a dozen bingo cards. He held out his arm and squired me into the ballroom filled with the remnants of wars past. On one side, a furious game of bingo was going on, complete with cussing and threats. I knew from Aunt Miriam that bingo was practically a contact sport. On the other side, a swing band played my favorite Glenn Miller song, "Chattanooga Choo Choo". In the middle, a bunch of guys were arguing around a king-sized map with pins and arrows all over it. At first I thought it was a WWII map or maybe Vietnam. But when we got closer, it proved to be a Civil War map, centering mostly on Fredericksburg, Virginia. From what I could tell, the Union was getting its ass handed to them. Two men stood nose to red nose, clinging to rickety walkers hollering about General Burnside's performance. They both seemed to think he was an idiot, just how much of one was in question.

"That's Carl and Lamont," said Mr. Avery. "They love to hate Burnside."

"No kidding," I said.

"I see your toe tapping. Care to cut a rug?"

"Why not?" I took Mr. Avery's hand, and he swung me out onto the dance floor. Not bad for an old guy and considerably better than any young guy I'd ever danced with, including my boyfriend Pete, who pretended dancing didn't exist.

The "Chattanooga Choo Choo" goes on forever, in a good way, and by the time it finished I was out of breath and panting. Another man took my hand, and we jitterbugged until he passed me to someone else. Somewhere along the line, the crowd started clapping, and I felt it down to my toes and out to my fingertips. I was just plain happy. Gavin wasn't dead. I wasn't doing grunt work for Dad. I wasn't tired, and I definitely wasn't having my period. I was perfect. I never felt so good swinging around, laughing, and dancing in a world before my time.

The band stopped playing, saying they needed a break. Half the brass section bent over and wheezed past their instruments, red-faced and trembling. Mr. Avery insisted on taking my picture with one of his buddies. I bent over and kissed his soft, lined cheek, and then smiled as Mr. Avery clicked away. I posed with other vets until my cheeks hurt and Mr. Avery took pity on me and stopped the picture-taking.

"How about some dessert?" he asked.

"Love some," I said.

I inhaled a piece of chocolate peanut butter pie and spied Gerald Smith coming out of the bathroom.

"Excuse me," I said. "I see Mr. Smith."

I got myself ready to chase him out the door once he saw me, but Gerald just smiled. "I guess you got me."

"Yep, time to pay up."

"I thought your mother collected the bills, but I guess you'll do," said Gerald.

"Whatever. Just write me a check for four hundred dollars," I said.

Gerald pulled out his checkbook, filled out a check, tore it off, and handed it to me. It was even for the correct amount. I expected him to give me a check for forty instead of four hundred. Dad said he was a wily old bastard.

"How about a picture to commemorate the moment," said Gerald.

"You want to commemorate paying your bill?" I asked.

"I'm eighty-nine. I commemorate taking a whiz."

"Whatever." I turned and smiled at Gerald, who kept peeking down my dress. "That's it. I've got to go."

The whole room stood up (those that could stand) and clapped. I bowed low, gave them a finger wave, and flounced out the door.

Score. I couldn't believe it'd been that easy. I'd never had fun when doing something for Dad. I'd have to remember this one, because it wouldn't happen again. I climbed into my truck, kicked off my heels, and smiled into the rearview. I'd done Dad's crappy errand, and it was almost like a good deed. God, I was good.

It took me another day to get to the morgue. Not that I couldn't make the time. I was up on eight doing orthopedic work. I could've gone down anytime I pleased, but I wasn't a big fan of morgues. It was a good thing nursing school didn't include a course in gross anatomy. I never would've made it. Dad, on the other hand, ate rare roast beef sandwiches during organ weighing. I didn't inherit his strong stomach, not that I missed it. Also, I wasn't crazy about using Dad's name to get information. It made me feel like I was back in fifth grade forging his name on my permission slips. My procrastination skills were working great until Aunt Miriam told me Gavin's chart review was done and the body was ready to go to the funeral home.

I sucked it up and went down into the bowels of St. James on Tuesday afternoon. As usual, it was quiet and took awhile to get some attention. Then I found myself in an office that looked like Vera Bradley had decorated it, and it wasn't a good thing. There were no less than five dried flower arrangements, a wreath, two framed needlepoint canvases of cabbage roses, and a deep-pile lavender rug on the floor. The name on the desk was A.M. Forester, so I expected a woman to walk in. A. wasn't an Alice or Anne, but Alan and he looked like a young Mr. Rogers gone homicidal. With that décor, who could blame him? I assumed his wife was at fault. At least I hoped so. Pictures of a pretty woman with enormous 1980s permed hair hung in a series behind the desk. Her pink and purple eye shadow said Vera and cabbage roses to me.

"Afternoon. I'm Dr. Forester." He looked up from a chart he was holding and did a double take. I'd seen that look a million times, the stunned fascination, the struggle for words. There were times I thought I'd rather not meet anyone new. Better that than deal with what inevitably came next.

"I've heard about... You know you look just like...Marilyn Monroe," he said.

Because this wasn't one of those times, I widened my eyes, crossed and uncrossed my legs. I admit the effect would've been better if I wasn't wearing scrubs, but I got my desired result. He was thrown off balance and I could probably get anything I wanted out of him.

"Mercy Watts," I said. "How are you today?"

"Fine, fine. I guess you hear that a lot."

"Occasionally." Also known as every freaking day.

"Sister Miriam said you'd be coming down. She didn't say you... what you wanted."

"Gavin Flouder. His wife is concerned about his cause of death. He was only fifty-five and had a clean bill of health three weeks ago. What did your review turn up?"

"Myocardial infarction. No doubt about it. I went to Washington University, you know." He gestured to his diploma framed in some kind of doily matting. I guess I was supposed to be impressed with his super expensive education. I wasn't. Dad had arrested more than a few dirt-bags that went to Wash U. A couple were doctors, as I recalled.

"I see that. So what did you do? Double check levels? I understand he was on thinners."

"I don't think you need to worry about that. I'd enjoy a cup of coffee. Can I interest you in our lovely cafeteria?"

"I PRN here. I get enough of the cafeteria. I do want to know what you turned up in your exam."

"I can't release information to you."

"Didn't Sister Miriam tell you to cooperate with me?" I put my fingers on his desk and leaned forward — a little cleavage never hurt anyone.

"Well, she doesn't have any real authority here."

"She'll be pleased to hear that." I stood up straight.

"You don't need to bother Sister Miriam about this."

"She's my aunt. I live to bother her. Is Dr. Grace in?"

"No." Dr. Forester looked over my head towards the door when he said it.

"Are you sure?"

"Absolutely," he said.

"I don't believe you."

"I'm not accustomed to being accused of lying."

"Well, get accustomed, because I'm not changing my opinion. Where's his office?" I asked.

"You really have no business being here."

"I sure do. If the family wants you to tell me your results, then you have to tell me, or didn't they teach you that at Wash U?"

"You should go now. It's time for my lunch." Forester gestured toward the door.

"It's three-thirty."

"I eat late."

"Right. I guess I'll have to find Dr. Grace on my own." I stood up and walked out the door without another word.

Who the hell did he think he was? As if I'd go to coffee with a man who'd hit on me while surrounded by pictures of his wife. Bastard. Actually, not only was he a bastard, he was damned unhelpful, too, and I started to get a feeling. My feelings aren't about mess, but about getting a huge pain in the ass. Like Dad and his feelings, I was rarely off base about my ass.

Dr. Grace's office was easy to find and, as luck would have it, he was in it, sitting behind a stack of charts so high that at first all I saw was a mop of iron gray hair and horn-rimmed glasses.

"Excuse me, Dr. Grace?"

"Yes. Can I help you?" He straightened up, and I got the full view of an unsurprised man. One who didn't find me particularly out of the ordinary. He must've met Mom.

"If you're not too busy. I'm Mercy Watts. I believe you know my father, Tommy Watts."

"Good old Tommy. How's he doing these days? Still making the rounds as a PI?"

"Sure is, and he told me to look you up as a favor to him."

"About a case of his?" Dr. Grace's eyebrows went up.

"Not really. It's more of a family matter. Gavin Flouder was a partner of his in the old days. Dad worked with him for a while when he went private. We were wondering if you could take a look at him for us," I said.

"Gavin Flouder, Gavin Flouder," he said as he thumbed through a stack of paper on his desk.

"He died on Sunday."

"Right. Here he is. Forester had his case. Have you talked to him?"

"You could say that," I said.

"Not very forthcoming, I take it."

"Not at all."

"What are you looking for?" Dr. Grace asked.

"He supposedly had a MI. We'd like to make sure. He did have a heart condition, but Dad has a feeling."

"Tommy and his feelings. Not that I doubt him. I've known him too long for that. What about you? Do you have a feeling, too?"

"Let's just say I don't like it."

"That's good enough for me. I'll take a look. I'll call you and we'll go over the results together." Dr. Grace got up and walked me out his door to the elevator. While we were walking, I could see him giving me sly glances. He wanted to throw out the Marilyn comment, but was too polite to do it. Instead, we chatted about Dad and the declining state of the police force. I left feeling better about Gavin's case, but worse about my ass.

CHAPTER FOUR

D r. Grace held Gavin's body for two days and then called me down from orthopedics for a talk, as he put it. I arrived at ten in the morning, and the morgue was hopping. There were no less than five detectives, a police photographer, and a couple of beat cops standing around drinking coffee. My cousin by marriage, Chuck Watts, was one of the detectives.

Chuck saw me and, before I could react, he walked over with his patent self-assurance that never failed to irritate me. He looked good, as he always did. He once told me that only ten percent of the world's population is attractive. He definitely considers himself in the top ten percent, maybe top five. I hated to admit it, but he was right. Chuck was a pleasure to view with his sinewy muscles, broad shoulders, and hooded blue eyes. Still, Chuck couldn't be considered conventionally handsome. He had thinning hair and pockmarks on his cheeks, but those flaws added to his allure. Dad said it was lucky he had them or he would've gotten nowhere on the force. It doesn't pay to be too good-looking in a job like Chuck's.

"Hey, Mercy," he said and gave me a hug that lasted a couple of seconds too long. No one else seemed to notice.

"Back off, you stink," I said.

"Is that any way to greet your favorite cousin?"

"You're not my favorite cousin. We're not even blood-related and your mom divorced Uncle Rupert forever ago."

"Even better." Chuck smiled the smile that melted the hearts of every single one of my friends, including my best friend Ellen. She took him to our prom. I haven't quite forgiven her for that one.

"Give it up." I shook his arm off me.

"Mercy girl, what are you doing here?" asked Dale Crudup from the corner.

"Hey, Dale. Just here to say hi to Dr. Grace."

"Oh, yeah?" Dale raised his eyebrows and came forward to give me a more welcome hug. "Didn't know you knew Grace."

"Through Dad. You know how it is."

"How come you don't mind Dale's stink?" said Chuck.

"I don't mind Dale in any form."

"I say she doesn't mind because Dale stands as far from the slab as possible." A detective I didn't recognize came forward and shook my hand. "Chris Nazir. You must be Mercy Watts."

"My reputation precedes me," I said.

"Your description anyway. You do look great on film," said Chuck.

"What are you talking about?"

"You should wear that leopard bra more often."

"I don't have a leopard bra and, even if I did, you'd never see it," I said in a manner I hoped was convincing. I loved my leopard bra.

Detective Nazir blushed and said, "It's nice to meet you, Mercy."

Chuck gave me a sly, knowing grin that made me feel like I needed a shower, and the rest of the crew shuffled their feet in the following silence.

"So what are you doing here? Big case?" I asked.

"Um, yeah. We pulled a couple more bodies from Sternberger Lake," said Nazir.

"Five detectives for two autopsies?" I said.

"We're up to four bodies now and Watts caught the bride, too," said Dale.

"Bride?" I said.

"You know, the bride strangled in the crying room right after her wedding reception," said Chuck. "And the lake's a nasty one. I earned this stink."

"You guys should bring a change of clothes with you," I said.

"Nah. It doesn't bother us. I'd think you'd be used to it too. I bet your dad came home smelling worse than us plenty," Dale said.

"I imagine he did, but Mom made him come in through the basement. He'd shower and change down there," I said.

"Glad my wife hasn't thought of that yet," said Nazir.

Dale clapped Nazir on the back. "Shit, she's probably just glad to see you. Nazir here is following in the steps of Tommy Watts. Twenty-hour days and all."

"He'll get over it," said Chuck.

"You haven't," I said.

Chuck was my father's protégé. He filled the sad vacancy I left when I decided against the family business. Chuck is the son I refused to be.

"It's a dirty job, but I love it," said Chuck.

"That's because you have a dirty mind," I said.

"Don't you know it."

"Actually, I don't and I don't want to."

"Burn," said Dale. "You gotta love a girl like that."

"On that note, I'm off to see Dr. Grace. Good luck on the lake case."

I went down the hall to Grace's office, knocked and received a quick "Come in."

"Hi. Are you busy?" I said.

"No more than usual. Glad you're here. I just finished Mr. Flouder." Dr. Grace took off his glasses, rubbed his eyes, and yawned. "Sorry, I've been here all night."

"Not on my account, I hope."

"No, on Mr. Flouder's actually."

"Did you do a full autopsy?"

"Had to. It's a suspicious death now."

"Why?"

"It seems Dr. Forester wasn't as thorough as I would've liked," said Dr. Grace.

"Meaning?"

"Meaning, the cause of death is no longer certain."

"How come?"

"Walk with me." He stood up, rubbed his eyes again, and we walked down to the autopsy suite. Someone was still on the table. I presumed it was Gavin. A glimpse of a foot was enough to get me to avert my eyes.

"Sorry. I shouldn't have brought you in here. For some reason, I was thinking of your father," Dr. Grace apologized.

That was a new one. I'd never gotten confused with a six-foot-four redhead before.

"It's okay. I can take it. If you would've brought Dad in here, then you'd better show me what you would've shown him."

"Are you sure?" he asked.

"Uh huh." I was by no means sure, but I knew it would get around that I wussed out. If Chuck could handle autopsies, then I could, too.

"Let me get a sheet," said Dr. Grace. He covered Gavin, and I was able to look up.

"At first I expected just to do a quick review and exam, but should've known it wouldn't be that easy. Your father is rarely wrong," said Dr. Grace.

"What did you turn up?"

"I believe Gavin had an MI, but I doubt it was natural."

"Why do you say that?"

Dr. Grace assumed a lecturing pose, and the teacher in him surfaced. I was going to find out more than I wanted to know.

"First, I reviewed his blood work, all within normal levels. I went over his chart and then examined the body. Come here." He gestured to the table. I made myself walk forward and stand beside him. He lifted the sheet back while I counted the tiles on the wall, careful not to look at Gavin's torso.

"At first glance, everything appeared normal. Nothing to indicate trauma other than the staff's attempts to revive him. Sometimes that can be violent in and of itself, as I'm sure you know. See the minor bruising along the midline?" Dr. Grace pointed, and I looked down.

"He has two broken ribs as well. All of this is from the paramedics and ER staff."

"How can you tell?"

"I took tissue samples of the bruising from here, here, and here." Dr. Grace pointed to three cuts on Gavin's chest. I found the longer I stared at Gavin, the less it felt like him. It was just a body. The man I'd known for most of my life wasn't there, lying on cold metal. I could get through whatever it was Dr. Grace wanted to show me because it no longer mattered to Gavin what was done to the flesh. It only mattered to Dr. Grace, me, and the detectives catching the case.

"Okay," I said.

"Come look at this." He led me to a microscope. I looked, but all I saw was a typical tissue sample. Granted, I wasn't a whiz in the lab, but it looked normal to me.

"What am I supposed to be seeing?" I asked.

"All the red blood cells, no white. The body never tried to repair itself. That and the fact the bruising is minor tells me that all this bruising," he waved his hand over the Y incision, "is from resuscitation."

"Didn't you already know that?"

"Yes, but when I examined the rest of the body, I saw this." Dr. Grace went back to the table with me in tow, rolled Gavin on to his side and pointed to a shaved section of his shoulder. There was a large reddish bruise outlining the shape of his shoulder blade.

"Resuscitation did not cause that," said Dr. Grace.

He took me back to the microscope, changed slides, and I took another look. I could see some white cells among the red. Dr. Grace smiled at me when I straightened up. "The repair process had begun, but it didn't get very far. There was at least an hour between this bruise and those the paramedics gave him. This is pretty deep damage. It took some force to cause it. I don't believe it was from a fall resulting from the MI. There's also a similar bruise on the back of the head."

"Gavin was in a fight?" I said.

"Doubtful. If it was a fight, as you say, it was short-lived."

"It caused the MI?"

Dr. Grace shook his head. "I don't think so."

"Why didn't Forester notice this?"

"Your friend Gavin here was pretty hairy. I didn't notice it at first glance either, and Forester didn't have the benefit of Tommy's feeling either. He was looking for an ordinary MI and that's what he found."

"He was sloppy," I said.

"Yes, and no."

"Give him the benefit of the doubt, in other words."

"I think we have to, in this case. I could've missed it myself," he said.

"I doubt that."

Dr. Grace smiled and led me to the other side of the table.

"Tell me what you see," he said, pointing to Gavin's chest.

I looked over the area slowly, not wanting to miss anything and let Dad down. Whatever was there, he wouldn't have missed it. I saw another shaved area next to Gavin's neck. It was small, the size of a quarter. Inside the area were two quarter-inch-long marks, identical and about a half inch apart.

"What's that?"

"Can't be sure yet, but if I had to guess, I'd say burns from a stun gun."

"Like in that Maryland cop case?"

"You read," he said.

"An unfortunate habit of mine."

"And a good memory, to boot. Ever think of a career in forensics?"

"Not for a minute," I said, wrapping my arms around myself.

"Too bad."

"How on earth did you notice these with all this black and gray hair everywhere?"

He tapped the side of his nose and smiled. "I smelled them."

"Say what?"

"I have a very sensitive sense of smell."

"Bet you wish you didn't." The smell in the room, although mild, was getting to me. Death has its own unmistakable odor. The antiseptic wasn't helping the situation either.

"Not at all. My sense of smell has helped me on a number of occasions like this one. The instrument used to make those marks burnt the hair on top of them. I smelled the hair. Now look at his mouth."

Oh crap. Do I have to?

"Come on, I have to show you."

I looked at Gavin's face and was surprised at how different he looked in death. Like his wife, he needed wakefulness to make him recognizable as the man I knew.

"You shaved his beard," I said. Dixie was going to be pissed. Gavin had a beard for as long as I could remember.

"Couldn't be helped. After the burn marks, I started looking for a cause of the MI, needle marks, something like that."

"Just being attacked couldn't have caused it?"

"Maybe, but I had to be sure there wasn't a direct cause from an outside source. I think we can assume whoever stunned him didn't do it for kicks."

I leaned over the table to get a better look and saw a portion of Gavin's thigh was shaved. "Is that a puncture?"

"Yes. I believe they injected him with something that brought on the MI."

"Like what?"

"Could be any number of drugs or poisons," he said. "I'm waiting for more extensive labs to come back now."

"Did you call the cops?"

"Your dad's old shop, to be exact. Called them before I called you, but they've got their hands full today and he isn't going anywhere. Should've called before the autopsy, but I was hoping I wouldn't find anything. I should've known better."

"You didn't break any rules bringing me down here, did you?"

"Depends on who you ask. Don't let on, though."

"No problem." He pulled the sheet back up over Gavin's head and we left the room. I thanked Dr. Grace in the reception area that was now empty and left the hospital. I went straight to my parents' house to see if Dixie was awake and willing to give me her house keys for no good reason. I wasn't ready to tell her that her husband had been murdered.

CHAPTER FIVE

Uncle Morty's jeep sat at my parents' back gate, parked cattywampus as usual. I gritted my teeth and considered turning around. I was not in the mood for Morty. He asked too many questions, and I had no answers, at least not yet. But there he was, and it wouldn't do to avoid him, as if that were possible for any length of time. Uncle Morty liked to turn up when I least wanted to see him. He was a total bloodhound and my father's best friend, if you didn't count my mother. Plus, he wasn't my real uncle, which made him more annoying than blood family and just as hard to get rid of.

Uncle Morty waited, in ambush, on the back porch. I was halfway up the garden path when a drizzle started, making the long grass shiny green, and the sky took on a thick purple cast. The wind picked up, swirling the leaves and lawn clippings around my feet. The heavy air and dread slowed me as I walked the twenty yards toward him.

Uncle Morty waited, not moving a muscle. He stood at the edge of the stairs, a menacing statue with his arms crossed and his driving cap tipped low on his forehead. Given the rest of his getup, the hat should've looked ridiculous. He wore a gray sweat suit washed within an inch of its life, a pair of Nike high-tops circa 1985 and a Members

Only jacket that hadn't fit in ten years. I doubted Morty noticed he was carrying another person around his middle.

I stopped at the foot of the stairs and looked up at him. Rain dripped off the brim of his hat and he looked at me from behind thick glasses. I couldn't read his expression. The rain fogged his lenses, and he made no attempt to wipe them. He stood and waited, and I wished my eyes would stop burning.

"You coming up or what?" Morty said.

I grasped the railing and put my right foot on the first step.

"Get a move on. Shit. I ain't got all day."

I climbed the stairs, pulled out my key, and unlocked the back door. I walked into the butler's pantry with Morty close at my heels and hung my rain-soaked jacket on the coatrack by the door and watched as Morty rummaged through the cabinets. The pantry was wonderful with its floor-to-ceiling cabinets, secret drawers, and odd-shaped cubbies. As a little girl, I spent hours trying to find the pantry's secrets. I doubt I'd discovered them all. The man who built our house was a master woodworker, and I suspected deeply crazy. There were secret drawers and doors all over the house. His masterpiece was the pantry with its beveled glass, hidden hinges, delicate carvings, and unique temperature. The small room was freezing. Josiah Bled designed his house to keep the pantry at a steady forty degrees. It didn't matter if the doors to the kitchen and dining room were left open; it never warmed. Dad spent hours trying to figure it out. Architects were called. Structural engineers examined it. No one had a clue. Every couple of years, Dad attempted to discover the secret, but he couldn't make any headway.

I rubbed my shoulders and watched Morty pulling out drawers. Morty liked the pantry too, but only because Dad kept his booze in there. Then he stopped, shut a drawer with a flip of his wrist and looked at the liquor cabinet. The cabinet was original to the house, although it was fifty years older. It was tucked in a cubby in a bank of built-ins. It looked like Josiah Bled placed the liquor cabinet in there and the rest grew in around it. It stood four feet high on delicate cabriole legs that looked as if they might snap under its weight. The front had four false drawers inlaid with five different types of wood in a star pattern. The sides were probably inlaid too, but we couldn't see them. Josiah built around the cabinet with only one millimeter to spare, and it couldn't be removed. Wooden hands and vines came out from the built-ins and wrapped around the legs. You'd have to snap off the legs or break the woodwork to get it out. Josiah made sure his cabinet would never leave.

Uncle Morty turned the key in the top drawer, pushed the top up and laid the front down. The door revealed an open space for wine and other bottles, but Mom used it for her old cookbooks.

"There you are, you little bitch," he said.

"What is it?" I asked.

Morty held up a slender wine bottle with a wooden cork. He rubbed the dust off the label with his jacket, smacked his lips, and closed the cabinet.

"Just what the doctor ordered."

"Wine?" I asked.

"Not just wine. It's the peach stuff Tommy ordered from Germany a couple of years ago. I knew he was holding out on me. Bastard said there wasn't any left."

Imagine that.

"Let's have a glass and toast to Gavin. God bless him."

"Maybe we should wait for Dad."

Morty ignored me and walked into the kitchen. I followed and sat down while he filled a couple of juice glasses with a flourish. He handed one to me. "Here's to Gavin. A good man gone to his reward."

"I didn't know you were religious," I said.

"I ain't, but Gavin was, so bottoms up."

He drained his glass, and I sniffed mine. It smelled too good to drink. A hundred ripe peaches smelled like they were squashed in there. The scent filled the kitchen and breathing it was enough to get me tipsy.

"Sit down Mercy, and let's us have a talk," said Morty.

Great, just what I wanted.

"You tell Tommy yet?"

"Tell him what?"

"That Gavin was murdered." Morty poured a second glass.

"That was quick. How'd you know?"

"Sources."

"You must know Dr. Grace," I said.

"Don't know the man from Adam. You told Tommy?"

"Not yet. I just got back from the morgue. Seriously, how'd you know?"

Morty took off his glasses and wiped them on a dish towel. He poured another glass of wine and sipped it.

"You might as well wait till he gets back. No use working him up when he can't do anything on that damn boat anyway."

"Fine with me," I said.

"Meanwhile, we better get moving on this thing."

We?

"Dixie upstairs?" he asked.

"Yeah. Why?"

"See if you can get the keys out of her, so we can check out the house before the Keystone Cops."

"Pass."

"Get the keys," he said.

"Let the cops handle it. It's their job, for heaven's sake."

"You want to let the cops handle Gavin's murder?" Uncle Morty banged his glass on the table.

I didn't, but I couldn't stand having Uncle Morty dogging my every footstep either. No keys for him. I'd check out the house by myself.

"I don't know," I said.

"Tommy will kick our asses if we don't move on this."

Before I could think of a reasonable answer, the doorbell rang. What luck! Morty shot me an irritated look as I left the kitchen. I went down the hall into the receiving room. On the other side of my parents' enormous front door were two tiny figures. They could only be the Bled sisters, Millicent and Myrtle. They were nieces of Josiah Bled and lived down the street in another of his creations. Millicent and Myrtle were also my godmothers. Once when I was ten, they told me Josiah didn't design the pantry to stay cold, but caused it all the same.

Josiah's mistress disappeared in 1921. It was a big news story at the time since Bernice Collins was rumored to be a former prostitute, and Josiah was heir to the Bled Brewery fortune. Josiah was never charged with any crime, but his nieces told me he might've killed her in the pantry, hence the constant cold. My parents have Millicent and Myrtle to thank for most of my childhood nightmares.

One of the sisters rapped on the stained glass. I ran my fingers through my hair, pinched my cheeks, and attempted to straighten my damp shirt. It was hopeless.

I unlocked the door and opened it to find two tiny elderly ladies clutching enormous handbags, umbrellas, and casserole dishes.

"Mercy dearest, we heard and came as soon as we could," they said.

"What did you hear?"

"About Mr. Flouder, of course. Sweet man, such a shame," said Millicent.

Both she and Myrtle waited in the doorway, and I was at a loss. If I let them in, they'd plant themselves, and I'd never get to Gavin's house. If I didn't let them in, they'd tell Mom, and I'd never hear the end of it.

"Please come in. What a nasty day today," I said.

"Yes, dear. Bad weather accompanies bad news, don't you think? Is dear Mrs. Flouder here?" said Millicent.

"I'm here."

I turned to see Dixie coming down. Her eyes were dry, and she'd fixed her hair.

"I do hope we're not intruding. We wanted to pay our respects," said Myrtle.

"Not at all." Dixie hugged them and herded us all towards the parlor.

Morty stomped out of the kitchen bellowing, "What the hell is taking so long?" He stopped short when he saw the Bled sisters. Morty had an unnatural respect for "The Girls", as they were known on the Avenue, and was on his best behavior when they were around.

"Ladies, I didn't see you there. How are you?"

"Morton," they said.

"Why don't we all go into the parlor?" I led Dixie and The Girls to the parlor while Uncle Morty stood in the hallway, shuffling his feet and giving me pointed looks. I supposed he wanted me to abandon my guests and finish our discussion. Fat chance.

We sat down on Mom's odd, mismatched collection of sofas and wingback chairs. Millicent and Myrtle covered their knees with a pair of lap blankets kept there especially for them. They were cold no matter the temperature and expected blankets would be afforded them wherever they went. They were rarely disappointed. Morty came and stood in the doorway with his arms crossed. I ignored him and listened to Millicent's intricate description of her casserole. Before long, my mouth was watering. The Girls could cook. People were always surprised when they discovered Millicent and Myrtle were Bleds. The Bled Brewery was a St. Louis institution, and the name had a certain mystique. No one expected elderly ladies raised with nannies and private tutors to make the hell out of a casserole, but they could.

"Miss Bled, you're making me hungry," said Dixie.

"Now, dear, I told you at Christmas, call me Millicent. Why don't we have some? Mercy?" said Millicent.

"Sure. Sounds great. Let's go to the kitchen." The Girls followed me down the hall close at my heels. They thought eating in the kitchen quite daring. Dixie set places, Morty poured drinks and soon the table was covered with chips, dips, relishes, rolls and, of course, casseroles. Morty sat as far from The Girls as possible and kept giving me sullen looks. Despite his displeasure, he ate half a casserole and finish off the peach wine. Millicent and Myrtle ate the other half. I'd never seen them eat so much at one sitting.

"Dixie, dear, I hope you don't mind my saying so, but you're looking thin. You must eat more. Your dear husband would want you to take care of yourself," said Myrtle.

"I don't mind, but it's the clothes, not me. I've done nothing but eat since I got here. I'm wearing Carolina's things. They're a bit large on me. I haven't gone home yet."

"Poor thing. Such memories there. Sometimes it can be difficult to walk in one's own home...without remembering," said Millicent.

My mother's clothes engulfed Dixie. She lacked Mom's generous hips and chest and needed her own clothes, but who could blame her for not wanting to go home? Morty let out a loud cough, and raised his eyebrows at me while muttering, "Excuse me."

Duh. Why hadn't I thought of that? It was the perfect cover. I'd pick up clothes for Dixie and search the house while I was at it. All I had to figure out was how to get rid of Morty and from the look of him, it wouldn't be easy.

"You know what I'm in the mood for...whiskey sours. Anyone else?" I said.

"Don't mind if I do," said The Girls.

"Sounds nice," said Dixie.

Morty ignored my suggestion and got up to make coffee.

"Come on, Uncle Morty. Don't make us drink alone." I made my eyes as big as possible and batted them twice. This move worked on plenty of men, including my father, if he wasn't wary. The eyelash batting wasn't my favorite maneuver, but occasionally it was necessary. Uncle Morty wasn't easily swayed. His mouth twisted, and his eyes went to the ceiling. Then he looked at me like I'd just stuffed a potato chip up my nose. I'd have to pull out the big guns.

"Miss Millicent, Miss Myrtle, don't you think Uncle Morty needs a drink? After all, he was quite close to Gavin, and has been grieving excessively." The Girls stood up, and with looks of extreme compassion on their faces, went to Morty.

"My dear man. What have we been thinking? You've been so quiet. Come have a drink. Perhaps you would favor us with a story about Gavin. I'm sure Dixie would like to hear a good memory," said Millicent.

"Yes, do tell us," said Myrtle. She tucked her arm around Morty's and led him back to his chair. I made the fastest batch of whiskey sours, extra strong, of my life. When no one was looking, I filled my own glass with water.

"This is pretty strong, Mercy," said Morty.

"I'm sorry. I guess I got carried away." I sipped my water and made a face. "Should I make another batch?"

"No, no, dear. They're fine, just fine," said Dixie.

"I think they're very good," said Millicent.

Three pitchers of whiskey sours, three glasses of water for me, and Uncle Morty was in no condition to go anywhere.

"Dixie, why don't I go pick up some of your clothes? That way you won't have to worry about it," I said.

"Wonderful idea. Make some more drink things before you go. My keys are in my purse, but I don't know where that thing's got to," said Dixie, her voice slurring.

"Don't worry about it." I made a fourth pitcher and poured another round. Morty watched me with a glazed expression. He knew I was up to something, but he couldn't connect the dots.

Morty swayed in his chair. "Sign anything away lately, Marilyn?"

"No, I didn't. And never call me Marilyn."

"You sure about that?" He belched and laughed at the same time. It made him sound like a Budweiser frog.

"Whatever. Bye, now." I saluted him and he swayed again.

I jogged around the house looking for Dixie's purse, and praying the cops hadn't beat me to Gavin's house. The purse sat in the receiving room under a pile of coats. I took two steps at a time up to the second floor and Dad's office. His collection of crime scene cameras sat on a shelf above the desk, coated with dust and looking lonely. Dad had it covered from the 1970s on. His favorites got prime position in the front. A Konica Minolta, an ancient Polaroid, and a hefty Nikon with an auto advance sat alongside high school basketball trophies, various plaques, and an unbelievable number of books on crime. Dad had it covered from footprint analysis to profiling. A thin layer of dust covered the camera. Dad wasn't taking a lot of crime scene photos anymore, but back in the day, he was known for doing the crime scene photographers' job for them. Dad always said, learn from your mistakes and improve. On Dad's first murder as the primary detective, no one bothered to document the scene thoroughly. They took shots of the body, the scene of the struggle and point of entry, or what they thought was the point of entry. Later on, Dad discovered they had it wrong, and an element of the crime was lost, and the conviction along with it. Dad never forgot the mistake, and he took it to heart. He bought the Konica and used it well. Dad shot everything from the front door to the trash cans, and he solved a few cases because of it.

I chose the less-loved, but totally rocking Sony Cyber-shot, since my phone would probably die. Dad preferred film over digital, but bowed to the practicality. He liked the smell of the film canisters and said that there was something magical about hearing the film advance. He was nuts.

I put the camera and Dad's work iPad in a backpack. I went over everything he'd told me about shooting a scene as I left without saying goodbye. I doubt they noticed. I snuck through the dining room and used the servant's door to the pantry to escape unnoticed. Uncle Morty was telling an old story about Gavin and the naked burglar. I heard them laughing all the way to my truck.

CHAPTER SIX

D ixie and Gavin's house was a trek from my parents' house in
the Central West End, and that one of the reasons Dad and
Gavin didn't stay partners for long. Both of them wanted
home offices, and they couldn't decide which would be the primary
location. So Dad stayed in the city and Gavin out in the burbs.

Florissant was filled with strip malls and planned communities. The
houses were nearly identical one-story fifties bungalows on curving,
confusing streets. I think the planners did that so the owners would
concentrate on where their house was, rather than how it looked like
every other one on the block. People told me my parents' neighborhood was creepy. The huge trees, mansions dripping with wrought
iron, and flickering street lamps unnerved them. A lot of the houses
may have had a certain Scooby Doo quality, including my parents, but
at least they didn't look like something out of *The Stepford Wives*.

I parked in Gavin's carport behind a police cruiser thirty-five
minutes later. Damn, I was too late. It shouldn't have taken so long to
get there, but I made three wrong turns. The house was on Orchard
Avenue. I turned on to Orchard Street, Orchard Boulevard, and
Orchard Lane before striking gold. The planners thought up about ten
names for their roads and used them well. I got out of my truck and

listened to the quiet of suburban life. It was too quiet, unnatural. At least my parents had the distant hum of Kingshighway traffic and the foot traffic of stylish people on their way to little shops selling everything from vintage clothes to French chocolates. Florissant had nothing going and I mean nothing. I swear even the leaves were limp with boredom.

I peeked in the cruiser. Empty. I snapped shots of the house's exterior, driveway, and trees. No one saw me. If someone had, I wondered if they would've cared. No one appeared to be involved in anything save their own square plot of earth. A couple of cars drove by, but the drivers didn't even turn their heads. Of course, it might have been that texting was more interesting than me snapping pictures.

It wasn't often that I didn't merit a second look, and no cop came out to yell at me. I felt luckier every minute. The property wasn't cordoned off, and the doors were free of crime scene tape. It was practically an invitation, so I unlocked the side door, and went into the cheerful yellow kitchen with its alphabetized cookbooks and shiny stainless appliances.

"Hey," I yelled. "Is anybody here?"

There was no answer, and I felt free to snoop.

My cell vibrated, and it wasn't a text. Some weirdo was actually calling me and it wasn't my mother.

"Hello," I said.

"Is this Mercy Watts?" a male voice asked.

"Yes."

"Hey, guys, it's really her. So what are you wearing?"

"What the hell?" I hung up.

My cell rang again, and I had a similar conversation with a guy who identified himself as Russell the Love Muscle. I hung up on Russell and ignored my ringing phone. I didn't waste time with less than witty prank callers.

Dixie's kitchen was neat and clean with a few dishes in the sink, but that was the only sign that something unusual happened. She never left dishes unwashed normally. I shot the kitchen with special attention to the door and windows. The living room was the same, no signs of a struggle or a break-in. The windows and front door were locked.

On Dixie's new leather sofa, a book lay open with its binding cracked and pages face down on a worn afghan. I'd read *Alive* by Piers Paul Read forever ago and never again. That copy was dog-eared. I guessed it was Gavin's. Dixie read romances of the Danielle Steel variety. I took a picture of the book on its afghan. I tipped up the book with my fingernail. Gavin was halfway through. I took note of the page. For some reason, it was comforting to know what he'd last read. Carefully, I lay the book back as I found it.

All three bedrooms and the two bathrooms were unremarkable and undisturbed. The shower and sink drains were clean. I didn't expect to see splashes of blood or the killer's hair in the drain, since it wasn't that kind of murder, but you never knew. Plus, I knew Dad would've looked. I wasted more time in those rooms and moved on to Gavin's office, taking pictures of the door, both sides, and the view into the office. It was messy as I expected. For a small room, Gavin packed a lot in. Three of the four walls had floor-to-ceiling bookcases filled to over-flowing. The bay window seat was stacked with how-to manuals on home improvement. Gavin collected how-to books like my father collected crime manuals. Some of the books were scattered on the floor. Gavin wasn't a neat freak, but I doubted he'd let his books fall and not pick them up. I shot the window seat from several angles and continued to look around. The chair was across the room about four feet from the desk, and there were several papers and a couple of file folders on the floor.

I got Dad's iPad out of my backpack and noted the names on the folders. The files appeared to be intact, so they probably didn't mean anything. They were just in the way. I went through the papers and books on the desk, using my fingernails to lift and shift. I wrote down every name and phone number I found.

My phone kept ringing nonstop. I gritted my teeth and answered. All I heard was raucous laughter and rude noises. I hung up, switched to vibrate, and threw the phone in my backpack. I feared turning it off altogether, in case Mom or Dr. Grace called.

I shook off the freaky phone calls and pressed the play button on Gavin's old school answering machine with my pen. The machine said, "No Messages." That was odd. Dad usually had a ton of messages. I flipped up the lid and found the cassette holder empty. The landline was only used for business, so I guessed I was looking for a client or someone who knew a client. If the killer had thought to take the tape, he'd want to take his file, too. I hadn't thought much about Gavin's files. The drawers were closed, and there were no signs of the struggle around it. I checked it out anyway and opened the top drawer.

Gavin was an organizing freak when it came to his files. I'd done some office work for him a few years ago during college. Each drawer was divided with hanging green files. Inside the hanging files were manila folders tagged and dated with the client's information. Gavin kept several folders per hanging file. He liked to divide the case into aspects with files for billing, handwritten notes, transcribed notes, dictated notes, interviews, research, and so forth. Filing for Gavin was a pain because each file was unique. He used one cabinet in the office, but there were several more down in the basement. He kept the active and recent files upstairs. There were four drawers. I started at the top and worked my way down. I used my nails to let my fingers do the walking. From what I could tell, all the files in the first two drawers were intact. I got lucky on the third drawer. S had two empty hanging files. Since the hanging files weren't tagged, I couldn't tell what belonged there. Gavin didn't allow empty files, so someone took them. The fourth drawer didn't yield anything new.

While I was on my knees, I glanced at the wall to the right of the cabinet. A black smudge started at five inches above the floor and ended at the carpet. It looked like a mark from the sole of a shoe. I crouched with my face a foot from the wall and studied it, looking for anything. I slowly got to my feet, and when I was standing straight, I spotted some tiny fibers snagged on the textured paint. They were short and dark blue. About five inches above the fibers were three hairs caught on the rough paint. The hairs were between two and three inches long. One was gray and the other two were dark brown. They matched Gavin's shaggy head. The police crime scene team would probably find skin cells. A swell of fear began in my stomach. That was where it happened. Gavin didn't die in that exact spot, but it was where the crime occurred.

I stood up and took a deep breath. I figured it out. The thought should've made me feel better, but instead, it made me feel worse. The crime happened in Gavin's own home, his safe place. What if Dixie had been there? I couldn't think about it. I wouldn't. Not now. Later. Much later.

My backpack vibrated nonstop against my hip and I started thinking that maybe it was Mom or Dr. Grace wanting to tell me the murder had been solved. I could go home and take a nap. So I answered and got a woman asking about my rates and travel stipend requirements. I told her I didn't know what she was talking about and hung up. My phone immediately vibrated again. For crying out loud.

I'd been in Gavin's house for a half hour, and it was time to get out before someone finally noticed me. I shot the wall as closeup as I could. I wanted to take some hair and fiber evidence, but let's face it, I wouldn't know what to do with it if I had. Plus, taking it had the distinct disadvantage of being a criminal offense, tampering with evidence or something. I left the fibers alone and took a last look, spotting Gavin's cell phone was on top of the filing cabinet. I pulled up the last twelve numbers Gavin dialed with my pen. Three were Dad's office, and the rest I didn't recognize. I put the numbers on the iPad and went to the bedroom to pack Dixie's favorite outfits and toiletries. On the way out, I checked the answering machine for the personal line. No tape. My guy took no chances.

The vibrating was getting ridiculous. I couldn't take it anymore and answered, praying it was Mom or Morty. Heck. I'd even take Chuck. Instead, all I got was weird sucking noises and moaning for my trouble.

"That's it," I said and turned the phone off. Mom would just have to leave a message.

I locked the side door, put Dixie's bags in my passenger seat and my backpack on the floor. A couple of cars pulled up in front of the house behind me. Male voices came to my ears, and I said a quiet, "Shit." I shoved the backpack under the seat as far as it would go.

"Where the hell are the uniforms?"

Shoes crunched on leaves as I crawled in the passenger door and tried to slither across the seat. I don't know why I bothered. It's not like my rear is easy to miss.

"Imagine finding you here. I knew I should've skipped lunch," said my cousin Chuck.

I peeked over my seat back and saw Chuck standing at the end of my truck with his notebook and pen ready. No iPad for him. Chuck liked to think he was a throwback to the golden age of detectives, some sort of Sam Spade in Levi's. Whatever. Detective Nazir and some crime science team members came up the walk behind him. Nazir waved at me and smiled. I responded in kind. One of the crime science guys took out his phone. The other one looked and began chortling. The rest of the team stopped and watched me from a distance. They smiled and whispered to each other. It was weird even for me. Chuck glanced back at them, and he wasn't smiling.

He came around the truck and watched as I slithered out and tried to look innocent.

"What are you doing here?" he asked.

"I could ask you the same thing."

"What are you doing here?"

"Aren't we cranky today? I'm picking up some clothes and stuff for Dixie, if you must know," I said.

"You'll have to give me that bag." Chuck didn't smile at me, and he usually did. The kind of smile that makes you feel oily.

"Why? What for? What are you doing here?" I was glad I'd stowed the camera in the backpack. I couldn't afford to lose those pictures. Dad would never forgive me.

"Evidence," he said.

"Evidence? Hand lotion and panties? What's going on?"

"Don't bullshit me, Mercy. You know exactly what's going on, and God help you if you've disturbed the scene."

I put my hands on my hips. "A scene you didn't bother to tape off, but don't panic. I only disturbed Dixie's closet and the medicine cabinet."

"Yeah, and what else?"

"Tell me what you're looking for, and I'll let you know."

"Give me that bag." Chuck advanced on me until we were toe to toe or maybe a better description would've been boobs to stomach.

"Seriously, Dixie needs this stuff."

"Fine. Let me take a look." Chuck went around me and pulled the bag out, totally neglecting to look under the seat. What an amateur. He rifled through Dixie's underwear and said, "I guess it's OK. You better hope you didn't mess anything up. But if you did, I'll let you make it up to me." Then he smiled.

"Don't hold your breath, Upchuck," I said.

"Upchuck? I'll remember that the next time you need a favor," said Chuck.

"Whatever. Can I go now?"

"Yeah, but we need to talk later. Same with Dixie. Has she said anything to you?"

"Nope, but I haven't told her yet." I put the bag back in my truck and walked around to my driver's side door.

"Why not?" he asked.

"Isn't it your job to deliver the bad news?" I looked at him over the bed of my truck, a nice, safe distance.

"You can't ever make anything easy, can you?"

"Not if I can help it. See ya." I got in and backed out the driveway before Chuck thought of a reason to keep me. As I drove off down the block, I saw a uniform running full out towards Gavin's house with his tie undone and pants unzipped. Somebody was in trouble, and I couldn't stop smiling. It was like Dad always said luck has everything to do with it.

On the way back to my parents' house, I called Dr. Grace.

"I have a couple of quick questions. Do you have a minute?" I asked.

"Shoot."

"First, is the toxicology back yet?"

"Not yet. Next?" Dr. Grace asked.

"Can you tell me what Gavin was wearing when he was brought in? We haven't picked up his effects yet."

"Hold on. Let me take a look."

I waited for five minutes until Dr. Grace came back on the line.

"He was wearing a blue polar fleece pullover, a white T-shirt, and jeans."

"What about shoes?" I asked.

"Hiking boots."

"What color are the soles?" I heard some rustling in the background, like Dr. Grace was looking through a bag.

"Black. Why?"

"Just curious. Is it possible to tell if hair was ripped out in a struggle?"

"Yes, if the root is intact, and by the placement of the hair? I have a bad feeling you're doing something you shouldn't."

"If you're worried that I messed up some evidence, don't."

"But you saw some."

"Could be," I said, still smiling.

"So I can expect a call from the detectives any minute."

"Oh, yeah."

"Good luck and be careful," he said.

"Thanks, Doc. You know I will," I said.

Back at my parents' house, The Girls and Dixie were snoozing in the parlor. They'd found more of Dad's peach wine and drained the bottle. Uncle Morty was nowhere to be found. He was probably out plotting revenge for me ditching him. I went up to the office to put the camera away and noticed the light on Dad's answering machine blinking like mad, as usual. I sat down with my pen ready and pressed the button. It was unlikely that Gavin would've left anything interesting on an answering machine, but you never knew.

The first four messages were from Dad's stable of detectives. The business grew so much in the first ten years; he had three detectives working for him. Denny Elliot and Suzette Montag worked insurance fraud and various white-collar crimes. Stark Evans worked everything else, mostly domestics. None of them worked with or for Gavin, as far as I knew. I took down the information and moved on to the rest of the calls. The next two were from clients, big industrial outfits asking about some background checks. Then I heard Gavin's voice come through the recorder, tinny and thin. It was unlike his voice in person, but it was him.

"Tommy. Gavin. I have a situation. I'm driving back now. Call me on the second cell," he said. Both Dad and Gavin carried several phones with them, in case of a problem.

"Tommy, where the hell are you? Call me ASAP. I'm four hours out."

"It's me again. God damn it. This is irritating. Don't make me call Chuck. Meet me at the house if you get this."

The first call came in at midnight, the second at two-thirty A.M. and the third at five. Gavin must've forgotten about the cruise. He never called Chuck, or he'd probably still be alive. I sat down in Dad's big chair and kicked my feet up on the beast. I grabbed my pack and looked at his last calls, three to Dad, two to information, and the rest I didn't recognize. Gavin called three numbers twice.

I dialed the first one and heard a voice say, "Rockville United Church of Christ. Nancy speaking."

"Hi. Did you say this was a church?" I said.

"Yes. This is the Rockville United Church of Christ. How may I help you?"

"I'm not sure. What denomination are you?" I asked.

"We're Protestant. Are you looking to join a congregation?"

I was so surprised I could only mutter, "I'm just doing a friend a favor. Thanks for your time."

Gavin called a Protestant church? He was Episcopalian. It had to be a case, but I couldn't exactly ask good old Nancy, "Hey, my friend was murdered. Can you help me out?" I'd have to call Nancy back and be a little more coherent.

I dialed the second number after forming a game plan. After all, Gavin could've been calling anyone, so I had to be less dufus and more Dad.

Like most of my game plans, it didn't help. The phone rang forever and finally a familiar voice said, "Hello?"

"Hello, who is this?" I asked.

"Who is this?"

"I asked you first," I said.

"Mercy?"

"Chuck?"

"How in the hell did you get this number?"

"Is this your cell?" I asked.

"You know it's not," he said.

"Whose is it?"

"First, tell me where you got this number." Chuck was grinding his teeth. Not a pleasant sound on a phone.

"Fat chance." I snorted.

"I'm not playing, Mercy. How did you get this number?"

"Got to go."

I hung up before he could threaten me and dialed the third number.

"Good afternoon, Student Administration. This is Angela speaking."

"Uh. I'm sorry, I'm not sure who exactly I've reached. Where are you?"

"This is Student Admin. Are you a student?" asked Angela.

"No. Is this a college?" I asked.

"This is the University of Nebraska at Lincoln. Is there something I can help you with?"

"I hope so. Were you answering the phones last Friday?"

"No. I was out sick. Why?"

"If I knew I'd tell you," I said.

I wouldn't, but she didn't know that. People like a little hopeless honesty.

"What's wrong? What can I help you with?"

"I have a friend who called you on Friday and I'm trying to figure out who he talked to and why."

"Well, like I said, I wasn't here," she said.

"Do you keep records of phone inquiries?"

"No."

"Who would've been handling calls while you were gone?"

"I think they sent someone from personnel down."

"You don't know who," I said.

"No," she said.

"Could you find out?" I asked.

"I suppose so." She didn't sound too sure, so I decided to throw out some bait.

"I'm a private detective, and this is part of a very important investigation. I'd really appreciate your help."

"Really? What's the case?"

"That's my client's private information. I'm sure you understand," I said.

"I do, I do, and I can't give you any personal information, either."

"I understand completely. I just need to know why you were called in the first place."

"OK. I can ask personnel who came up." She was so excited she could hardly breathe.

"That would be great." I gave her my name and cell number. Angela said she'd find out what she could.

I pushed my feet off the desk and let myself spin in Dad's big chair. What did I know? Not much. For details, I'd have to rely on Dixie. She might know where Gavin was before he returned in such a lather, but then again, she might not. Dixie wasn't like my mother. She had nothing to do with the business, to the point that she didn't answer the business line.

I wrote my sad little list and doodled on it, drawing a pattern of paisley around the words and sentences. Gavin liked paisley. He wore paisley ties when he wore ties, which wasn't often. He gave Dixie a paisley scarf for Christmas two years ago. I'd seen it knotted around her throat a hundred times. She'd had it on at our Easter brunch a few weeks before and Gavin unknotted it several times, causing her to go to the bathroom and reassemble herself. He loved to pester her.

I couldn't remember who said what or who ate what at Mom's brunch, but we had a good time. Gavin smiled a lot. Dixie too. They held hands when they walked out the door. I watched them from the bay window as they walked down the steps and through the gate. They turned left, got in their car, and drove away. I would never see him alive again. I wished I'd known it at the time. I would've told him some things. How I liked his magic tricks and his barbecued ribs. I'd thank him for remembering that I only like dark chocolate with nuts. No one else ever did. Just little things, things that don't matter much when people are alive, but become important when they're not. I missed him, and I didn't know if it would go away. Time heals all wounds, they say, but I'd seen plenty of evidence that it didn't. I didn't think Dixie would heal. Hers wasn't a flesh wound, and I hoped to God it wasn't a mortal one either.

I dug out my cell phone and checked my messages. Sixty-eight. I hadn't had sixty-eight messages in the last month. Heck. The last six months. On the upside, the first one was from Pete, the invisible doctor.

I called him, and he actually answered. It might be a first.

"Hey. Where are you?" asked Pete.

"Mom and Dad's. Where are you?" Like I needed to ask.

"Your apartment."

"Wow. I thought you'd be at the hospital. I'm starting to think they have you on a choke chain." I didn't try to keep the sarcasm out of my voice.

"It's not that bad," he said.

"Right."

"Don't be like that. I can take an hour at six. Let's get some dinner."

"Ooh, a whole hour."

"What's wrong?" Pete asked.

"Nothing," I said.

"Don't give me that. What's wrong? And don't say it's my schedule because I know you don't care."

That wasn't exactly true. I wanted to see him more, but I understood. Being a cop's daughter taught me the value of independence. I lived my own life much as my mother had and fit Pete in whenever I could.

"It's been a bad day."

"The Siamese piss on the sofa again?"

"Not yet." I hadn't seen the cats. They were snots and had issues with being left in my care. They'd been known to pee on Mom's favorite sofa to show their displeasure. Invisible cats weren't a problem for me; as long as food disappeared from their bowls, I was happy.

"Well..."

"Gavin died."

"MI?" Pete didn't sound surprised. He was training to be a surgeon and people dropped dead around him all the time. I was the same way, but I knew Gavin and he didn't.

"Sort of."

"How do you have a sort of MI?"

"It wasn't natural."

"Define unnatural."

"He was murdered." I heard a gasp behind me. I turned and saw Dixie standing in the doorway with her hands over her mouth. Her eyes were round, and her knuckles were turning white.

"Oh, crap," I said.

"What happened?" asked Pete.

"I'll call you back," I said, and hung up.

Dixie dropped her hands and yelled at me, "Shut up! You shut up. That's not true. It's not true, so you just shut your mouth."

I couldn't speak. Anything I might have said evaporated.

"You think you know. You think you know, like your father, but you don't. You don't. He had a heart condition. So you don't know and shut up."

"Dixie, I'm so sorry," I said.

"I said, shut up!" She brought her hands to her mouth, hard enough to knock her head back, and she screamed into them. She didn't move.

She stood in the doorway screaming and looking at me with rage. It overwhelmed me. I knew for the first time what it was like to be scared of someone you love. I stood up and walked to her with my hands in front of me.

Before I reached her, Dixie's eyes changed, her screaming stopped, and she walked out of the room. I followed her down the hall, trying to find the right apology inside of me. I wanted, no, I needed to say the right thing for the both of us. Instead, I followed her to my parents' bedroom. She was drunk and unsteady on her feet. She lurched towards the stairs, over corrected, and before I reached her, she bumped into one of Mom's framed needlepoint pictures. Mom had worked on the canvas for a year and it hung in a prime viewing spot. Tough luck for it because it fell off its hook and shattered at my feet. Dixie glanced at it and continued down the hall, slower and less sure with every step.

In the bedroom, she reached for the Ativan bottle I'd refilled in a fit of stupidity.

"That's not a good idea, Dixie." I took the bottle from her hand and put it in my pocket.

"What else am I supposed to do?" she asked.

"Just lay down for a while."

I pulled back the covers. She sat, and I took off her shoes. She lay back against the fluffy pillows. Mom's small reading lamp lit the room and Dixie's eyes shone wide and watery in its dim glow. In the near darkness, she looked as young as me; maybe younger because the unexpected had happened, and no explanations were forthcoming. Her eyes showed her confusion.

"Do you want the TV on?" I asked.

"What will happen?" she asked.

"With what?"

"Will they find out who did it?"

"Yes," I said, confident in that, at least.

"Will you?"

"Yes, I will. I'll do anything you want."

"I think I want to sleep now," she said, closing her eyes and turning her face from me.

I turned off the lamp and went downstairs. It was rare that I felt bad about anything. I mean, really felt terrible. Normally, I could negotiate with myself; tell myself it had to be done, things like that. But this was one of those rare occasions when I had done something with no excuse available. I needed chocolate and fast. There was only one place to go when I needed chocolate and comfort with no questions asked. Thank God Aunt Tennessee was always home.

CHAPTER SEVEN

Aunt Tenne lived in Chesterfield about a half hour from my parents' house, far enough for me to calm down and form a plan. Halfway there I pulled over and looked up the Rockville United Church of Christ on my phone. I couldn't help myself. I had to know why Gavin called them. The church was a quick detour on the way to Aunt Tenne, and I could take the guilt until then.

Due to my keen sense of direction, it took longer to find the church than expected. I drove around backstreets a good fifteen minutes before I found the right avenue. Then the traffic moved like a tortoise, when I was dying to be a hare. A block away, I saw why. Crime scene tape cordoned off the church, and everyone was slowing down to get a look. The St. Louis County Medical Examiner's van sat in the parking lot, and there were half a dozen cops and crime scene analysts moving around the building. I parked across the street and walked over to a couple uniforms doing guard duty.

Too bad I didn't take the time to spruce up a little. Dad would shake his head in dismay if he knew. He had no shame when it came to gleaning info out of cops or anyone else. The younger cop would probably appreciate my Marilynness. I should've been able to take advantage, but I was wearing a pair of jeans and a T-shirt. The jeans weren't even low rise. I just had to go for comfortable. What an idiot. The T-shirt did have a scoop neck, and I was wearing a lacy bra. A little bra goes a long way. I reminded myself that this was for Gavin and tugged at my shirt, exposing the top of my secret weapons, and then added a little extra swing to my hips. The cop locked in on me at twenty paces. He straightened up and swaggered over to the barricade.

"Hey there," I said.

"Hello, what can I do for you this fine afternoon?" he asked while thrusting his badge out at me.

"I was just driving by and saw all the hoopla. What's up?"

He gave me what I supposed was his sexy look. It could've been confused for his I-just-took-NyQuil look. "Crime scene."

Duh.

I flipped my hair back. "What happened?"

"Murder."

"Really? How totally awful." I ran my fingers through my hair and let some thick, blond locks fall in my face. They ended at my lips. How convenient. "What happened?" I said.

"I don't think you want to know. It's pretty brutal. You don't want that kind of thing on your mind, do you?" He fingered his gun holster.

No, no. I'm too busy thinking about my manicure.

"Ooh, tell me. I'm dying of curiosity," I said.

"Well, if it isn't Mercy Watts."

While I was busy setting feminism back twenty years, the officer's partner snuck up on me. His name tag said Parker, and he'd seen more than a few crime scenes if I went by his craggy face and wrinkled uniform. Life'd been rough on Parker.

"Do we know each other, Officer Parker?" I asked sweetly.

"Not exactly, but I know your pop. You'd better stow it, Ameche," he said.

"Who's your dad?" asked Ameche.

"Her pop is none other than the famous Tommy Watts."

"No shit, I mean, no kidding," said Ameche.

"No kidding," I said. "So what's this crime scene, a trade secret?"

"It's no secret. I suggest you go home and watch the news if you're so curious," said Parker.

"Yeah, that'll be accurate," I said.

"Maybe it won't be accurate, but it's the best you're gonna get," he replied.

"Isn't Tommy Watts some kind of hero?" said Ameche.

"He is, but she ain't." Parker sneered at me.

"Aw, come on," I said.

"Forget it. Tommy's a PI now. Give them an inch and they'll take a mile." Parker hitched up his belt and tried to look substantial. He'd need a few more sandwiches for that.

"Are you a PI?" said Ameche.

"Nurse."

"Give a lot of sponge baths, do you?" He gave me another NyQuil look with his close-set hazel eyes.

"You've been watching too much porn," I said. "I do put in a load of catheters, though."

"Oh, yeah? I could go for a little of that action," said Ameche.

"Shut up, dumbass," said Parker. "A catheter involves sticking a tube up your dick."

Ameche stepped back. "You do that?"

"It's a dirty job," I said.

"No shit," said Ameche.

"So about this scene?" I asked.

"Forget it, sweetie pie. We got a job to do. Go thread some wieners," said Parker.

"Thanks for nothing," I said.

"Anytime," Parker said over his shoulder as he started to walk the line again. I could feel Ameche's eyes on me as I walked to my truck. I gave him an extra swish and wiggle just for fun. You never know when you might need a contact in the department.

I drove away from the church with nothing, but the hairs raised on the back of my neck. A murder in the church Gavin called. Coincidence? I doubted it. Might as well go on to Aunt Tenne's and indulge my secret desire to eat an eight-thousand-calorie-a-day diet. Aunt Tenne was a 911 operator on the graveyard shift and a woman without a hint of a social life. She was good for sympathy and snacks. Mom liked to call her a big girl, but at fifty-five she wasn't a girl, and big didn't quite cover it. Aunt Tenne had to turn sideways to get into her closet, which is to say she was morbidly obese. Of course, no one used those words to describe her. I'd heard plump, overweight, big-boned, but I never heard fat or obese, although I imagine she suffered it plenty.

I walked up to her door and paused. Inside, Aretha Franklin hit the high notes while Aunt Tenne sang along. I knocked and waited. She opened the door five minutes later. "Mercy, just the girl I wanted to see."

"Hi, Aunt Tenne. Why'd you want to see me?"

She moved back to let me through, and I went into the living room. Aretha was singing about respect.

"I'm taking a vacation. Well earned, if I do say so myself," Aunt Tenne said.

"Where are you going?"

"Cruise. Want to go?" She turned to grab a diet coke off an end table as she asked. Otherwise, she'd have seen my expression, and I doubt it was pleasant. She turned back around and I had a fixed smile in place. I hoped it looked genuine. The thought of cruising with Aunt Tenne brought on visions of buffets and judgement. I'd spend the whole time fighting the urge to smack smug faces and trying to keep my favorite aunt out of the earshot of the nastiest voices. Still, if I didn't go, who would? She'd rather stab herself in the head than ask my mother, her sister, to go. Aunt Tenne liked to say that Mom was born with a spotlight trained on her. I agreed. I'd felt the glare of Mom's glow plenty. No one compared to her, not even me, and I was a dead ringer for both her and Marilyn Monroe. I'd inherited the spotlight, but I hadn't quite grown into it yet. Aunt Tenne said it got worse as Mom got older. Last year, she caused a three-car pileup when she went out for a jog. Dad bought her a treadmill, so we wouldn't get sued.

"When are you going?" I asked.

"I'm thinking sometime this summer."

"Where to?"

"Virgin Islands or the Bahamas. What do you think?" she asked.

"Er...I'll have to see if I can work it out financially."

And mentally.

"I have brochures." Aunt Tenne spread a dozen booklets across the coffee table and looked at me hopefully. I felt sick to my stomach.

"I'm thinking about the Bahamas. Everybody goes to the Virgins," I said.

"Just what I was thinking. Are you hungry? I'm starving." She led me into the kitchen, and I had a childhood flashback. God, I loved Aunt Tenne's kitchen. It was snack food heaven and stuffed to the gills. Mom's kitchen was more wine sauces and vegetables.

"What are you in the mood for?" she asked.

"Calories and lots of them." She turned away from the cabinets and brushed the hair out of her eyes. Her eyes got me. They were the same brilliant green as Mom's, but without the scrutiny. Mom wouldn't adopt Aunt Tenne's look of concern without being sure that I hadn't done anything wrong first. Aunt Tenne thought I could do no wrong. Little did she know.

"Gavin?" she asked.

"He died." I ducked my head and swallowed hard.

"I know. Aunt Miriam called. I left you some messages."

"I'm sorry. It's been crazy since it happened."

"What was he, fifty something? That's so young," she said.

"Not too young to get murdered," I said. Good, good to have the word out of my mouth, past my lips.

Aunt Tenne grasped her chest and looked around for a seat. She sat and slowed her breathing while tears rushed down her cheeks. She reached for me. I took her hand and sat on the arm of the love seat. Aunt Tenne was the only one person I knew with a love seat in her kitchen.

"Honey, sweetie pie. What happened?" she said.

"I don't know. The M.E. thinks he was poisoned with something that caused an MI."

"Something he ate?" Aunt Tenne produced a candy bar from somewhere. She ate it without noticing what she consumed. I wondered if any M&M's were stashed in her cushions. Or better yet Ding Dongs. I loved Ding Dongs.

Once after Thanksgiving dinner, I found six Ding Dong wrappers in the guest bathroom trash can. I was incensed. We had Ding Dongs and Mom was holding out on me. I marched around the house and found Mom in the pantry.

"How come I didn't get any Ding Dongs?"

"What are you talking about? Go entertain Grandma J," Mom said without turning around.

"Mom."

Who knew the word "Mom" could be so long and irritating?

"Mercy, please. Go somewhere."

"I want a Ding Dong."

"We don't have any Ding Dongs. Go on now." She looked up from the apple pie she was cutting and glared at me.

"Mom," I repeated.

"What's wrong, girls?" Dad said from the doorway. He leaned on the frame, his arms crossed over his chest. He smiled so his dimples cut deep into his cheeks, and I thought he was the coolest guy ever. That was before I saw Clark Gable in *Gone with the Wind*.

"Mom won't give me a Ding Dong," I said.

"We have Ding Dongs?" Dad asked.

"No, we do not have Ding Dongs. How many times do I have to say that?" asked Mom.

"Yes, we do. I saw the wrappers in the bathroom."

So there. I had evidence. Try and hold out on me? We'll see about that.

"You saw Ding Dong wrappers in the bathroom?" Mom looked at Dad. His dimples disappeared.

"Carolina, you can't fix it," said Dad. "It's always going to be there until she finds a way to get past it."

I touched Mom's arm. "Fix what?"

Mom ignored me. "That place was supposed to help her, really help her with the whole thing."

"What whole thing?" I asked.

"Well, you know, she's bound to have setbacks, Carolina," Dad said.

"Well, I wonder how many setbacks she's had. Mercy?" Mom's hands went to her hips. Her knife was pointed at me and dropped bits of crust on the floor.

"What?" I said.

"How many wrappers did you find?" Mom asked.

"Six."

"Great, just great." Mom covered her eyes with her free hand, and Dad took my arm. He pulled me out of the pantry into the empty kitchen. He sat me in a chair and made coffee.

"You know how Aunt Tenne was on vacation the last couple of weeks?"

"Yeah," I said.

"Do you know where she was?"

"No."

"She was at a weight-loss clinic," Dad said.

"So how come Mom gave her Ding Dongs?"

Dad made me a hot cocoa. He glanced at the pantry door before adding a tiny bit of peppermint schnapps. "She didn't. Aunt Tenne brought them with her."

"It's Thanksgiving. Mom made six pies and a chocolate trifle."

"I know," he said.

That was the moment I realized Aunt Tennessee had a problem and probably more than one. Fifteen years later; nothing had changed.

I looked around Aunt Tenne's kitchen for my beloved Ding Dongs, while Aunt Tenne chewed. They could be anywhere — the microwave, freezer, toaster oven — but she was better than she used to be. She confined food to the kitchen. Food used to be all over the house, including the bathroom. She lost fifteen pounds after the change.

Aunt Tenne munched on chips and asked through mouthfuls, "What do we know so far?"

I got two snack cakes out of the microwave and settled for them. "Not much. He was poisoned at home but died at the hospital. He was working on a case out of state and came home in a hurry. Oh, and on his cell phone, recall I found the numbers of a church and University of Lincoln student services."

"Was he in Lincoln before he came home?" she asked.

"Don't know, but I did run by the church on the way over here. It's a crime scene. The cops wouldn't tell me anything, though."

"What church is it?"

"Rockville United Church of Christ," I said.

"Oh, yes. I know that one. You know that one. Everybody knows about that one."

"I don't."

"Sure you do. You have to. It was the bride who was strangled right after her wedding on Saturday." Aunt Tenne shoveled in more chips and hiccuped.

"That's the day before Gavin died and he called that church. It was one of his last calls. Holy shit."

"Mercy." Aunt Tenne frowned at me.

"Sorry. I can't believe I forgot about that. What an idiot," I said.

"I knew you knew."

"What's her name?" I said.

"Who?" she asked.

"The bride."

"Oh, yeah. Simple, no no, it's Sample. Rebecca Sample. I think she was about your age, twenty-five or twenty-six. Maybe she was from Lincoln or went to school there," said Aunt Tenne.

"I didn't think of that. I knew I came here for a reason."

Other than the snacks, that is.

"I'm so sorry about Gavin, sweetie." Aunt Tenne wiped her eyes again. "He was like family. Have you called your parents yet?"

"Yeah. They're coming home as soon as they dock and get a flight."

"When's that?"

"Tomorrow, I think." I polished off my cakes and scanned for a second helping.

"Then there's no reason to get excited."

"What do you mean?" I lowered my eyes.

"I mean, there's no reason to keep after this. Tommy will take care of it," she said.

"I don't know what you're talking about," I said as I spotted another snack cake.

"I suppose you went to that church to find religion."

"Not exactly."

"I know you loved Gavin, but let Tommy handle it or the police. That's what they're there for," said Aunt Tenne.

"You know what Dad thinks of that."

"I know, I know. He's sure the whole system has fallen to pieces without him. Well, let me tell you, it hasn't. Besides, Chuck's on it."

"Please." I rolled my eyes.

"You know he's good. Even Tommy thinks so."

"I guess. Wait a minute. Chuck said he caught the bride case. How'd you know?" I asked.

"I saw him on the TV. He said a very eloquent, 'No comment'."

"Chuck's on the case. Chuck's on the case."

"Mercy?" Aunt Tenne knitted her eyebrows.

"Give me a second," I said.

She got up and put a pizza in the oven. I let my mind wander in an attempt to connect the dots. It was a slow process, given my sugar-saturated brain.

"Chuck answered the phone," I mumbled.

"What's that, sweetie?" asked Aunt Tenne.

"I called a number off Gavin's recall and Chuck answered."

"So what?"

"It wasn't his phone, and he said as much. He wouldn't tell me whose phone it was, but he kept asking where I got the number. Gavin called the church and then he called that number. I bet it was that bride's phone. It was left at the crime scene."

"Wouldn't that be in an evidence locker?" she asked.

"Detectives check out evidence all the time."

"Sounds good to me. You want a Coke?" she asked.

"Sure. And there was an S missing from Gavin's files. Sample was probably a client. I can't wait to tell Dad."

"The sooner, the better. One thing I know is you are not supposed to be rummaging through crime scenes," said Aunt Tenne.

"I didn't rummage. I was picking up clothes for Dixie."

"With a detour through Gavin's files?"

"Yeah, well, you know how it is," I said.

"Yes, I do know, and I want you to let it alone. Don't you have some nursing to do?"

"You sound like the cop at the scene."

"What did he say?" she asked.

"He told me to go thread some wieners," I said.

"Couldn't have put it better myself." She laughed and fresh tears appeared at the corners of her eyes. "How's Dixie handling it?"

"Not well," I said.

"Anything I can do?"

"Maybe you could come over and stay with her for a while tonight. I have some stuff to do."

"I will, but it better not be Gavin stuff. Go see Pete or something."

"Pete. Oh crap. We're supposed to have dinner. I have to go," I said.

"What about my pizza?"

"Eat it for me. I'll see you later."

I went out Aunt Tenne's front door and walked towards my truck when someone tapped me on the shoulder. "Ahhh!" I jumped away and turned around to find Aaron, a friend of Uncle Morty's, standing there.

"Hi, Mercy," said Aaron.

"What the hell are you doing here? You scared me to death," I said, clutching my chest.

"My car broke down." Aaron looked at me with the guile of a newborn calf, and I resisted the urge to slap my forehead. Aaron had a way of turning up when least expected. I can't say I ever desired his company, but I sure spent plenty of time with him.

"Since when do you have a car?" I asked.

"Thursday," he said.

"What happened to your scooter?"

"Front wheel fell off."

"No kidding." As long as I'd known him, Aaron rode a scooter manufactured during World War Two. He rode it in all types of weather and looked it. I had thought his hair resulted from scooter riding, but apparently not. He looked the same that day as every day before. The front of his hair was plastered to his head. The back stuck straight up. The enormous lenses of his thick glasses were smudged. He probably bought the glasses in 1983. They went well with his Izod shirt (collar up) and stonewashed jeans. Put the whole look on a five-foot-four, moderately obese body, and you get the picture.

He stood in front of me, blinking slowly and fiddling with his belt loops. If he was thinking at all, Dungeons and Dragons strategy was my number one guess.

"Do you need a ride?" I asked.

"Great. Where's Pete? Have you seen Pete lately? I want to run something by him."

Oh Lord!

He scratched his head and said, "You see, I've been working on this new character, and she's got these wild powers."

He went on and on through the entire drive. Half the time, I didn't know what he was talking about. Aaron didn't notice when I pulled out my cell and texted Pete. I told him to meet me at Kronos and then went back to nodding and grunting answers to Aaron.

I parked in front of Kronos fifteen minutes later. It was hard to believe, but Aaron was a successful restaurateur. Kronos was a Star Trek-inspired burger joint renowned for its sandwiches and décor. Aaron owned Kronos with Rodney, a Dungeon and Dragons pal, and close friend of Uncle Morty, which is how I knew both of them. Rodney was a taller and slightly more sophisticated version of Aaron. Rodney said Aaron was the brains behind the glamour. I'd never figured that one out. Neither one of them showed a tremendous amount of brains and, as for glamour, forget about it. It's doubtful Kronos would even be in business if it wasn't for my dad.

Fifteen years earlier, Rodney had the brilliant idea to open Kronos. It turned out not to be so brilliant because nobody ate there. In a fit of desperation, he asked Dad what to do. Rodney saw my father as the solver of all problems. I'd like to think that wasn't true, but I couldn't think of a problem he hadn't solved. Kronos was a case in point. Rodney painted what Dad told him over the inside of the front door in English and Klingon.

"Make Good Burgers."
Det. Tommy Watts, STLPD

So Rodney set to work on the perfect Tommy Watts burger. It took eight tries, but he nailed it, and Dad said he'd send some business over. Dad never does anything by halves. He told the class he was teaching at Saint Louis University about a weird little burger joint in the Central West End and the rest was history.

Aaron and I walked into the evening rush. Every night is a good night for Kronos. The twenty-five-foot walnut bar, salvaged from a turn-of-the-century pub, was packed with off and on duty cops, firefighters, and paramedics. They clumped in groups and told tales with large hand gestures and laughter. The tables were full, but with civilians. There was a lot of head swiveling at the tables as the customers checked out the décor. Rod was right about the Star Trek decorating. People loved it. The walls were covered with everything from vintage movie posters to cases containing Spock ears. Star Trek did good by Rod until he had a second brainstorm. He added cop memorabilia. So between autographed pictures of Captain Picard and Data, there were framed newspaper clippings like, "Rookie Cop Solves Triple Homicide." The cop business, never lacking, boomed. Soon he added paramedic and firefighter garb and clippings. If there was a place to expand, Rod and Aaron would've expanded long ago.

We only got a few feet in the door before a hush settled over the crowd and the sound of my heels clicking on the hardwood filled the empty air. Then the entire bar stood and cheered. A group of cops my dad worked with stood on their chairs and whistled. Aaron and I looked at each other. I think my face mirrored his dumbfounded expression. Usually, Kronos clientele didn't pay much attention to me. I was in there all the time. They knew me.

After a good five minutes, the crowd calmed and went back to their groups. They laughed and patted each other on the back while stealing glances at me. It felt like an out-of-body experience. Was I really in Kronos? Did that really just happen?

"Hey you!" Pete yelled over the din and waved me over. Aaron disappeared into the kitchen, and I sat down under a new display suspended from the ceiling in a Plexiglas box, a complete firefighter's uniform including boots, a small shovel, and several framed photos of firefighters looking grim beside a burnt-out factory hung over our heads. Pete leaned over the table and kissed me. He smelled terrible, a mixture of sweat and disinfectant, but I enjoyed it just the same.

"Okay, what the hell was that all about?" I asked, brushing his dark blond off his wire-rimmed glasses.

"You don't know?"

"Obviously not."

Pete picked up his phone off the table and pressed a couple of buttons. He handed me the phone and sat back like he expected something to explode.

"Check it out," he said.

I looked down at the small screen and saw myself bending over an old guy with my leopard bra showing. The tiny caption said, "Marilyn Lives."

"Oh my God," I said, clapping my hand over my mouth.

Pete leaned forward. "It gets worse."

"How can it get worse?" I asked from behind my hand.

"There's a website and you're all over YouTube."

I dropped my hand. "YouTube? Mom's going to kill me."

"It'll blow over. You want to see more?" asked Pete.

"God no," I said, shaking my head.

Stanley Thigpen, a paramedic, swaggered over, put his hands on the table, and leaned over me, filling my airspace with the stench of sour beer.

"How much for a dance?" he asked.

"Shut up, Stanley," I said.

Stanley made a move like he was going to sit down next to me. "Are you saying I can't afford you?"

Pete stood up and towered over Stanley. "No, I am."

Stanley backed off with his hands up. "Come on. Your dad could always take a joke."

"You're lucky he's not here," I said. "You'd be taking your teeth home in a cup."

"Get back here, Stanley, you dumb fuck," yelled an EMT at the bar.

"Sorry, sorry. Jesus, a guy can't even make a joke around here."

"He can if he's funny," said Pete.

Stanley shrugged and walked away.

"Still think it's no big deal?"

"It's a medium deal, but it will blow over," Pete said.

"It better blow over before Mom gets back because it will hit the fan. How did you find out?"

"I heard a couple of techs talking about you this morning. It was like they found out Batman's secret identity."

"I think this might be Mom's worst nightmare, everyone looking at me, thinking things about me," I said.

"But it's not yours, I mean, not your worst nightmare?"

"I'm not crazy about it, but there are worse things."

Pete pushed my glass of water to me and raised his own. "To worse things," he said.

I drank to that and ignored the catcall coming from the other end of the bar, not to mention the grimace on Pete's face.

"She's a beauty, ain't she?" said a voice.

Pete's grimace disappeared. "Yes, she is."

"They don't make rubber like that anymore." Pete and I looked up to see Rodney standing with his hands on his hips, grinning at the ceiling.

"Er, I guess not," Pete said.

"Damn shame," I said.

Rodney looked at me. "I can take it out if you want to touch it."

"That's okay."

"Fine then. You hungry or what?" He looked disgruntled that we didn't want to touch his rubber.

"I'll have a triple tribble platter and a Coke," said Pete.

"Worf burger, cheese fries, and a metamorphosis malt," I said.

Rodney turned and waded through a large group of cops screaming with laughter about a guy named Cleason.

"I was starting to wonder what happened to you," said Pete.

"Sorry. I got a little sidetracked," I said.

"I thought that was my line."

"You'll have to share. How long do we have?"

"A half hour or so. Slow night. How are you doing?" he said.

"Okay, I guess. I still can't believe he's dead, though."

Pete picked up my hand and stroked it with his long fingers. "You're sure it was murder?"

"That's what the M.E. said. Plus, Dad had a feeling."

"What does that mean?"

"It means something isn't right," I said.

"He could be wrong," Pete said.

"Yeah, right. I've been waiting for that for twenty-five years and I bet there are some guys here that have waited a hell of a lot longer than that."

"Who's the M.E.?"

"Simon Grace," I said.

"I know him," Pete said.

"Oh, yeah?"

"Well, I know who he is. He's good. Makes me think about special-izing in pathology."

"Ick." I made a face.

"What, you don't want to date a cutter?"

"Not just no, but hell no."

"I thought you love me no matter what," Pete said with a smile.

"I do, but let's not get crazy," I said.

"What about surgery? You'll barely see me for the next five years. What then?" Pete asked with a look bordering on serious.

"At least I wouldn't have to smell dead people in your hair," I said.

"I'll wash it."

"There's not enough shampoo in the world." I wrinkled up my nose and made a hacking noise.

"You know you don't always smell rosy." He made a hacking noise of his own and pinched his nose.

"You really know how to sweet-talk a girl."

Aaron came with our platters and started jabbering about a flame-throwing goblin as I plowed my way through a mountain of cheese fries. I looked around the bar and caught the eye of a few friendly faces. They waved and, thankfully, stayed where they were. Then I heard Pete ask a question, a real question, not just a grunt or a vague agreement. I turned back to Pete and Aaron in time to see Pete arrange his face into a look of studied boredom. Rodney came out from behind the bar and yelled for Aaron. He kept on about aerial tactics until Rod threw a roll at his head. Nailed him, too. Right in the ear. Aaron left, dragging his feet.

"What was that all about?" I said.

"What?" Pete stared down at his plate and pushed his house-made tater tots into a line opposite a row of garlic green beans. The whole thing looked like a chessboard, or dare I say a battle plan.

I narrowed my eyes at him. "You were starting to actually sound interested."

"I'm not interested. I'm polite. You should try it sometime," Pete said.

"Sorry. Point taken." I wasn't sure I was buying it, but sometimes it's better to let things lie and hope they go away.

"Alright then. If we eat fast, we could go back to your place for a little while." Pete cocked one of his eyebrows at me.

"How long is a little while?" I asked.

"Long enough."

"Oh, yeah? Long enough for who?"

"You, me, mostly me, but maybe you too. I'll throw in a foot rub."

"Fifteen minutes isn't long enough for a good foot rub, much less anything else," I said.

"I had to try," said Pete with a low-wattage smile.

"I understand." I waved to Rodney behind the bar.

"What are you doing?"

"Getting to-go boxes."

"Really?"

"You know I can't resist you in your lab jacket. Especially with all those stains," I said.

"Thank God for that," he said.

CHAPTER EIGHT

Fifteen minutes was not long enough, but since we bagged dinner, we stretched it to twenty-five, which bordered on reasonable. It goes without saying that I didn't get my foot rub.

Pete stretched out beside me and stoked my thigh. I put my head on his shoulder, drawing his smell deep into my lungs until they were full to the point of pain. The stench was gone, banished by the thin sheen of fresh sweat on his skin. After letting me breathe him for a couple of minutes, Pete said, "I have to go."

"I know. See you in a month," I said.

"Sorry, babe. But I do have a break after this rotation. Two weeks. We should go somewhere."

"I have to go on a cruise."

"A cruise with who?" he asked.

"Aunt Tenne just asked me, and I can't afford two vacations," I said.

"Why do you have to go?" he asked.

"Well, she asked, and who else is going to do it?"

"Your mom could go."

"She's on a cruise now and, besides, cruising with Mom isn't Aunt

Tenne's idea of a good time. The looks, the comparisons. You know how it is," I said.

"You look exactly like your mother, so how are you different?" asked Pete.

"I'm not her sister."

"I guess I don't get the whole girly competition thing."

"All I can say is Mom's a lot to handle even for me, and I don't weight three hundred plus."

"I don't even get that," he said.

"I don't have the energy to explain girls to you," I said, rolling over and shoving him off my bed.

Pete walked into the bathroom muttering. I looked after his long, lean frame for a moment and then picked up the phone on the first ring.

"Mercy, it's Mom. You're not answering your cell phone."

"Sorry. I turned it off because...dinner. I was having dinner. I guess I forgot to turn it back on."

"I'm surprised you're home. I expected you to be with Dixie. She shouldn't be on her own," said my mother in the special disappointed voice she saved just for me.

"She is not alone. The Girls were at the house when I left," I said with my 'I'm a good girl' voice.

"No one answered the phone," she said.

"Maybe they didn't hear it. So what's up?" I asked.

"Dad wants to know how it's going. Have you talked to Dr. Grace yet?"

"Where's Dad?"

"Right here." She offered no explanation. It wasn't like Dad to let Mom do the talking. He just plain had too much to say.

"Is something wrong?"

"Well, he's a tad under the weather," she said.

"Dad's sick? No way!"

Dad sick was a once in a decade occurrence. Injuries happened all the time, but Dad considered illness an insult.

"Try not to sound so pleased," Mom said.

"I'm not pleased. I'm surprised. What's wrong?"

"The flu, I suppose. It's going around."

"Norovirus?" I asked.

"They're not willing to go that far yet," she said. "Back to the case. This is costing us a fortune."

"Okay. I talked to Grace. Dad was right. Gavin's MI was induced. Tox screen isn't back yet." I heard a murmur, and Mom repeated what I said. Dad cursed, and Mom came back on the line.

"Dad okay?" I asked.

"He's fine," she said.

He didn't sound fine. The background, previously quiet, was filled with loud hacking and thumping furniture.

"What's he doing?"

"He wants the phone," she said.

"Give it to him before he has a conniption."

"Absolutely not. He might vomit on it and then where would I be."

"That bad, huh?" I said.

"Worse. What else have you done? Nothing illegal, I hope."

"Of course not. I got some things for Dixie and documented the house. That's the crime scene. I found a couple of missing files, a scuff mark on the wall, fibers, and hair. No blood."

"You didn't touch anything." Mom's voice rose an octave.

"No, I did not touch anything. I'm not an idiot, Mom."

"What else? What files?"

"Two S files. I'm not sure who the clients were yet. Gavin's cells were there. One was dead, and I copied the last ten numbers dialed on the other."

"Whose numbers were they?"

"Dad's office, the Rockville United Church of Christ, and the University of Nebraska, Lincoln. I'm not sure about the last one." I didn't want to tell her about Chuck and the bride's phone number. If I brought him up, she might tell me to drop it and give Chuck what I had. Since I wasn't doing that, it was easier to omit than disobey.

"Rockville United Church of Christ? Have you been by there yet?"

"Yeah and get this, a bride was murdered there the day before Gavin died. Does Dad know what Gavin was working on?" Mom asked Dad and through the coughs, I thought she got a positive response.

"Deadbeat dad case," Mom said. "Not very exciting."

"It may have just gotten exciting," I said.

"He doesn't think so, but you should check it out anyway."

I got up and put on a robe. "What about the University?"

"He doesn't remember Gavin saying anything about that. Have Mort run Gavin's credit cards," said Mom.

"When are you coming home?" I could feel Mom's hesitation, and then I heard concern in her voice.

"Well, dear, we're docking this evening, but I don't know..." There was a yell in the background that sounded like Dad finally having his conniption fit.

"Your father seems to think he can fly back immediately, but I don't know if they'll let him on a flight."

"Let me know," I said.

"I'll call later for another update. Be safe and, for God's sake, stay under the radar." That was Mom's way of saying, don't get arrested. I have been arrested a few times, but somehow my paperwork always gets lost, never to be seen again. Can't say I worry much about getting arrested anymore.

We hung up as Pete came out of the bathroom amid billowing steam. His damp scrubs stuck to his skin and showed me the outline of his abs under the fabric. I followed him into the kitchen and watched him toast a bagel. He slathered it with whipped butter and wrapped it in plastic for later. He turned to me and said while putting on his lab coat, "I'll call you later." Pete's later meant some time in the indistinct future.

"You can't wear that," I said, poking his chest.

"What?"

"That lab coat is disgusting. You can't treat sick people in that. They feel bad enough already," I said.

Pete looked down, his head moving side to side while smoothing his jacket. "I think it's okay."

"You would. What's that?" I pointed to a three-inch yellow stain on his right sleeve.

"Orange juice, I think."

"What about this?" I picked up his hem and brought it chest high. It was gray, and the stitching was falling out.

"I'm going to be a surgeon, not a seamstress," he said.

"Leave it here. I'll fix it. Imagine that. The poor thing has probably never seen the inside of a washer." I slipped the jacket off his shoulders and threw it in my washer.

"When can I have it back?"

"I'll let you know. You better go."

After Pete left, I washed the jacket all by itself with lots of deter-gent, bleach, and hot water. I didn't want it contaminating my unmen-tionables, even though I had a pile of them waiting to be washed. While I waited for the jacket to finish, I showered and pondered the few pounds I'd put on. It's hard to ignore that kind of thing in the shower. The pounds made me look softer, but I don't think Pete noticed. A previous boyfriend once described me as squishy. That was the end of him. I'd adopted my mother's yoga habit, so despite my so-called squishiness, I was pretty fit. The more I thought about Pete, the more I thought I'd better keep him, schedule and all. How often did I meet a man who didn't compare me to Marilyn? Who didn't even seem to care that much about how I looked or that I was a YouTube laugh-ingstock? That alone was a feat. Actually, I was more Marilyn than the genuine article. My body curvier, taller with bigger breasts and hips, not to mention that I'm a natural blond, differences the average Joe didn't get. Pete never once thought I was Marilyn. He touched my curves like he wanted to paint them. Not like he was living out a fantasy.

I turned on the hair dryer and ran it over my body, removing the last bit of moisture, and then dried my hair. My curls tamed with the help of a round brush, I added mascara, a touch of blush, and a ton of lip gloss. The effect was spot on and just what I needed if the church was still a crime scene and hadn't been released yet. I had to pull out the big guns if I was going to get past the cops and into that church.

First, I had to go back to my parents' house. Emphasizing my Mari-lynness wouldn't help me interview Dixie. In her state, I doubted she'd notice if I wore Dad's clothes. Also, my mother was her best friend, so she was used to it. Mom was more Marilyn than any sane person would hope for, and I was going the same route. Plus, I was getting Mom's attitude. Why fight the power when it can be so useful?

I put on a lacy bra, no padding necessary unless I wanted to injure somebody, and a tank dress, clingy yet loose. I wanted to teeter at the top, but not go over it. A low sandal and a clutch and I was ready for anything, or at least I thought I was.

CHAPTER NINE

I drove to my parents' house with the windows rolled down. The breeze felt like silk on my skin. Seven-thirty was a good time of night in the Central West End. The street lamps lit the dusky shadows of evening making golden orbs for me to follow home. In the warmth of that June evening, I allowed myself to feel good.

The streets were parked up early with Porsches and every other expensive car imaginable. Lucky for me, I didn't have to park on the street. I bypassed the trendy restaurants and antique shops, turning down the alley behind my parents' house. Their street, Hawthorne Avenue, was the best section and had alleyways between streets. The houses had servants' staircases and high-six-figure price tags. Dad lucked into our house in the seventies. He did the Bled family a favor, and my godmothers practically gave him the house as a thank-you. He never could've afforded it any other way, even when the area was at its lowest ebb. Hawthorne Avenue was an island of exclusion.

I parked in the garage and walked up through the garden to the back porch. Happily, Uncle Morty wasn't there waiting for me, but the kitchen lights blazed. Strains of Vivaldi's *The Four Seasons* wafted through the screen door. The summer section, I think. It felt like home and, in the deepest part of my heart, I still considered it my home, although I hadn't lived there in four years. I wasn't sure if another house could ever supplant it in my affections.

When I got closer, I smelled bacon frying mixed with the scent of damp soil. Someone had over-watered the potted plants that lined the stairs and a trickle of water went down to a small pool on the brick walkway. I went up the stairs, my hand sliding on the smooth, worn wood of the handrail, then I pulled open the screen door and walked into the frigid pantry. Several ingredients lay on the marble counter, heavy cream, strawberries, mushrooms and a Ghirardelli Sweet Dark Chocolate bar. Aunt Tenne was making a decadent dinner to soothe Dixie's soul. According to her, food was the only way to go. Where my mother might have called a priest, Aunt Tenne called the calorie cavalry.

"Don't even think about it."

I turned around to see Aunt Tenne standing in the doorway. She stood with her arms crossed and a sad smile on her face.

"Don't think about what?" I asked.

"The chocolate bar. I'm making ice cream and I only brought the one." She waved me into the kitchen. It was alive with her presence with thick-cut bacon frying in a large iron skillet, homemade avocado mayo, and lettuce draining in the sink. Aunt Tenne started slicing an enormous tomato from Mom's garden out back.

Umm BLTs.

I poured myself an iced tea, plopped in a couple slices of lemon and sat down at the table. Aunt Tenne didn't speak and continued to slice slowly and deliberately. I sipped my tea and thanked God Dad wasn't there to pester and order me about. Dad was great, but when he had an important case, it was all hands on deck. Actually, it was more like hand on deck. Dad loved a free lunch, and I was his favorite waitress. He could get me to do work that he'd have to pay for otherwise. It was my own fault. My pride wouldn't let me be lousy at the tasks he assigned, so I kept getting more difficult jobs like this thing with Gavin. If I'd proven to be a goofball, I'd have been scot-free. As it was, I was in up to my eyeballs and the water was rising.

"So what have you been doing?" Aunt Tenne asked.

"Nothing."

She made a disbelieving grunt under her breath.

"No, really. I had dinner with Pete. That's it."

Well, not exactly just dinner, but my other activities were off the record.

"Glad to hear it. Are you eating?"

"Absolutely. Where's Dixie?"

She forked the last bacon slices onto a paper-towel-covered plate and said, "Upstairs. Taking another nap." I could tell by the way she said it that she wasn't crazy about the multiple naps. But who was she to judge? When was the last time she had a spouse murdered?

"Do you want me to wake her for dinner?" I asked.

"I'm here." Dixie walked in with a shawl around her shoulders and a face that said head cold.

"Are you okay?" I said.

"I'm fine. A bit tired."

She sat down at the table, and I poured her a glass of tea. Aunt Tenne assembled the sandwiches, slathering thick coats of mayo on the bread.

"Dixie, I need to ask you about some things, but if it's not a good time, we can do it later," I said.

"Later won't change a thing, will it? Go ahead." She looked so tired I thought she might lay her head down and go to sleep on the table.

"Mercy, why don't you give it a couple of days? The detectives are coming back tomorrow," said Aunt Tenne.

"Who was here? Chuck?"

"Yes, it was Chuck with somebody else, dark-complected, young. I can't remember his name."

"Nazir?"

"That's him."

"How'd you get them to back off?" I asked.

"It wasn't hard. Dixie was asleep. They're coming back first thing tomorrow," Aunt Tenne said.

"Dixie, I'm sorry," I said. "Dad wants me to talk to you and now is better than later."

"Fine." Dixie held her glass under her chin like a basin and she looked like she might throw up in it.

"Okay. Tell me everything about what Gavin was doing on Sunday before you found him."

"I'm afraid I can't be much help there," she said, holding the glass a little tighter. "He wasn't home. I only saw him for a bit."

"Where was he?"

"Out on a case."

"Deadbeat dad?"

"Maybe. We didn't talk much about his work, you know."

"Did it have anything to do with Lincoln, Nebraska and the University there?" I asked.

"He went to Lincoln, but he didn't say anything about the school. Why?" Dixie set her tea down and leaned forward. Her eyes focused, and she was back from wherever she'd been.

"He made two calls to the University. I saw them on the cell phone recall. Don't tell Chuck I said that." I touched Dixie's hand, and she nodded. "Gavin didn't mention the University?" I asked.

"No. Never. I can't imagine why he'd call there."

"When did he go to Lincoln?"

"Thursday and he got back Sunday morning."

"What time was that?" I stood up and rummaged around Mom's junk drawer for a notepad and pen.

"Let me see. I think it was around five because I was in bed. I get up at six," Dixie said.

"Tell me everything that happened with times, if you can." I sat down with my pen poised above the pad.

"Well, like I said, he came home at five. I got up at my normal time and then I made breakfast. Wait a minute. First, he made some phone calls. We probably ate at six-thirty."

"So the calls didn't take long," I said.

"No, not at all," she said. "Less than ten minutes."

"Then what?" I leaned back as Aunt Tenne put a large dripping sandwich in front of me.

"Well, we ate, of course, and talked, and then I went for my walk." Dixie paused, her brow wrinkled. "I can't remember what we talked about. Nothing important. Normal things." Her hand brushed her cheek for the tear that wasn't there. "I wish I could remember exactly what he said, every single word."

"I'm sorry, Dix. I'm so sorry." I reached across the table and grasped her hand, mindless of the mayo dripping off my fingers.

"I know, honey. I know. You'll do your best, won't you?"

"You know it," I said.

Aunt Tenne blew her nose into a napkin and said, "I just can't stand it. Why did this have to happen? Why? Why?"

"It didn't," I said.

"What?" said Aunt Tenne.

"It didn't have to happen."

"I see what you mean. It's just so hard," said Aunt Tenne.

I looked at Dixie and watched her face closely. The spark of attention vanished.

"When did you go for your walk?" I asked.

"I don't know. After seven, because *The Today Show* was on."

"And Gavin didn't say anything about his case or who he called? Did he seem excited, worried, upset?"

"No. He was worried about the muffler in my car. I guess I have to buy a muffler. I've never bought a muffler in my life." Dixie seemed to shrink and get smaller and smaller on the chair.

"I'll take care of it," I said.

"What do you know about mufflers?" asked Aunt Tenne.

"Enough to go to a muffler shop."

"Well, I can do that," said Dixie.

"But why should you have to?" I asked. "I'll do it."

"Alright, honey. I'm so tired. I think I'll go lie down for a bit." Dixie stood up, clutched the shawl tighter around her thin shoulders, and turned to leave.

"Wait, Dixie. Did Gavin bring in his briefcase when he came home?"

She thought for a moment and said, "If it wasn't in the office, he probably left it in the car. He was forever going out to get it."

"Where's the Marquis? I didn't see it at the house," I said.

"I drove it to the hospital. I guess it's still there." Dixie left. Aunt Tenne and I listened to her footsteps die away in the hall.

"She took maybe two bites. All that sleeping and now she's not eating. I just don't know," Aunt Tenne said.

"What don't you know? Her husband just died. You can't make her eat."

"We'll see," said Aunt Tenne. "So...you're famous."

"You heard."

"I saw."

"Is it bad?" I asked.

"See for yourself." Aunt Tenne gestured to Mom's laptop on the other side of the table.

I went around to the computer and stopped short when I saw the screen. My family, all my family, the best and worst of them, smiled at me from in front of last year's Christmas tree. Chuck gave me a lecherous look. Uncle Morty drank out of a container that must have held at least a quart of buttered rum, and Aaron had half a piece of cake in his mouth. My dad hugged Grandma George. And Gavin was there with his arms slung around Dixie and Mom, his head thrown back in a laugh. I heard that wondrous, jolly laugh bouncing around in my head.

My fingers brushed the keyboard, and a shot of my barely restrained boobs bloomed on the screen.

"Shit," I said.

"That's what I said." Aunt Tenne watched me from the stove with her hands on her hips.

A slide show started, featuring me, every part of me from every angle. I sat down with a thump.

"Those nasty old bastards," I said.

"You're very popular with the over-eighty set," said Aunt Tenne.

I clicked on a link, which brought me to a page with my head pasted on what looked like Britney Spears' body (back in the day) dancing with an enormous snake.

"I can't breathe."

"And that's one of the nicer ones."

"They planned this. Those old nasty bastards planned this," I said. "And I fell for it."

I laid my head on the table and moaned. One of those moans that comes up from the feet and sounds like a dying cow.

"What's Mom going to say?"

Aunt Tenne rubbed my back. "I'll pray for you."

"Pray for Dixie," I said. "I deserve this. I'm too stupid to breathe."

"What about a therapist?" asked Aunt Tenne, still rubbing my shoulder.

I lifted my head. "For me?"

"For Dixie. Do you think she'll eat the ice cream?"

"Maybe," I said.

"She likes chocolate, right?" asked Aunt Tenne.

"Definitely. When do you have to go to work?"

"Ten forty-five, no later. Why? Where are you going?" Aunt Tenne furrowed her brow.

"I thought I'd check out that church again."

"I thought the cops told you to beat it."

"They did. New shift, second chance. It won't take long. I just want to get a look at the layout for Dad," I said.

"You don't really think that bride has anything to do with Gavin?"

"Covering the bases like Dad says."

"You've got a feeling," Aunt Tenne said. It wasn't a question.

"You could say that," I said.

"Don't be too long. Dixie shouldn't be alone."

"That's what Mom said."

Aunt Tenne didn't say anything. She hated being compared to Mom, even in the most benign fashion. I thanked her for the sandwich and shot out the back door before I got trapped in a conversation about their differences. I knew from experience that was a no-win conversation.

I sat in my truck and closed my eyes, but images of me, at my most Marilyn, kept popping up in my mind. That's how the world saw me, would see me forever. I guess I didn't believe it could go so far until then. I never saw myself like that. I was just me. The shape of my lips and the size of my eyes weren't of much consequence. I hadn't worked at it. I didn't dye my hair nor have my lips chemically plumped. Call it lucky, call it a curse. It was what it was. Now I'd revealed myself and people in India knew my name. I was such an idiot for thinking I could walk through the world unnoticed or do whatever I wanted. Mom never thought that. Why did I?

My hand fell on my purse, and I felt my cell phone through the leather. No point in ignoring it. I pulled out my phone and listened to a profusion of messages ranging from the obscene to polite inquiries. Then I got to message ninety-three.

"What did you do?" asked my mom.

I'd only heard her tone a few times before, like when I stuffed a nickel up my nose in the first grade.

"The room service guy thinks I'm a prostitute, the cruise line wants to hire me to lip-synch cabaret songs, and I've gotten three hundred obscene emails in the last two hours."

People thought Mom was me. Of course it was possible, even probable, but I never considered she'd have trouble on the cruise. Did people watch YouTube on cruises? Shouldn't they be learning to luau and playing shuffleboard? I knew she'd find out, but I thought a concerned (also known as interfering) friend would do the deed, not the cruise line.

"It could be worse," I said to my steering wheel. "And it will be when Mom comes home and kills me."

But I was right. It could be worse. I could be a widow. The thought of Dixie popped me out of my maudlin state and I remembered what I was supposed to be thinking about, Gavin and only Gavin. He was my job and maybe my ticket to redemption.

Darkness had fallen by the time I drove to the Rockville United Church of Christ. St. Louis in June had a tendency to be warm during the day and cool at night. Perfect wedding weather, or so I'm told. The wind tousled my hair, blowing strands into my mouth, and I blanked out for a bit about where I was going and why. I sang along to Christina Perri's pretty pain on the radio and felt alive and satisfied. Moments like that were all too short. I arrived at the church parking lot in record time. It was near empty, just a police cruiser, a church minivan and a Buick. I hadn't paid attention to the church itself on my previous visit. It was well named with rough-cut rock walls and a low-slung roof. Crime scene tape crisscrossed the front entrance. I hung a left and walked around the side, lots of windows, but no doors. At the back was a playground bathed in darkness and a door. I reached for the knob, and heard a voice say, "Hey, what do you think you're doing?"

Crap.

I ran my fingers through my hair, careful to let some curls fall forward and brush my lips. I turned and was surprised to see one of the officers from the dayshift coming toward me with his hand on his nightstick. It was the younger of the duo, thankfully.

"Officer...Ameche. I didn't expect to find you still here."

You're still here. Great, Mercy, very smooth.

"I didn't expect to see you so soon either," he said with a slight hitch of the pants and touch of the hat. "I'd of thought you'd be busy signing autographs."

"Do not mention YouTube or anything to do with Marilyn."

Ameche took a step back. "Okay."

"Where's your partner?" I asked.

"Carl went home. You need to leave. This is still a crime scene."

"I'm not here to cause problems. I was hoping to talk to the reverend. Is he here?" I hoped it was a reverend and not something else. I was a lapsed Catholic and could barely keep my own religion straight, much less any other one.

"She's here. She, not he," he said. "Why are you really here?"

"I told you," I said.

"No, you didn't."

"I need to talk to the reverend," I said.

"What about?" Ameche asked.

"That's a personal theological matter."

"A personal, theological matter that you have to talk about, at nine o'clock at night, at a church you've never been to before with a reverend you don't know."

"You've got it, so excuse me, and I'll let you get back to your duties." I did an about-face and made for the knob again.

"Hey!" Ameche grabbed my arm and spun me back around. I faked a fall into his chest, complete with a little gasp.

"Let go," I said, looking up and gazing into his eyes. I've been told I'm exceptional at that angle. You know, the big eyes, slightly parted lips with my hair tossed back. Men could be such suckers for the dramatic, but I couldn't help loving them for it. It was nice to know romance wasn't dead among males, no matter their claims.

"Sorry, sorry." Ameche let go, backed up, lifted his hat and ran his fingers through his dark hair before settling it back on his head.

"It's okay. Can I go now? Please?" I rubbed my arm and pulled my top a bit lower. Ameche took in the complete picture and heaved an exasperated sigh.

"What do you really want?" he asked.

I calculated my odds, and they weren't good. He wasn't stupid or horny. Or, more likely, good old Carl had given his partner an earful after my earlier appearance and Ameche wanted to follow his instructions. It was my last at bat, so I decided to go for a homer. Why not? I had nothing to lose and everything to gain. Plus, I was starting to like Ameche. He hadn't tried to cop a feel when the chance presented itself. With a body like mine, I appreciated a man with a sense of decency; there were so few around. He looked honest. The honesty was useless, but he also looked ambitious. That I could use.

"So Carl filled you in on my dad?"

"Yeah. What about it?" asked Ameche.

"So you know he's got tremendous pull in the department."

"Are you trying to bribe me?"

"I'm trying to help you," I said.

"I'm not a total fucking idiot. You don't want to help me. You want to get in the scene and you can forget it."

Damn it.

Ameche was getting brighter by the minute, but, then again, that made him even more ambitious.

"Let me guess, you want to be a detective, right?"

"And you're gonna help me make it. You must think I'm a complete asshole," he said.

"Not at all." I reached in my purse and fished out my wallet. I opened it and held out a picture. "That's Gavin Flouder and my dad at his retirement party. They were once partners. Gavin was murdered on Sunday. You hear anything about that?"

"I might've."

"I think Gavin's death has something to do with the murder here. My dad is on a cruise, barfing his brains out, or he'd be here talking to you. Actually, he wouldn't. Chuck Watts, my cousin, would've already given him the keys to the kingdom. Now Dad wants me to do this, so I'm damn well gonna do it. Gavin wasn't just Dad's partner twenty years ago, he was our friend. He and Dixie had Easter dinner with us, for Christ's sake. That was the last time I saw him unless you count the slab, something I'm personally trying to forget. So cut me some slack here, and I swear Dad will talk you up. Unless you have a dozen high-profile busts under your belt, I'm guessing you need it," I said.

"And if I don't?"

"Don't expect help on anything, ever. Dad has a long memory, as do I."

Ameche considered his options carefully. I'd seen that look before and I knew it'd go in my favor. In my senior year of high school, I asked Werner Schneider to homecoming. My best friend, Ellen, told me not to, but, me being me; I did it anyway. Werner was good-looking, in a geeky sort of way, but that wasn't why I chose him. First, if I didn't ask a guy, I'd have no date, again. I scared guys for some reason. Second, I liked Werner for it because we'd had several conversations in Chem class, and he'd never once looked at my boobs. Ameche had the same look Werner had when I said, "Hey, want to go to homecoming with me?" He wanted it, oh yes he did, but he also had a certain standing to uphold. In Werner's case, he was supposed to be above all the trivial society gatherings of all us peons. He was an academic. Ameche was afraid of getting caught and never being left on his own again.

"What exactly do you want to do?" Ameche asked.

"Check out the layout. Do some timing and look at where the body was found. I won't touch anything. Come with me."

"Your damn skippy I'm coming with you."

Ha! Got him. Another guy dancing against his better judgment.

"One more thing," I said.

Ameche let out a low groan, and said, "Now what?"

"Did you get a look at any of the evidence?"

"Like what?"

"Did they bag a cell phone?" I asked.

"I didn't see what got bagged. What's the deal?"

"I need to know if they found a cell phone near the body and, if possible, whose it is."

"Why?" His fists were on his hips and I thought I might've gone too far.

"Long story," I said.

"What do you expect me to do?" Ameche lifted his hat and ran his fingers through his hair again.

"Get a look at the evidence list or the evidence itself. Chuck might have it on his desk. He likes to look at stuff while he's working things out in his head."

"How do you know that?"

"Cause my dad does the same thing and Chuck's his protégé," I said.

"If Chuck's your cousin, why don't you just ask him?"

"I would, if he'd tell me, which he won't. We don't get along all that well."

"Why not?" Ameche looked at me like I might be worse than he thought, if my own cousin didn't trust me.

"We have this thing. He hits on me. I insult him. It's like that," I said.

"Your cousin hits on you," Ameche said, his upper lip curling in distaste.

"He's not my real cousin. His mother married my uncle. He adopted Chuck and then Delilah divorced him about fifteen seconds later," I said. "He just does it to piss me off."

"Works, huh?"

"Oh, yeah."

"I'll be sure to remember that." Ameche smiled.

"Swell. Now, are you going to get a look at that cell for me or what?"

"I'll see what I can do."

"And there's one more thing," I said.

"Of course there is," said Ameche.

"I need to know who my dear cousin was interviewing the morning after Sample's death."

"Dare I ask why?"

"If Chuck was interviewing them, they couldn't have killed Gavin."

"That shouldn't be too difficult," said Ameche.

"Okay then. Let's go." I moved towards the door, but then thought better of it and motioned for Ameche to lead the way. He gave a quick look skyward, as if to say, "Please God, don't let me get caught." Then he opened the door, and I went inside.

Ameche switched on the light. We were in an antechamber used for storage. Racks of choir robes, stacks of chairs, and boxes of children's books, bibles, and hymnals littered the floor. There were no signs of a forensic technician going over the place.

"Didn't they search this area?" I asked.

"It was locked at the time of the murder. This way to the crying room. That's where the body was found." Ameche led me down a hallway past several doors into the main section of the church. He closed the door behind me and said, "That door was locked after the ceremony and was still locked when we showed up."

We walked down the aisle of the chapel, still decorated for the wedding. Small bouquets of flowers garnished each pew along the center aisle and the white satin runner covered the floor. The smell of rotting gardenias lay heavy in the air, making me remember why I hated gardenias. Ameche opened one of the entry doors to the chapel, the one the bride goes through on her way to her vows. The heavy walnut paneling didn't quite match the understated elegance of the chapel with its white walls and tasteful bible scenes painted fresco style at regular intervals. A six-foot-tall golden cross with no decoration sat behind the simple altar. It couldn't have been more different from the cathedral I attended as a child. Everything was bright and crisp with no hint of pain or sacrifice. All blissfully guiltless, but it felt wrong to me without the intricate mosaics, rich colors, and stained glass. The chapel might've been pure in its devotion, but I missed the mystery.

Ameche ushered me through the doors into a little antechamber. To my left and right were two more identical doors. Each had finger-print powder residue at strategic points and were open. Ameche put his hand on the small of my back. "Don't touch anything. The geek squad has been here three times already. All I need is for them to find new fingerprints."

I clasped my hands behind my back and walked in. It was a typical crying room with two rocking chairs, a small round table and chairs, and a changing table. All of which had been dusted for prints and, from the look of it, they'd found plenty. Four red plastic numbers at the far right end of the room marked specific evidence. The bench against the right wall had a number one marker next to it. On the back wall was the changing table with the numbers two and three on the floor next to the leg nearest the bench. In the center of the room was the last number, four, next to a bloodstain about two feet in diameter. The stain wasn't a pool. It looked more like someone had gone over the floor with a bloody mop.

"I thought she was strangled," I said.

"She was, but she took a pretty good blow to the head on the bench, too."

"But strangling was the cause of death?"

"As far as I know," Ameche said.

Other than the evidence markers and blood, the scene was relatively undisturbed. The rocker nearest to the changing table lay on its side, but that was it. Not a bit like I imagined it would be. I expected the scene to look like a cyclone had torn through there. Get a damp sponge, right the rocker, and the room would be good to go.

"Lot of fingerprints," I said.

"Yeah, dozens. It'll probably take those techs a while to sort through them."

"And probably to no avail."

"How come?" asked Ameche with a frown. "They think this was a crime of passion. I doubt he took the time to put on gloves."

"Most people get killed by people they know. Everybody she knew was probably at the wedding and could come up with a reason for being in here."

Ameche nodded. "The whole bridal party got dressed in here. I think I heard the photographer used it to store some equipment, too. It's all bagged and down at forensics."

"Okay. How many exits?" I asked.

"I don't know."

"Well, let's take a look, shall we?" I led him back into the hall and through the opposite doorway. It was a cloakroom with hanging racks and a couple of boxes of stray hats, gloves, and boots. More folding chairs were stacked against the wall. It was windowless like the crying room and hadn't been dusted for prints. Presumably because there would've been no reason for the killer to have used the room since it had no exit or it'd been locked. Ameche watched me while I walked around the room and then followed when I exited. I went over to the chapel's front doors. They were massive, lightly carved, and had dusting powder on the hand panels and surrounding area.

"Unlocked at the time?" I asked.

"Yeah," he said.

Dad wouldn't be happy. An easy exit at night. Fantastic.

"Let's take a look at the other exits."

We went back into the chapel this time, walking down the other side towards a door at the right of the altar. I motioned to it. "Locked?"

"No, it leads outside," he said.

"Let's go."

Ameche pushed open the door and waved me through it. It opened to an empty antechamber, probably where the groomsmen waited for the wedding ceremonies to begin. Directly opposite the door was another door. Ameche opened it for me and I stepped out, breathing in the warm night air and enjoying the feel of it on my skin. The killer might have done the same, so he wouldn't look suspicious. We went down the short flight of stairs to a sidewalk until it branched off in three directions. One walk wrapped around the back of the chapel towards the parking lot. Another went alongside the chapel towards the front and a third led straight to a low stone building about twenty yards from the chapel.

"Reception hall?" I asked, leading the way.

"You got it."

"Do you have the key?"

"Don't need one. It's open." Ameche opened the door for me, reached inside, groped around for a moment, and flipped a light switch. "They're done with this area. Finished yesterday."

Any evidence of the wedding was gone. All tables and chairs were stacked neatly against the wall. It didn't take a genius to figure out anyone could've slipped out of the reception, gone to the crying room, strangled the victim and been back before anyone noticed. I could ask Dad how long it takes to strangle someone, but I imagined not more than ten minutes, less if she was knocked unconscious before being aware of the killer's presence. On the other hand, they might've argued, struggled before the blow to the head and who knows how long that could've taken?

I started to ask Ameche another question, but stopped myself.

"What?" he asked.

"Nothing," I said. "I was going to ask about more exits, but I don't think it matters."

"Why not?"

"Because if the killer was one of the guests, then he returned here after doing it. He didn't need an escape route. He would've stayed till the police came. He would've been interviewed."

"What about the blood?" asked Ameche.

"There wasn't any spatter. The blood was just smeared around, like with her hair, as she struggled. He might not have gotten much on him, except for the hands. He could've just washed up in the bathroom and rolled up his sleeves," I said.

Ameche elbowed me. "It could be a she, you know."

"It's not beyond the realm, but, come on, how many women stranglers have you heard of?" Ameche shrugged and I continued, "If it wasn't someone from the party, they'd have gone out the front door and it still doesn't matter."

"I guess. How do you know all this stuff anyway?"

"My dad likes to talk things over. Helps him think about the possibilities when he says it out loud."

"He discusses cases with you?" Ameche narrowed his eyes at me, and I could see my dad was dropping in his esteem.

"Hardly." I smiled.

Ameche relaxed.

"My mother was always his sounding board, but he did like to tell me his general method, and I have an unfortunate habit of eavesdropping."

"You're kidding."

I punched Ameche in the shoulder and said, "Shut up and tell me about the guests."

"How can I do that if I'm shutting up?"

"Oh, for heaven's sake. Just tell me. I don't have all night."

"I do," he said.

I groaned and rolled my eyes. "Are you going to tell me or not?"

"Nope, cause I don't know a damn thing." His grin took over his whole face.

"Why not?"

"Cause I've been on the force for eight months. I direct traffic," he said.

"Right. I don't know what I was thinking," I said.

"Look, I'll tell you anything I pick up."

"In for a dime, in for a dollar?"

"May as well. If anybody finds out about this, my ass is grass. Your dad is really going to put in a good word for me, right?"

"Absolutely," I said. "We pay our debts and remember our friends."

"Friends?" Ameche's eyebrows went up under his hat.

"Sure, why not? You're not so bad."

"Very complimentary."

"I try," I said.

"You better go. I've got to get back out front," he said.

"No problem, and thanks."

"Mention it, please mention it."

We headed back towards the door. Ameche reached for the door-knob, but we both froze with a jolt when we heard a woman's voice say, "What are you doing here?"

Ameche wheeled around. I studied his face to figure out how deep a shit we were in, but he betrayed little. Mild surprise at best. Not "My life is over. Someone shoot me." We could save the situation and, if we could, it was up to me. I was probably a more accomplished liar than Ameche. Helping Dad out gave me plenty of practice. I turned with a fixed look of mild interest on my face, praying she wouldn't recognize me.

Don't look scared. Don't look scared.

A woman stood ten feet away from us under an archway that had an exit sign over it. She crossed her arms. "Well?"

"Hi. I'm Mercy Watts and this is Officer Ameche. Have you two met?" I walked the ten feet, extending my hand to her. She shook it briefly and put her hands on her hips.

"Not formally, no. I'm Reverend Coleman," she said.

"Pleased to meet you, Reverend." Ameche extended his hand. She shook it and her hand snapped back to her hip.

"What are you doing here? I wasn't told about any more people coming tonight," said Reverend Coleman.

Think fast. Think fast.

"Are you with the forensics team?" A furrow formed between the reverend's eyebrows and I knew I was fast missing the window where she could learn to like me. In a split second, I had to judge her by looks alone.

Did the reverend have a rough past, causing her to suspect everyone of everything? Did I have to lie and get the hell out before she called Chuck? Or was she an average person with average experiences who'd take me at my word and give up some information?

Reverend Coleman looked like a nice guy. She had a lot of Aunt Tenne's elements and if there ever was a nice guy; it was her. The reverend was tall, at least five eleven, and a good fifty pounds overweight. She knew how to wear it well in varying shades of gray and a scoop neckline. Nothing pinched or pulled. Despite her bulk, she looked smooth. Her makeup was low key and well applied. But it was her eyes that showed her desire for goodness. They were blue with crinkled corners. They were probably the cause of people saying behind her back, "She'd be so pretty, if she'd just lose some weight."

I decided Reverend Coleman was normal (aka not a criminal or victim), and to listen to my dad. Don't tell him I said so. Dad says that normal people live normal lives where major lying isn't an everyday occurrence. Non-criminals assume you're telling the truth and want to believe you. In fact, they'll go to great lengths to believe.

"No, I'm not with forensics. Actually, I'm working on another case." I smoothed my dress and tried to look super honest. It was a stretch. "Do you think we could talk for a couple of minutes?"

Reverend Coleman relaxed, and Ameche let out a long-held breath.

"Sure. My office?" she asked.

"That would be great."

"Do you need me for anything else?" Ameche asked me.

"Not at the moment. Thanks."

"I better go patrol the grounds." He nodded to the reverend and left.

"I'm sorry. I'm not familiar with the layout. Where's your office?" I asked.

"In the main building. Follow me," said Reverend Coleman.

We walked back over to the church and took the path around the rear to the door that Ameche and I had first entered. She opened the door, and I noticed fingerprint ink on her hand. She led me down the hallway to a plain door with two dozen drawings and finger paintings on it. Most of them had her name and various versions of her face and body on them. The kids were a little too accurate for my taste and I wondered how the reverend felt about them. Maybe she was a big enough person not to care, but her careful dressing and makeup said different.

Reverend Coleman offered me a cream-colored armchair and sat behind the desk. She sighed, rubbed her eyes carefully so as not to smudge her mascara, and put on a pair of glasses.

"What can I do for you, Miss Watts?" she asked.

"I'm not sure to tell you the truth, Reverend. I'm just fishing here."

"You said something about another case. Please, tell me this isn't going to get any worse."

"It's been pretty bad then?"

"Oh, the cameras and reporters. They have no decency, no shame. I don't know when we can start services again. I don't want them bothering our parishioners."

"I don't think you can prevent that," I said.

"I suppose you're right. What's the other case?"

I fished around in my purse, slipped Gavin's picture out of my wallet, and handed it to Reverend Coleman. "Do you recognize the man on the right?"

She hesitated, shook her head no, and peered at the picture again.

"He'd be a bit older looking and much thinner," I said.

"No, I'm sorry. Has he been here?"

"Not that I know of, but he called here probably on Saturday. Do you keep records of incoming calls?"

"It depends on what the caller wanted," she said. "Are you sure it was on Saturday?"

"I believe so," I said.

"That was Rebecca's wedding day."

"Did you know her well?"

"Why do you ask?" The reverend rubbed her eyes again.

"You referred to the wedding as Rebecca's, as though you knew her personally."

"Did I? Of course I did." Her eyes got misty, and she cupped her palm over her mouth, her fingers spread over her cheek. She looked at her lap for a moment, and then dropped her hand. "I knew her quite well. She volunteered here for the last three years. We had such fun planning the ceremony. Was he calling her?"

The question startled me. My mind had wandered to Gavin, and I'd forgotten what we were doing, what we were talking about. A flush of grief rushed to my face and my answer came out as a strangled croak, "I can't be sure, but I suspect he was. Who was on the phones then?"

"No one. Everyone was at the wedding and reception. We were all invited, of course."

"Of course." I cleared my throat. "Well, someone answered the phone. Any idea who that might've been?"

"No, but Rebecca wouldn't have spoken with him unless he was on her list."

"What list?" I asked.

"Rebecca only took calls from certain people. We were very careful never to say whether she was here or not. She was grateful, I think, not to have to worry about that here," she said.

"What exactly was she worried about?"

"She had some trouble a while back. Some man was bothering her. I think he threatened her. She moved and changed her phone number, but he wouldn't let her alone."

"Did she make a police report?"

"Dozens, for all the good it did. One of the cops said he was extremely good or they would've been able to get him."

"They never got a name or a description?"

"She never saw him and, obviously, he didn't leave a name," she said.

"Right," I said. "I suppose you told all of this to the detectives working her case?"

"Yes. Do you want the list?"

"That'd be great," I said.

"We keep it in her file in my secretary's office next door," she said.

We stood up, walked out of her office and into the door to the right. It, too, was covered with drawings and some photos of church gatherings. Inside was a waist-high wooden partition with a bell, in-and-out trays and a stack of flyers advertising a new bible study group. We walked around the partition to a triple set of filing cabinets. Reverend Coleman opened a drawer and thumbed through a manila folder.

She murmured something under her breath.

"What's wrong?"

"It's not in here."

"Could it have been taken into evidence?"

"Maybe, but I don't remember mentioning the list to anyone. I should've. Evelyn might have told the detectives. Evelyn's my secretary." She looked at me, her brows furrowed.

"That's probably it. Do you remember who was on the list?"

"Her parents, of course. Her sister, some friends, people where she worked," she said.

"A lot of names?"

"No, not a lot. Maybe fifteen or twenty."

"Do you remember if Gavin Flouder was on the list?" I asked.

"Doesn't sound familiar, but I hadn't looked at the list in a long time."

"Why's that?"

"I don't answer the church phone much, so I didn't need to look. Rebecca did say he stopped bothering her."

"When was that?"

"About the time she met Lee. She was so relieved, I can tell you," she said.

"Who's Lee?"

"Her fiancé, I mean husband. Poor man. I don't know how he's going to get through this."

"Have you seen him since it happened?"

"Twice. He couldn't stop crying the first time. Kept saying he didn't want to live without her. The second time he was on something to calm him down, I think."

"Did he say anything that time?" I asked.

"Not really. I couldn't understand him," she said.

"When did you say they met?"

"Six months ago. A few days after Thanksgiving, I think."

"Short engagement."

"I thought so too, but they were so in love and so happy. I can't tell you how good he was for her. He got her out. She wasn't afraid when she was with him."

"So Lee got rid of the stalker?"

"Stalker? Yes, I guess he was a stalker. Rebecca never called him that. She just said 'that guy' or something to that effect. I guess Lee got rid of him. I never thought about it. That guy must've figured out that bothering Rebecca was pointless, don't you think?"

"Unless he didn't," I said.

"You think he did it, too? I can't imagine anyone else. We all loved her. She was a good person. She'd never hurt a fly." Reverend Coleman turned to a corkboard on the back wall, pulled out a stickpin, and handed me a snapshot of a young blond woman surrounded by smiling children. "The kids are taking it hard. She organized most of their activities and chaperoned. We're having counselors here during Sunday school next week."

"That's an excellent idea," I said, as I looked at the photo. Rebecca Sample had blond hair and a shy smile. She didn't look like a stalker's favorite target. Not being famous, beautiful, or anything I imagined stalkers to go for, but I knew nothing about stalkers except what I'd seen in news magazines. Dad had only had a couple stalker cases in his entire career, and I didn't remember him saying much about them.

I handed the photo back. "She was lovely."

"Yes, she was."

"If you come across that list or think of anything, please call me." I rummaged around looking for my business card that didn't exist and pulled out my pad instead. "I guess I'm out of cards. Let me write down my cell number for you."

"Thank you, I will. Do you think Rebecca's murder is connected to your case?" The reverend hesitated over the word murder. She looked like she had a hard time believing she was saying it in connection with someone she knew.

"I doubt it, but I have to cover all the bases," I said.

"Can I ask what that case is about?"

"Sorry, I can't say."

"I understand," she said.

Reverend Coleman walked me to my truck and thanked me for working so hard for the public. I felt like a schmuck and thanked her for being so cooperative. I drove away and reminded myself that I was doing it for Dixie and Gavin, and it didn't matter what I had to do. The truth was the only thing that mattered.

CHAPTER TEN

On the way back to my parents' house, I stopped at a mini-mart. It was in a bad neighborhood and I took perverse pleasure in going against Dad's advice. He'd warned me about the area. He was forever warning me about something or the other. Sometimes I listened, mostly I didn't. I bought the *Post-Dispatch* and a bottle of water, resisting the call of the candy bar rack. The way I'd been eating, I'd be more than squishy if I didn't watch it.

At home, the lights were out except for the ones that turned on when they sensed motion and Aunt Tenne remembered to set the alarm. I was late and going to hear about it. I coded myself in, unlocked the door, recoded, relocked, and walked into the kitchen. Aunt Tenne had left a terse note on top of Millicent and Myrtle's casserole dishes saying I needed to return them. Dixie was asleep and Uncle Morty called for me four times. She underlined the Uncle Morty part. I took it to mean he wasn't happy, but I wasn't worried. Morty being happy was as rare as snow in April. It happens, but you can't count on it.

I spread the paper out on the table and breathed in the ink. I could've read about Rebecca Sample's murder on my iPad, but it just wasn't the same, less real somehow. On paper, Rebecca wasn't virtual.

She wasn't to be confused with entertainment. I read with my stomach in a hot knot. She was twisted up with Gavin now and her death covered the front page. As expected, it was full of lurid details the public shouldn't have and didn't need. I, on the other hand, did need them. I broke out a notepad and wrote out the details in bullet format. Rebecca Sample, age twenty-five, was married at two P.M. on Saturday. The body was found during the reception in the crying room at six-thirty P.M. by the groom. The groom started looking for her a half hour earlier. No witnesses. No break-in. Nothing heard or seen. Victim was stalked previously, but situation resolved itself. No suspects. Candlelight vigil to be held on Wednesday.

The article went on to discuss Sample's life in general with plenty of quotes from co-workers and friends. I scanned without really reading until my eyes latched on to the words "University of Nebraska at Lincoln."

Holy shit. Aunt Tenne was right.

Sample graduated from the university three years before with a degree in marketing and was recruited by a local firm. I wrote down Sample's graduation date and the firm name. I twirled the end of my pen in my mouth, listening to the clink of it against my teeth. It could've been a coincidence. Dad used to come home and have a stiff drink after chasing his tail all day. He'd say, "I can't believe it's just a coincidence. I can't believe it." That kind of thing happened more than you'd think. Dad went through a period when Mom thought he might develop an alcohol problem. Dad said it was amazing the amount of connections people had when on the surface they appeared to have no common variables at all.

So Gavin was in Lincoln right before he died and happened to call a church where a bride who graduated from Lincoln was about to be murdered. So what? Weird things happen. Of course, there was the missing S file, and that made it harder to dismiss. In spite of myself, I wanted to hear what Chuck thought. Maybe he'd run across the same connections I had. If he wasn't such a sleaze, I would've called him. I knew where that would get me. We'd insult each other. He'd make a comment, and I'd have to shower it off. Then he'd take my information and use it with no quid pro quo. Pass on the Chuck experience.

I called Uncle Morty instead, expecting little better, but at least there wouldn't be any sleaze.

"Hi, it's me," I said.

Uncle Morty grunted a response, so it was going better than expected. He might've gone straight to curses.

"Sorry about yesterday."

Grunt.

"I took a ton of pics. You want to see them?"

Double grunt.

"I talked to Mom. Dad's sick as a dog, but they're coming back ASAP."

Grunt.

"So...I could use a little help."

Silence

"I need some background on Rebecca Sample, the bride that got murdered. I need some addresses, friends, family. Maybe check out her credit cards. See if she's been to Lincoln recently. I think there's a connection between her and Gavin. You know the drill. So...can you do that?"

"You Fiked me," Uncle Morty said.

Michael Fike was my dad's first partner. He couldn't stand Dad and ditched him whenever he had the chance. Dad got ditched so much the squad started calling it getting Fiked.

"Um, well, that's one way to look at it," I said.

"Give me another," he said.

"It's not that big a deal."

"Say you're sorry for Fiking me."

"I didn't Fike you," I said and a voice behind me said, "Who got Fiked?"

I screeched and fell out of my chair. Aaron stood in the kitchen doorway eating a Twinkie and wearing a hairnet.

"What are you doing here?" I said, picking myself off the floor with as much dignity as I could muster.

Aaron looked at his Twinkie and then at me. "Eating."

I smacked my forehead and said to Morty, "Aaron's here."

"Yep."

"You sent him?"

"Yep."

"Thanks a million," I said.

"The least I could do. Now, what do you say?" Uncle Morty's tone made the hair on the back of my neck stand up. He was actually mad.

"I'm sorry I Fiked you."

"You sound real sincere."

"Yeah, it was such a terrible thing."

"You left me with a bunch of old broads." Uncle Morty slammed something and let out a string of curse words.

"You seem to have survived intact," I said.

"Just barely."

"What'd they do, force-feed you Metamucil and file your bunions?"

"Shut up," he said.

"So about Rebecca Sample?" I asked.

"Yeah, yeah. I'll email the stuff to Tommy's address."

"Thanks."

Uncle Morty grunted and hung up. I supposed my weak sorry hadn't quite made up for a drunken afternoon with The Girls.

Aaron got another Twinkie out of the freezer and sat down across from me. He'd brought supplies. That could only mean he'd been instructed to stay awhile.

"Did you bring extra drawers?" I asked.

"Huh?" Aaron looked confused, and I thanked the heavens. If he didn't have a change of underwear, I could Fike him sooner rather than later.

"Who'd you Fike?" he asked.

"Uncle Morty."

Aaron snorted into his Twinkie and I saw a wheel, just one, turning behind his eyes. It was a rare sight, and I was transfixed for a moment. He was probably thinking of ways to torment Morty at their next Dungeon and Dragons meeting. Morty was their Dungeon Master and Aaron thought Morty was giving his magical troll (or whatever he was) a bad shake in the game. Aaron thought revenge was in order. I thought the chances of him making Morty feel stupid were slim.

"I'm going to bed," I said.

Aaron didn't answer. He continued to chew placidly as a cow and blinked as if blinking required concentration.

"So I'll see you later."

More blinking.

"Night," I said.

"Night, night, sleep tight. Don't let the bedbugs bite," said Aaron, his mouth full of Twinkie.

I went upstairs and paused briefly to listen for Aaron leaving. He didn't, but I imagined I could hear him chewing all the way to the third floor.

The third floor was my domain. It consisted of four large square rooms, all interconnected by a series of arched doors and a walk-in closet in the center of the four. I never moved out of the nursery. That's what my mother called it, the nursery. When I went to college, she threatened to move out my stuff, but she wouldn't, if only to avoid carrying my junk down three long flights of stairs.

I went into my room. My main room, I should say. It was the one the stairs led up to. My queen-sized white wicker bed dominated with a matching desk and wall unit. My high school memorabilia was still in evidence as were the mountains of teenager clothing I'd left in the closet. The other rooms were filled with toys, four sets of bunk beds for my slumber parties and books, lots of books.

I went into the closet and rummaged around to find a tattered football jersey. I stripped and pulled it over my head. I sniffed the sleeve and felt a longing in the pit of my stomach. The boy smell. It was amazing how his scent lingered in the fabric after years of wear and washing. David was still in there and still in me, it would seem.

I cranked up the air-conditioning to obscene levels and got into bed, pulling the covers up to my chin. Thoughts of Dixie, downstairs in The Oasis, crept into my head. I wondered if she was awake or if she was dreaming of her Gavin, gone as David was to me. I couldn't imagine her loss, but I'd had a hint. A mist of tears filled my eyes when I thought about her down there, alone. I fell asleep, crying for Dixie and David, or maybe it was for me.

CHAPTER ELEVEN

I woke in sunshine streaming in from the two windows on either side of my bed. I'd forgotten how bright it could get if the shades weren't down. Quarter to seven. Damn, it was early, especially since I didn't have to go to work. I took off David's jersey and tucked it under my pillow the way Mom instructed me a thousand and one times. She hated it when I left my pajamas all over the place. She thought I should know exactly where they were, not that losing them bothered me. I found a pair of wrinkled tan shorts that mostly fit and a white tee with only one hole.

I slipped on my old worn-out kimono and ran down to a guest bath. A boiling hot shower turned me bright red while I resisted the urge to inspect my thighs for telltale dimpling. Once my hair was dry and pulled back in a barrette, I looked in the mirror and sighed. It was hopeless. I was tired of looking like me. I thought about dying my hair red, black, or brown, but it'd been tried.

My mother attempted to disguise herself, and pictures in our family albums bore the evidence of her failures. She looked weird or obvious. She once told me, as I picked up a hair color called Copper Penny, that people only noticed her more when she changed her hair and that was no good. I didn't buy the dye and resigned myself to being blond.

Being blond wasn't so bad. It had its advantages, none of which would be evident at the muffler shop I was going to.

I walked past Mom's bedroom door. It was closed. Hopefully, Dixie was still sleeping and not crying. I didn't hear anything, so I crossed my fingers and ran downstairs. High doses of caffeine were in order. I went straight to the coffeemaker, rubbing my neck as the scent of hazelnut filled the room.

"Smells good."

I jumped and screamed, "Ahh!" Chuck and Aaron were sitting at the kitchen table. An anvil formed in my stomach when Chuck's scent enveloped me.

"What the hell are you doing here?" I yelled.

Chuck put his hands behind his head and pushed his chair back on its hind legs. "Waiting for you, of course." He smiled, but it wasn't friendly.

"And what about you?" I asked, pointing to Aaron.

Aaron stopped and looked at the Pop-Tart he was about to shove into his mouth.

"Never mind," I said. Sometimes it doesn't pay to ask.

Aaron ate his Pop-Tart in one mouthful and chewed, never taking his eyes off me.

"How's it going?" Chuck asked.

"Swell. What do you want?" I asked.

"Where are you going so early?"

"Muffler shop, if you must know."

"What?"

"Dixie needs a new muffler. I'm taking care of it." I poured myself a cup of coffee and blew the steam at him.

"Right. You're up at seven a.m. to buy a new muffler."

"Yeah, I am. What's it to you?"

"What were you doing at the church last night?"

"What church?"

"Cut the crap, Mercy. I know you were there. What I want to know is why."

"If you're so smart, figure it out."

Chuck dropped his chair onto the floor and slammed his fist on the table. Aaron jumped, but kept chewing.

"You're pissing me off now," Chuck said.

"So what's new?" I said.

"Leave it alone. I'm not fooling around. They are not going to be happy if you impede this investigation, and they will have you charged."

"They? They who? And what investigation am I impeding anyway? If you think I'm doing something wrong, go ahead and arrest me. In the meantime, get out."

"Do you have to be so difficult?" Chuck asked.

"Yes. Get out," I said.

"I think I'll have some coffee first. If you don't mind."

"I do mind. Get out."

"Nah." Chuck stood up and stretched. He walked over to me and reached over my shoulder for a coffee cup. His breath smelled like my dad's, beer and wintergreen gum. He brought the cup over my shoulder, then reached for the pot with his other hand. It didn't bother me at all, I swear. I hardly noticed his pecs.

"Want some more?" he asked.

"I made it, didn't I?"

He topped off my cup and reached for the sugar over my shoulder again. I slipped under his arm before I did start to notice all sorts of things.

"That's not very neighborly of you," he said.

"It would've been neighborly to tell me about the website," I said.

"What for?"

"So I could get an injunction or something before it went too far."

Chuck stood and watched while I fried an egg, made toast, and started to eat. "Won't work, I tried," he said softly.

"You tried?" I asked.

"I did." Chuck moved closer and my anvil got heavier.

"Yeah, well, I still don't want to be neighborly with you."

"Yes, you do." Chuck stood and watched while I fried an egg and made toast.

"Aren't you going to offer me any?" he asked.

"Nope."

"So when's Gavin's funeral?"

"I have no idea. Straatman's are trying to strong arm Aunt Miriam over some sort of short notice fee. Gavin's still at the morgue."

"Let me know. I'd like to be there and remember what I said."

"It's seared into my memory," I said.

Chuck saluted me, gave Aaron a pointed look, and left through the pantry. Aaron watched me eat and devoured three more Pop-Tarts.

"Don't you have to go to Kronos?" I asked.

"We don't open until eleven."

Great.

I cleaned up, threw my purse over my shoulder. "Well, I'll be seeing you."

"Yep," said Aaron, but he didn't move.

I went out the back door and reset the alarm. The day was glorious, blue skies with a couple of white puffy clouds for effect, my favorite kind of day. I walked down the brick walk that I'd spent a significant portion of my childhood weeding and paused to smell the bluebells with their perfect waxy forms and light scent.

I went on, meandering this way and that through the flower beds to the garage. I'd left it unalarmed and unlocked. Dad would kill me, if he knew. Lucky for me, he was barfing his brains out thousands of miles away. I got in my truck and twisted around, watching the garage door go up. I turned back around, put my truck in gear, and my passenger door opened.

"No, no. What are you doing, Aaron? Seriously?" Aaron climbed in next to me, shut the door and put on his seatbelt.

"Aaron, hello?"

"Morty said you need some watching."

"Are you kidding me?"

"Where are we going?" he asked.

"I'm going to fix Dixie's muffler. You're going to work."

"We don't open till eleven."

"I don't need watching. Morty was messing with you." I banged my hands on the steering wheel with each word.

"I don't think so. You need help."

"I don't need help, really," I said.

"Which muffler shop?"

Christ almighty.

"I don't know. I have to get the car first."

"There's a good one on I-70."

"Fine."

And there it was, short of physically booting Aaron out of the car, I had a babysitter.

CHAPTER TWELVE

G avin's Grand Marquis sat in the St. James Emergency parking lot untouched by the police crime lab techs.

"We can't break in," said Aaron.

"We're not. I have Dixie's keys," I said.

I unlocked the driver's door and popped the trunk. Dad kept his briefcase and any loose material in the trunk. It was harder to get at that way. Gavin did the same. His trunk was neat and organized with a toolbox, jumper cables, first aid kit, a shopping bag with a Nebraska sweatshirt and a cookbook, and his briefcase. The briefcase was new, a birthday gift from Dixie, but it was the same style he carried throughout his career. It looked more like an English professor's case than a retired cops with soft buttery caramel leather and brass buckles.

I picked it up, shut the trunk, and went up front to Aaron, who sat in the passenger seat chewing a wad of grape bubble gum and smacking his lips.

"What's that?" he asked as I slid Gavin's briefcase behind his seat.

"Don't worry about it," I said.

"Isn't that evidence?"

"Must not be or the cops would've taken it."

Aaron gave me a smile and blew a huge bubble. He directed me to the muffler shop that he knew well. I couldn't imagine why. His scooter had its original muffler and it could be heard for miles around. The shop was a mom-and-pop affair with no waiting. Pop recognized Gavin's car and knew what it needed. He didn't know Gavin was dead. When we told him, he got quiet and said the new muffler was on the house and he'd get right on it. I walked him out to the car, got Gavin's briefcase, and handed over the keys.

Aaron and I went into the waiting room, a standard automotive repair shop waiting area with dirty cracked linoleum, orange plastic chairs, and multiple vending machines. I bought a can of iced tea with a disgusting lemon additive and found the cleanest seat in the place. Aaron sat down next to me in what looked like an old spill of soda that nobody bothered to clean up. He leaned back, crossed his ankles, and looked at me out of the corner of his eye.

I hesitated. I didn't want to go through the case with Aaron watching me, but it was too late. He'd report back to Morty every single thing I did, so I might as well be up front about it.

I unbuckled the case and rifled through Gavin's stuff. There were two manila folders labeled Sendack, Doreen. The rest of the case didn't yield anything interesting. It contained a bottle of Tylenol, some tissues, and a notebook. The notebook was brand new and didn't have so much as a doodle. I was surprised that Gavin hadn't free-handed some notes. I'd filed plenty of his scribblings in the appropriate folders.

"Maybe he had a second notebook," I said.

"What?" said Aaron.

"Nothing. Just thinking out loud."

I opened the first of Doreen Sendack's files. It was the support case Dad mentioned. Doreen was trying to get a line on her ex-husband. He owed thirty thousand dollars for the support of three children he hadn't seen in over two years. Bart Sendack was a swell guy that ran out on his wife and had been dodging her ever since. Doreen heard through a cousin that Bart was living in Lincoln. Gavin must've gone there to check out the lead. Bart's picture was included in the file. He was thin with a long, narrow face and a buzz cut. He'd have been handsome if he gained thirty pounds and changed the hair.

The second file was for accounting purposes. It denoted Gavin's mileage and the number of meetings with Doreen. He'd also run a records check on both her and Bart. Doreen came up empty. She had a couple parking tickets, but that was it. Bart, on the other hand, covered all the bases, speeding, assault, assault with a deadly weapon, robbery, domestic violence, and carjacking. He'd been out on bail for the carjacking incident when he ditched Doreen. I didn't see how Doreen expected to get a dime out of Bart. Maybe it was the principle of the thing.

"Anything interesting?" said Aaron.

"Maybe." I got my own notebook out of my purse and wrote down Doreen's vitals and Bart's crimes. Then I slipped Bart's picture in my purse and put Gavin's stuff away. Fifteen minutes later, the muffler guy came out and said he was finished.

We returned Gavin's car to the hospital parking lot with his briefcase in the trunk. I drove Aaron to Kronos and tried to persuade him to get out of my truck.

"Come on, Aaron. It's ten to eleven," I said.

"I'm off today."

"No, you're not. You're never off."

"I'm off."

I said an "Ah crap" under my breath and parked in Aaron's scooter spot.

We went in and I asked Rodney for a salad at the bar. Aaron followed me to a table and sat down across from me. He replaced his gum with a fresh wad and sat blinking at me like a toad. He needed to be Fiked. Desperately.

"I have to go to the ladies," I said.

Blink.

"Order me a slice of key lime pie, okay?"

Blink.

I went down the hall to the restrooms, looked over my shoulder at Aaron's back, and hung a right out the back door. I jogged the three blocks home. I found Dixie sitting in the living room, swallowed up in one of The Girls' afghans. It wasn't cold in there.

"Hey, how are you doing?" I asked.

"Fine. What do you want?"

"Ah, nothing, um, I had the muffler fixed."

"Great." Dixie's swollen eyes stared at the used tissues scattered over the coffee table. She sat rigid, as if she were expecting a fight.

"Do you need anything?"

"No, I don't." She dismissed me without her eyes ever wavering. I left her with the E! network yammering on the TV to keep her company and went up to Dad's office. His message light was blinking again. There were messages from a couple clients and one for Denny Elliot. I wrote down the particulars for Dad's records and texted Denny. The second-to-last message was from Mom. She was so pissed at me she could hardly speak. She managed to choke out their flight number and that they expected to arrive in Lambert at five p.m. She didn't say how Dad was. The last message was from a surly Uncle Morty. He wanted to know if I'd reviewed his information yet. I hadn't. I'd forgotten all about it.

I booted Dad's computer and called him.

"Hey, it's me," I said.

"Yeah," said Morty.

"So, I got the Sample info." I logged into Dad's email account.

"No, you didn't."

"Yes, I did."

"I put a return receipt on it. You haven't opened it yet," he said.

Crap.

"Now you have," he said. Of course, Mort was online and got the update the second I opened his email.

Sample lived a boring life on paper except for frequent moves and telephone number changes. She'd had six addresses and eleven phone numbers during the three years she lived in St. Louis. Her credit card usage was average. She didn't carry much debt and her charges went down considerably in the six months she'd known her fiancé. He must've done most of the paying. I like that in a man. There were no recent links to Nebraska in either her charges or phone records. I felt the familiar itch to know how Morty got his information. But if it was too easy, I'd be paranoid for the rest of my life. Better to think of Morty as a genius than find out he was one of many.

Uncle Morty made a hacking noise.

"Sorry, I was reading," I said.

"Not much there," he said.

"No, not much at all. You busy?"

He snorted into the phone. Morty was a bit of a snot when it came to his availability. He liked me and everyone else to think he was up to his eyeballs and would squeeze us in if he could. He was busier than I liked to admit. His alter ego wrote high-fantasy bestsellers, but when he was between books, he worked for Dad and bothered me.

"Well, are you or aren't you?" I asked.

"What do you need?"

"Background on Sample's fiancé. I'm thinking she was doing a lot through him. A link to Nebraska might show up through his records."

"Yeah, I had the same thought. What's the name?"

"Lee something. I don't remember the last name. It was in the *Post*."

Snort.

"I can't do everything, you know," I said.

"Try doing something," he said. "Something besides being notorious."

"I am. It's not like I wanted to be on YouTube."

"Then why'd you sign that release?"

I cradled my head in my hand. "I didn't know what would happen."

"Really? You didn't know signing the rights away to your image and likeness wouldn't have, say, consequences?"

"Fine. I'm an idiot," I said.

Uncle Morty snorted and said, "Saw you on BBC World today."

"Just look into Bart and Doreen Sendack again, will you?"

"What do you mean again?"

"You did their backgrounds for Gavin, didn't you?" I smiled. Morty didn't know what I was talking about. That meant Gavin used one of his competitors.

"Son of a bitch." Morty banged his fist on his desk.

"Sorry." I wasn't sorry, but what the hell?

"Bastard," he said.

"So about Bart and Doreen Sendack?"

"Yeah, yeah."

He hung up on me. I did a couple mouth movements. My cheeks hurt from my huge smile. I shut off the computer, went downstairs, got a soda, and went out the back. No point in talking to Dixie. She sure didn't want to talk to me. I trotted out to the garage. Dad's 300 waited for me in his spot next to Mom's Z coupe. Time to use up some of Dad's gas. It was the least he could do since he'd never pay me for doing anything. I slid in, not realizing that it was already unlocked and just about jumped out of my skin when I saw Aaron sitting in the passenger seat.

"Ah crap!"

"What's wrong?" he said.

"What's wrong? What's wrong?" I said with my head in my hands. "Ah nothing."

"Where are we going?"

"To talk to Doreen Sendack," I said.

"Got your salad and pie." He blew a bubble that popped and covered half his face.

"Swell."

It was all I could do not to give him a swift whack to the head. I doubt he would've noticed. The man didn't notice that I'd tried to Fike him.

Christ, what an idiot.

CHAPTER THIRTEEN

Doreen Sendack lived in West County, home of big hair and strip malls. It was a little bit of Jersey in the Midwest. I plugged Doreen's address into Dad's GPS and it began talking to me in an Australian accent. Dad does love Australian women, preferably in bikinis. It's a good thing Mom doesn't have a jealous streak.

We made record time, and for once, I didn't get lost. Doreen lived in an apartment complex built in the seventies. It had avocado green panels under the windows and a brick façade with a hint of orange. The building was in good condition, but it said low rent all the same. Aaron followed me up to apartment 3F and waited, smacking his gum while I knocked. No answer. I could've called and saved myself the trip, but some of Dad's lessons worked their way into my subconscious. I made choices without knowing I did it. Dad said to do X, so I just did it. Never let them know you're coming, and face to face is better were two of his favorites. I wasn't sure whether they applied to both suspects and witnesses. Dad never spoke of such differences. Everybody was in the gray area. There was no black and white.

I knocked again and turned to Aaron. "Guess she's not home. We'll try her work."

Aaron didn't reply, but followed me down the stairs. What would he do if I took off running? Don't think I didn't consider it.

Back in the car, I plugged in my iPod, but before I could touch play, Aaron started talking. I should've expected it. He'd been so quiet on the ride over. Once he got going, Aaron covered a dozen subjects, including his all-time favorite, "What's in hot dogs?" He refused to believe that they were all meat, and that I didn't care. The ride to Conrad's Crab Shack took a half hour, physically and a year mentally. He told me about a secret recipe that he and Rodney were working on for Kronos's own handmade dogs. He'd just gotten my interest piqued when we arrived, and I was about to hear the secret ingredient. It was a sick kind of interest like stopping to get a good look at an accident or having your buddy pull back his Band-Aid so you could see his pus.

We parked and got out. I had to know. What was it? Dog food? Tuna? I looked over the hood at that weird little dude. "So what is it?"

"Huh?" said Aaron.

"The secret ingredient. For the dogs?"

"Oh, yeah. Rodney won't tell me."

"For crying out loud! Are you trying to drive me insane? You just spent ten minutes telling me about this great recipe."

"Maybe he'll tell you."

Since Rodney was weirder than Aaron — I mean, who would choose Aaron to go into business with — the answer could be anything from one small cockroach to jalapenos, so it was better left alone. I threw my hands in the air and walked toward the restaurant. At least, I hoped it was the right place. The parking lot was half empty and the only sign was a large unlit neon sign on a utility pole saying 'Eat.' No name, no hours, just 'Eat' and an arrow pointing roughly to a building.

"You think this is it?" I asked Aaron.

"Yeah. I heard about this place."

"You're kidding."

"They got great crab." He rubbed his hands together and grinned.

"If you say so."

A sign saying "eat" didn't exactly inspire confidence. The place did remind me that I needed a tetanus booster.

Aaron led the way and opened the door for me. There were more customers than the parking lot portrayed. Mostly working-class guys clustered in huddles and a few suits thrown in for good measure. Sawdust and peanut shells covered the floor and the overwhelming smell of crab, never one of my favorites, emanated from the kitchen each time a waitress went through the swinging doors.

We walked past the sign that told us to seat ourselves and found a table underneath a five-foot dartboard. I checked out the waitstaff. They wore plastic name tags with punched-out plastic letters and stained white butcher-type aprons. I didn't know what Doreen looked like and all the waitresses looked like they'd be smart enough to marry Bart Sendack. Aaron picked up a menu and started making pleased murmuring sounds. I picked up one, too. I had to see what the fuss was all about. Crab. All crab. Not a single thing on the menu, besides drinks, that did not include crab.

"What are you having?" asked Aaron.

"Nothing. I hate crab," I said.

"Then why are we here?"

"Doreen Sendack works here, remember?"

"Uh-huh. Well, I'm ordering." Aaron buried his face back in the menu, and I flagged down a waitress. Carla.

"Hi, is Doreen working today?"

"Yeah. What'll you have?" Carla asked.

"You have iced tea?"

Carla nodded and scribbled on her pad. She looked back at me.

"That's it for me."

I kicked Aaron and he looked up from behind the menu. Carla looked surprised and said, "You?"

"Super crab platter, double hush puppies, onion rings, and a vanilla shake."

"That it?" asked Carla.

Aaron said yes. Carla looked back and forth between us a couple of times with furrowed brows.

"He's rich," I said.

Carla made a face that said, "Oh, I get it," and left.

"I'm not rich," said Aaron.

"And it wouldn't make any difference if you were."

Aaron gave me a puzzled look and went back to the menu. A couple minutes later, Carla came back with my iced tea and Aaron's shake.

"What do you want with Dorie?" she asked.

"It's business. I'm an associate of Gavin Flouder's. Could I speak with her?" I asked.

Carla shrugged and went to check on a couple of tables. I inspected my tea. No crab, although the glass had a slight odor to it. It might've been my imagination. I really hated crab.

Aaron sucked down half his shake in one breath. "So what do you think, chicken or tofu? I don't know about those chicken dogs. They don't say what part of the chicken. They might use the whole thing. I think I got a toenail once."

I gagged and tried not to imagine biting into a hot dog and finding a giant toenail in it. Fail.

"You want to see it?" asked Aaron, suddenly looking super happy.

"You kept the toenail? Why?"

"It's kind of cool."

"OMG. You are so weird."

"So you want to see it?"

"No!"

Carla waved at me from the kitchen door, and I left Aaron to ponder chicken toenails alone. She pointed to a woman bending over a skillet, sniffing the contents. Carla picked up a large platter and left. I watched Doreen pour half a can of beer into the skillet. She moved her hips side to side with the rhythm of the bluegrass music playing on a portable CD player above the stove. She moved quickly from skillet to pot to oven to grill and back to skillet again. There were several others in the kitchen, but Doreen was in charge. She yelled orders every few seconds and shuttled plates back and forth from the stove to the prep area.

I walked up behind her. "Excuse me, Doreen Sendack?"

Doreen turned around and gave me the old once-over. She yelled for someone named Ken, told him she was taking a break, and gave him a set of rigid instructions that a rocket scientist would've had a tough time following. Ken looked terrified, and I didn't blame him.

Doreen motioned for me to follow her and we went out the exit door to a stoop in the alley. Doreen lit a cigarette and leaned against the rusty metal railing. She looked me over again, her mouth clamped around the cigarette.

"Who're you?" she said.

I released a tense breath. Anonymity, my favorite thing.

"I'm Mercy Watts. Sorry to bother you at work, but I need to ask you some questions about your case."

"You really work for Flouder?" She raised the brows that she'd painted on with a careless hand. The left wasn't quite even with the right. The rest of her appearance ran in the same vein. She'd colored her hair a medium blond one too many times, and it had a greenish tint. I knew Doreen was thirty-one from her file, but it was hard to get a handle on that number from her face. I would've put her in her early forties at least. The orange-tinged base and heavily lined eyes didn't help.

"Yeah. Who'd you think I was?" I said.

"I thought maybe you were one of Bart's girlfriends. They show up every once in a while." She paused and took a long drag. "To get a look at the competition, you know." Her mouth twisted into a smile around the cigarette. She didn't think she was anybody's competition anymore.

"I've never met your ex."

Doreen relaxed and flicked the ash off her cigarette.

"Flouder getting closer to finding that shithead yet?"

"I don't know. That's why I'm here. Mr. Flouder died last Sunday."

"No shit? I wondered why he didn't call me. He was pretty good about checking in. Nice guy. What happened?"

"He was murdered."

"Holy crap. You don't think Bart did it, do you?"

"Not at this point. What do you think?"

"No way. Bart is a serious asshole, but he'd never kill anybody."

"He's been arrested a lot, including assault with a deadly weapon."

"That was his stepmom. She's a real bitch."

Well, that makes all the difference.

"When was the last time you talked to Gavin?"

"Huh?"

"Mr. Flouder."

"Who are you exactly?"

"I'm the daughter of his best friend. My dad's a detective, but he's out of town. He wants me to figure out what Gavin, Mr. Flouder, did in Lincoln, Nebraska, right before he was murdered."

"Sorry. I had to ask. Are the cops going to be coming around on this?"

"I have no idea, but I wouldn't count it out. Do you know why he went to Lincoln?"

"Sure. I told him to."

"Why's that?"

"My cousin Dave calls and tells me that Bart the shithead asked him for money. What a fucking idiot. Dave don't have a dime. He pays his support."

"And Bart said he was in Lincoln?"

"Yeah. Staying with some chick, of course."

"You remember her name?" I asked.

"Yeah, Tina Shipley. Didn't get an address, though."

"Did Dave give you any other information?"

"No. Just that Bart was in Lincoln with that chick."

"He didn't call you from Lincoln? You never heard whether he found Bart or not?" I pulled out my notebook and wrote down Tina Shipley.

"Nope, not a word. What's gonna happen with my case? I need that child support. You think your dad might take it on?"

"I'll mention it to him and see what he says."

Doreen dropped her cigarette and ground it to dust with her toe. "I'm getting so sick and tired of this shit. Why can't Bart be a man and pay up?" She looked at me like she expected a reasonable explanation. I guessed that the best explanation was that a man that would assault his stepmother with a deadly weapon wasn't much of a man to begin with and she ought to have known that. But since she had kids with him, I imagined she didn't.

I leaned on the rickety railing and crossed my arms. "I have got to ask. From the look of your file, Bart doesn't have two nickels to rub together. How do you expect him to pay thirty thousand dollars of back child support? It doesn't look like he's had a real job in years."

"His family owns Ace Bailey Trucking. All I got to do is find him, have him thrown in jail, and they'll pay up." She smiled. "I've got to get back."

"Thanks for your help. I'll let you know what happens," I said.

She reached for the door handle, but stopped and looked at me. "You know, I can't understand it. You'd think he'd want to help out. He loves his boys. I can say a lot against him, but he loves his boys, and he knows I ain't got a pot to piss in."

"I doubt he gave a thought."

Sadness filled her eyes, sadness for her boys, not herself. She looked like she was doing alright. The boys might be another matter.

I followed Doreen inside and watched Aaron take an hour to polish off his crab feast. He was still moaning in ecstasy when we got in the car. I told him to calm down, but it did no good. Aaron was nothing if not passionate about food. Crab stink radiated off him, and I had to crack the window to keep from gagging.

"That car's following us," said Aaron.

"Which one?"

"Gray one."

Not a big help. Every other car on the road was gray, including Dad's.

"You want to give me more specifics?" I asked.

"Two cars back. Left lane," said Aaron.

"How can you tell?" I asked.

Aaron shrugged and licked a bit of crab off his lip.

I had to look in the rearview twenty times before I believed him. I don't know how Aaron knew, but he was right. The gray Escort stayed with us at a discreet distance.

I pulled the 300 up in the front of Kronos. "Well, it's been...something. See you later."

Aaron looked at the restaurant and settled in. "Where to next?"

"The airport. Surely I can be trusted to pick up my parents on my own. I am a big girl."

Aaron considered my request and put in another wad of gum. The smell of grape and crab combined, and I made an involuntary horking sound.

"What's wrong with you?" Aaron asked.

"Can't you smell that?"

He tilted his head in the air and sniffed like a hound. "Smells okay to me."

"Forget it. Now go on." I pushed his shoulder towards the door.

"Okay, okay. Call me later."

"I will call you later." I waved at Rodney in the doorway and hit the gas before Aaron could change his mind.

Call him later. Why would I call him later? I'd never called him in my entire life. Still, he did notice the Escort when I didn't. Maybe I owed him something for that, because it was still behind me, three cars back.

I drove three miles before I realized that crab stink wasn't going away. Aaron had left a lovely sweat stain on Dad's leather seat back. I rolled down the windows despite the heat and wished I had some VapoRub to stuff up my nose. That crab had staying power. Aaron owed me. Uncle Morty owed me. Everybody owed me. God, I hate Crab.

CHAPTER FOURTEEN

I arrived at the airport at a quarter after four in the crab car and discovered the airport was on some kind of alert. It took me a half hour to get through the nimrod security designed to stop terrorists without two brain cells to rub together. Like barricades and checkpoints were really going to help. All a terrorist needed was a fake ID and the ability to turn a corner and he would be allowed to park. It was inconvenient at best and rip-roaring annoying at worst. The Feds couldn't decide what to do, so they settled for looking like they were doing something. Since I couldn't go to the gate, I settled at a bar, ordered an iced tea and waited for my parents to walk by.

A half hour later, a glut of passengers passed, but my parents weren't among them. I waited, and the passageway cleared. I went and checked the arrivals monitor and sure enough, their flight was in.

Ridiculous thoughts popped unbidden into my head. Things I usually was able to keep under wraps, like some ex-con murdered Gavin and poisoned Dad for revenge and my parents were lying in a ditch somewhere. That's what Mom used to say when I was late for curfew. "You could've been dead in a ditch somewhere, young lady." I thought that was stupid when she said it to me and before I knew it, I was thinking it about her. It must be something about being an adult that makes you go to the worst-case scenario instead of the best, like they missed their connection.

An announcement came over the intercom, "Carolina Watts, please come to Concourse A security. Carolina Watts, please come to Concourse A Security."

My stomach twisted into a bow tie. I dropped a five on the table and jogged down the passage. Like my mother, I should never run in public. There's not a bra manufactured that can stop my breasts from bouncing like a couple of kids on a trampoline and the little lace number I had on was barely enough to keep them from knocking me out. A businessman dropped his briefcase, and I saw a wife smack her husband on the back of the head as I passed.

I rounded the turn and saw Mom and Dad standing on my side of Security. Mom seemed okay, but Dad looked like he'd been pulled from my imaginary ditch half alive. Some guards stood near my parents, looking at me with their mouths hanging open. The guards were all men except for one large black lady with Lynette on her name tag. She was also looking at me, but without the whoa expression on her face. She smiled as I ran up out of breath and said, "Girl, you should be against the law. Look at these fools. As if your mother wasn't bad enough."

"Sorry," I said, panting.

"Don't be sorry, girl. If you've got it, flaunt it. Just don't run. The world can't take it."

I turned to Mom. "What happened? What's wrong?"

Mom fluffed her hair and looked at Dad out of the corner of her eye. "We're fine. We could use some help with the carry-on luggage, though."

"Fine? Are you nuts? Dad looks like he should be in the ICU," I said.

"I can hear you. I'm standing right here. How about a kiss for your dear old dad?" Dad leaned on Mom and held out his hand. His skin had the translucent look of greased paper and his veins showed the effects of several needle sticks. Large purple bruises spread across the back of his hands and up his wrists, ending in large Band-Aids. I was glad I wasn't the one who had to find a reasonable vein for an IV.

Dad wasn't a guy who had a lot of color to begin with, but his freckles stood out like stars in the night sky. There were deep purple grooves under his eyes and his eyeballs looked too small for their sockets. The lower lids hung away from the eyes, showing the blood-red rims. His red hair wasn't brushed back, sleek as a seal, but stuck up in every direction in odd clumps. There was a spot of crusty yellow on the front of his polo shirt and his jeans were about to fall off him.

"I think I'll pass. Can we get a wheelchair over here?" I asked Lynette.

"You could, but he won't sit in it. I already tried." Her mouth turned down into a disapproving frown, and her arms crossed over her own substantial chest.

"I don't need a wheelchair," said Dad. "How old do you think I am?"

"Dad, it's not your age. It's your condition. You look like you're ready for a toe tag. Can we have that wheelchair, please?" I looked at Lynette. She shrugged and went into a storage room.

"No wheelchair," said Dad as Lynette wheeled a chair up behind Dad and opened it up.

"Dad, if you don't sit in that chair, I'm taking you straight to the ER instead of home. What do you think of that?"

"It sucks," he said.

"Damn straight. Sit down."

Dad looked at me with his basset hound eyes. "To think I could've had a vasectomy."

"Tommy, for heaven's sake." Mom looked at the ceiling. "I'm sorry, honey. It's been rough."

Dad looked at the two of us. "I'm not sorry. She's a pain in my ass. Always has been. Who do you think you are? I don't take orders. I give them."

"Dad, please."

"Don't you talk to me." He looked at the guards. "Do you know what her name is? We call her Mercy, not Carolina, Mercy. Why do we call her that? Because she screamed for twelve hours straight the day we brought her home. All I could say was, 'Have mercy.'" And that's what we call her. My wife wanted to have another one. Another one?

Are you crazy, woman?" Dad looked at Mom and passed out cold. Luckily, he dropped straight back into the wheelchair. I checked his pulse and respiration. They were fast, but not dangerous.

"Should we wait until he wakes up, so he can order me to push him to the car?" I asked Mom.

"Be amusing on your own time. Push the chair."

We got Dad out of the airport and into the back of the car before he woke up. I covered him with the emergency blanket he kept in the trunk.

Mom glanced at Dad's closed eyes and whispered, "Tell me you took care of that problem."

"Well..."

"Don't well me. You fix this. Now," said Mom.

He opened his bleary eyes and started struggling with the blanket. The only word he uttered that I could understand was barf. Mom and I pulled his head and chest back out of the car. He vomited a thin, yellowish liquid onto the pavement. It's the kind of stuff that comes out of a stomach that's been ill and empty for too long. He continued to dry heave for ten minutes, then I dried his mouth with a tissue and checked his pulse again. Dad was getting into the scary range and I had to make a judgment call. We put him back into the car and I asked Mom, "Didn't they put him on anything?"

"Of course they did, but he keeps throwing it up."

"What about a suppository for the nausea?"

"No, they said he was better."

"This is better?"

"Your father was putting on a bit of a brave face. We had to get on that plane."

"It's not going to make any difference where he is in this condition. You should've stayed there." I felt Dad's forehead and tucked the blanket in around him.

"There's no reasoning with him. We've been married for twenty-six years and I've never seen him this belligerent. Well, maybe when Cora died, but mostly he was just crazy," said Mom.

I ran my thumb over the lines on Dad's forehead. I hadn't thought about Cora in years. She was one of Dad's partners and the only female. Cora got shot in the head when she walked into a robbery in progress in her own house. Dad loved Cora. He thought she was the best he ever worked with. I was ten at the time and her death changed him in ways I didn't understand.

If he was as bad as when Cora died, it was serious. "I think we need to take him in," I said as I fired up the car.

Mom got in and wrinkled her nose. "Do you smell something? What is that?"

"Aaron."

"Poor guy."

"Aaron is not the victim here. He's quite happy, as a matter of fact."

Mom found an old air freshener in the glove compartment and swung it around. "I can feel sorry for him if I want to. He can't help it if he stinks."

"Yes, he can. That's what soap and not eating crab is for."

"Fine. Now, are you sure we have to take your father in? He won't be happy."

"Nothing would make him happy right now, and I don't know what we're dealing with."

"The ship's doctor said it was some kind of flu-like virus. He has to ride it out."

"How many people got it?"

"Quite a few, I gathered."

"How many is that? Ten, twenty?"

"More like a couple hundred. It was on the news," said Mom.

"Haven't been watching a lot of CNN lately."

"I'm sorry. Has it been very bad here? How's Dixie?"

"I really don't know," I said, feeling my throat constrict at the thought of Gavin and Dixie.

"She's out of her head, honey. She doesn't know what she's doing."

"You talked to her?"

"Once. Two days ago. She says she yelled at you. What happened?" Mom twisted in her seat and looked at me. I was merging onto I-70 with the Escort right behind and took the opportunity to concentrate on that while forming a reply. Mom wouldn't be happy with how Dixie found out about Gavin's murder, but I'd feel worse if I lied to her about it. Mom would find out in the end, so I gave it up.

"She overheard me talking to Pete about what happened to Gavin."

"That's how she found out he was murdered?"

"I didn't mean for her to hear. It just happened."

"You should've been more careful." Mom turned back towards the front and crossed her arms. She looked up at the ceiling. "What else can happen?"

"Don't say that. We could have an accident on the way to the hospital."

"Heaven forbid. Are you still seeing that Pete what's-his-name?"

"Yes. I'm still seeing what's-his-name."

"He's a doctor, isn't he?"

"Yeah. Why?" I asked.

"Could he come by?"

"You want to meet my boyfriend now?" I couldn't believe it. My parents, mostly Dad, had a long-standing rule about meeting boyfriends. He couldn't hate them if they didn't exist.

"No, I mean yes, I want to meet him, but I was hoping he would take a look at your father."

"You don't trust my medical opinion? I'm your own daughter."

"Pete's a doctor. I'd like him to take a look."

"Instead of taking Dad to the ER, you mean," I said.

"Exactly."

"Is he that crazy?"

"You have no idea. If we take him to the hospital, we may as well book him into the psych ward straight away."

"My phone's in my purse."

Mom got out my cell phone and texted Pete a 911. He called back immediately and agreed to come to the house. Pete wasn't thrilled about meeting my dad, period, but he still agreed to come. I must've sounded desperate.

After I hung up with Pete, Dad started making gagging noises.

"Pull over. Pull over," Mom yelled.

I couldn't. We were on the highway into the city, and there was nowhere to go. Mom panicked. She opened her purse and dumped it out on the floor. It was her favorite Prada bag, but Dad could not barf all over the car. If that happened, there would be repercussions, to say the least. Mom started to crawl into the back seat.

"Wait. I have a salad in the glove compartment. Toss it and use the container."

Dad's long arms waved around as the gagging got worse.

"Why do you have a salad in the glove compartment?"

"Who cares? Hurry!"

"What do I do with the salad?" Mom looked around with the Styrofoam box in her hands.

"Throw it out the window."

"It'll get on the paint."

"Christ, Mom. It has six thousand coats of wax on it. Just toss it."

Mom flipped my salad out the window, and it flew straight back. A Buick swerved and dodged it and my salad splatted onto the Escort's windshield. Much honking and, I imagine, cursing ensued as the Escort ended up on an off ramp and we sped away.

"Mercy, look what you made me do. You could've caused an accident," Mom yelled.

I could've caused an accident. She flew Plague Man halfway around the world, and I could've caused an accident. I was sure all the people from the plane who would be barfing their brains out in a day or two would think I was the bad one. Recycled air was the curse of all travelers.

Dad made a chest-deep honk like a water buffalo. I'd never heard a water buffalo, but I was sure that's what they sounded like, low and phlegmy.

"Mom!" I yelled as Mom crawled into the back and murmured soothing sounds into Dad's ear while he spewed into my salad box. When he was done, she came back to the front seat with the box.

"I suppose you want me to throw this out the window too," she said.

"I do not," I said.

Actually, I did, but I could live with the smell for another ten minutes in order to take the high road.

I pulled into the alley in record time and saw Pete leaning on his ancient Saab parked next to our trash bins. He looked wonderfully cool and confident. The sight of him made me want to cry with relief.

"Is that him?" Mom asked.

"That's him," I said with more than a little apprehension.

"Nice, and he drives a Saab. Your father will be pleased."

"I'm sure that's what Pete was going for."

"Don't be snide. I'm saying it's a good thing."

"I know."

I parked in the garage, got out, and kissed Pete. Then I turned to Mom and introduced the two of them. Mom shook his hand, apologizing for both calling him and her appearance. She was stunning, as she well knew, and Pete said so. That brought a smile to her face, and we were off on the right foot.

Pete listened to Dad's heart and lungs, took his blood pressure and pulse in the car in case we had to take him in. He pronounced him safe to keep at home for the time being and asked me to get a bag out of his back seat. Pete and Mom slid Dad out of the car, and Pete carried him into the house. There was a lot of strength in that skinny body. I never would've guessed it.

There was no sign of Dixie or anyone else as we walked up the stairs to the second floor. Mom decided to settle in the largest guest room, since Dixie was entrenched in their room. Dad lay on the bed semiconscious while Pete unpacked his bag. It was filled to the brim with hospital supplies, IVs, several bags of saline, some lancets, tubes for collecting blood samples, several prescription bottles, syringes, and liquid vials from the pharmacy.

Mom took off Dad's stained shirt, and we got a view of his sunken chest. Mom and I pulled on a fresh pajama top. I'd never seen him wear one before. Dad had pajamas, although he never wore them. He usually slept in boxer shorts and he wasn't shy. He was known to answer the door first thing in the morning without adding to his wardrobe. And by God, if he wanted to get the paper like that, he did. As a teenager, I complained that my friends didn't want to see him in his skivvies. Dad couldn't see why they'd care. He couldn't care less what they wore. Half the time, I would've sworn that he didn't see them at all, unless they said something that interested him, which was rare.

Since I was the nurse, I had to do the IV. Dad's arms looked like he'd been bludgeoned. I hated the idea of poking a needle into those traumatized arms. I might've asked Pete to do it, but I'd look like a wuss. So I pictured Dad as an intravenous drug user — he had the body — and got started. I blew three veins and got lucky on the fourth stick. Dad was so out of it, he barely complained. I hooked the bag on a coat hanger and hung it on the headboard. Pete measured out a dose of Zofran and injected it into the IV line.

"That should take care of the nausea and vomiting," Pete said. Then he looked at me. "You can give him another two cc's in a couple of hours, if you think he needs it. We'll see how he's doing then and reevaluate."

"So you don't think he'll need to go to the hospital?" Mom asked.

"I don't think so, but he's right on the edge. It depends on how he responds to the Zofran and if we can get him hydrated in a reasonable amount of time."

"What's a reasonable amount of time?" said Mom.

"I'd like to see him hold something down within two hours. Apple juice or a cracker will do."

"I'm certain he'll be able to do that now that he's medicated. Why don't you two go downstairs while I put his pajama bottoms on?"

Pete and I went down to the kitchen. I found Dad's last can of C4 Black Cherry for Pete and made hot chocolate for myself. I needed it, even if it was ninety degrees outside.

"I can't believe an airline would let him fly in that condition," Pete said.

"Dad can be very persuasive."

"I still don't see how he talked them into it."

"Let's just say he knows people," I said with a smile.

"People in high places?"

"And low places. All layers of the stratosphere, really, and they all owe him or want him to owe them."

"Airlines have regulations about illness and injury. It doesn't matter who you are or know. Someone wasn't doing their job." Pete frowned at me. I didn't respond immediately, and his gaze hardened. People shouldn't break the rules and certainly not because they admired or feared someone. Debts should never be considered. Rules were rules and for the world to run correctly, they must be obeyed. Pete didn't live in Dad's world. I didn't either, but I visited on a regular basis.

"Well, you know how overworked all those airline people are. They're more concerned with keeping weapons off planes than viruses, I imagine." I looked into Pete's blue eyes and tried to look as innocent as possible. I loved his big eyes with their heavy fringe of lashes, almost feminine in their thickness. His expression changed from suspicious to affectionate, and he relaxed. He pushed back and balanced his chair on its hind legs. He looked elegant and easy. I could smell his scent despite the distance between us. I filled my lungs with it. Pete smelled like the color forest green looks.

"Light day?" I asked.

"Yes, we're nearly empty. Why do you ask?"

"You smell good," I said, and Pete laughed quietly. Mom walked into the kitchen. She had a funny look on her face, like she was intruding, which she wasn't.

"I just thought I'd get some juice and crackers for Dad," she said as she walked past us into the butler's pantry. We listened to her search until she came back into the kitchen empty-handed. "I think we're out of saltines."

Pete stood up. "I'll get some."

"Good. Could you pick up some smoky cheddar, too? Tommy likes it when he's sick."

"How do you know?" I asked. "Dad hasn't been sick in twenty years."

"Well, he liked it twenty years ago. Stop arguing. You're as bad as he is and drop those casseroles on your way." Mom pointed to the dishes that The Girls had brought their famous casseroles over in. Pete picked them up, and I told Mom we'd head to The Girls' house first.

CHAPTER FIFTEEN

The Bled mansion lorded over the avenue six houses down and across the street, past the invisible line that separated the upper class from the truly rich. Hawthorne Avenue was a gated street, so from the outside we were all lumped in together. It takes bucks to be gated, but on my parents' half of the street those bucks could've been earned the hard way. Doctors, lawyers and businesspeople owned those houses. The rest of the street was another story. Those people didn't work for corporations, they owned them. Their mansions ran in the high seven figures, but it was rare for one to come on the market. The last time was five years ago and caused quite a stir. Highpoint House went for a cool million seven to the heir of the Lange auto empire and a sigh of relief was breathed by the neighborhood. They lived in constant fear that someone would buy in and try to commercialize their world for boutiques or bed-and-breakfasts.

Myrtle and Millicent Bled didn't worry about such trivial concerns. I doubted they realized anyone could or would want to change the world in which they'd lived their entire lives. They lived in the house they'd been born in, been raised by nannies in and received their ultra-private tutored education in. As far as I could tell, they had no desire for a different kind of life, but they would hardly have spoken to me about it if they had. In many ways, I was like their child. I, too, was born in the Bled mansion, delivered by a private medical staff and surrounded by an unbelievable collection of art, including framed leaves from the Gutenberg bible, a Matisse, a Degas, and a Vermeer sketch. The Girls said I should be born in the presence of greatness and so I was. The Girls had insisted on caring for my mother at the end of her pregnancy. They liked to call it her confinement. Neither of my parents denied The Girls anything, since they loved them and owed them for their entrance into the exclusive world of Hawthorne Avenue. Neither Myrtle nor Millicent said that we owed them. They didn't operate that way. I think they fell in love with my parents and did as they pleased. The Girls wanted to give them a house, so they did. They wanted to care for my mother and they did that, too. There was no question of Myrtle and Millicent's intentions — they were good, always good, even if they infringed on our lives a bit.

"I love this street," said Pete as we crossed Hawthorne Avenue. "I never knew it was here until we met. It's like another world."

"It is another world, believe me."

My phone rang, but it was an unknown number, not Dad having a seizure. I let it go to voicemail. I could check the heavy breathing later.

"It must've been strange growing up here with all these rich people and your dad being a cop. No offense, but you know what I mean."

"I do and it was, but I think they always liked having us here. Dad made them feel safe when the neighborhoods around them were going down the crapper. He used to check out their security for them and install new locks. The rich can be pretty paranoid."

"Did they pay him?"

"Are you kidding? The rich don't pay; they expect."

"That's nice. All the money in the world and they won't pay some guy to put locks in for them. They make your dad do it for free."

"It's not about the money. It's about trust. Dad's a known entity. He's a cop and lives here."

"He's one of them."

"Sort of. Close as a regular guy can get and still be able to install locks."

"Does he still change their locks for them?"

"He would if it came up."

"Which house is it? Or should I say mansion?" Pete shifted the dishes to one arm and put his arm around my shoulder, rubbing it gently.

"It's the next one. The one with the green marble columns."

"Whoa. I've seen it before in some book. I can't remember which one," he said as my phone rang again.

He took it out of my hand and said, "Hello."

"Who is it?" I asked.

"Do you do private parties?" Pete asked with a big grin.

"Shut up!"

"They'll pay three thousand for two hours."

"That'll happen." I took the phone and switched it off. Dad probably wouldn't die in the next ten minutes.

We stopped at the front gate, and I pushed the buzzer. It made a little buzzing noise that made me think I was about to be electrocuted. A couple minutes later, there was another buzz and the eight-foot-high black wrought-iron gate swung open. We walked through the gate and I looked up at Pete. He stared up at the house, his eyes jumping around as if they didn't know where to land. I'd seen plenty of people look at the house that way. It was that kind of house. It wasn't unusual to see a tripod set up across the street with a camera clicking away or an art student working over a sketchbook. It wasn't hard to see why; the house was just plain weird. Nicolai Bled, The Girls' father, built it in 1920 after Prohibition was passed. He took the act as a personal attack since the family fortunes were linked with the consumption of beer. The house was his act of defiance against the whims of public opinion. He wanted it to be noticed, and it was.

I stood by Pete, looking up at the mansion with my own feelings of devotion. It was big by Art déco standards, but whether it truly was Art déco was difficult to say. The mansion was two exaggerated stories high. In any other building, it would've been three. The main structure was rectangular with a flat roof and rounded corners with the exterior covered in pale gray stucco. Four green marble columns decorated the front façade. It was the columns that caught the passerby's eye. They were huge and spanned the height of the building and bowed out against the house like a child blew them up with a tire pump. Large green ceramic tiles, each with hand-painted palm fronds, edged the top and bottom of the house all the way around. All the many windows were covered in black wrought iron in geometric shapes. None of the windows matched and on either side of the building were glass rooms that The Girls called conservatories. Neither conservatory had walls, only iron columns that held up the flat ceiling. The panes of glass were held in place with elaborate ironwork that suggested Egyptian hiero-glyphics, although there were no people done in iron.

It was dusk in the Central West End and a single light above the front door beckoned us to come forward. It wasn't the welcoming sight I was used to. The conservatories were usually lit to show off their beauty. The Girls liked light. They rarely turned off any switch. In recent years, Dad had gotten them hooked on a computerized lighting system. They liked to fiddle with it and turn the lights to different intensities, have some go on or off at special times of the day. The last I'd heard, Millicent was trying to program the garden walkways to follow a musical program. But that night, it was all dark, even the stained glass windows. I felt weird about going up to the door. The Girls were home; they buzzed us in, but the house was all wrong. I looked around and realized the grass was uncut and there were leaves floating in the four fountains, the water, for once in my life, not gushing.

"It looks abandoned," said Pete.

"I know. It's weird. I wonder if the lighting program got fried," I said.

We walked up the marble steps to the oversized front entrance. The doors themselves were recessed by a foot and encased in more ironwork. I reached through and lifted the iron crow that served as a knocker. I dropped it and it made a heavy plinking noise that would echo through the hallways. A second later, Millicent opened the right door half a foot and peered out at us.

"Hello, dear. How are you this evening?"

"I'm fine, Millicent. This is my friend, Dr. Peter Linderhoff. We wanted to return your dishes." I waited for her to invite us in. She didn't.

"Thank you, dear. So kind." Millicent reached back, and I heard a buzz and a click. The iron door slid back into the wall. Millicent took the dishes from Pete, apologized for not being more hospitable, said Myrtle was ill, and bade us goodnight. Before I knew it, the door closed and the iron door slid back into place.

"Okay. I know they're like family, but that was odd," said Pete.

"Something's wrong. They love me. They love men. I figured we'd be here until midnight if we weren't careful."

We walked back past the neglected fountains and out the gate. Stern's, the grocery that existed only to serve Hawthorne Avenue, was six blocks away. I held Pete's hand, and we walked there in silence. Pete bought Dad's crackers and cheese while I tried to think of a way to get in that house.

CHAPTER SIXTEEN

My parents' house was silent when we got back. On the second floor, I could hear Mom and Dixie talking in the master bath. It was their habit. If the worst happens, go hang out in the bathroom. I couldn't throw stones. My best friend, Ellen, and I spent plenty of hours in there, getting ready to go out and discussing our so-called problems. Mom's bathroom was a sanctuary with a huge claw-footed tub, a dressing table with a velvet bench and an archway into the dressing room. Dixie was probably crying in a bubble bath, while Mom listened and applied a moisturizing mud mask.

Pete and I went into the guest bedroom and found Dad sleeping. My mother's cats had emerged from their hiding place and were sitting at the foot of the bed looking like a couple of Egyptian statues.

"So that's them. The sofa pee-ers," Pete said, gesturing to the cats.

"Uh-huh. That's Swish on the left and the other one's Swat." I glared at the cats, but they didn't acknowledge that we'd entered the room.

"Swish and Swat?"

"They have real names on their pedigrees, but we call them like we see them."

Pete sat on the edge of the bed and looked at the cats. Neither responded. They both stared at Dad and were expressionless. That might sound odd, but those cats had definite expressions. Maybe it had something to do with being well-bred Siamese. My own cat, Skanky, had no expressions. He barely had a brain.

Pete took Dad's pulse and blood pressure. When he finished, he pronounced him marginally better. As we looked at Dad, Swat stood up, stretched languidly, and walked up the length of Dad's body. He stood on Dad's chest. After a few seconds, he sniffed Dad's nose, sat down, stuck his leg straight up, and cleaned his butt.

"I need a camera," I said and ran to the office. When I came back, Swat was biting his butt, and Pete was stifling a laugh.

Pete turned red. "I can't stand it." He ran out of the room and I heard him laughing in the hall. I shot pictures from every angle until Mom heard the laughter and came in.

"Don't take pictures, Mercy. That's not nice," she said.

"I want to remember this moment."

Mom shooed the cats off the bed. Pete got paged and left for the hospital. We woke Dad for the cracker test an hour later. He was groggy, but ate half a saltine.

"Why are you smiling?" he asked with narrowed eyes.

"No reason, honey. Go back to sleep," Mom said.

Dad ignored Mom. "How's the case?"

"Fine. Try to get some sleep," I said.

"I don't need any more sleep. I didn't come home to sleep."

"He is better."

"He's no better." Mom pulled the covers up and Dad shooed her away like she shooed the cats.

"Tell me," Dad said.

"Okay. I photographed the scene, fixed Dixie's muffler, walked through the church, and talked to Gavin's last client." When I said it like that, it sounded like I'd been sitting on my ass.

"That's all?"

"I went to the morgue, too."

Dad growled and tried to sit up. "I'll take over from here."

"That sounds like an excellent plan. Goodnight, Mercy dear," said Mom.

"An excellent plan? Dad can't take over stink."

"It'll be fine. He might be well enough tomorrow."

Swat jumped up on the bed and licked his chops. He had an interesting expression on his pointed face. I could've sworn he was thinking, "I just cleaned my ass on you. You're not going anywhere."

Mom grabbed me by the arm and steered me out of the room, down the stairs, and into the kitchen.

"Can't you let anything go?" she asked.

"He's sick as a dog. He's not going to the bathroom by himself."

"I know that. It won't hurt to let him think he's going to take over, and then you just keep going."

"What if I don't want to keep going?"

"Please. I don't have the energy for this." Mom rolled her eyes and rubbed her head. Her hair, which had been damp when she came out of the bathroom, had dried into soft curls around her face. She was pretty, much prettier than a woman her age had a right to be. I thanked God for my fortunate gene pool, mixed blessing, though it was.

"What am I expected to do now?" I asked.

"What would you have done if we hadn't gotten a flight?"

"More interviews, I guess."

"Then it's settled. Do that." Mom handed me my purse and indicated I shouldn't let the door hit me on the way out.

"You want me to leave?"

"Don't you have to feed Skanky?"

"He has a self-feeder and Dad might get worse."

"You're three blocks away. I think I can handle it."

"Fine, but I want to give him the next dose of Zofran in a half hour. That way, we won't have to worry about nausea during the night and I'll be by first thing in the morning."

Mom nodded her assent. Thirty-three minutes later, I was out the door and walking home. The door didn't hit me.

CHAPTER SEVENTEEN

I woke the next morning in my own bed with Skanky curled beside me. He slept with his mouth open and made little kicking motions with his feet, dreaming about feline heroics, no doubt. I took a drink from my water glass that I have to have next to my bed or I can't sleep. That's on the neuroses-that-Mom-gave-me list. Skanky woke and did a long stretch with his butt in the air and let out a big curly-tongued yawn. I patted him while I called Mom. She said Dad had a good night and was sleeping. She wanted me to get on with the investigation. I told her about Millicent's odd behavior the night before, and she dismissed me as a worrywart. I hung up feeling a bit like a hysteric. Everything in the last few days was a crisis, and I was starting to see them everywhere I turned.

"Don't look at me like that," I said to Skanky. "Your biggest problem is where to take a nap today. You don't even have balls."

He sneezed, fell over, and began cleaning between each and every one of his toes. Cats never listened to me. I searched around until I found my cell phone in a pile of dirty clothes. I needed to check my messages in case I got one from someone other than a pervert. The first three texts were from Suck, We're Horne, and Horney 4 Mercy. You know it's bad when the perverts can't spell horny. The rest followed in the same vein. I could've changed my number, but that was such a pain. I deleted every one and called my agency. Dolores wasn't thrilled that I didn't want to work for a while, but she'd live.

I got into a hot shower and lathered up while listening to Skanky mewing at me for food through the glass door. Being yelled at in the shower doesn't make for a good time, so I cut it short and fed the beast. He ate, cleaned, and immediately went back to sleep. His life is hard. The landline rang. I could tell it was Uncle Morty just from the grumpy ring.

"How's Tommy?" he said.

"Pretty sick. Good morning to you too," I said.

"Yeah, yeah. I got your info on the dead bride's husband."

"Great."

"Yeah, swell, who's paying for this?"

"It's for Gavin."

"Don't you give me that crap. This is a separate crime, and I got a business to run."

"Fine, put it on my tab." Vintage Uncle Morty. Never mind that a dear old friend got axed; who's paying?

"No tabs."

"The check's in the mail, then."

"You know I can't be handing out no more freebies. Got it?"

"Fine. What'd you find out?"

"Nothing. Well, close to nothing. The guy is a serious bore. He don't gamble, drink, drug, or sleep around, and he's a vegetarian."

"I don't do any of that stuff, except drink. Am I a bore?"

"You ain't no vegetarian, and you got Tommy for excitement."

I didn't know about excitement. Most of what Dad roped me into was grunt work he didn't want to pay for. There was no point in bringing that up with Uncle Morty. He was squarely on Dad's side in the free-lunch department, as long as he wasn't serving.

"Yeah, it's a thrill a minute in the Watts family," I said. "I thought you had something."

"Don't get your panties in a twist. It ain't much. He had a hundred buck charge from a company in Lincoln three months ago."

"Who was the payee?"

"Wilson Novelties. Like I said, it ain't much."

"Did you come up with anything else on Sample?" Before he could answer, my cell phone rang. I told him to hang on while I checked the name. Ameche. Yes.

"Hello, Ameche," I said.

"Mercy Watts?"

"None other. What's up?"

"You remember me," he said.

"Sure." I never forgot people, but people always thought I would forget them for some reason. "So do you have something for me?" I asked.

"As a matter of fact, I do. There was a cell phone logged into evidence and better yet, a couple days ago, it rang and pissed off Watts."

"How do you know it pissed him off?"

"Afterward he cussed up a storm about not having a trace on the phone."

"Excellent," I said. "What about Sunday morning? Any interviews?"

"Just one was recorded. Lee Holtmeyer, the husband. That help you out?"

"More than you know."

"You remember our deal, right?"

"Absolutely. I'll tell Dad you did us a good turn and hand over your numbers. Thanks, Ameche."

"Anytime. Well, maybe not any time, but you know where I am." Ameche chuckled. "By the way, you look fabulous in jeans."

"When did you see me in jeans?"

"I want to do Mercy dot com," he said, laughing full out.

"Thanks, I so needed that," I said.

"Anytime. I'm here for you."

"I'll remember that, jerkwad."

I would remember too. Ameche came through for me (despite his attempts at levity). Lee was off the list. He couldn't have killed Gavin. The connection between Sample and Gavin cemented. He knew her. I just had to figure out how.

Uncle Morty's gruff voice brought me back to reality. "What was that about?"

"You heard?" I asked.

"I heard you pissed someone off," Uncle Morty said.

"Yeah, I did."

"Who?"

"Chuck."

Uncle Morty made a flappy spitting noise with his lips.

"I know, I know, but this time there was a point. I found a connection between Gavin and Sample."

"Oh yeah. What?"

"He called her cell the day she died."

"Sweet. What else?"

I told him about the call to the church. He gave me some numbers and addresses of Sample's friends and family.

Before he hung up on me, I said, "There's one more thing. I've got a guy tailing me."

"Gee, I wonder why," said Uncle Morty.

"Can you check him out?" I gave him the plate number and description of the car.

"So why haven't you changed your number yet? It's all over the Net."

"Do I really have to? Won't the idiots just give up after a while?" I asked.

"There are enough idiots to last you a lifetime," he said, before hanging up on me.

I pulled my laptop from under the bed and googled myself. I got over thirty thousand hits on my name alone and over twenty thousand on Mom's. I didn't know how I was going to break it to Mom that she had to deal with this because of me.

I called my cell provider and had them change my number, but since they knew who I was, I figured I had two hours before my new number was posted. I was wrong. It took thirty-eight minutes. No more answering the phone just because it rang. I would have to screen until I figured out a better way. I should've had Uncle Morty get my cell. His name was on everything else, one of Dad's precautions. He'd put away some pretty nasty characters. The Watts' name was on nothing, except cell phones. We used a post office box for those.

I went back into the bathroom to decide on the right approach with Sample's associates. The friends were girlfriends and women didn't generally appreciate the Marilyn thing, but you have to work with what you've got. I blow-dried my hair into a sleek bob, dusted on some powder and applied nude lipstick. A black pencil skirt, flats, and a crisp white shirt completed the look. Skanky came sliding in the room and sat on his rump while I buttoned my shirt.

"How do I look?" I asked him.

Skanky looked at me and licked his chops. Not exactly the response I was going for, but what did the cat know? He attacked himself in the full-length mirror at least twice a day.

I checked my list. ASB Systems looked like a good place to start. Rebecca Sample had worked there. It was the only job she'd held since college. According to Morty, Rebecca's best friend Helen Card worked at ASB with her. Rebecca and Helen had been close for several years and were roommates for some period of time. Helen was the maid of honor at the wedding. Since her best friend was killed less than a week ago, Helen probably wouldn't be there, but it didn't matter. Co-workers were a good place to start.

I walked from my apartment to Kronos to get my truck and then headed to ASB Systems. It was a small but profitable design firm specializing in websites and online marketing. I parked on the side of the building so I wouldn't be seen getting out of my truck. I wanted to appear professional, and I wasn't sure a 1958 Chevy truck was going to do it for me. This was one of the few times I considered buying a regular car, something that didn't belong on permanent display at an auto museum, but I liked the surprise on people's faces when I got out of it. That wow factor wasn't something Dad anticipated when he bought that truck for my sixteenth birthday.

The year before I turned sixteen, I pestered Dad within an inch of his sanity, asking for a car for my birthday. "Please, Daddy," I'd say. "I need a vehicle. Everybody else has one." Note the use of *Daddy* when begging. I had no pride when it came to getting a car. I don't have much now, come to think of it. And I was right about everyone having a car. Myrtle and Millicent had insisted on sending me to Whitmore Academy at their expense. It was a twenty-thousand-dollar-a-year school and upper class, to say the least. Dad always said he'd live to regret my going to Whitmore and, of course, he did. I wanted a car like everyone else had in my class, a BMW, a Mercedes or, at worst, a Toyota. But I was young and not quite clued into the way men's minds work. But I knew I couldn't say exactly what I wanted, so I said vehicle. I thought it implied transportation, instead of deathtrap.

Dad latched on to that word, vehicle, and didn't want me to have one. He'd scraped too many teenagers off the pavement to want me behind the wheel. So Dad, thinking he was smarter than the average teen, bought me a 1958 red Chevy pickup. It was cherry, but old as hell. I nearly cried when I saw it. That is, I nearly cried until I saw Dad's face. He stood in the driveway with his arms crossed and a twisted smile on his face. I knew then what he was up to. That cherry truck with the optional rear glass and chrome plating wasn't for me, it was for him. Not for the first time, Dad underestimated me. I ran to him and threw my arms around his neck. I told him I loved it, snatched the keys out of his hand, and drove off. I saw him in the rearview and knew he'd never be the same. I was driving off with his truck.

I didn't expect to drive the truck for long, but I found people thought it was cool. It grew on me, and it drove Dad crazy. I couldn't ask for more than that, so nine years later, that cherry Chevy was still mine.

I patted the curvy hood, rounded the corner, walked through the automatic sliding front doors and went straight up to reception. I could've skirted the desk and roamed around asking questions, but sometimes it's nice to be invited. That time I felt I had the right.

The girl at the desk looked up from her nail filing, and her mouth fell open. "Oh, my God. I know you. You're that Marilyn Monroe impersonator."

"No, I'm really not," I said.

"I'm sorry. Are you like offended or something?"

I wished for an espresso or a Xanax. "No, it's fine. I'm looking for Helen Card. Is she in?"

"She is. You're really not that Mercy Watts?"

"I work for a detective agency and Helen Card's name came up. I'd like to ask her a few questions." I fished one of Dad's cards out of my wallet and handed it over. She glanced at it and said in a low tone, "Is this about Rebecca Sample?"

"It may relate to her case. Did you know Miss Sample?"

"Yes, of course. Everybody knew Rebecca. She was so nice. I can't believe someone would want to hurt her."

"She wasn't having any trouble with anyone around here?"

"No way. Rebecca was great."

"Has anyone mentioned a theory?"

"Oh yeah, but I can't talk about it. So do you have implants?"

"No. Why can't you talk about it?"

"The police came and interviewed us all and told us not to tell anybody. I guess they don't want reporters to hear."

"Which detective did you talk to?"

"I don't remember his name. He was real good-looking. Kind of like a movie star."

"Chuck Watts. He's my cousin."

"No kidding. He seemed real nice." She glanced down at Dad's card in my hand long enough to find the name Watts. "Watts. You are the Marilyn impersonator. I saw you on YouTube."

"Fine. That was me on YouTube, but it was all a mistake. I was just trying to be nice to a bunch of geezers and they put me all over the internet. I am a detective and I am very interested in your theory of the murder. I'd ask Chuck what you figured out, but he's so busy. He doesn't even have time for a girlfriend."

"Oh, really. That's so sad." She fluffed her hair.

Finally. Chuck was coming in handy. About time.

"It's hard to meet the right kind of girl when you're in his line of work," I said.

"I bet it's real hard."

"Maybe I should have him come back and interview you again. See if you've thought of anything new."

"Do you think he would?"

"He might. It depends on how interesting the theory was to begin with," I said.

"I guess Chuck wouldn't mind me telling you, since you are his cousin and all."

"I promise I won't tell a soul."

"Rebecca used to have a stalker," she said.

"Did you ever see him?"

"No, but he left flowers on my desk a couple of times and a box with a dead bird."

"How'd you know they were for Rebecca?" I asked.

"They had cards."

"Handwritten?"

"Yeah, but printed in big block letters."

"Did you talk to Rebecca about him?"

"Not really. We weren't that close, but I did find her crying in the bathroom a couple of times."

"Did she say what was wrong?"

"No, just that she had a bad night. I don't know what that means. I figured it was something to do with him because she would remind me not to let any men I didn't know back to her office and not to put through any unknown callers," she said.

"Did he call her here a lot?" I asked.

"She didn't really take calls. Everything went through her voice mail, so she could screen."

"Can you think of anything unusual happening just before the wedding, any suspicious packages, calls, or visitors?"

"Chuck asked me that, too. You're good." She smiled at me and checked her reflection on her computer screen. She'd be ready when Chuck came back.

"Was there anything odd?"

"Nope. Not a thing."

I thanked her, and she gave me directions to Helen Card's office. I promised to mention her to Chuck, and I thought I might actually do it. If he got a girlfriend, maybe he'd stop being so obnoxious.

Helen Card sat in her cubicle, holding a peanut butter and jelly sandwich in her hand. Comfort food, unless I missed my guess. Helen had taken two bites, and she was looking at those bites like she didn't know how they got there.

I hated to intrude and waited, hoping she'd notice me, but Helen remained hunched over. She was small, even compared to me, and I'm no super model. She had short, dark, cropped hair that lay flat against her head. There were dozens of pictures pinned up on the gray carpet that lined the cubicle walls. I spotted several of Rebecca. In the photos was a very pretty dark-haired girl with flamboyant spiked-out hair. I thought it was Helen, but the hair didn't seem to match the head I was seeing. I coughed. Helen jumped and looked up.

"Sorry, I didn't mean to startle you. The receptionist sent me back," I said.

"It's okay. Do we have an appointment?" Helen quickly scooped up a dozen used tissues off her desk and threw them in the trash can under her desk.

"No, we don't. I'm Mercy Watts." I waited for a reaction.

Helen just sat there. Thank goodness. No implant questions.

"I'd like to ask you a few questions," I said.

"What about?"

"Your friend Rebecca Sample."

"I'm not supposed to talk to anyone about that."

"Detective Watts tell you that?"

"Yes. He was very specific."

"He's my cousin. I know how specific he can get. I have to be honest with you. It's not Rebecca's case that I'm interested in." I decided to stick with the honest approach. It'd been working like cash money, as Grandpa would say.

"Why are you asking about Rebecca, then?"

"I think she's connected with a case I'm working on." I took Gavin's picture out and handed it to her. "Do you recognize the man on the right? He'd be older and thinner."

"Oh yeah. I know him, but his name escapes me. Who is he?"

"Gavin Flouder. How do you know him?"

"I went to meet him with Rebecca. He's a detective."

I wanted to jump up and do a happy dance, instead I said, "Did Rebecca hire him?"

"Yes, but I can't talk about that." She reached up and rubbed under her eyes. She'd been crying and her mascara had run. Her eyes were large and round. The mascara made her look like an owl.

"She hired him to track down her stalker, didn't she?" I handed her one of Dad's cards as I said it.

"You're not a reporter?"

"Not even close," I said.

"Who's Tommy?"

"My dad. He's Gavin's old partner."

"Why do you care if Rebecca hired him? I already told the cops," Helen said.

"Because Gavin was murdered the day after Rebecca and I think there's a connection."

Helen's eyes widened.

"I'm guessing my cousin didn't let you in on that fact," I said.

"No, he didn't."

"Look, you've already told the cops everything you know, right? So it won't hurt to tell me. I'm not a reporter. My dad and I just want to find out who killed Gavin. I suspect it's the same person who killed Rebecca."

"It's not going to make any difference. They're not going to catch him, and neither are you."

"What makes you say that?"

"That guy tormented Rebecca for three years and the cops never got so much as a glimpse of him. Your friend, Gavin, didn't have a clue either. No offense."

She rubbed her eyes, spreading the mascara further down her cheeks. She wiped her fingers with a tissue and tucked her shaky hands into her armpits. I felt like an ass. Who the hell did I think I was, making her think about all this?

"Well," she said.

Gavin. Just remember it's for Gavin.

"I admit it. You might be right, but I have to try," I said. "I do think you're wrong about Gavin. He did have a clue, and that's why he's dead."

"You think he knew who it was?"

"Definitely. He was trying to get in touch with Rebecca the day of the wedding. Can you please give me a break and tell me what you know?"

"Why not?" She rubbed her eyes again. "She did hire him to find that guy, but he never did."

"Did he come up with anything?"

"Nope."

"What kind of things did this guy do to Rebecca?" I asked.

"You name it, he did it. He called her all the time and left nasty messages on her machine. He sent her emails, letters, dead flowers and, once, a dead bird. She was so freaked."

"She had no idea who it was," I said.

"No. He had to be certifiable to do that stuff. Did you know he burned a big heart with an arrow into our lawn with weed killer? That's when I moved out. I couldn't handle it anymore."

"How long did you two live together?"

"About six months. We met when I started work here. He'd been bothering her for a while already. She told me about it, but I wasn't worried. I'd had a couple guys bother me, and I thought if she had a roommate, he'd back off."

"He didn't?"

"No. It got worse. The calls were nonstop. The week after I moved out, he broke every window in the house with bricks. She moved into a secure building after that," Helen said.

"How many times did she move?"

"Four and I don't know how many times she changed her email address and phone number. He got worse every time she changed it, like it insulted him or something."

"It probably did. When did it stop?"

"Right after she met Lee. Have you met Lee?"

"Not yet. I didn't know if he was up to it," I said.

"He'll be up to it. He'll do anything to catch that guy."

"Would you mind introducing me?"

"I know I shouldn't, but I kind of like you." She smiled for the first time and blew her nose.

"I grow on people."

"Like mold." She smiled and dabbed at her eyes.

"You know it. Do you think I could see Lee today?"

"Probably. I'll call you and let you know." I took the card back from her and wrote my cell number on it.

"One more thing. Was Gavin still working for Rebecca at the time of the wedding?"

"God, no. She fired him, sorry, after she met Lee. But there was another guy. I completely forgot about him," said Helen.

"What guy?"

"Emil something. He used to deliver UPS packages to our office. He asked Rebecca out a couple of times. He wasn't nasty or anything, but I think he scared her. He was pretty persistent."

"Did you tell Chuck, I mean the cops?"

"No, I just remembered him. Should I call them? It was a long time ago."

"Definitely call. How long has it been? Before she met Lee?"

"Oh, yeah. Maybe a year, a year and a half. Can I ask you something?"

"Sure," I said.

"How do you do that?" Helen made a gesture around her face.

"You mean the Marilyn thing? I was born this way. I can't help myself."

"That must be weird."

"You have no idea."

I thanked her and practically patted myself on the way out. The connection with Gavin was clear, but if he was fired six months ago, I couldn't figure why he'd be calling Rebecca at all, much less on her wedding day. Dad would be happy, though. He does love a suspect and now we had the UPS guy.

I walked through the glass doors to the sound of manic clicking. A tall guy with a beaky nose advanced towards me, holding a large camera.

"Okay, good. Can you give me a profile?" He smiled like we were old friends.

"What the hell? Who are you? Have you been following me?"

"You noticed."

I put my hand in front of his lens. "Get lost."

"Can't. It's my job," he said.

"If taking pictures of me is your job, you need professional help."

"You can help me with a big smile on those luscious lips and maybe pull up the skirt," he said.

I brushed past him and jumped into my truck all to a symphony of clicks. I peeled out of the parking lot and called Uncle Morty, ignoring the three million messages.

"Hi, it's me," I said. "I've got a name."

"I'll add it to your bill," he said.

"You're swell. You know that?"

"What's the name, cheapskate?"

"Emil something. He worked for UPS a year and a half ago and delivered to ASB Systems."

"That it? Emil Something?" Uncle Morty sounded disgruntled that my lead was a first name, and it gave me perverse pleasure. Let him work for my money. Cheapskate indeed.

"Yep," I said.

"I don't know. It ain't much to go on."

I said I had every faith in him and hung up before he had a chance to double my bill, then drove to my parents' house without any specific plan in mind.

Mom opened the back door. "I think he needs more of that anti-nausea medication."

"Why didn't you call me?"

"He wouldn't let me." Mom sat down at the kitchen table with her coffee.

"Wouldn't let you? What's he going to do? Rip the phone out of the wall?"

"Mercy, please. I can't fight with you right now."

"Sorry." I started to leave the kitchen, but Mom held me back.

"Let's wait a minute. The beast needs to calm down."

I sat down next to her and watched her blow into her cup. She was tired. Tired beyond the usual. Mom's life wasn't a quiet affair, but I guess she'd rather have the usual insanity than the sickbed.

"So what's been happening?" I asked.

"The usual. Vomiting, diarrhea, crying, and cussing."

"Dad was crying?"

"No. That was Dixie. The rest is your dear father," she said.

"He doesn't sound so dear."

"At this moment, no."

"Dixie's crying again?"

It was a stupid question. Mom thought so too because she rolled her eyes at me and went back to blowing on her coffee.

"I got her a script for Ativan, but she was taking too many." I took the prescription bottle out of my bag and handed it to Mom.

"She told me. Another thing for her to feel bad about."

"She feels bad about taking the Ativan?" I couldn't do anything right when it came to Dixie.

"No. She feels bad that you had to take it away from her."

"Sorry. I guess I shouldn't have given it to her in the first place."

"No, you were right. She needs something. She just doesn't need to be in control of it. I couldn't get her calmed down last night and I ended up giving her a couple antihistamines." Mom looked at me for approval and I was happy to give it. It was rare for Mom to look to me for advice.

"Well, let's go check Dad," I said.

"I hope he's not awake."

"Why?"

Mom gave me a pained look. "Because he'll talk."

I knew Dad wasn't awake from the doorway. If he was, the Siamese wouldn't have curled up on either side of his head. I changed the IV bag and gave him another dose of Zofran. When I turned around, Dixie stood outside the door. She'd cleaned up and looked comfortable in her own clothes. She waved me into the hall and gave me a hug.

"What's that for?" I asked.

"I'm sorry I yelled at you. I don't know what's wrong with me." She brushed a tear off her cheek and looked me in the eye. It seemed like forever since she'd looked at me without ducking her head or screaming.

"I'm the one who should be apologizing. I should've been more careful."

Dixie began to cry in earnest. Large tears rolled down her face, soaking the collar of her blouse. "It's just I can't believe it's true. I tell myself it is. It happened, but I don't believe it. It's like he's on a trip and forgot to phone. I know he's not, but that's what I keep thinking."

Mom took her arm, and I followed them down the stairs into the kitchen. I made tea while they sat in silence at the table. I set Dixie's teacup in front of her. "I was thinking yesterday about how he was going to laugh at Dad being sick. Then I remembered, and I didn't know what to do with myself."

Mom said, "I think we're all going to have moments like that, but pretty soon we won't have to remind ourselves anymore and it'll get better."

"I'm not sure I want it to get better," said Dixie.

Suddenly, I wanted to clean something, anything, even a toilet would do. I hated cleaning, so I could only assume I was going insane. I talked myself out of the toilet and settled on dishes when my phone vibrated. It was Helen Card. Lee would see me at his apartment in a half hour. Thank goodness I had something to do, and it didn't involve scrub brushes.

"I have to go," I told Mom and Dixie.

"How's it going?" Dixie changed from weepy to brittle and angry in a second.

"Pretty well. I don't think you'll have to worry about it for much longer."

"Really?" She didn't look optimistic.

"Really." I was no Tommy Watts. That I admit. But I would get the job done. I'd give her peace one way or another. Me, not Dad.

CHAPTER EIGHTEEN

I left my truck parked next to my parents' garage and took the 300. Dad's navigation system helped me make it to Lee's apartment in record time. Before I could get out, my phone vibrated. It was vibrating almost continually at that point. I may as well have kept it in front of my face. Screening wasn't working out for me.

"Hello," I said.

"I got a bead on that guy," said Uncle Morty. "Name's Emil Roberts."

"Already? That was fast, even for you."

"Yeah, yeah. You want the info or what?"

"Did you get his address?"

"I got his home and work addresses. No connection to Lincoln, but he has a record. A harassment charge five years ago. Pled out with community service and he had an indecency charge in the eighties. He got a couple of months for that one."

"The eighties? How old is he?"

"Forty."

"That's a juvie record. Wasn't it sealed?"

"Yeah. What of it?"

"Never mind. Roberts sounds promising. What do you think?"

"Worth an interview," Uncle Morty said, just before he hung up on me.

Worth an interview? Definitely.

Helen waited for me outside Lee's door. She'd washed off the smeared mascara and applied a new thick gloppy coat. Amazing that she could hold her eyelids up.

"How's he doing?" I asked.

"What do they always say? As well as can be expected."

"I'm getting more and more familiar with what that looks like. What's his last name? I don't remember it."

"Holtmeyer. Are you ready to go in?" She looked at me with those heavy red-rimmed eyes and I considered calling the whole thing off. If she looked like that, how would Lee look? I wasn't sure I was up to another grieving spouse. I could pretend my phone rang, and I had an emergency. There was always the attack of diarrhea fake out. I'd used that to great and embarrassing success. Helen would get over my bugging out, but Dad and Dixie wouldn't. I had to get this interview for them, so I nodded and tried to arrange my face into appropriate lines. I didn't know what to ask, but then again, I rarely did.

Lee Holtmeyer sat in the middle of the sofa, staring out of a window. He didn't acknowledge our entrance or move. He seemed frozen. Every hair on his dark head was in place and his blue oxford was freshly pressed with sharp creases down the sleeves. I would've thought he was ready for work, if it weren't for the look on his face.

"Lee," Helen whispered. He turned and for a moment I wasn't sure he saw us, but then he said, "Sorry, I was just thinking."

"It's okay. This is Mercy Watts, the girl I told you about. Is it okay?"

"Of course. What do you want to know?" Lee's face was blank, and I wondered if he was on something.

"I'm sorry to bother you. I wouldn't if it wasn't necessary," I said.

"I really loved her, you know. I don't think she understood that. I tried to tell her, but I don't think she really understood."

"What makes you say that?"

"I couldn't say it the way I wanted to, to make her understand."

"She probably understood more than you know, and she loved you."

"She did love me. She did." Lee smiled, but it looked like it took a lot of effort.

"Did you ever meet Gavin Flouder?"

"I thought she fired him," he said.

"She did. Did you meet him?"

"No."

"Then she hadn't rehired him?"

"Why would she?"

"I thought maybe the stalker had started up again," I said.

"No. That was all over. I don't think she thought about it anymore."

"So she hadn't had any problems recently?"

"No. She would've told me. Do you know something?"

"Not really. I'm here because Gavin Flouder was a family friend, and he died on Sunday."

Lee leaned forward, his eyes intense. "Do you know what happened?"

"It isn't clear, but he was murdered. I think it has something to do with Rebecca."

"Why?"

"He called the church and her cell phone the day of the wedding. Did she mention that to you?"

Lee crossed his arms. "No. Why does it matter?"

"Because he called her from the road and he died shortly after arriving home. Was there anyone at the wedding that you didn't know? Did anyone look suspicious or out of place?"

"Not at all, and I would've noticed. It was small, just about seventy people," he said.

"Seventy-five," a voice said.

I looked up and saw a man and woman standing beside my chair. I hadn't heard them come into the room. They stared at me, their mouths pulled down into fierce frowns.

"What?" I leaned back away from them, trying to get some distance. Apparently, they hadn't heard of personal space.

"There were seventy-five people at the wedding," said the woman.

"Oh," I said and turned to Lee. He seemed to shrink in their presence and he avoided meeting my eyes.

Helen stepped up and said, "Mercy, this is Darrell, Lee's brother, and Rhonda, his mom."

"It's Mrs. Holtmeyer, if you don't mind." Lee's mom straightened her lilac blouse, ran her finger along a long string of pearls, and turned her icy gaze on Helen. "Who ate peanuts?"

Helen immediately stepped back and looked at the floor. "I had a sandwich. I'm sorry. I forgot about your allergy."

"You've been told how to behave," said Mrs. Holtmeyer.

I stepped in front of Helen. "I'm sorry to trouble you at such a time, but — "

"Then why are you?" Lee's brother leaned forward, his eyes raking over my breasts. My skin flushed and tightened. I wanted to shrink away, but the Dad in me wouldn't allow it, so I looked Darrell full in the face. He resembled his brother down to the pressed pleats, but all of Lee's soft good looks were hard and edgy on Darrell. He leaned farther over me, mere inches from touching me.

I stood up, causing Darrell to jerk backward.

Step off, asshole.

"It's OK, Darrell. I said she could come," said Lee. He was back to staring out the window.

"It is not a good time," said his mother.

"Then I'll be brief," I said.

"You don't take a hint, do you?" said Darrell, leaning in again.

"Neither do you," I replied. "Now Lee, do you think you're up to telling me what happened during the reception?"

Mrs. Holtmeyer sat beside Lee and put her hand on his leg. She squeezed his knee until her fingers dug into his leg.

"I feel like I've told it a hundred times, Mother. One more won't make any difference." Lee glanced at me and removed his mother's hand. It didn't go easily.

"We were all at the reception. Dinner was over and she went to the bathroom. At least, I think she did. She was gone awhile, and I looked for her. Mom said it was time to cut the cake, but nobody knew where she was. Helen went into the bathroom to look for her." Lee looked at Helen. She bit her lip so hard, I expected blood to gush out.

"She wasn't in the bathroom," I said.

"No," said Helen.

"Obviously she wasn't in the bathroom. What's the point of this? We've talked to the cops five times already," said Darrell.

"Go ahead, Lee. She wasn't in the bathroom, and then what?" I said.

"We looked for her and we found her. The end," said Darrell.

"I asked Lee," I said.

Lee straightened up on the sofa. "We all started looking for her and somebody suggested we check in the chapel. I thought she might be praying."

"Did she do that a lot? Go to the chapel alone, I mean?" I asked.

Lee looked back out the window and sighed. "I guess so. I don't know. She prayed a lot. It calmed her."

"Who found her?"

"I did. She wasn't in the chapel, so we went into the crying room."

"Who's we?" I asked.

"Me and Darrell." Lee covered his eyes for a moment. "Rebecca was lying on the floor, but I didn't think she was dead until I picked her up. She was so heavy and limp. Then everybody was there. I don't know what happened after that. It's a blur."

"You picked her up?" I asked.

"Yes. I remember somebody telling me to put her down. I don't know who. Was it you, Helen?" asked Lee.

Helen shook her head no.

"It was me," said Darrell, his face reddened and, for a moment, anguished.

"I loved her so much, so much." Lee continued looking out the window and I heard Helen crying beside me, but I couldn't move. It was the first time I'd ever done that, interviewed a mourning spouse, unless you counted Dixie. The moment was bizarre, like being inside a painting, clear and blurry at the same time. I would remember every detail and want to forget it, the way the June sun came through the window, the smell of lemon cleaner in the air. It was all perfect and horrible at the same time.

"I think it's time to go," I said to Helen.

She nodded and followed me to the door.

"About time," said Darrell.

His mother didn't say anything. She looked at me like I'd taken a dump on her floor.

Lee didn't look up when I said goodbye.

Helen leaned on the wall outside the apartment and sucked in a deep breath. I took a spot next to her and said, "I don't think they liked me very much. Darrell and his mom, I mean."

"They don't like anyone," said Helen.

"Including Rebecca?"

"I think they tolerated her, but Mrs. Holtmeyer was definitely in charge of the wedding and everything else." Helen wrinkled her nose when she said Mrs. Holtmeyer.

"I'm not crazy about the brother either," I said. "How was he to Rebecca?"

"Okay, but he treats Lee like he's disabled or something. They both do."

"Yeah, I got that," I said.

"Did this help you at all?"

"Don't know yet. How long was Rebecca missing?"

"I don't know. I hadn't seen her for at least a half hour when Lee asked me to go into the bathroom."

"Were you there when he found her?"

"No, just Darrell. I was in the chapel when I heard Lee. He was screaming."

"Did you go into the crying room?"

"No, just to the door. It was horrible. I wish I didn't see it," she said, biting her lip again.

"How many people were there?"

"Everybody, I guess, except the kids, of course."

"How did everyone seem?"

"Upset. What do you think?"

"Besides that. Did anyone strike you as acting odd?"

"No, but I was with Lee and Rebecca's mom."

"You've talked to her mom. Does she have any ideas?"

"No way. I think she's more shocked than the rest of us. She didn't even know about the stalker," she said.

"Why didn't Rebecca tell her?"

"She thought it would upset her and it's not like she could do anything about it."

"What about the rest of the family? What do they think?"

"It's just her mom, an aunt, and a couple of cousins. They're clueless too."

"Could I speak to her mom?" I asked.

"I imagine so, but she's back in Decatur now. I could call her for you."

"Never mind. You're probably right. She's out of the loop."

I believed Rebecca's mom was out of the loop, but it was my innate laziness and fear of another interview like Lee's that kept me from driving the two and a half hours to Decatur. It'd already crossed my mind that somebody would have to retrace Gavin's trip to Lincoln. I'd assumed it'd be Dad, but that was out of the question, so I was back on the front lines.

I grabbed Helen's arm. "Wait a minute. I forgot something."

Helen knocked on Lee's door, and Mrs. Holtmeyer opened it a couple of inches. The chain was on.

"What do you want now?"

"I'm sorry," I said. "I forgot to ask Lee something. Could you ask him if he or Rebecca went to Lincoln, Nebraska recently or if she said anything about it in the last few weeks?"

She hesitated, but turned and repeated my question to Lee. She probably figured I wouldn't leave if she didn't. She was right. I heard Lee answer no. He'd never been there and Rebecca hadn't been back since her graduation.

Mrs. Holtmeyer turned back to me with the dump expression on her face again. "No, and Lee's never been there. Don't bother us again."

She shut the door in my face.

Helen closed her eyes. "My god, she's a bitch. I can't believe Rebecca was going to be her daughter-in-law. What a nightmare."

"Thanks again and I'll try not to bother you anymore."

Unless I did. Me being me; it was likely, but it sounded nice anyway.

I left Helen standing in front of Lee's building, looking miserable and lost. I'd had a taste of how she felt and it was bad. She didn't know what to do or who to be. It takes a while to move forward without feeling like a strong wind is buffeting your every step. I felt a little like that when I saw Gavin on the gurney, but I had a job to do and Helen didn't have the benefit of purpose. My purpose just then was to interview Emil Roberts. Maybe I'd get lucky, and he'd confess. Then I wouldn't have to go to Lincoln. But the trip was getting more intriguing, like a mini-vacation. With no one to pester me, I'd be able to think and maybe start to feel better.

CHAPTER NINETEEN

I drove straight to Roberts's work address. He was still with UPS, but no longer delivering. I walked in and stood in line behind three people with large packages. The girl behind the counter was slow and methodical. I began to feel my hair turning gray when I saw a man step out of the back. He joined the girl at the counter and his name tag identified him as Emil. I watched him without guile as he assisted the customers ahead of me in rapid succession. He was the kind of guy who was hard to describe, not because he was unusual looking, but because he was so unremarkable. I'd have a hard time recalling what he looked like the minute I left his presence.

Roberts was small, maybe an inch or two taller than me. He had hair that was neither blond nor brown, but some in-between color that defied easy categories. My mother would've called it dishwater or dirty blond. Neither seemed quite right to me. His hair hung in lank waves and he hadn't bothered to wash it in a day or so, but he didn't seem dirty or unkempt.

His eyes lit on me when it was my turn at the counter. They were pale blue and set far apart on his thin face. His eyes should've been his best feature, but they made me think of tortoises and inbreeding.

"Can I help you?" he asked.

"I hope so. You're Emil Roberts?"

"Yes. How can I help you?"

"I'm Mercy Watts and I was wondering if I could interview you about the Rebecca Sample case." I hoped her name would provoke some kind of reaction in him. It didn't.

"Are you a policewoman?" He looked doubtful.

"No, private investigator, and I'm actually working on a case that's related to the Sample case. Do you have a moment?"

He looked at the girl who was still helping her first customer and said, "Sure, but it'll have to be quick."

"No problem," I said.

I followed him into a back office, where he motioned for me to sit down. He sat on the edge of the desk that had a reading lamp and an in/out basket on it. The out basket was full, and the in was empty. His name was carved into a triangular block of wood and it named him as the store manager.

"What can I do for you?" Roberts looked over my head when he asked and it unsettled me.

"I understand you knew Miss Sample," I said.

"I did, but not well."

"Did you ask her out?"

"Yes, but she said no."

"I hear you were pretty persistent."

"It depends on what you consider persistent," he said, looking past my right shoulder.

"I consider persistent to be asking repeatedly beyond reason." I tried to catch his eye as he switched to looking past my left shoulder.

"Then no. I wasn't persistent. I asked her out two or three times. She said no and that was it."

"Why did you stop delivering to her office?"

"I got a promotion."

"You don't seem surprised that I'm asking you about this."

"I'm not. When I saw what happened to her on the news, I assumed I'd be questioned, although I thought it would be the cops doing it."

"They'll be around. You can count on it. Were you at the wedding?"

"No. Why would I be? We weren't friends and I haven't seen her since I was delivering to her work," he said.

"Any idea who would want to hurt her?"

"No. If you don't mind, I have to get back."

We both stood up and his eyes shifted to the floor to the left of my feet. I should've shaken his hand or something, but I couldn't bring myself to touch him.

"Well, thanks for your time," I said.

He nodded, and we left the office. The girl at the counter banged on the credit card machine and Roberts went to help her. As I went out the door, I glanced over my shoulder and saw him looking at me. When he saw me, his eyes went back to his work, and I left.

I got in the 300 and sat for a moment. Roberts wasn't in the clear, but I didn't have a feeling one way or the other about him. He'd been straightforward with my questions. The eyes bugged me, but other than that he was a normal guy doing normal things. The more I thought about it, Roberts didn't fit. The stalking started before he asked Sample out and continued after. I just didn't see a psycho like that stopping his behavior long enough to politely ask her out and then starting it up again. Besides, I didn't think I had to deal with Roberts. Chuck would be on him as soon as Helen called, and I was happy to leave him to it. Now I had no excuse to avoid Lincoln, so I'd be getting my traveling shoes on.

CHAPTER TWENTY

Cats are hard to find normally. Trying to find a cat when you're holding a travel carrier is near to impossible. My apartment didn't help either. It had plenty of dark corners and crevices just big enough to hide a six-pound feline with nerves of spaghetti. Stale air and the smell of mold snaked around me as I searched. There wasn't enough Febreze in the world to fix it. My building was built in the twenties and what it lacked in light and ventilation it made up for in character. At least that's what I told myself. Crown molding is important. Damn it.

So I searched for Skanky in the semidarkness, packed, searched, and then searched again. After a can of Fancy Feast didn't produce results, I started thinking that he'd gotten out. Panic had just set in when I heard a faint 'yow' in the bedroom closet. Skanky was hiding in an old shoe box in the back. He hadn't cleaned his fur recently and looked freaked out. He always had an element of freak, but that day it was more than average. His yellow eyes darted around and his claws were extended for no reason. When I reached for him, he jumped out of the box and buried his claws into the deep carpet. It took ten minutes to pry him off. Then I gave him a good brushing and put him in his carrier. I was a bad mama, but my mama would have to make it up to him.

Skanky yowled and hissed when I put him into the 300. He'd been a desperately ill kitten when I rescued him and he never liked being in a vehicle. He always thought we were going to the vet or worse. Worse being a visit to the evil Siamese.

"Quiet," I said. "We're not going to the vet."

Skanky went bat shit crazy at the word 'vet', banging his head against the door and flipping over to claw the top. All the while yowling like he was in the middle of an anal gland exam. It's a good thing I didn't mention the Siamese. He probably would've tried to bite himself to death.

He continued the insanity for the few minutes it took to get to my parents' house. I did feel guilty, but enough was enough. After a couple of days with the Siamese, he'd be happy to see me. That is, if he survived. The Siamese weren't partial to company, human or otherwise. They liked to tag team him when Mom's back was turned.

"Sorry, boy. I don't have time to find a kennel," I said.

Skanky's yowling went to a higher decibel as I spotted Pete's car in the alley next to my truck. That couldn't be a good thing. I didn't think he would voluntarily see my parents without me unless something was seriously wrong with Dad. I parked and sprinted up the back walk, leaving Skanky yowling in my wake.

Mom and Pete sat at the kitchen with iced teas in hand. They were calm and looked at me with mild surprise.

"Hello, sweetie," said Mom.

"Where's Dad?" I said.

"Right here." Dad sat on the window seat propped up with Mom's sari pillows and covered to the chin with afghans.

"What happened? What's Dad doing down here?"

"Nothing, and we helped him down. He's getting stir crazy. What's wrong with you?" Mom looked at me with her perfectly sculpted eyebrows raised to points.

"Well, what are you doing here?" I looked at Pete, feeling angry and stupid at the same time. Damn them for being so obtuse.

"Your mother asked me to come over and take out the IV," Pete said.

"That's it?"

"Something wrong with that?" Pete shrugged his shoulders and raised his palms at me. "I could've done it," I said.

"You were busy," Mom said.

"Not that busy. So he's better?"

"He's sitting right here." Dad glared at me, tried to raise an arm and gave up after a feeble attempt. I walked over, the fear draining out of me with every step. I touched his forehead and tucked the afghan in around him. He smiled. "You were worried."

"I was not." I sat down on the floor and lay my head on the seat cushion. "God, I'm tired."

"Not too tired to go to Lincoln," Dad said.

"What makes you think I'm going to Lincoln?"

"Your cat yowling in the car."

Skanky's yowls got all the way through the yard, butler's pantry, and into the kitchen. His voice was the biggest part of him.

"Go get that animal before the neighbors start complaining," said Mom.

I tromped back to the car to get him. Skanky thanked me by peeing out the back of the carrier and narrowly missing my leg.

"I should've left you in the car, you ungrateful wretch."

Hiss.

"Fine, let the Siamese eat you. See if I care." I opened the cage and tossed him into the kitchen.

"Are you talking to that cat again?" Mom never called Skanky by his name. I wasn't sure if she disliked the name or the cat.

"Yes. Unlike everyone else in this family, he listens."

"If that isn't the pot calling the kettle black. When was the last time you listened to me?" asked Mom.

I had to think. I was sure I had at some point, but I couldn't narrow it down.

"See what I mean," she said.

"Well, the apple doesn't fall far from the tree." Dad wavered on his seat, but looked better. His eyes had lost their hound dog look, and the color was back in his face. "Have you packed?"

"Yes, I've packed."

"You're really going?" Pete looked at me with astonishment. He must've thought Dad was joking.

"I have to. Dad can't, and it needs to be done quickly."

Dad nodded his approval and closed his eyes. Pete frowned, but, being sandwiched between my parents, he wasn't in a position to make a fuss.

"I'll be fine. It's just fact-checking really," I said.

"How long?" Pete said.

"Two days tops."

"Better hit the road." Dad was never one to put off the inevitable.

"I'll go tomorrow. I have some things to take care of."

"Like what?"

"I want to see The Girls, for one thing. I still think something's going on with them." I looked at Pete. "Walk me out."

We said our goodbyes, and Pete was thanked and thanked again. For some reason, I felt like I was being reprimanded for my unavailability for the IV removal. Probably paranoia on my part. It wouldn't be the first time. Parents.

"So how about I come over later?" Pete opened the car door for me and leaned against it in his lean, graceful way.

"I'd love it, but I won't be there."

"Why not?"

"I'll be in Lincoln," I said.

"You just said you're leaving tomorrow."

"Yeah, well, let's just keep this between us."

"Your parents should know," he said.

"I don't want them hassling me with advice and instructions."

"Can't somebody else do this?"

"Yeah, but I'm going to. Gavin was family. It's our job. Since Dad's not available, it falls to me." I saw that he didn't get it, but he bowed to my position anyway. Then he kissed me and closed the car door. I watched him in the rearview as he watched me drive away.

CHAPTER TWENTY-ONE

I parked in front of the Bled house and stood at the gate for a moment. A soft breeze swayed the branches of the gigantic oaks that lined the street, but nothing else moved. The house was dark and lifeless as before. The lawn hung over the edges of the flagstone walk and the house was beginning to look abandoned. I rang the gate bell multiple times and was ignored. Mom gave me the emergency key, but we'd rarely used it and never for an actual emergency. Was this an emergency? Maybe. Maybe not. But I had to know what was going on. I decided to take a walk, just a little snoop, around the perimeter. After that, I wasn't sure.

Leaves crunched under my feet as I walked through the overgrown lawn and peeked into the left conservatory. Everything was neat and tidy, but the absence of light bothered me. The Girls weren't conservationists. They were known to leave TVs on for days, if not weeks, at a time. The darkness made me feel weird and itchy. Dad used to talk about that feeling over dinner. The crime scene feeling, sometimes it meant something, sometimes it didn't. I was damn sure it did this time, but still I doubted The Girls were lying in a pool of blood in the living room. I needed to go in, but I didn't really have the time.

I headed back towards the front when I heard, "Hello, Miss Watts."

Caught in the act. At least I wasn't climbing in a window, which I'd been known to do. I turned around to find Mrs. Haase smiling at me from behind her fence. Mrs. Haase was a big smiler. It doesn't necessarily mean you're in the clear.

"Hi. How are you?" I smiled, too. It didn't mean much with me either.

"Very well, and you?"

Oh, great. Just standing in the azaleas.

"I'm good," I said.

"The Girls left an hour ago, if you're wondering."

"Then they're fine, thank goodness."

"Worrying they'd been mutilated by a maniac?"

"I was beginning to wonder."

"You're not the only one," said Mrs. Haase.

"Really?" I asked, while treading on bluebells and callas on my way to the fence.

"Indeed. Ronald and I have become concerned. They've been acting so odd."

"What did they do?"

"They didn't come to our church fete, the lights are always off, and Millicent won't let me in, even though we had a lunch date on Monday. She didn't remember to cancel or send a note. And there was this man at the door yesterday." Mrs. Haase's eyes opened wide with a look of suspicion and disdain. Who were these people coming onto Hawthorne Avenue? The nerve.

"Who was he?"

"I don't know. He banged on the door and tromped around in the garden like you."

Great, I had something in common with a weirdo harassing The Girls.

"The Girls weren't home?"

"No, they were there, and he knew it. He kept yelling that they couldn't ignore him forever and for them to open the door," she said.

"They never came to the door?"

"I don't think so. He was quite angry, and he drove away in a Ford."

Ah, the final condemnation. He drove a domestic car.

"Do you know where The Girls went?"

"No, but a cab came for them. I haven't seen Lester in weeks."

Lester was The Girls' driver. He was old as dirt and could barely see over the steering wheel. Dad had wanted them to retire poor old Lester for years and get someone who could see as well as drive. He'd never had any luck. Lester's absence was the final straw.

"Have you seen anything else that bothered you?" I asked.

"No, but something's wrong. I can feel it." Mrs. Haase removed her gardening hat and touched her thick gray hair. I admired that mane of hers. It didn't know the meaning of hat hair.

"They haven't said anything?"

"Exactly. They won't say a thing. Millicent looks embarrassed and Myrtle looks to have been crying."

"When?" I asked.

"Every time I see her. Which isn't often, might I add. You will do something, won't you?"

"Dad'll figure it out." I tried to look unconcerned.

"Is he still under the weather? I've been meaning to call."

"He's better, and he'd love to see you."

Strictly speaking, that wasn't true or untrue. Dad was pretty neutral on most people, but Mom loved visitors. For Mrs. Haase's sake, I hoped Dad would still be in bed. If not, he might answer the door in the dreaded underwear. She'd never recover. I had several friends who still talk about my weird dad and I couldn't even defend him. It was weird.

"I was grieved to hear about your friend. Mr. Flouder, was it?"

"Yes. Thank you," I said.

I left Mrs. Haase to her roses with a promise for an afternoon call. I walked around the rest of the house. All was in order and I didn't know what to look for anyway. I walked down the flagstones and stopped midway. The 300's passenger seat was occupied. The tinted windows were enough to obscure the person's identity. I sprinted down the walk, flung open the gate, and then the car door.

"How you doing?"

Aaron.

"What in the hell are you doing here?" I said in a low voice. I had the feeling Mrs. Haase was watching from the hedgerow.

"What?" Aaron's eyebrows shot up from behind his smudged glasses.

"What do you mean 'what'? What are you doing in this car?"

"Heard you had a trip," he said.

"Who told you that?"

Aaron blinked and opened the glove compartment. "I brought snacks."

"You can't come. Get out."

"You didn't say please," he said, pulling out a carton of chocolate milk and opening it.

"Please," I said.

"Nope. I'm going. I never been to Lincoln. Heard it's nice. Does it snow there year-round, or is that Alaska or maybe Canada?"

God help me.

"You hungry? I got dogs." Aaron smiled at me and I knew it was hopeless. Dad had sicced him on me, but for what purpose I couldn't guess. Maybe my father secretly hated me. The thought that Aaron could protect me was ludicrous. No, Dad hated me.

"No hot dogs in the car." I slid into the driver's seat, breathing in the aromas that accompanied Aaron wherever he went: hot dogs, chili cheese fries, and some kind of drugstore cologne that I couldn't name. It was kind of a nice combo, but I'd never say that under oath.

My cell phone vibrated, and Aaron answered it. Then he pressed the off button, tossed the phone on the floor, and went back to rummaging around in his snack bag.

"Who was that?" I asked.

Aaron shrugged. "They hung up."

"Well, don't throw my phone on the floor. You'll break it."

Aaron shrugged again and ate a Snickers bar.

The drive to Lincoln was seven hours long. Between Aaron's bathroom breaks and hankering for diner food, it took us eight and a half. If it wasn't for the constant talk of snack food and Dungeons and Dragons, the drive would've only taken two days off my life instead of three.

Aaron booked a couple of rooms for us at the motel that Gavin used. It wasn't far off the highway in a commercial district. We checked in, and I called my cell provider for another number change. A scant two minutes after I hung up, Aaron banged on my door.

"What's the plan?" he asked.

I'm going to Fike you, bub.

"No plan. I'm going to wing it."

Emphasis on "I".

"Wings sound good," he said.

"You can't be hungry."

"Or ribs. Wings or ribs, what'll it be?"

"All you did for the last eight hours was eat. You are not hungry," I said.

"I have to check out the competition." Aaron plopped down on one of my beds and began flipping channels. It was late. All I wanted was a boiling hot shower and a bed in a room absent of Aaron.

"Are you completely gone? We're in Lincoln. They're not your competition. What do you think, a couple guys are going to say, 'Hey, you want to go to the rib joint on the corner or drive seven hours to St. Louis for Kronos?'"

"Got to keep current," said Aaron.

"Current on what? Rib joints in Lincoln?"

"So it's definitely ribs. You ready?"

I threw up my hands. "Fine. Fine. Yes, I am ready. I am absolutely ready." I grabbed my purse, avoided my reflection in the mirror over the desk and stomped out to the car. Aaron followed me, thumbing through a restaurant guide and giving me choices that I didn't give a shit about. With minimal help, he picked a rib place with a chuck wagon theme. He forced me to admit the food was superior and, instead of shower and sleep, I came up with a plan as my cell phone rang. The caller moaned and hung up. My second new number was out in record time. I had to figure out how to block everyone but friends and family. Uncle Morty didn't fit neatly into any category, but I called him anyway.

"Hey, it's me," I said in my best, most cheerful voice.

"Do you know what time it is?"

"You weren't asleep."

"I could've been," Uncle Morty said.

"No, you couldn't. You're like a bat or a wolverine." It was true. Morty's sleeping habits were the subject of speculation, because he rarely slept and, if he did, it was during the day. When I was a kid, I convinced myself, and most of my school, that Morty was a vampire. That was before I read Anne Rice and realized that vampires are supposed to be sexy.

"What do you want and who's paying?" he asked.

"Did you find out who's following me?"

"Bernard Rey, known as Nardo. Has-been paparazzi," Morty said.

"How can paparazzi be has-beens?" I asked.

"He used to get the big shots of Jennifer Aniston sunbathing topless. That kind of shit. Now he can't. You're his comeback."

"How do I get rid of him?"

"You don't."

A headache bloomed in the back of my skull. "That's bullshit. He can't stalk me and take pictures of me all the time."

Morty snorted. "Sure can. You signed that release, like a freaking moron, and now you're a personality like an actress or something."

"Aw, crap."

Morty laughed, a booming, throaty guffaw.

"Wait," I said. "If I'm boring, he'll go away, won't he? I mean, there'll be nothing to take pictures of."

"You be boring? That'll happen," said Morty. "What else you got?"

"It's about The Girls."

"I don't give a shit. Who's paying?"

"Me or Dad. Somebody'll pay, alright?"

"I'm listening."

"I want you to look at The Girls' financials," I said.

"Why? Hoping the old bags bought you a tiara for your birthday?"

"No, smartass. I'm just worried. They're acting kind of weird."

"News flash, they're rich old bags. That's what they do," he said.

"They won't let me or Mrs. Haase in. The lights are all off. The gardens are a wreck and nobody's seen Lester for weeks."

"Maybe they killed him. I'm telling you, it's *Arsenic and Old Lace* over there. Those women weird me out."

"So does Aunt Miriam. Do you think she's been out killing, too?"

"I wouldn't put it past her. Would you?"

"Well, that's more likely than The Girls killing Lester," I said.

"Yeah, yeah. I'll take a look. You in Lincoln?"

"Yes." Was there anyone who didn't know where I was?

"What'd you find out?" Uncle Morty asked.

"Not a thing. We're still eating," I said.

"Wings or ribs?"

I cut short a discussion on the merits of Lincoln's restaurants and paid the bill. Aaron wanted to go for ice cream, but I was bloated and we called it a night.

CHAPTER TWENTY-TWO

In a fit of get-up-and-go, I set my alarm for five. I showered and got dressed in my best give-me-some-information-people outfit. A pair of black pants with a perfect, non-flashy fit and a button-down made me look professional, while hiding my boobs. Boobs are never a good thing when trying to get information from women. Mom taught me that. Last, I donned one of Mom's jackets from last season to make me look like I had two nickels to rub together. Rich is better than poor. That was another of Mom's lessons and it helped me out on more than one occasion. I expected to be dealing with women at the university and then I'd check out Bart Sendack's girlfriend. I doubted they had anything to do with Gavin's death, but he found something that led to Sample's stalker. Maybe that something was Sendack. Plus, Doreen deserved a favor, and I felt generous, despite my overwhelming need for coffee.

At a quarter after six, I decided to make a break for it. I'd never seen Aaron before eight in the morning, so I figured he'd be sleeping. I opened my door and, pow, there he was, leaning on the railing. If I hadn't looked out my peephole during the night, I'd have thought he'd stood there for the last seven hours. He certainly looked like it with his hair standing on end, not to mention the clothes. He probably slept in them, although it might've been a different shirt. It was hard to tell, but the new one was free of rib sauce.

"Hi Aaron."

"Hey. Ready? Let's go to this diner on 12th. I hear it's got the best omelets in town."

"Where'd you hear that?"

"Janitor," he said.

"You've been talking to the motel janitor?"

"Nope. He works in an office building," he said.

"Whatever. Let's go."

Aaron directed me to the Kissimmee Diner. I guess somebody had a hankering for Florida. The color scheme was blinding. The bright oranges, greens and yellows made my head hurt, and I wasn't crazy about the plastic palm trees either. The place was more than half full of college students trying to wake up after a long night, truck drivers and business types getting an early start. The omelets were as advertised and we lingered while trying to clean our plates. Aaron managed, but I gave up. I'd have to join Weight Watchers if I kept letting Aaron order for me. He knew what I liked and ordered in volume. It might've been my imagination, but that volume was showing on my hips.

After breakfast, I decided to hit the university first. Since it was summer and early, not many students would be there and hopefully the ladies would've had their coffee. Aaron looked up the address on his phone. I didn't know he was technically savvy, but I was beginning to suspect there was a lot about Aaron I didn't know. He input the address into Dad's navigation system and it proceeded to tell us where to go. I started thinking about getting a newer vehicle. There was something to be said for climate control and a glove box cooling system. Then again, the words 'car payment' made me queasy.

We drove through the university's well-planned streets shaded by mature trees and watched the early birds go after their worms. Aaron talked. I don't know what he said. I became a master of the well-placed, "Oh yeah," and "Sounds good." Parking was brutal. I wondered if any architect ever thought about how many cars people actually use or maybe they're too busy designing archways and fountains to worry about how people would get to them. I found a space a good half mile from Student Administration and it was eight o'clock in the morning.

"Why don't you stay here?" I suggested to Aaron as he munched on a soft pretzel he'd produced from behind his seat.

"No way," he said.

"Why not?"

"You're trying to Fike me."

True, so true.

"How can I Fike you? You're in the car?" I asked.

"You could get a rental."

Damn.

"I won't get a rental." I gave Aaron the big eyes, but he didn't look convinced. "I swear, cross my heart and all that."

"Nope."

Double damn.

I needed to Fike Aaron and not just because he was a pain in the ass. I was trying to look professional. Aaron's look said tons, but nothing close to professional or even clean.

"Look Aaron, I have to get information out of these women. Do you really think you can help me do that?"

"No."

"Then why don't you stay here?"

Aaron didn't answer. He didn't need to. We both knew the reason. Dad asked him to watch me and he was damn well going to do whatever Dad asked.

"Fine, you can come, but for heaven's sake, be inconspicuous. Can you do that?" I had my doubts, but Aaron nodded. I got out of the car and walked towards the administration buildings. I forced myself not to look back. I didn't hear Aaron's breathing or smell him, and I took that as a good sign.

Student Administration inhabited a large brick building with a well-manicured lawn and trees. Students lounged under the trees, eating Pop-Tarts and cramming useless data into their heads. I felt a familiar sting of regret as I passed them and jogged up the stairs. I'd gone to a private nursing school. It wasn't all girls, but pretty close to it. There were no parties, no frats, none of the stuff you'd associate with the college experience. I had fun, but it was harder to come by. We didn't even have a campus to lounge on. I suppose I regretted that the most, the long walks to class, playing Frisbee on the quad, all that stereotypical crap that I fantasized about in high school. My friends that went to regular schools told me I was out of my mind. The walks sucked. They froze their asses off in winter and they never once played Frisbee. Still, I would've liked to have tried it.

According to the directory, I needed the third floor and in honor of Aaron's omelet; I took the stairs. I felt like barfing on the second floor, but I made it. A mixed bag of women watched me stagger in. They whispered to each other. I get that a lot. There was a blue hair that looked like she had one foot in retirement, one girl who looked college herself, and a mom type. Dad would've chosen the old lady. They dig him for no good reason. On the other hand, old ladies don't like me unless they've known me since birth and even then, it's not a sure thing. The blue hair was out. The college age girl blew a huge bubble which smacked all over her face. Forget her. I needed brains.

The mom eyed me with both suspicion and interest. I had a winner. Walking over, I pulled one of Dad's cards out of my purse.

"Good morning. I spoke to someone a couple of days ago and she said she could help me out with some information. Her name was Trish."

"What kind of information? Are you a student?" she asked.

"No. Private detective." I handed her dad's card. She looked at it and interest piqued in her eyes.

"I'm Carol. What do you need?"

"It's very simple actually."

The college girl stuck her head over the partition. "Hey. That's me."

The mom rolled her eyes as the girl picked purple gum off her cheek and stuck it back in her mouth.

"Who are you?" I asked.

"I'm Trish. You wanted to know about that murdered guy. So lucky I'm filling in for Barb today."

"What murdered guy?" The mom looked worried and on the spot.

I took out my photo of Gavin and Trish snatched it out of my hand before Carol could take it.

"Do you recognize him?" I asked. "He'd be thinner with less hair."

"Nope," said Trish, as she handed the photo to Carol.

"I remember him." She looked at Trish. "This is the guy you were talking about?"

"That's him. What did he come in for?" I said.

"Class schedules," Carol said.

"Who for?"

"That I don't remember. He told me he was working on a case and that it was important to a young lady. Is this between us? You're not going to tell anyone, are you?"

"I won't. Trish?" We looked at Trish and she crossed her heart. I took that as a promise for silence and continued. "What did you do?"

"I looked up some schedules for him. I'm not supposed to do that, but he seemed desperate," Carol said.

"How many schedules did you look up?"

"Two. One for a boy and one for a girl. At least that's what I think."

"Rebecca Sample ring a bell?"

"Yes, yes. I think that's the girl. How'd you know?"

I smiled and handed her Sample's picture. "Just a guess."

"Is that her?" asked Trish.

I nodded. "Do you recognize her?"

Both women said no and looked disappointed. We stood in silence, thinking. I suspect Trish was thinking of the hot guy that walked in for help, but she didn't move to assist him.

"Gavin, that's the detective. He called you twice. What was that about?"

"It was for the schedules," said Carol. "When he came in, my boss was here and I couldn't look them up. He had to call back twice before I could do it."

"And what? Did you tell him about the schedules? What was he looking for?"

"Continuity, he said. He wanted to know if they shared any of the same classes," Carol said.

"Did they?"

"Yes. Two or three, I think."

"What did he say when you told him that?"

"Not much, just that I'd been a big help," she said.

"Did he sound upset or worried?"

"More angry." Carol brushed her bangs out of her eyes and leaned forward. "Do you think it's my fault he got killed? I know I shouldn't have told him anything."

"No, it wasn't your fault. If you hadn't told him, he would've gotten the info another way."

"How? Nobody has access to our records."

"Believe me, there are ways," I said.

Carol looked both relieved and uncomfortable. I knew how she felt. We all liked to think records are confidential. They're not, but it's easier thinking that.

"I think that guy's watching you," Trish said, pointing at a potted palm that did nothing to disguise Aaron's rotund form. So much for the brains behind the operation.

"Believe it or not, he's my bodyguard."

"He's your bodyguard? What's he do, sneak up on people and sit on them?" asked Carol.

"Mostly, he just annoys me."

I thanked them and pulled Aaron out from behind the palm amid protests that he was incognito. It was my turn to roll my eyes as I pushed him towards the stairs.

"What'd you find out?" Aaron asked.

"That Gavin knew."

"What'd he know?"

"Who Sample's stalker was," I said.

We walked towards the stairs slowly. Aaron eyed the elevator, but I ignored his silent pleas.

"They told him?"

"No. They confirmed it. I think he already knew. He came to Lincoln looking for Bart Sendack. He must've come across Sample's guy accidentally," I said.

"Are you gonna answer your phone?" asked Aaron.

"How did you know it was vibrating?"

"I can see it." Aaron pointed to my shaking pocket.

"They won't leave me alone," I said.

Aaron held out his hand, and I handed my phone over. He hit a few buttons and held it up. "This ain't Mercy Watts, you freaking losers. Stop leaving me messages or I'll sue your stupid asses." He stuck my phone in his pocket and jogged down the stairs.

When I managed to close my mouth, I followed and found Aaron at the bottom, bent over and gasping.

"Aaron, you sounded just like Uncle Morty." I grinned at him. "That should scare some of them off. Thanks."

Aaron shrugged and when he caught his breath, he said, "Let's find Bart Sendack."

Like most things in my life, it was easier said than done. We went to the address Gavin wrote in the file. Bitsy Meyer, Bart Sendack's girlfriend, moved out two months before and left no forwarding address. The apartment manager remembered Gavin coming by and told him the same thing he told us. Good riddance. Meyer and Sendack had lived at the address for six months. Their rent was late, if it showed up at all. Sendack grew pot in the window boxes, barely disguised by geraniums. The manager called the cops and Sendack and his plants disappeared. The girlfriend, Bitsy, stayed on for another week, which she didn't pay for, and then she left too. The only helpful bit of information was that Bitsy worked at Denny's, but he didn't know which one.

I drove back to the motel after lunch. Aaron belched in the passenger seat, bringing up unpleasant reminders of his blackened catfish and onion rings. I had a salad, and it was a good thing. Something greasy might've come back up. I sent Aaron up to his room for a good mouth washing. He must've sensed I wasn't up to anything because he didn't protest. For once, I could've Fiked him, but I didn't have the energy and went to the motel lobby instead.

The lobby was low budget and over decorated, as if a lot of fake plants make people forget they're fake. No customers waited at the desk. I leaned over it and coughed to get the attendant's attention. Her name tag said "Venus" and it was appropriate. She was out there. Venus could've passed for a crack addict in a Spike Lee Joint.

"What?" asked Venus.

"Hi. I'm in 120. I need some information." I showed her my key, but she couldn't have cared less.

"Uh huh."

"Do you recognize this guy? He stayed here about a week ago for several days." I handed her Gavin's picture, and she stared at it. Her eyes didn't focus, and she yawned.

"Nope."

"Could you look in the computer and see who checked him in?"

"Why?"

"They might remember him," I said.

Venus sat pondering that, when a guy came out from the back. His name tag identified him as Ted the manager.

"Can I help you?" asked Ted.

"I hope so. Do you remember him?" I took Gavin's picture out of Venus's trembling hand and gave it to him. He looked at it and handed it back.

"Sure. Nice guy. Private detective, as I recall."

Hallelujah.

"Did you talk to him much?"

"And who are you?"

"Room 120. I'm also a detective." I gave him one of Dad's cards.

"This says Tommy Watts."

Damn.

"I'm his daughter. I don't have my own cards yet. Mr. Flouder was my dad's old partner. He was murdered last week."

Ted took a step back. "Not here."

"No, in St. Louis. It was shortly after he came home from Lincoln. My dad thinks he ran across something while he was here."

"Why isn't your dad looking into it, or the police?"

"My parents were on a cruise when it happened and my dad caught a wicked shipboard virus. As for the cops, I imagine they'll be around, eventually."

"Which ship was he on?" he asked.

"*Star of Freedom.* Why?"

"Just checking. I saw that ship on the news. Couple hundred came down with it. How's your dad?"

"Miserable, but better. He hates being laid up."

"I hear that. What do you want to know?" He looked at me steadily. I'd seen it before. He looked directly into my eyes, so he could ignore the rest of me. Great. As far as I was concerned, anything that kept his eyes off my boobs worked.

"What did you talk about? Did he ask you for directions?"

"He asked for restaurant recommendations and a phone book. I think his phone was dead. And he needed to stay an extra day," said Ted.

"Did he say why he needed to stay an extra day?"

"No, just that he had the luck of the Irish, which doesn't make sense to me. The Irish never seemed lucky with that potato famine and all. He was happy, though."

"Which restaurants did you send him to?"

"Only one. Albert's on Oak. He wanted a good French dip."

"What'd he need the phone book for?"

"Denny's. Personally, I don't know anybody who would need Denny's."

"It was a lead. Can I see that phone book?"

He handed me the book, and I wrote down all the numbers and addresses of all the Denny's in Lincoln.

"Thanks. If you think of anything else, let me know."

"I will. I'm sorry about Mr. Flouder. He was a nice guy. I enjoyed talking to him."

I thanked him again and practically ran out the door. Tears welled up and my throat closed to a millimeter. I'd forgotten what it was all about again. Gavin was gone and when I finished we might know why, but he'd still be gone.

"What's wrong with you?" Aaron snuck up on me.

"Nothing, just thinking about Gavin." I rummaged around my purse for a tissue that I didn't have.

"What happened?"

"Nothing. I just remembered he's dead."

"You forgot?"

"Sort of."

"You hungry?" Aaron rubbed his stomach.

"God no. Is that all you think about?"

Aaron scratched his chest and looked confused. Perhaps there really wasn't anything else.

"We need to go to Denny's."

"Denny's?" Aaron looked horrified, but followed me to the car. He started making numerous restaurant suggestions until I broke down and told him I was following a lead, not looking for fries.

Lincoln had Denny's out the ass. I supposed the college crowd accounted for it. We went to four without any hits, but got lucky on the fifth. Bitsy Meyer worked there when she bothered to show, which she hadn't that day. I weaseled her new address out of the manager, who *never* looked at my eyes.

I was ready to check out the new address, but by then Aaron was starving. I relented and went to Albert's on Oak for that famous French dip. If we had to eat, at least I could cover another base. Aaron approved, despite the fact that he hadn't received the tip.

The dips were great, but the info was lousy. A waitress remembered Gavin because he came in several times and ordered the same exact thing, plus he left large tips each time. She didn't know anything about his business and he didn't meet anyone in the restaurant.

We left and, in a fit of irritation, I let Aaron drive to Bitsy's new address. That was a big no-no in Dad's book. He didn't like people driving his car, period. He couldn't say a thing about me since I was doing him a multitude of favors, but Aaron was out of the question. I wondered if Dad thought it through when he sicced Aaron on me. Aaron left grease stains wherever he went. The sight of Aaron's stumpy fingers wrapped around Dad's steering wheel would've given him fits.

But despite eating two Twinkies and a Ho Ho while drinking a grape soda, Aaron got us to Bitsy's in one piece and in good time. The steering wheel wasn't so lucky. The filth would have to be scrubbed off.

I'd have to say the same for Bitsy's new place. She'd moved from a decent apartment complex to a trailer park. Her fortunes were failing, and I wondered how much of that had to do with Bart Sendack.

Aaron drove between trailers on a dirt road filled with ruts and rocks. I started to feel nervous, not for us, but for the car. She was too nice to be in that neighborhood. Of course, Dad was a detective, and he'd been in worse places, but if something happened to the car, it was my ass. Aaron must've felt the same way because he drove so slowly I could count every rock we drove over.

Bitsy's trailer sat at the end of a crooked row half obscured by weeds and a pile of old tires. The porch had collapsed and a rickety metal step stool gave entrance to the door, which looked ready to fall off its hinges. I wondered if she bothered to lock it.

"This is it." Aaron sounded worried and not in his usual "can I get to food quick enough" way.

I got out and walked to the step stool. My feet crunched broken beer bottles and kicked empty ketchup bottles and slimy hot dog wrappers. I put my hand on the side of the trailer to steady myself and mounted the stool. Paint and slivers of wood stuck to my palm. The trailer was disintegrating before my eyes. I knocked and held my breath, hoping the door wouldn't fall in. I don't know if I was hoping Bitsy'd be home or not. Mostly, I wanted to leave and wash the car. A voice yelled from inside. It sounded like, "Come in," but I wasn't about to do that.

"Don't go in there," said Aaron.

"Don't worry," I replied.

The voice got louder and more irritated. I knocked again, and the door flung open, knocking me off the stool into the weeds. A hot pain radiated up my arm from my wrist. Aaron grabbed me under my arms and lifted me to my feet.

"Holy shit." A woman stood in the trailer door with her hand over her mouth. It wasn't Bitsy Meyer, or at least I didn't think so. The woman looked fifty, and she'd been rode hard and put up wet, as Dad would say.

"You're not Bitsy Meyer, are you?" I asked.

"No. Are you okay?" She stepped down from the trailer and took my hand. I screeched as a fresh pain went up my arm. I had pebbles embedded in my palm and the start of a killer bruise, but that wasn't causing the pain. My wrist had an impact fracture. It ballooned up as we stared at it.

"I think that's broken," said Aaron.

"You think?" I said, trying to remember if I'd seen a hospital nearby.

"Holy shit. Don't sue me. I didn't mean for you to fall." The woman looked at me with watery blue eyes and began wringing her hands.

"I'm not going to sue you." What would be the point? The woman didn't have a pot to piss in. "Who are you?"

"Tiffany Meyer, Bitsy's mom," she said.

"Is she living here with you?"

"You got to go to the hospital, honey."

"I will. Does she live here?" I asked through gritted teeth.

"Sometimes."

"What about Bart Sendack? Does he live here too?"

Tiffany's lips curled back to reveal yellow teeth and red gums. I took it she wasn't fond of Bart.

"So does he or doesn't he?"

"He's here when she's here. Which ain't much, I'm happy to say. Who're you?"

"Mercy Watts, private detective. I'm looking for Bart, not your daughter."

"I don't give a God damn which one you want. Take them both. They're pieces of shit."

Note to self: hug Mom.

"Do you know when Bart will be back?"

"Never, I hope. Dickhead. He ruined my Franklin Mint plate of President Reagan. God damn bastard used it as an ashtray. I should've shot him in his skinny ass."

"So he won't be back?" My eyes watered from the pain in my wrist, but I didn't want to come back to that dump.

"Yeah, he'll be back. Bitsy left some shit here, and he's coming to get it."

"When?"

She stopped wringing her hands. "Why do you want to know?"

"His ex-wife wants him arrested for back child support."

"He'll be back tonight. I don't know when."

"They've got a new place?"

"Yeah, some apartment. Got a pool. Like they need a pool," she said.

I pulled out one of Dad's cards with my good hand and gave it to her. She looked at it like she couldn't read. By the looks of the trailer, it was a possibility.

"Ain't got no phone."

"Nevermind then." I turned to leave. Aaron held onto my arm and, for once, I was glad he was there.

"Thanks for your help. Don't let on that I've been here," I said over my shoulder.

"Don't worry and don't be sending me no bill. I ain't got no money."

Aaron situated me in the car and found a hospital in record time. I threw up right after we got out, narrowly missing the 300's intact paint job. It came through the trailer park just fine, even if I didn't.

CHAPTER TWENTY-THREE

The ER sat empty waiting for the nighttime accident crowd and I was ushered into a bed posthaste. Aaron came back with me and fussed like it was his fault. I'd rather have been alone.

"What am I going to tell Tommy?" he asked again.

"Dad won't care. What are you worried about?"

"I'm supposed to watch you," he said.

"So he did send you." I narrowed my eyes at Aaron, but he was too freaked to notice.

"What am I going to tell Tommy?"

"Stop saying that. Now get my phone out of my bag and go back to the trailer park," I said.

"No way. I'm not leaving you. Tommy'd kill me."

"Give me a break. Dad will kill you if you let Bart Sendack get away."

"Tommy doesn't know about Sendack," said Aaron. "We're here for Gavin."

"Yeah, and Gavin got killed 'cause he was chasing Sendack. Don't you think we need to find him?"

Aaron sat on my bed and produced a Snickers bar from his jacket. He chewed it slowly, mulling over my argument.

"Look, we don't have all day. Go back to the trailer park and wait for Sendack. Try to be unobtrusive. Park behind that orange trailer so he won't see you, then follow him to the new apartment," I said.

Aaron was unmoved. Such is the power of Dad.

I had one shot left, and it had to be a good one. "If you do it, I promise to eat at whatever restaurant you want and eat whatever you want. Except crab. No crab."

Aaron smiled as someone padded around the other side of the curtain. They paced back and forth, stopped, and a camera peeked around the curtain edge and began clicking away.

"You!" I yelled, pointing a finger at Nardo the paparazzo. "Get out!"

"No way," he said. "This is too good. 'Sex Kitten Sidelined with Crushing Injury.'" He swept his hand up high and beamed at his imaginary headline.

A transporter came in to take me to Radiology and pushed past Nardo. Aaron swallowed the rest of his Snickers whole, tossed me my phone, grabbed Nardo by the ear, and dragged him out the door.

I had my doubts about Aaron's abilities, but he had his moments. Maybe he would be able to tail Sendack successfully. He'd helped Dad out quite a few times, but it takes more than one car to properly tail a suspect no matter what they show on TV. Hopefully, Sendack would be unsuspecting and make it easy on Aaron.

After an hour, my doctor came back and showed me my films. I had two fractures, but they were fixed and didn't need to be set. I was flying on Demerol when my phone started rattling around on the side table.

"Lo," I said.

"Mercy, why haven't you called?" My mother, at her most irritated, sounded like the southern belle she was. Usually, Mom's years in Missouri helped her hide her New Orleans beginnings.

"Hey y'all." I mimicked her with a nice slur from the drug.

"Don't you make fun of me, girl. I've been getting calls nonstop. They think I'm a man or I'm made up."

I giggled.

"Mercy, I'm not laughing. I've been avoiding this since I was fourteen and now I have photographers following me to the grocery store," said Mom. "What are you doing about this?"

"Nothin'. I'm in the hospital."

"Oh, dear Lord. I knew we shouldn't have sent you. Oh, my Lord."

"Like you had a choice. Calm down. I just fell and broke my wrist," I said.

"Did they catch him?"

"Who?"

"Whoever broke your wrist."

"I told you I fell." Talking to my mother brought me out of my stupor and reminded me Aaron was on his own. I was worried about Aaron. How did that happen?

"Alright then. Did you give them your insurance? You did bring your card with you, didn't you?" Mom spoke faster and with a deeper accent the more worked up she got. Normally, I enjoyed a good fluster, but that time it made my head hurt. Painkillers didn't agree with me. I didn't like the separated-from-the-world feeling that others enjoyed so much, and Mom's voice made me feel woozy.

"Oh, please stop talking," I said.

"Sorry, honey. Let me talk to Aaron."

"Not here."

"What? He's supposed to be watching you," she said.

"Please, do you really think Aaron can watch me, Mother?"

"He's better than nothing."

"You'd think so, but no," I said.

"Aaron's a sweetheart and you best not have Fiked him. Do you understand me?"

"Whatever and I didn't Fike him. He's following a suspect," I said.

"Who?" Mom sounded interested. I heard her take a drink and settle in for an explanation.

"Bart Sendack. He's the one Gavin was looking for."

"Did Gavin find him?"

"I don't know. His notebook is missing. Anyway, tell Dad it's going well. How is he?"

"Better. He's sleeping," Mom said.

"Tell him hello for me. I've got to go. The doctor's coming in."

Liar, liar, pants on fire.

Mom hung up, and I felt a twinge of guilt. I should've told her everything I found out — maybe Dad would be able to follow up on his end -- but there was a chance, a good chance Mom wouldn't tell Dad. She might tell Chuck, and then where would I be? I couldn't stand the idea of Chuck using my work to his advantage. No, it was best to keep it to myself. I laid back on the adjustable bed and let sleep overtake me.

When I woke up, Aaron stood over me like a vulture. A vulture that smelled like ham hocks.

"You ate," I said.

"Just a little. There's this great place on Taverna Avenue, and the stuff they can do with a pig. You hungry?"

"You're supposed to be watching Sendack. Can't you..." I looked at my watch. "Can't you concentrate for two hours?"

"I got him. You hungry? I brought soup and a sandwich." He waved a Styrofoam container under my nose.

"No. I'm not hungry. What happened with Sendack?" I swallowed to get rid of the copious amounts of drool that threatened to spill over my lower lip.

Aaron waved the box again. "You know you want it."

I snatched the box from his hands and scarfed down the best ham sandwich of my life. It's a good thing I didn't have an affinity for drugs because I'd have gotten huge.

After I finished, Aaron handed me a piece of paper with Bart's address. It smelled of pork and I wanted to eat it, but I needed the address. That kept it out of my mouth, but just barely. It was a good thing because the doc came in and I'd have hated to explain why I was eating paper. I might've ended up in the psych ward and deservedly so. As it was, he discharged me with a lovely purple cast and prescription for Vicodin. I'd have to take it for a couple of days and resigned myself to Aaron driving. It wasn't a pleasant thought, but at least I'd have a good excuse if something happened.

Actually, something had already happened to the car. It smelled like the inside of a roast pig and trash covered the floor. I don't even want to talk about the steering wheel and keys. Aaron slid into the driver's seat. Maybe the drugs were stronger than I thought, but it sounded like Kajagoogoo on the stereo.

"I fixed your iPod," he said. "You got it all now."

All of what?

Aaron burnt rubber out of the parking lot and I pictured Dad's face when he saw his expensive Italian tires. I'd never hear the end of it.

Aaron finally slowed down when we pulled into a parking lot so bumpy it felt like a gravel road. Bart and his beloved Bitsy had moved into an apartment that wasn't much better than the trailer park. Tiffany would be pleased to know her daughter wasn't getting above herself. The faded paint had a faded seventies motif, complete with a jazzy stripe around the middle of the building. I thanked God for letting me miss out on the seventies. But the apartment building that sat in the middle of a sea of cracked asphalt and weeds did have a pool. Glorified bathtub would've been more accurate.

Aaron pointed out a window with a screen hanging half off and no curtains. Made sense. I doubted Bitsy or Bart cared much for the niceties of curtains.

"Are you sure that's it?" I asked Aaron.

"That's it. What now?"

"I guess we call the client."

"We have a client?"

"We have Gavin's client. Doreen Sendack."

I called the Crab Shack and waited, listening to at least five waitresses yelling orders in the background as the owner went on about Doreen's awesomeness. She worked every shift, and I felt a warm fuzzy come over me as I prepared to give her the news.

"Yeah, what?" Doreen asked.

Not exactly what I was expecting.

"Doreen, this is Mercy Watts. We spoke the other day about your ex."

"Yeah. What is it now?" Doreen barked orders at someone named Fred. The background noise was deafening, and I didn't have her interest, much less her attention.

"I found him," I said loudly. Screams erupted in the kitchen and they weren't screams of joy. Somebody yelled for an extinguisher. I'd picked a bad time. It was a talent of mine that usually worked out for me.

"What'd you say?" asked Doreen.

"I found Bart."

Doreen yelled for everyone to shut up and then said, "You sure?"

"I'm sure. Want the details?"

"Yeah, yeah I do." She sounded misty and overwhelmed. That's the stuff I was looking for.

"He's living with a girl named Bitsy Meyer at 3351F North Fredericksburg Road in Lincoln. They just moved in."

"Does it have a pool?"

"Yes. Why?"

"Bart needs a pool. Thinks it shows he's classy," she said.

"This isn't a classy pool."

Doreen laughed, and I pictured her standing in the greasy Crab Shack kitchen smiling and looking a little less tired.

"Bart never had a clue about real class," said Doreen. "What do we do now?"

"Call the cops and have him arrested," I said.

"Can you do that? I want my name off of it cause of my boys."

"I'll take care of it and call you when he's in custody."

"Thanks, Mercy. I never expected you to do anything. Nobody else ever did," Doreen said.

"Nice surprise, huh?"

"Oh, yeah."

We hung up, and I basked in the warmth of my own goodness for a few minutes until Aaron started asking about dinner. We had a deal, and it was time for me to pay up. If I'd known what restaurant Aaron had in mind, I'd have had second thoughts about the whole thing. We picked up burgers and fries from some dive in the worst location I'd ever seen under a biker bar named Bloodsucker. The clientele looked like the cast from *The Walking Dead*, except not as clean or friendly. The burgers were delicious, so good I was afraid to think what might be in them. Aaron said he found something suspicious in his. I quick took a painkiller before he could tell me what it might be and fell asleep with a fry dangling out of my mouth.

CHAPTER TWENTY-FOUR

The next morning, Aaron woke me at seven with more takeout. We ate buttermilk pancakes and home fries while I mentally flogged myself for forgetting to report Bart. Then I remembered. Who would I report him to?

I called home, and Dixie answered the phone. I tripped over my own tongue until Mom got on the line.

"Hi Mom," I said with relief.

"How's your wrist, honey?"

"Achy, but better. Does Dad know about the whole Marilyn internet thing?"

Mom's voice got hard. "No, he does not, and you aren't going to tell him."

"No worries there." I'd rather chew off my foot than tell Dad what I'd done.

"Are you calling to tell me that you've fixed this situation?"

"Not quite. I need to know if Dad has any contacts in Lincoln," I said.

"Why do you need to know that?"

"Mom."

"Fine. I'll get him."

After a couple of minutes, Dad came on the line with a round of coughing that sounded like someone was plunging a toilet.

"Jesus, Dad. Have you called Pete?"

"As a matter of fact, he was here this morning and I'm good," he said between coughs.

"Right. You know I can call him."

"He says I need a chest x-ray."

"So when are you going in?" I asked.

"Right after you solve the Lindbergh kidnapping."

"I'll get right on that. Go in, Dad."

"Yeah, yeah. How's Lincoln?"

"I broke my wrist. Other than that, I think we got a good line on Gavin."

"You need to be more careful." Dad went into another fit of coughing that covered the sarcastic noises I made at that advice. Dad never got sick, but he got hurt on a regular basis. He'd had everything from broken bones to a light coma in the eighties.

"Do you know anybody in Lincoln?" I asked.

"No, why?"

"I need a guy arrested," I said.

"Did he do anything?"

"Of course. He's the deadbeat dad. I found him." I waited for congratulations. None were forthcoming.

"Call the local precinct," he said.

"Yeah. I was going to, but then I realized they wouldn't exactly rush on over to grab him up, would they?"

"No, probably not. Let me see what I can do. I'll call you back."

I took a nap and an hour later, Dad called back with more than what I needed. He gave me a number of a retired cop with a kid on the force in Lincoln. Better than that, Dad told me Bart had been busy. He had several outstanding warrants in Nebraska. I called Dad's contact, who arranged for me to meet his kid at a coffee shop in an hour. An hour wasn't enough time to make me presentable in a way that might help, but I did the best I could. A nice scoop-neck tee and low-rise jeans would have to be enough.

I opened the door, and Nardo leaned on the balcony railing, grinning and chewing on a toothpick.

"Where're we going?" he asked.

"Straight to hell," I said. "You first."

"That's not very original. I'd expect better from you."

"Bite me." I walked past him with Aaron trailing behind me, humming the *Star Trek* theme song.

"Come on. We can work together," said Nardo.

"No. We really can't. We're not the same species."

"Listen to this. I know I'm scum and you're an artist or whatever, but this relationship can benefit us both."

"There's no relationship, unless you count harassment and disgust," I said.

"It is a relationship, whether you like it or not." Nardo ran in front of me and blocked the stairs. "I'm the talent. You're the face. We'll make millions."

"Get out of my way." I forced my way past him and nearly pushed him down the stairs. I jogged to the car, ignoring the honks from the road.

Nardo yelled out behind me. "If you won't work with me, maybe your mom will."

I got in the car, closed my eyes, and swallowed. I wouldn't think about it. It was too horrible to be contemplated.

Nardo pounded on my window and yelled through the glass. "My partner says the camera loves her."

"Leave my mother alone," I yelled back.

"Yep, she looks great, as good as you, and he has all the time in the world."

Aaron got in the passenger side and I rolled down the window an inch. "Call him off."

"Then we'll talk," said Nardo.

"Fine, just get away from me," I said.

Nardo stepped back, saluted me, and smiled.

I looked at Aaron and asked, "Well?"

"What?"

"Aren't you going to say something?"

"About what?"

"Never mind," I said.

Aaron drove us to the coffee shop, whining about his need for a snack. I shut him up with a promise of carrot cake and fluffed my hair. As it turned out, I needn't have bothered. Nic Serena didn't need convincing. She sat down across from me without introduction or hesitation. She was a surprise and an interesting one. Nic Serena had to get as many second and third looks as I did, although we couldn't have been more different. She had dark blond hair that looked natural, café au lait skin, a broad nose, wide shapely lips, almond-shaped eyes, and a body that looked like a bag of hangers. She was all angles and edges with cheekbones that could've sliced meat.

"Mercy Watts. Nic Serena. Why am I here?"

"To do me a favor, I hope," I said.

"You need somebody arrested?"

"Yeah, a deadbeat dad with some warrants for check kiting and larceny."

"Sounds like a minor character. What's the deal?"

"I don't know what you've been told, but a family friend was murdered last week."

"So?"

"I think he found something out accidentally about an old client while he was here. He started calling her while he drove back and she was murdered right after he got through, and then he was. I need to know whether Sendack saw Gavin and what happened."

"Any connection between the dead client and Sendack?"

"Not that I know of," I said as I pulled on a sweater. I felt obvious and stupid in my scoop neck next to Serena in her sleek black suit. I guessed she didn't use sex to get answers. She probably scared guys into talking. She scared me.

"You don't know if he located Sendack?"

"Gavin's notes are missing along with the client's file, but he probably did. I did," I said.

"Not difficult?"

"Just legwork. So what do you say?"

"I'll pick him up and do the questioning," she said.

"Why can't I talk to him?"

"Because I'm a cop and you're not. There's nothing you can get out of him that I can't." She looked at me, waiting for further protests. I couldn't think of any, but I felt slighted just the same. I'd gotten plenty of guys to say plenty of stuff.

"So how about giving me that address and Sendack's particulars?" asked Serena.

I gave her everything I had on Bart and she left, promising to call when she had him. As she walked out, heads turned, and I was quickly aware that we'd been watched for our whole conversation. I'd been so busy looking at Serena I hadn't noticed being noticed. It was a new sensation, and it felt good to have been anonymous, even if it was in my own mind.

I spent the early afternoon on my rock-hard motel bed with a pillow over my head. Aaron waxed on about Dungeons and Dragons' strategy, oblivious to the pillow and my occasional snoring. The painkillers were doing a number on me even though I was down to a half dose. Serena hadn't called back yet, and I started to question whether she would. The less I had to do, the more I thought about Gavin and Dixie. My wrist hurt more than I would admit, and I wanted to be home in the cocoon of The Oasis with my mother making it all better.

Serena called at three and asked me to come down. Nardo followed us to the station at a discreet distance but didn't come inside, thankfully. Aaron dumped me at Serena's desk and disappeared.

"Where'd your little guy go?" Serena asked when she showed fifteen minutes later.

"I'm afraid to know."

"What's the deal with him?"

"Family friend and my dad thought I needed help," I said.

"He's helping you?"

"He's driving."

"That's something," she said.

"It's the only thing. You pick up Sendack?"

"He's in a room with my partner. Nice guy."

"I bet. Did Gavin find him?"

"Not that he knows of. Tell me more about the client that got murdered."

"Rebecca Sample, graduated from UNL and worked for an internet marketing company in St. Louis. She was strangled during her wedding reception, not long after she talked to Gavin. A stalker pestered her for a couple years but quit when she met her fiancé. The stalker's the prime suspect, but the cops are weeding through the guest list, too."

"Any decent physical evidence?"

"Some, but I don't know what it shows," I said.

"What did your friend die of?"

"Heart attack brought on by an injection."

"No idea what the substance was?" she asked.

"Labs aren't back yet," I said.

"Will you know when they are?"

"Why?"

"Just curious why you know so much about an open and actively pursued investigation run by your cousin."

"You didn't call him, did you?"

"No. Should I?"

"Why are you asking me about him, then?" I rubbed my arm above the cast and thought about my next painkiller.

Serena drummed her fingers on the desk. "You shouldn't be involved in this at all and Chuck Watts is heading this way."

"Great. Just what I needed and I'm not involved. I'm nosy."

"Well, you've got a great nose because from what I can tell, you're a couple of days ahead of your cousin," she said.

"He's been busy. Triple homicide or something. Is this all you wanted me in here for?"

"No. I need a picture of Mr. Flouder." She looked at the picture I handed her. "Is this recent?"

"It's around a year old. He lost a lot of weight and some hair before he died, but he looked basically the same."

"Would you like to check out Sendack while we take another run at him?"

"Sure. I've never seen the guy in person."

Serena led me to a viewing area with one-way glass. It was empty and smelled like Simple Green, the industrial cleaner that Dad used to clean the bottom of his shoes after a nasty crime scene. Stuff gets through the booties if you walk through enough of it. I hated that smell once I was old enough to know what it meant.

Bart Sendack lounged in an orange plastic chair with a cup of coffee and a smile. Bart's picture didn't do him justice. He was relaxed and in control. I liked him with an instantaneousness that startled me. He was still the thin, sleazy guy from the picture, but his voice, his smiling eyes changed everything. Bart'd gotten through life on a wink and a smile and, if he knew the jig was up, he wasn't concerned about it.

"I don't know him, but he looks familiar," said Bart. "I might've seen him on the street. Who is he?"

"Private detective hired to find you. He's dead," said Serena.

"I didn't kill him."

"Been to St. Louis lately?"

Bart shrugged, still smiling. "Nope. My ex lives there. I'm not her favorite person. I don't blame her, but it's best to stay out of her hair."

"We'll find out if you made any quick trips to the Show-Me State."

"I didn't. You can ask Bitsy. She'll tell you. Am I being arrested for something?"

"I'll let you know," Serena said as she left the interview room.

She came into the viewing area and watched Sendack with me.

"Interesting," she said.

"I can't help it, but I kind of like him," I said.

"Me, too. Some guys just have it. I don't think he knows a thing about Flouder."

"What did you pick him up for?"

"Back child support, but we'll book him for everything."

"Can you hold off on that and just stick to the child support for a couple days?"

"Why would we do that?" asked Serena.

"Just a favor to me. His ex thinks his family will pay his back support if he's arrested for it. They might not if he's got other charges and won't get out whether she drops her charges or not."

"How long do you expect us to stick to that?"

"Couple of days, max. I'm guessing he'll call for a bailout and let them know the situation. They'll call Doreen to see if a deal can be made. I doubt he'll tell them what else he's been up to."

"I'm sure he won't. How do you know this woman, the ex?"

"I don't really, but she's decent and struggling because of Bart. Plus, she was Gavin's last client. It's a loose-end kind of thing."

"I think we can let Mr. Sendack twist for a couple days. Let me know what happens with the ex." Serena handed me her card and I took a last look at Sendack. It was about time a woman got one over on him.

Aaron drove me to the motel. Nardo still followed us, but there wasn't a hint of a camera. He stayed in his car when we went inside. Aaron watched and complained as I packed, but it didn't take long. We were on the road in an hour against his protests. He wanted to sample another rib joint, but I couldn't be swayed. I wanted home, my home with the Target curtains, hand-me-down furniture, and Skanky purring in my ear. I didn't want to talk or hear or think. Lincoln was a bust and once that thought came to me, I couldn't get rid of it. I took a full dose of painkillers in an effort to sleep it away, but it didn't work. I went in and out of consciousness. The thought that I'd failed Dixie was waiting for me every time I came to.

Day faded to night and the rhythm of passing headlights mesmerized me, but failed to soothe. What would Dad have done? He would've found something or had a decent lead.

"I can't believe this," I said, interrupting Aaron in the middle of an explanation for his latest brilliant idea, a hash brown stuffed dog. A bad idea if I ever heard one.

"We could add egg."

"No. Gross. Nobody is going to want egg and hash browns stuffed in a hot dog. There's something wrong with you."

"I think it sounds good."

"You would," I said.

"What's wrong?" asked Aaron.

"Nothing unless you count the fact that I just wasted two days for nothing."

"What for nothing?"

"We don't know anything, Aaron."

"We know stuff."

"Oh yeah. What?" I asked.

"We know Gavin knew who the stalker was, and I got that recipe for blueberry pie."

"I forgot. Now it's all worth it." I rolled over, putting my back to Aaron. But a little thing like a back wasn't going to stop him. He told me about that blueberry pie until I fell asleep again.

CHAPTER TWENTY-FIVE

The Central West End was quiet for a Friday night, but then again it was three in the morning. Aaron double parked and lifted me out of the car. Not bad for a fat little guy.

I don't remember getting in bed and pouring the glass of water that sat on my bedside table. A gentle hand woke me the next morning, and that glass was the first thing I saw. Skanky had his head halfway in with his pink curled tongue, making lapping noises.

"Aw, Skanky."

"I'll get you another glass." Pete sat on the edge of my bed in yet another stained lab coat.

"Didn't I leave him at my parents' house?"

"I picked him up for you. I thought you'd want him home," Pete said.

I rolled over and rubbed his thigh. "Were the Siamese tormenting him?"

"I guess so. Your mom said she couldn't take the yowling anymore."

"Was there biting?"

"Maybe a little," he said.

"Those damn Siamese. Why can't they leave my little guy alone?" I

stroked Skanky's head while he kneaded my stomach, his claws snagging my tee.

"They're territorial. I know how they feel. The whole world's falling
in love with you." Pete bent over and kissed me. He looked like he
hadn't shaved since I left for Lincoln and his bristles poked my face.
He pulled back and said, "Somebody keeps calling your cell. Your new
message isn't scaring them off."

"Who was it?"

"I don't know. They hang up on me," he said and waited for me to
comment.

I shrugged.

"Has that been happening a lot? The hang-ups, I mean," said Pete.

"It's no big deal. Just some weirdoes," I said.

"That's what I'm worried about." Pete touched the fingers sticking
out of my cast and flexed each one slowly.

"It doesn't hurt," I said.

"Good, just checking. How many pills did you take last night?"

"Two."

"That's it? I had a hard time waking you."

"I'm sensitive."

"Since when?"

"Sensitive to painkillers, dufus. What are you doing here?"

"Your mom called. Wanted me to check in on you," he said. "She
had a photographer following her too, but apparently he got bored."

"Getting pretty tight with the parentals, aren't we?"

"I wouldn't say that. Let's get you up." Pete spoke to me like a
patient. His carefully modulated voice made me smile.

"I'm not critically injured, you know."

"I know." He kept his doctor voice while drawing a bath for me. I
undressed, slightly embarrassed to find I'd slept in my clothes. Aaron
was a bad influence.

"You smell like hot dogs and cheap perfume," Pete said as he
poured in a liberal amount of bubble bath.

"You smell like an armpit."

"It's been a rough couple of days. What's your excuse?"

"Aaron."

Pete laughed and helped me into the bath. I watched while he stripped off his lab coat and scrub top. He gave himself a quick sponge bath and wet his hair. Rivulets of water ran down his back while he shaved.

"I find this kind of sexy," I said, squashing my breasts against the side of the tub.

"Careful with that cast."

"Uh, huh." I batted my eyelashes and tugged on his pant leg.

"I have to go. There's a gallbladder in an hour I want."

"That's all you have to say to me?"

"Check your landline messages. Morty called, and he didn't sound happy."

"He never does." I set my breasts on the edge of the tub and rested my cheek on my good hand. "You really have to go?"

"I shouldn't be here right now." He redressed and kissed my forehead. I recognized the already gone look in his eyes.

"Call me tonight, if you can." I could be a good girl with effort and Pete left with a flash of his lab coat.

I soaked in my tub for a good hour until the water went cold and the phone started ringing continually. No rest for the wicked, as my mother would say. I washed and went to unplug the damn thing. Caller ID said Uncle Morty. I was relieved until I answered. Another freak might've been more pleasant.

"Finally. What took so long?" Uncle Morty yelled. Did I detect a bit of worry in his voice? Not hardly.

"I have a broken wrist," I said.

"I've been calling all morning. Get dressed and meet me at Kronos."

"Why?"

"I'm hungry." He hung up with a click so loud it hurt my ear. I lolled on the sofa in a weak attempt to feel rebellious, but curiosity got the better of me. Breakfast at Kronos was a new one. Aaron and Rodney didn't serve breakfast as of two days ago. Maybe Morty found something, and it wasn't for the phone. Then again, paranoia was his friend and it might end up being nothing.

I put on a polo dress that my mother considered ill-advised. I liked the straight lines meant for a straight body, but I knew I was fooling myself. The dress pulled in all the wrong places. My breasts and hips shortened the hem, so I couldn't bend over. Oh well, Pete liked it and his gall bladder would be over by lunch. I could stand the hospital cafeteria, if he could.

When I walked into Kronos ten minutes later, Uncle Morty waved me over to his favorite table under a display of firemen boots suspended from the ceiling. He says they remind him of a mistake he made that got him kicked in the head. I feel that way about the back seats of Honda Civics, but I didn't want to sit under one.

"It took you long enough." Morty glowered at me, motioned to the opposite seat, and handed me a paper menu.

"What's this?"

"Rod decided to work up a breakfast menu." I gave him a doubtful look and scanned the menu for hash brown stuffed hot dogs. Happily, they weren't there. Rodney came out of the kitchen, pulled up a chair, and mounted it like a horse.

"What do you think of the menu?" he asked.

"Looks good. What started this?" I asked.

"Cops been coming in asking for breakfast before we open. We've been fixing them up. If we're gonna be doing it anyway, we may as well add it. Did Aaron tell you about his dog idea?"

"Please don't do that. It's too gross to be considered," I said with a well-placed gag noise.

"Dog idea?" Morty looked at Rod with a curled lip. He reminded me of a cartoon bulldog.

"Aaron wants to stuff a hot dog with hash browns for breakfast. Nasty, but if he changes it to a house-made split breakfast sausage on a sourdough roll heaped with browns and eggs, we might have something." Rod smiled, his eyes crinkled and his eyebrows went to points. He looked like the Grinch getting ready to steal Christmas. Rodney had a great feel for what people, particularly men, would eat.

"I could go for that," Morty said.

Rodney leapt up and looked at me.

"Why not? Go crazy," I said.

Rod clapped his hands and sprinted into the kitchen, happy as all get-out.

I glanced out the front window and damned if Emil Roberts wasn't loitering across the street, fiddling with a parking meter, and looking suspicious as hell. I turned to Uncle Morty, and he snorted.

"Took you long enough," he said.

"How long has he been there?"

"The whole time. Probably followed you from your apartment. You got instincts, you do." He looked at me like I was too dumb to breathe. There was no point in reminding him that I was trained in IVs and illnesses, not detecting tails. Being that I was Tommy Watts's daughter; much was expected. Plus, I wasn't expecting to be followed. Nardo promised to back off, and he had.

"Shut up," I said.

"I got to give credit where credit's due."

"Thanks. I appreciate that. So why am I here?"

Uncle Morty stretched and took a sip of coffee. His expression changed from a look of amusement to restrained anger. "You need to change your number again."

"I already did it twice," I said.

"Yeah, and you emailed the numbers to everyone you freaking know."

"What am I supposed to do?"

Uncle Morty slapped a cheap throwaway cell on the table. "You use this. I email the number out. We don't trust your provider anymore."

I picked up the phone. Definitely wasn't a lux model, but it came without crazy freaks. "You rock, Uncle Morty."

"How's the wrist?" he asked with another frown.

"Fine. So, what's going on? I assume you didn't bring me here just for the phone."

"Who you want to start with?" He drummed his fingers on the table, each strike a hard thump.

"What are my choices?"

"The Girls or Gavin," he said.

"Gavin," I said.

"Did you check out Wilson Novelties while you were in Lincoln?"

"No. Why? Was I supposed to?"

"Would've saved some time, but no. Another charge posted on Gavin's account." Uncle Morty's fingers drummed harder. The sound echoed off the walls of the near-empty restaurant.

"Wilson Novelties? Isn't that kind of late?" I asked.

"Paper charges take longer and I guess the owner wasn't in a big hurry."

"Sample's fiancé ordered her something from there, right?"

"Yeah, but Gavin didn't know that. He wasn't working for Sample anymore," he said.

"So he was really shopping," I said. "He had a sweatshirt and a cookbook in his trunk."

"That's the stuff. I cross-checked his motel bill against the new charge." Morty took another sip of coffee and paused for effect. He wanted me to jump to the bait. I was determined not to, but before I knew what I was doing, I said, "Well?"

"Twenty minutes after the charge at Wilson Novelties, he extended his stay by a day. That extra day he went to the university."

"So he found something. Any idea what?"

"Nope. Owner doesn't remember Gavin," he said.

"Please don't tell me you want me to go back to Lincoln." I put my head in my good hand.

"Somebody's got to check out that store."

"Well, it's not going to be me. Why couldn't you've given me this information yesterday?" I asked, my head still in my hand.

"I got it when Visa got it," he said.

"Crap, shit, fuck."

Morty smiled, a rare thing, but he likes to hear me cuss.

"So, was that the good news or the bad news?" I asked, dreading the answer.

"It's all bad," he said.

"Great. Let me have it."

"I found out about The Girls."

I straightened up. The idea of helping someone alive had appeal.

"There's a freeze on their bank accounts, all the accounts," said Uncle Morty.

"Credit cards?"

"Frozen."

"Lines of bank credit?" I asked.

"Frozen. They don't have access to a freaking dime and they have a shitload of dimes," Uncle Morty said.

"Who did it? Did you talk to them?"

"Hell no, I didn't talk to them. I talked to Big Steve."

Big Steve was the biggest badass lawyer in St. Louis and a good friend to my parents. Mom used to be his legal secretary when I was little. My parents trusted Big Steve, and that trust was returned. Big Steve called them when his son, Stevie, got in trouble. Stevie was a disaster, and I was grateful for every one of his scrapes. He made me look good.

"What did he say?" I asked.

"Rumors mostly. Somebody's trying to take over the family trust," he said.

"Can that be done?"

"It ain't easy, but yeah."

"What do you do? Get them declared nuts or something?"

"Basically," he said.

"I can't imagine anyone who would want to do that," I said.

Rodney brought me a cup of coffee, and I took a slow sip. Somebody wanted to hurt The Girls. I couldn't wrap my heart around it.

"It's family, whoever it is," he said.

"Family," I repeated.

"Yep. Only family has that kind of pull. Got any candidates?"

"I don't know most of the family. There's Lawton, but he's a sweetheart."

While both of the girls had married, only Myrtle had a child. Lawton was in his mid-fifties and childless. He lived in Cambria, California, a small tourist town on the coast filled with artists and retirees. He came home several times a year, spending weeks gardening and shopping. Lawton loved to shop, and my mother was his Barbie doll. He took full responsibility for Mom's collection of outlandish hats and he got miffed if she neglected her nails. Lawton considered Mom a work of art. I was a work in progress, slowly making my way towards greatness. A couple of years ago, he told Mom that I would be fab if I'd just stop wearing cutoffs. I'm still not fab.

"It ain't Law. I checked him out this morning." Morty looked disappointed. Lawton tried on a yearly basis to reform Morty's wardrobe. He had less luck with him than he did with me. Morty avoided Lawton like he carried Ebola.

"There are some cousins, but they're all rich. Why would they want to screw over The Girls?"

"Shit, who knows? Maybe somebody's gambling or bought too many houses in Tuscany," he said.

The red alert signal from the Enterprise echoed through the bar. Rodney had changed the door buzzer from my favorite tricorder beeps to the much more obnoxious red alert. I looked up to see my mother coming through the door. Beyond her, across the street, Nardo chewed on a toothpick and eyed Emil Roberts. Mom wore jeans and a tank, which meant it was a bad day. On the other hand, her hair was done. She walked to the bar without seeing us and asked Aaron for a cup of coffee when he came out of the kitchen.

"Check it out," Uncle Morty said with a nod to the front window next to the door. Emil Roberts had disappeared, but two guys in their forties stood peering in through the glass with their hands cupped around their eyes. They were dressed in business suits and looked too old to be stalking my mom, but she gets all kinds.

I started to stand up to tell them to get a life when they caught sight of me. Both their hands and their jaws dropped. They looked from Mom at the bar to me and back again. They did it so fast they banged their heads together, and they rubbed their foreheads while looking at us.

Rodney walked out of the kitchen carrying two steaming platters. He set them in front of us and marched to the window.

"Get out of here, you freaking losers. We don't open til ten-thirty." Rodney wiped his hands on his apron as the businessmen ran away.

"I guess they were really hungry, huh, Rodney," I said, trying not to be too sarcastic.

"They're hungry alright." Morty rolled his eyes and dug into his pile of hash browns.

Across the street, Emil Roberts yelled at Nardo and a second later they were bitch-slapping each other. I snorted and Morty's eyes left his plate to see my stalkers going at it. He shook his head and shoveled in more hash browns.

"Must've heard we're starting a breakfast menu," Rod said.

"That must be it," I said.

Mom came up behind Rod and pursed her lips. She wasn't the fan of sarcasm that I was.

"I'm glad you're here," Mom said.

Uh oh.

"You need to drive Aunt Miriam to the funeral home tomorrow."

Score.

"I can't. I'm taking narcotics. Sorry." I concealed my smile by stuffing my mouth full of sausage.

"I'll drive you."

I looked up and saw Aaron standing next to Mom, smiling.

Double score.

I swallowed my sausage. "Um, well, if Aaron is driving, then you don't need me, right?"

"Wrong. We finally got Gavin a spot at Straatman's and Aunt

Miriam needs help with the casket. You know her cataracts are giving her trouble," Mom said.

"Why aren't you going or Dixie, for heaven's sake?"

"Stop arguing. Dixie doesn't want to go there until she absolutely has to. So we need you to go and you're going. Or would you rather stay home with Dad and Dixie? She may stop crying by then."

"Fine, I'll go," I said.

"Thank you, honey. Make sure Aunt Miriam takes plenty of pictures. Dixie wants to see the choices." Mom slid into the booth next to Uncle Morty and looked back and forth between us. "So what is this all about?"

"I can't even remember." My eyes roamed around the restaurant, watching Rodney turn on the ceiling fans one by one. A chilly breeze washed over us and I shivered.

"We were talking about The Girls," Uncle Morty said as he handed me his jacket.

"Oh yeah. I guess I'm supposed to do something,"

"Don't you want to help?" asked Mom. "The Girls are family. They practically raised you."

God help me.

"I'm so disappointed in you." Uncle Morty smirked at me.

"You could deal with it." I smirked back.

"I'm going to Lincoln," he said.

"Enough. Mercy, you'll deal with The Girls' situation." Mom leaned back and crossed her arms. Discussion over.

"I thought I was going with Aunt Miriam."

"That's tomorrow. You can speak to The Girls today. Rodney, do you have my order?"

Rodney jogged back into the kitchen to get it. Mom kissed me on the cheek and took her bag. "I have to go. Your father keeps trying to get out of bed. I caught him crawling towards the office this morning." Mom left, bringing traffic to a dead stop. She should never wear tank tops.

Aaron looked at my plate. "So...what do you think? How was it? Taste good?" He held his hands clasped in front of him. He would've looked angelic and sweet if it weren't for the hair, clothes, glasses, and everything else about him.

"It's okay." My plate was spotless. Okay didn't cover it.

"Maybe more hash browns or add cheese sauce?" Aaron asked.

"Fine. I admit it. Your dog disaster is delicious. Thanks. I'm going to gain a thousand pounds." I told Uncle Morty good luck in Lincoln and walked to the door with Aaron close on my heels.

"I'll drive you," he said.

"I'll walk." I left Kronos and went past Nardo and Emil, slapping each other and yelling insults about mothers. I angled away from them to cross the street in front of a Mustang. It started honking like crazy. The driver stuck his head out the window, made a V with his fingers and started doing a lovely tongue thrust through them.

Some days just can't get bad enough.

CHAPTER TWENTY-SIX

I walked into the breezeway between Stillman Antiques and a contemporary design studio. Stillman never locked the gate to the alley, bad for security, but lucky for me. The alley ran parallel with Hawthorne Avenue. I walked a block and crossed the street to where Lexington changed to Hawthorne. I liked the alleys. They were quick and convenient and hid me from assholes in Mustangs, not that there would be Mustangs on Hawthorne or Lexington. Still, I stayed in the alley, skirting trash cans and enjoying the quiet of the rustling trees.

I reached the rear of the Bled property in ten minutes. My low heels felt like stilettos and I wished I'd taken Aaron's ride. I felt a little pang of guilt for snubbing him. He was clueless, but it was possible, however remote, that I'd hurt his feelings.

I unlocked the garage and stepped into the dark. The alarm panel glowed green. I punched in the code and flipped the light switch on. The new Mercedes Lester drove sat in its place, recently waxed but unmoved. A few leaves littered the floor. If Lester had been around, he'd have swept them away. Nicolai Bled's 1921 Maybach had a thin layer of dust on its dark green paint. It was the same with the 1954 Borgwald Isabella convertible Millicent bought to drive around

Europe. A 1950 Morgan and a 1945 Jaguar sat in the other two bays, also dusty. I couldn't remember the last time they'd been out. Sometimes Lester or my dad drove them to make sure they stayed in working order. I'd never been allowed. The Morgan and the Jag belonged to The Girls' late husbands and there was an unspoken understanding that only men would drive them. Frankly, I didn't want to drive them or the convertible. I didn't have enough insurance to fix so much as a headlamp on one of those babies. I did make out with Junior Hassleburt in the Jaguar once. It really turned him on. A little too much, if you know what I mean.

I walked past the cars and into the stable section. The whole thing was designed to be a stable originally. Nicolai Bled didn't like cars. He kept two teams of horses for his personal use and ponies for Millicent and Myrtle. He only gave up on buggies for his primary transportation after his wife was hit in her chaise and four by a Model A and nearly killed.

The eight stalls had brass nameplates, straw on the floor and tack oiled and ready for use. It looked like the horses were out for a ride and could return at any moment. I took a deep breath of leather and hay, unlocked the door to the garden, and stepped out through the stone arch into the sun.

The garden bloomed with unchecked abandon. The gardeners had disappeared, along with Lester. Millicent and Myrtle couldn't keep up with the dead-heading and pruning on their own. From the looks of things, they hadn't tried. The rose arbor sagged under the weight of heritage blossoms and their petals littered the flagstone walk. All The Girls' flowers were antique and original to the house. The Bled garden was on the St. Louis garden tour and had been in umpteen magazines. They donated clippings to charity auctions and received unbelievable bids. Some of the flowers could be found nowhere else. I'd spent a lot of time in that garden, playing, talking, and, unfortunately, gardening. I didn't want to dig, prune, or plant. It was too much like work, but I'd done it just the same, side by side with Myrtle. Millicent didn't garden. She read magazines and commented on our work from the lounge chair that she continually moved to stay within talking distance.

My heels crunched leaves and twigs as I went up the walk. The house sat silent as before, but I looked through the door glass and spied Myrtle's purse sitting on the hall table. I rang the service bell beside the door and waited. Then I rang again. Being ignored was not one of my favorite things. I wasn't used to it and it grated. I pushed the button like a three-year-old in an elevator and paced the low stone stoop.

"That's it. I don't have all day," I said to the door. I punched the code into the security keypad and got the green light. The black iron door slid back at the touch of my hand and the door itself wasn't locked. I stepped into the cold, empty foyer and closed the door behind me. The windows let in a soft, diffused light, and the stale air lay heavy and silent. No heat. The Girls would have to be miserable. They needed the heat on year-round.

"Myrtle. Millicent. I know you're here." I walked down the hall past huge Grecian urns and flower arrangements that had gone south, their petals forming a carpet on the beautiful marquetry floors.

I checked the receiving room, the morning room, and formal parlor before heading to the kitchen. I hoped they were in the kitchen. I did not want to search the second floor. I pushed through the swinging rosewood door and found it empty. A clink of china led me to the servants' dining room, wood-paneled and the snuggest room they had. The Girls sat at the battered walnut table with cups of tea. I'd never seen them enter that room in my entire life. Things were really bad.

"Didn't you hear me?" I said, knowing full well they had.

Millicent sat her cup down with a careful clink. "We heard you, dear."

"Why didn't you come?" I was pretty sure I knew the answer to that, too.

"We thought perhaps you'd leave."

Bingo.

"You know me better than that. Since when do I give up?"

"There's always a first time." Myrtle put up the collar of her thick wool coat and crossed her arms. She didn't look upset or surprised to see me, neither did Millicent.

"Can I have a cup of tea? It's kind of frigid in here."

"Of course, dear. What are we thinking?" Myrtle said.

"What happened to your arm?" asked Millicent.

"I fell. It's no big deal," I said.

The Girls hugged me, and we went back into the kitchen. I perched on a tall chair at the end of the island, listening to their hushed voices talking about tea and thought about all the pie dough I'd rolled out on that marble slab. In Myrtle and Millicent's world, ladies didn't bake or cook, period. Making lemon tart with me was their form of rebellion and, as a result, I could make practically anything from puff pastry to tiramisu. I can't tell you how often that doesn't come in handy.

Millicent set an eggshell teacup, big for its age, in front of me. I picked it up like it might crumble to dust at my touch and sipped the jasmine tea.

"So, do you want to tell me, or should I start?" I asked.

They looked at me with wide eyes and said nothing.

Great.

"Mom sent me. She's worried."

"Your mother is sweet, but there's nothing to worry about." Millicent patted her thick silver hair. It was coiled in an elaborate fashion on the back of her head. It was going-out hair. I could always tell with her. Myrtle's hair stayed in the same marcel waves framing her face no matter what. But if something special was going on, Millicent would spend an eternity fixing her hair.

"Nothing to worry about?"

"No. Not a thing," Millicent said.

"You wouldn't be fibbing to me, would you?" I sipped my tea and peered at them over the gold rim of my cup.

"Mercy, dear, we're fine, but we are in a rush, about to go out, you know."

"You're going out?"

"Yes," she said.

"How?"

"What do you mean?" Myrtle asked.

"Neither of you drive, and Lester isn't here. Mrs. Haase says he hasn't been around in weeks."

"A friend is coming. We do have to go." They got up and looked at me. I didn't move.

"Look. I know you're having a problem. What's going on?" I set my cup on its wafer-thin saucer, stood up, and slapped my hands down on the marble tabletop.

"There's no problem." Millicent took my arm, steered me away from the table and out of the kitchen.

"Millicent, your accounts are frozen. I'm not just being nosy. We want to help." Well, mostly my parents wanted to help. I wanted to go meet Pete and help later.

"Mr. Cardiff handles our affairs." Millicent's voice was strong, but her eyes roamed everywhere except to meet mine.

"Mr. Cardiff couldn't handle his way out of a paper bag," I said.

"Mercy, please," Myrtle said with her hand on her chest.

"Sorry, but it's true. He does estate planning and taxes. You need a litigator. Somebody who can fight."

"Don't worry yourself," Millicent said.

Too late. I was officially worried.

Millicent and Myrtle flanked me through the servants' dining room, the cloakroom, one of the pantries into the family room and out into the hallway to the front door.

"Wait a minute. What was that?" I said.

Myrtle fidgeted with her hands while Millicent tried to push me towards the door.

"Nothing, dear. Have a nice day. We'll call your mother," Millicent said.

I sidestepped Millicent's hands at the small of my back and spun around. There at the door to the family room were two suitcases partially hidden by a potted palm. I walked to the suitcases and looked at the initials MB stitched into the hide of each of the cases. The Girls were going somewhere, but they weren't going far. The cases were part of two sets, twelve pieces each. There were hatboxes, trunks, and cases of every shape and size. I'd played with them, packing with old clothes for my imaginary adventures, and I'd watched The Girls pack their luggage for their many trips. They filled every piece. That luggage was serious. They'd bought it in the early sixties after one of the husbands died and Lawton was born. Myrtle had gone into a decline the way Millicent put it, and she decided they needed to get away. The trip started in San Francisco and circled the earth, taking two years and six months.

"Exactly where are you going? Not to lunch, I assume," I said.

Millicent opened her mouth, ready with a lie, but Myrtle reached out and touched her arm. "We're going to Prie Dieu," she said.

"Who died?" I asked.

"No one, thank our dear Lord," said The Girls, while crossing themselves.

"Then why are you going?"

The Girls looked around like they'd find the answer on the walls. I crossed my arms and waited. Prie Dieu was the Bled family's ancestral home, built in the 1820s as a tribute to a lost wife. I'd been there quite a few times, usually for funerals. It was a national historic home and the Missouri Historical Society ran it, giving tours and overseeing the reenactment of a small Civil War skirmish that took place on the grounds.

"Are you kicking out the Historical Society?" It sounded stupid even as I said it.

"Of course not. It's just that..." Myrtle said.

"It's just that we need someplace to go," Millicent said, her brown eyes fixed on my face, stoic, yet sad.

"Someplace to go? You can't stay here?" Blood rushed to my face, and my good hand went to my hip.

"We simply can't afford it," said Myrtle. "It's not that bad, dear."

"Not that bad? That's pretty bad. Who is it? Who's doing this to you?"

They looked away, and Myrtle started fidgeting again.

"You know I'll find out," I said. "You might as well tell me and save some time."

"We don't want to upset you," said Myrtle.

"That ship has sailed. Who is it?"

"Our cousin Brooks," said Millicent.

"Brooks! Who the hell is Brooks?"

"Mercy!" said Myrtle.

"Sorry. Who's Brooks? Do I know him?" I sat down on the long bench next to the cases and put my cast on the large Egyptian dog's head that made up the armrest. Across from me was a small, tasteful display of family pictures.

Millicent picked up a picture of an elderly lady wearing a hat the size of a garbage can lid. "You may have met at Great Aunt Eulalie's funeral."

"That was five years ago."

"He doesn't visit much," said Myrtle.

"Obviously," I said.

Millicent set the picture down next to my favorite, a black and white photo of an extremely stylish and beautiful couple standing next to a Venetian gondola. Stella and Nicky were the most interesting of all the Bleds and that was saying something, considering they had Josiah Bled to compete with. I was always Stella when I packed my bags.

"Promise you won't tell your mother," said Myrtle.

"I will not. Even if I did, she'd get it out of me. You know how she is."

"Yes, we do." They smiled at me, but I was unamused. The day was going downhill. The next thing I knew, I'd be breaking out in hemorrhoids.

"So what's the plan? You do have a plan?" I asked.

"There's a competency hearing next month," said Millicent.

"So Brooks is trying to say you're crazy." I rubbed my head. My painkillers had worn off, and my arm ached. I could've used that twilight feeling just about then.

"Incompetent, dear. He says we're incompetent," said Myrtle.

"Well, you're not incompetent or crazy. You don't talk to walls or wear tinfoil hats. You'll definitely win."

"That's why you shouldn't worry," said Myrtle.

"But Mr. Cardiff can't defend you," I said.

"He's very good." Millicent crossed her arms.

"He's good at taxes. When's the last time he was in a courtroom?"

The Girls looked at each other. I'd stumped them.

"You have to have a litigator. You can bet Brooks is gonna have one."

"You may be right. We'll think it over," said Millicent.

"So what's his problem? Did he gamble away his money or what?"

"No, he still has it," said Millicent.

"Then why's he telling everybody you're crazy, sorry, incompetent?"

Myrtle sighed and sat down beside me. She put her hand, soft as a feather, on my leg and said, "It's about the name."

"Your name? Bled?"

"He wants to start another brewery and use the name Bled. We head the family now, and we said no."

"How come?"

"Brooks isn't a brewer. He doesn't know the business. Francesca heads the brewery now. She worked beside her father since she was twelve and she was very upset," said Myrtle.

"Does Francesca know what Brooks has done?"

"Not at all. Francesca is...unpredictable. We can handle this," said Millicent.

I didn't blame them for not telling Francesca. She was absolutely fierce when it came to the Bled brewery. We were the same age, and she'd taken to her family business the way my father wished I'd taken to ours.

"And we can help you." I stood up and walked to the front door with them. "I'm telling Mom. She'll find you a good lawyer."

"If you must, dear," they said in unison.

I stepped through the doorway and into the warm June sun. It felt like life on my skin after the cold of the house. It'd be alright. The hearing was a month away. We had plenty of time to figure out a decent defense.

"Bye, dear. We'll call your mother from Prie Dieu," they called after me as the black iron gate closed, but I caught it before it latched.

"Wait. What evidence does Brooks have?"

"Hardly a thing. Don't worry yourself," said Myrtle.

Yeah, I'd heard that before.

"Come on. What's he saying?" I insisted.

"He doesn't like how we spend our money," Millicent said.

"Oh. Bye." I let go of the gate and it clicked shut. What was wrong with the way they spent their money? Nothing had changed as far as I knew.

I walked down the path past the silent fountains and heard a voice call over my shoulder. Mrs. Haase in her floppy hat waved a pair of pruning shears at me. I waved back and dashed through the front gate. Mrs. Haase wanted to hear some secrets, but I wasn't telling.

CHAPTER TWENTY-SEVEN

I took off my shoes and walked home barefoot under an archway of oaks. Home to Mom and Dad's house. If I'd turned left, I would've ended up in my apartment and in peace, but I didn't give it a thought. I went home. The bricks felt warm and soothed my sore feet. In a few weeks it'd be too hot to walk on, so I enjoyed the moment before the heat of a St. Louis summer came home to roost. The black iron street lamps flickered, their flames barely visible in the sunlight. I touched each lamppost, counting the number between the Bled mansion and home as I did when I was a child and managed to forget my troubles. I was ten again, not my mother's daughter yet. Just a little girl with braids and big eyes.

My feet automatically found the front walk of my parents' house. I looked up at it, my eyes examining the stonework, the ivy creeping over the façade and the open windows with their lace curtains blowing out. A song by the Eagles drifted in the breeze and drew me along. It felt like home and a place that never belonged to me at all.

My phone rang as I reached the front steps. No name on my screen, but a St. Louis number I didn't recognize. Why wasn't it blocked? I hesitated with my finger on the button to answer. I was sick of the hang-ups and the nasty messages. They didn't scare me as much as they just plain made me tired. If somebody wanted to mess with me, I wished they'd just go ahead and do it.

"Hello."

"Mercy. Thank goodness," said Tricia from my service. "I've been calling your apartment."

"How did you get this number?" I asked.

"Your Uncle Morty sent it to me. So you need to come in and handle some paperwork. And I have some shifts for you."

"I can't work right now," I said.

"I know you're having some kind of family thing, but we need you back," Tricia said.

"Fine. What do you have?"

"Three South at St. Mary's this week and Dr. Feinstein's office in South County next week."

"Twelve-hour shifts?" I asked.

"What else?"

"How many days at St. Mary's?"

"Three. Same with the office," she said.

"Is he a pediatrician?"

"Yep, your favorite," she said.

"I can't start till Tuesday," I said.

"No good. It has to be Monday."

"I have a funeral." I craned my head back and rubbed my neck.

"Let me talk to the charge nurse. I'll work something out. You're set for Feinstein's, right?"

"I guess," I said, feeling so tired I could've laid down on the front step and gone to sleep.

Tricia harassed me with more details. I grunted, and she decided to give up. I didn't want to work though I needed to. I called Pete and left a message, leaning my head against Dad's favorite stone pillar, the one with the peeing gargoyle. Pete didn't call back. He was probably still in surgery, so he may as well have been on the moon.

"Mercy." I turned around and Aunt Tenne stood in the doorway, a large carrot stick in her hand.

"What's with the carrot?" I asked.

"I have to look my best for the cruise, don't I?" She sat down beside me and I shifted my head to her shoulder.

"I forgot about the cruise," I said.

"I'll take care of everything."

Music to my ears.

The carrot looked a little floppy. It takes a good while for carrots to get floppy, so I guess she'd been contemplating that veggie for some time.

"Are you going to eat it or admire it?" I asked.

"You want it?"

Carrot, yes. Floppy carrot, no.

"Pass," I said.

Aunt Tenne reached up, cupping her hand over my cheekbone, and pressed my head into her soft shoulder. We looked at the carrot and listened to the bluejays having it out in the hundred-year oak that sat at the edge of the lawn.

I felt my mom before I caught her scent. People say she has a presence, like me. She didn't speak, and we didn't move. Then I smelled her perfume, White Linen same as mine, drift over and settle on us like a comfy blanket. Home. I loved home.

"Who wants lunch?" Mom said.

"Me," we said together as we turned.

Mom leaned on the doorframe with arms crossed and a toe pointed towards me like a ballet dancer. Pretty as a picture, Dad would say. I wanted to be in that frame, in that perfection, and feel the strength that she exuded. People thought I was like her, maybe they even thought I was her from time to time. People don't see the subtleties. Mom was Mom, looking perfect in a pin-striped shirtdress on a summer day. If somebody took a snapshot, people would say generations later, "God, what a great picture."

"Let's go out," I said.

"I'll see if Dixie wants to go," Mom said.

Aunt Tenne gave me a look that said "Crap."

"Since when do you call her Dixie?" I asked.

"Since she told me she likes it better." Mom turned and walked back into the house.

Aunt Tenne groaned.

"What's wrong? Is she bad again?"

"No. She's so sad she depresses me. I'll have to eat a whole cheese-cake to recover."

Somehow, I thought a whole cheesecake was on the menu anyway. Mom returned with Dixie and we walked to Mom's favorite little Italian place. They were out of cheesecake, darn the luck, but had plenty of carrots on salad, not that Aunt Tenne ordered one. She went for her usual, creamed asparagus soup (it has veggies, right?) and a grilled sandwich dripping with cheese. I, in one of my finer moments, had a salad. I'd been winded on the walk over, not a good sign, and Aunt Tenne sounded like she was having an attack of emphysema. Mom blessed us with silence on the matter and lunch was pleasant if you didn't count Emil Roberts, who I caught eyeing me over a parti-tion. I ignored the urge to fling a tomato at him and reevaluated my earlier opinion.

What did I know about stalkers? You couldn't really expect them to act in a rational manner, could you? I made a mental note to call Chuck and tell him about Roberts following me. I hated to do it, but I knew he'd take care of it since Dad wasn't available. Roberts was getting to be downright annoying. Something had to be done and, if Chuck had written him off, he needed to take a second look.

After an hour of stuffing ourselves, we walked home, smelling the flowers and watching the world hurry by. Mom and Dixie hooked their arms together, walking in step and silence. Dixie hadn't said a word the whole time, but she wasn't tearing up either. A few steps behind them, I hooked my arm with Aunt Tenne's. A man smiled at us from beside a stone pillar, but he didn't move or pull out a camera, so I smiled back.

Mom glanced back over her shoulder at me. "So did you talk to The Girls, Mercy?" "Can we talk about it later? I don't want to think about it," I said.

"Of course," Mom said. "They're not going anywhere."

Well...

I squeezed Aunt Tenne's arm. "Have you booked the cruise yet?"

"Who's going on a cruise?" Dixie said.

Nobody spoke for a moment. For my part, I was astonished and slightly embarrassed.

"Tenne and Mercy are. Have you booked, Tenne?" Mom said.

"No. I haven't decided on the Virgins or the Bahamas yet."

"I say we go to the Bahamas," I said.

"It's more expensive," said Mom.

"I feel flush."

"I've never been on a cruise. I always wanted to, but Gavin thought they looked boring," said Dixie.

Silence again. I swear, even the birds stopped chirping.

"Do you want to go?" said Aunt Tenne.

We walked on. The concrete sidewalk turned into the brick of Hawthorne Avenue and the wind picked up, whipping our hair around and lifting our hems. Emil was probably getting an eyeful.

"Yes, I think I do," Dixie said.

Mom unhooked her arm and squeezed Dixie's shoulders. "If you do, then I think I will, too."

What just happened?

"Are we all going, then?" I asked, a little hopeful, a little afraid.

"Looks like it," said Dixie.

"And it's the Bahamas?" said Aunt Tenne.

"It is," said Dixie.

Nardo came around the corner and walked towards us with long, loose-limbed strides. I thought his appearance might just be a reminder of our future talk, but he walked straight up to me. "Ready to talk?"

"No," I replied.

He grinned when I ushered Aunt Tenne past him.

"Who's that?" Aunt Tenne asked.

"Nobody," I said.

A camera clicked behind us and I wanted to nestle my head into Aunt Tenne's shoulder and keep on walking. Instead, I dropped her arm, did an about-face, and marched back to him.

"Stop. Enough," I said.

"It's not enough. I'm getting a hundred requests for prints of you a day and there's more of me coming. You got to learn to work it. You signed that release and there's no going back."

"I can't get used to this," I said.

Nardo leaned over and got in my face. "Listen to me." A breeze of industrial-strength mouthwash blew back tendrils of my hair, but his toothpick remained balanced on the tip of his lip like it was mounted by superglue. "You've got to. It's either me or them." He pointed to the guy by the pillar and a couple more by the shops. Three cameras and at least fourteen eyes were on me.

"Shit. I didn't even notice them," I said.

"I thought not, and more are coming."

"So I suppose if you take my pictures, they'll go away and leave my mom alone."

"That's the plan. It works for you?"

I glanced back at Mom, who tapped her foot and glared at the photographers slowly moving in on us.

I turned back to Nardo. "And you can make them go away, really?"

"A picture to seal the deal?" asked Nardo.

"Make them go," I said.

Nardo went around to each photographer and with a bit of haggling they left, one by one, then he pointed his camera at me. I smiled, flipped my hair back, and put my cast behind my back. Nardo took pictures from several angles, saluted me, and disappeared between two storefronts.

When I went back to Mom, she asked, "What was that all about?"

"Nothing," I said, but I think Mom knew and she was okay with it. Sometimes you've got to do what you've got to do.

"Don't trust him," said Aunt Tenne. "He looks like a slimeball."

"Oh, he's a slimeball all right, but he's my slimeball," I said.

"That does not make me feel better," said Mom. "But look at that."

Behind us, Nardo had emerged again and was blocking Emil Roberts from following us.

"Looks like he might be good for something. Maybe he'll put that other one in the hospital," said Dixie.

"Oh my God," I said. "Dad."

"What about him?" Mom asked. "He says he'd rather go shopping or take me to the gynecologist before he'd go on another cruise."

"No. We left Dad home. Alone."

"Sounds like you're afraid he'll get into the cookies or burn down the house," Dixie said with a little laugh that sounded part worn out and part sore throat.

"He might at that." Mom laughed, soft and musical. No sore throat there.

"He's sick, Mom. You left him alone."

"He's fine. Listen to you worry."

"He won't stay in bed. He might aspirate or something. Jeez, Mom."

"He won't aspirate. He hasn't vomited since yesterday and he's not unconscious. Stop being a mother hen."

"I'm not being a mother hen," I said.

Dixie stopped and looked over her shoulder. "Are, too." She smiled at me. Gray hair peeked out at her roots. She wore no makeup and deep, dark circles were tattooed under her eyes, but I saw Dixie in them, the Dixie I once knew and would know again.

Once I installed Mom, Aunt Tenne, and Dixie at the house and made sure Dad was alive and not eating cookies, I went home to my apartment and bed. If I couldn't have Pete, I could at least have a nap. Skanky slept on my pillow and he had missed me so much that he didn't notice when I laid down, but continued to have cat dreams. I imagine they had something to do with catnip with all the noise he was making.

CHAPTER TWENTY-EIGHT

I slept hard. It was one of those sleeps that leaves you disoriented and more tired than you were before, especially when you're interrupted. I usually was, so you'd think I'd be used to it. A rapping on my door broke into my dream slowly and I came to with a slobbery pillow and a thick head. I buried my head under a dry pillow and pretended I didn't hear it when the phone started ringing. Why didn't I unplug it? Idiot.

"Hello," I said, my voice phlegmy and deep.

"Answer your door," said my mother, and she hung up.

Crap. Double crap.

I rolled out of bed and lurched towards the front door, pulling down my dress and considering putting my bra back on. What the heck? Whoever interrupted my nap would just have to take me as I come, braless and slobbery. If I'd been thinking clearly, I'd have put on that bra. Mom wouldn't call for just anybody.

The rapping started up again, louder than before. I put my eye to the peephole. Nobody. Something hit the peephole, and I jumped back a foot and hit my cast on the edge of the breakfast bar.

"Shit."

"Mercy Watts, I heard that."

Groan.

I opened the door. Great Aunt Miriam stood with her left hand on her hip and a large four-pronged cane in her right. It was raised to the height of the peephole and she looked ready to clock me with it.

"Hello, Aunt Miriam," I said.

She stalked past me with her cane still raised and made a growling sound deep in her throat.

"So what can I do for you?"

Aunt Miriam looked me up and down with emphasis on my chest. "A nice young lady dresses properly to receive visitors."

Who ever said I was nice or a lady, for that matter?

"I wasn't planning on receiving visitors."

"You opened the door."

"I'll be right back." I went in my bedroom and put on the accursed bra. Then I went back into the living room and stood in front of Aunt Miriam like a recruit ready for inspection. "Better?"

"Hm," she growled.

"What? I put on the bra."

"You've no shoes and your hair, you look like you just woke up."

"I did."

"Hmm."

"Fine." I went to the bathroom and ran a comb through my hair. I washed my face and applied lip gloss and a fresh coat of mascara to be on the safe side. My feet begged to be shoeless, so we compromised and I put on sandals. Better, practically stunning, if I did say so myself.

I marched back to the sofa. "Better?"

Aunt Miriam narrowed her eyes and pursed her lips. God forbid I be fishing for a compliment. Vanity is a sin, you know.

"We will be late now, thanks to your nap." She pronounced nap like it was a dirty word. The kind I would say.

"Late for what?"

"Our appointment at four."

"The coffin thing? That's tomorrow."

"It's today. Hurry and we'll be on time." By on time she meant a half hour early. It was three o'clock.

"Mom said tomorrow."

Aunt Miriam stood up and marched to the door after giving me a scorching look, and I knew to drop it. She wasn't wrong and neither was my sainted mother. It wouldn't be healthy for me to suggest otherwise.

I followed her out the door and down the hall past Mr. Cervantes's open door. I caught a glimpse of him smiling under the chain. Mr. Cervantes both admired and feared Aunt Miriam much like the rest of the world. Unlike the rest of the world, Mr. Cervantes would've asked Aunt Miriam out for coffee if she weren't already married to God.

Aunt Miriam went straight to my truck and stood at the passenger door. She was eye to eye with the lock and she stared at it like she could open it by force of will.

I came up panting behind her and said, "I can't drive. Painkillers." I waved my cast beside her head.

She turned around, looked at my cast, and her lips relaxed into their usual thin line. "Bad break?"

"No. It's alright. Hurts though."

Aunt Miriam grumbled.

Come on, you're a nun. Give me a little sympathy, a pat on the head, something.

"Your mother didn't say how it happened," she said.

"I fell off the stoop of a wrecked trailer."

Her lips pursed.

"I was following up on Gavin's last case in Lincoln."

Aunt Miriam's lips relaxed, and she patted my shoulder. "We need a ride."

"Where's your car?" I asked.

"At the hospital."

"Alright then. Aaron said he'd take us tomorrow. Let's walk to Kronos," I said.

"Will he be there?"

"Where else?"

A ten-minute walk to Kronos was enough to make Aunt Miriam antsy. It was twenty minutes down Highway 40 and we already bordered on being late by her watch. When we walked in, Rodney stood behind the bar, wiping glasses and jawing with a couple business types. When they turned and saw me, their jaws dropped. It was the guys from earlier. I guess they doubled back in hopes of another Mom sighting. They simultaneously dropped fives on the bar and shuffled past us, murmuring something about appointments. Aunt Miriam glared at them and climbed onto a bar stool.

Rodney looked over his smudged glasses and said, "What is it with you?"

I could tell by his expression that he really didn't know.

"Maybe it isn't me. It could be Aunt Miriam," I said.

Rodney thought about that, and Aunt Miriam growled.

"We need a ride. The appointment for casket picking is today," I said.

Rodney yelled for Aaron who appeared from the storeroom with a smudge of ketchup on his chin and his glasses dangling from one ear.

"What," he said.

"We need a ride," I said.

"Okay."

No questions asked. I liked that in a man. Aaron fixed his glasses, wiped his chin, tucked in his shirt, which untucked itself in three steps and said, "I'm ready.

I helped Aunt Miriam off the stool. It was a good two-foot jump for her. She straightened her veil and marched out the door.

"What's with the cane?" asked Rodney. "She got the arthritis?"

"No. She thinks it gives her an edge in negotiations," I said.

"She wants a cheap casket?"

"You bet." I saluted Rodney and ran to catch up with Aunt Miriam and Aaron.

When I caught them at the curb, Aaron opened the 300's passenger door for Aunt Miriam. She settled herself in, adjusting every bell and whistle the seat had. She wiggled, made sure she could see over the dash, looked through the glove compartment, who knows why, maybe she thought I stowed some condoms in there. She's been looking for evidence of immoral behavior since I was fifteen. There's plenty of it to be found, but being a nun she didn't know where to look. I'd never put anything in a glove compartment. What am I, stupid? I don't think so. Besides, it was my dad's car. Ick.

Aaron put me in the backseat with the care he used with Aunt Miriam. He'd have belted me in, if I hadn't beat him to it. Aunt Miriam continued to adjust her seat, grumbling about her lumbar region. Since she drove an ancient Ford Escort, I didn't think it was the seat that was bothering her. She gave Aaron directions every fifteen feet and pointed out other cars and traffic signs that didn't pertain to us. I admired Aaron for his calm forbearance, but the truth is he probably didn't hear a word she said.

I lay down in the backseat and tucked Dad's emergency blanket under my head. I sucked in a lungful of Dad's scent and listened to Aunt Miriam critiquing the shape of a new Volvo driving by.

Twenty minutes later Aunt Miriam was still gabbing on, but this time about the size of a parking lot. It was too small, badly shaped and to top it all, full. Aaron parked on a side street and she didn't like that either.

Aaron helped me out of the backseat. "How long?" Maybe he had been listening to Aunt Miriam and couldn't take it anymore.

"Beats me."

"I'll stay here," he said.

Coward.

We left Aaron leaning on the 300 studying an elm and walked towards the funeral home. There must be one architect that designs funeral homes and he's obsessed with the South. This particular design was Tara, the one from the movie, not the book. The illusion was perfect down to the sweeping verandas and flowers. It was made to look old while at the same time being shiny and well-scrubbed. It gave me the creeps. Not because I knew what went on inside, but because it was all so fake and cheerful. I didn't think funerals should be cheery, well-scrubbed, and shiny. Death was miserable crap, at least they could own up to it, but I guess I was in the minority because the place was kicking. The lot was packed to the point of double parking. Some guy in an Excursion parked on the lawn. We walked up the front steps and rang the bell. I swear it sounded like the theme from *Gone with the Wind.*

A girl with sad eyes and frosted blue eye shadow answered the bell. We told her we had an appointment, and she promptly told us we didn't. Wrong answer. After Aunt Miriam scared the glitter off her, she went to get management.

A tall young guy, also with sad eyes, hurried out from the back. He stopped short when he saw us. That time I didn't know if it was me or Aunt Miriam. She'd called in some favors to get Gavin a spot and my guess was he'd already spent too much time with her.

He took a deep breath, straightened his tie, and smoothed back the remains of his hair. Okay, it was me, but at least I didn't have to do the talking.

"We're here, Mr. Altemueller," said Aunt Miriam.

"Yes, yes you are," he said, looking at me.

Don't look at me, bub. It's her deal.

"We're ready," she said loudly.

Mr. Altemueller jumped and flushed. "Well, Sister Miriam, you see I think there may have been a miscommunication with our dates. We were expecting you tomorrow and we have a large event today."

Event. Now death is an event. Super creepy. Of course he was talking to my boobs at the time.

"We're here now," said Aunt Miriam.

I couldn't see Aunt Miriam's face, but the back of her head scared me.

"Yes, I see that. Right this way," he said to my boobs.

We followed him past rooms named Remembrance One, Two and Three. They were packed with sobbing mourners and people drinking cappuccinos with extra foam. Mr. Altemueller led us down a ramp through double doors into the showroom. The showroom was empty save a dozen caskets on velvet-covered pedestals. The room was pure white with low lighting and little spotlights trained on each casket, but it was the least creepy room in the place. It was real and down to business. The business was death, but what of it. It had to be done, and we had to do it.

"Normally I'd walk you through the process, but it's a special day and I have to get back."

"Price list," said Aunt Miriam.

"Yes, right. Well, I'll send my assistant down in a few minutes to see if you've made a choice and we'll see what we can do."

"We'll see a price list. Send your assistant with that."

"We don't really have a price list per se. You see, we're offering custom burials."

Aunt Miriam pointed to a gold casket trimmed in oak. "So we can't buy that exact casket?"

"Yes, of course you can. That one is our Eternity Gold, and it's very popular."

"Why is it custom?" I couldn't resist.

"It's a special design," he said.

"What's special about it? Doesn't it come from the factory that way?"

"I...I have to get back. Please look around and..." Mr. Altemueller left mid-sentence. We weren't typical mourner material. Who but us goes in looking to bury a loved one on the cheap? Most people are probably so shell-shocked they'll pay anything just to get it over with and to not look cheap. Of course, those people wouldn't be from the Watts clan. Aunt Miriam had been taught by the Catholic Church and they took those vows of poverty and economy seriously.

"Special." Aunt Miriam grumbled and started walking from casket to casket. She took pictures for Dixie, scratched paint with her fingernail, tapped on lids, and tugged on handles. She put it into perspective. I mean, we were burying this thing after all. It should hold up.

Wait a minute. Why? What for? Presumably we weren't going to dig it up. Why not go for the old pine box? It ends up in the same place.

Aunt Miriam walked back to the double doors and turned around. She stared at each casket with the intensity of a chess champion. If she favored one, I couldn't tell. She stopped looking at the caskets and began pacing back and forth in front of them. She swung her cane beside her, occasionally snagging on the beige carpeting and irritating herself.

"Do you want me to get the assistant?" I asked.

"No."

Great.

The more I looked at those coffins, the more I imagined being in one. My hands were clammy, and I felt like I had a hole through my middle. Aunt Miriam kept pacing. The more she paced the thinner her lip line got. Yipes. I didn't know what I did, but it was bad.

"I think I need a coffee." I gave her a wide berth and went for the door.

"We're almost done."

"Err. Okay. You want the assistant?"

"No." She went to the small padded bench next to the door and sat down. She put her cane between her knees and leaned her chin on it. I sat down on the end of the bench and waited. Time goes slowly in a room full of coffins. I could hear the sounds of sorrow through the doors along with the piped-in music mutilating some of my favorite old songs. "Like a Virgin" should never be played in a funeral home. It's just not a good idea whether it's lyricless or not.

Then a sound rocketed out of my purse so loud it echoed off the walls and was magnified ten times. Being a cool customer, I screeched and fell off the bench.

Aunt Miriam looked at me, her chin still on the cane. "Answer your phone."

I did a mental bout of cussing, grabbed my purse, and pulled out my new, very loud phone. "Hello."

"It's me. Where are you?" It sounded like Uncle Morty chewing something big and wet.

"Who is this?"

"Who do you think?"

Aunt Miriam gave me the evil eye and motioned to the door. I got off my knees and walked out. The hall was filled with more mourners and I threaded my way to the door, trying not to get felt up or scorched by coffee.

"Uncle Morty?"

"Duh. Where are you?"

"Funeral home picking out the casket," I said. "What do you want?"

"You should've checked out Wilson Novelties," he said.

"We covered that. Where are you?"

"Lincoln. Where do you think?"

"That was fast," I said.

"Only for old ladies," said Uncle Morty.

"You didn't have Aaron with you. Never mind. What've you got?"

"Gavin signed the guest book. The clerk remembers he wrote down something out of it. It made the guy uncomfortable."

"What'd he write down?"

"Shit. I don't know. Probably a name and address. I spent the last hour going through the book. My eyes are killing me. These people have terrible handwriting."

"Any bells go off?"

"None, except Lee, but we already knew he bought a present for Sample here."

"Anybody else?"

"Listen to a few names for me and see if you recognize any of them. Leslie Baum, Corey Hampton, Jason Moore, Beth Simpson, Ali Musat, Jefferson Bell, Shelley Peterson, Emily Robere, Elian Katz and Rob Clemens."

"They don't sound familiar to me," I said.

"Those are all the names from Gavin's page and the one before. Those are the ones he would've naturally seen. Christ. I'm going to have to look up every one of these bastards."

"Better you than me." I hung up, walked back towards the coffin room and there he was, Emil Roberts, peeking at me from around a corner.

Christ. What a dickhead.

Without thinking, I pivoted and went for him. I'd had enough. You can follow me to Kronos. You can follow me home, to the grocery store, to my parents' house, but you cannot follow me to a funeral home.

"Look, you little creep. Get the freak off me. If I lay eyes on you again, I'm going to kick your balls into your throat. You got that?"

Roberts nodded with his mouth open and cappuccino slopping down his shirt. I turned from him and walked as fast as I could towards the coffin showroom. I spotted blue eye shadow girl on the way. Unfortunately, she spotted me too and did an about-face. I followed her into Remembrance Three and zigzagged through mourners and past the casket, the Eternity Gold. Nice choice. Pictures were grouped on the casket along with a ton of flowers. Mr. Alte-mueller was making a bundle off this event.

A large wooden easel sat at the foot of the casket. I was in arm's length of blue eye shadow girl and I reached out to grab her arm, when I saw the picture propped up on the easel. Rebecca Sample. It was the shot I'd seen in the Reverend Coleman's office. Rebecca Sample smiling with her long, blond hair draped over her shoulder and looking like nothing could possibly be wrong. The children that had surrounded her had been carefully edited out. Rebecca was alone in that picture, life size, but taken out of her life. The hole in my stomach returned. I hadn't missed it.

Blue eye shadow girl disappeared from Remembrance Three and mourners crowded me taking their turns at the casket. I got turned around and headed to where the lid was up. An old woman steadied herself with my arm and said what a shame it was. I tried to pull away from her, but found myself boxed in. I hadn't known Rebecca in life and I didn't want to know her in death. When you haven't got life to remember, death is all you've got. I was able to forget Rebecca while I investigated Gavin's murder, but if I saw her, she'd be there right along-side him forever. Gavin was enough.

Too late. There she was, lying in a box. Expensive and pretty as it was, it couldn't compare to Rebecca herself. She didn't photograph well. Rebecca was a beauty in person. The mortician hadn't caked makeup on her. She looked fresh and rested. A high-necked pink blouse covered her bruised neck and brought out the subtle blush of her cheeks. The crack on her head must've been in the back because there were no marks on her face.

"Charlotte wanted Rebecca in her wedding dress, but they couldn't get the blood out," said a woman behind me.

"Ellie, do we have to talk about that now?" asked a man.

"I'm just saying."

"Just saying what? God, I have to get out of here."

"Earl, Earl? Where are you going?"

I turned away from Rebecca and followed Ellie and Earl through the crowd. The sea of mourners parted for them. I guess it was Earl's distress that did it. His hand was over his face and Ellie was soon crying. They stopped at some rosewood sofas in Remembrance One. I passed them and went out the door into the hall. A line blocked my way. People were queued up to sign the guest book. A man bent over the book crying, his hands gripping either side of the desk and tears dripped down his nose. It was Lee Holtmeyer. I watched as Reverend Coleman rubbed his back and whispered in his ear. He straightened up, wiped his nose on a tissue and signed the book. He walked towards me with the reverend's arm around his waist.

"Excuse me," said Lee, his voice barely audible. I felt like he was looking through my head when he said it.

"I'm so sorry, Lee," I said.

"Excuse us, Detective Watts. We have to go in," said the reverend.

They brushed past me and I stood for a moment face-to-face with Lee's brother, Darrell. He glared at me and started to speak, but blue eye shadow girl came out of Remembrance One and did another about-face.

Not so fast, sister.

I chased her down. I wasn't going back into Remembrance Three no matter what.

"We need that price list now," I said.

She muttered some excuses, but I held her arm, and she relented. We walked into the hall, down the ramp into the showroom. Aunt Miriam started quizzing her on each casket, price, paint quality, availability. She talked and talked. The girl listened and would've agreed to anything just to escape Aunt Miriam. I knew the feeling. Blue eye shadow girl pulled out some paperwork from behind the Eternity Gold and asked Aunt Miriam to sign the order. Lee Holtmeyer popped into my head, him signing the guest book. Morty said Lee's name was in the Wilson Novelties book. He signed it. He was there. Lee was in Lincoln and he lied about it.

"Oh my God. Aunt Miriam. Oh my God."

"Mercy Watts, have some decorum and respect. I'm trying to negotiate here."

"But Aunt Miriam..."

"Please be quiet. It's nothing that can't wait."

"No. I'm telling you it cannot wait."

"Mercy, please."

"Fine." I pulled out my phone.

"Mercy, how many times do I have to tell you?" Aunt Miriam made a chopping motion towards the door. I glared at her and walked out. I wouldn't have thought it possible, but the hall was even more packed. I pushed through to Remembrance Two and gave up. I dialed Chuck's desk. It killed me to do it, but Dad was still out. Chuck, as sleazy as he was, was a great cop.

Somebody answered the phone, but I couldn't make out what he said. "Chuck. Chuck. Is that you? I'm looking for Detective Watts."

I couldn't make out a word. My phone was useless in there. No one would be able to hear me and I'd never make it to the front door. The exit in Remembrance Two was worse than the hall. I rotated and spotted an unmarked door. At the very least it led out of the crush, so I took it. It was a storage room packed with extra chairs, baseball equipment, broken podiums and, ick, more caskets. They should keep that door locked. Lucky for me it also had an exit. The red sign glowed behind a stack of chairs. I pulled on them and they fell over on a red casket creating a huge gash in the lid.

Great, just great. Wait, it wasn't my fault. They should've kept that door locked plus it's red. Who gets buried in red? Prostitutes and adulterers maybe.

I pushed on the metal bar on the exit door, and sunlight blinded me. I hadn't realized how dim it was inside. I leaned my hip on the door, thrusting it open further, and propped it open with a dented brass ashtray.

I hit redial on my phone.

"Detective Clancy."

"Detective Clancy? Isn't this Watts's desk?"

"Yeah it is. Can I help you?"

"No. I need Watts right now," I said. "It's an emergency."

"Tell me who you are and what the emergency is. Then I'll get him."

"Mercy Watts. It's about the Sample Flouder case. Get him now!"

"So which case do you want to talk to him about, Sample or Flouder?"

"Oh my god! They're the same case."

"Okay. Okay. Don't get your panties in a twist."

The door screeched open, and I slipped behind another stack of chairs. The door closed, and I heard the unmistakable sound of a gun cocking. I shifted sideways and peeked around the chairs. Darrell. Of course. Big brother come to fix the problem once again.

Darrell's eyes slid around the storage room and settled on the exit door to my left. "God damn it."

The baseball bats were across the room. I'd never get to them. Darrell came closer. If he went all the way to the door, he'd see me. I held my breath.

I'm not here. I got away. Go back.

He kept walking; slow, deliberate steps. He was at the door.

"Mercy!" Chuck's voice came out of my phone.

Darrell's head snapped to the left. Our eyes met. I grabbed the chairs and toppled them over on him. He yelled as he went down and I heard the metallic clunk of the gun hitting the concrete floor. The chairs settled. They covered Darrell completely, except for his gun hand which was empty and still. I put my hand to my ear and realized my phone wasn't in it anymore. Like Darrell's gun, it had disappeared in the avalanche of chairs. It also blocked the way to the door into Remembrance Two. I'd have to climb over caskets to get to it.

"Ah crap."

That was the last thing I said. White starbursts filled my vision and my hands were on either side of my head trying to press out the pain. I was on the floor, my cheek against the cold concrete. I think I was rolling back and forth from the pain, an involuntary movement I'd seen patients make after a severe injury.

Someone touched me. He didn't speak or at least I didn't hear anything. He grabbed my arm and pulled it away from my head and started dragging me. The starbursts got brighter and became streaked with red. Through the pain, I knew I was in big trouble. What did Dad say? Never let yourself be taken to the second location. I was going to the second location. I slid over a hump and something snagged my dress. He pulled my arm so hard; I thought it would come out of its socket. Something went through my dress and cut into me. A hot, burning pain went down my back slicing skin from muscle. It was one more pain in a nightmare and worse; I was now outside. Outside. Away from people. The second location.

My arm dropped, and I thought he left. My hand went back to my head and then he kicked me, not hard, not the first time. But there wasn't just one kick, but a half dozen in my ribs and the small of my back. The pain rivaled the pain in my head, but I couldn't do anything to protect myself. I couldn't move my hands from my head -- that pain was paramount.

One more kick, a big one, sent me off the edge of something. The fall was short, but it felt like forever. Long enough for me to think, "At least he's not kicking me anymore." Then I hit the ground. Apparently, the body can only take so much pain because it didn't hurt and it should've. I could feel sharp rocks under my face and chest. I'd landed sunny-side down. My hands were still at my head, my elbows digging into the ground. My stomach heaved. It wasn't forceful or even uncomfortable. Warm liquid spilled over my lips and pooled under my cheek, but nothing happened. No more pulling or kicking. The pain didn't subside or increase, and I began to cope with it. I felt my face and realized that my eyes were closed so I opened them. The pain powered through my head like Aaron through a crab cake. My vision went in and out with starbursts and red streaks going through, but I could see. I was outside on a gravel border about three feet from the funeral home lawn. Beyond the lawn was a stand of trees. I was alone. When I realized I could hear I listened for footsteps and there weren't any. He was gone, and I had a chance.

I rolled back over on my back and looked at the sky, pale blue with fluffy clouds floating past at a good clip. I took a deep breath and forced myself onto my left side. The building was in reach of my fingertips. I cocked my head back. The edge of the parking lot was twenty feet away. The other way was a small porch, the one I'd been kicked off. I couldn't go that way. He'd come back, and that's the way he'd come. I could crawl out onto the lawn and hope a mourner would spot me when they got in their car. Of course, the guy wouldn't have a hard time spotting me either, but he'd have to drag me back in a visible area. I could make for the parking lot. I'd be blocked by the cars but easier to hear. Then again, if he came back, he could drag me into a car and that'd be the end of me.

It came down to what I was capable of, which wasn't much. The pain in my head was getting worse, and every breath was fire. Damn it. I had to get moving. I didn't know how long he'd been gone, but it was too long. I looked up over my hand and saw a water spigot. The piping went up the side of the building and looked sturdy. Maybe if I could drag myself upright I could inch along, using the wall as a brace. It had to be faster than crawling, as long as my head could take it.

I belly crawled to the pipe and grasped the spigot. My hands shook so that I could hardly get them on it. I inched my way up the wall, maneuvered myself until I was in a seated chair position. It wasn't too bad. My head felt like the Fourth of July, but I was moving. I let go of the pipe and flattened my hands against the wall, spread eagle. I wiggled and slid toward the parking lot. I was feeling pretty good about it, all things considered. I was snail slow, but I could hear the sounds of the road. If I had to, I knew I could scoot around to the front.

Then I bumped into something cold and metallic, a drainpipe. I rolled on the wall and grabbed it with both hands and nearly fell to my knees. A couple of deep breaths and I was ready to move over it.

"Where do you think you're going?"

I opened my eyes. My nose touched the chipped gray paint of the drainpipe and my breath grew more ragged. She was back. Not him. She. I pulled myself closer to the pipe and put my cheekbone against it and I looked at her. Lee's mother stood so close I could count the large pores on her cheeks and the clumps of mascara on her lashes. I couldn't think of a thing to say. All my powers of sarcasm left me and all I had was hot breath and fear.

"You lied to us." Mrs. Holtmeyer moved in closer and I smelled her breath, coffee and Kahlua.

"Huh?"

"You said you weren't a cop."

"I'm not."

"Detective Watts, the reverend called you, Detective Watts. You lied."

"I lied to her, so she wouldn't tell the cops about me."

"You lied." She looked at me like lying was the worst thing in the world; worse than, say, murder.

Must stall. I'll be missed, eventually.

"Lee lied," I said through clenched teeth.

Her head jerked back a couple inches. "Lee does not lie."

"He lied to Rebecca."

"He loved her. He never lied to her."

"He sure as hell never told her he was fucking stalking her."

"He never hurt her,"

"You're a fucking idiot." I knew it was a mistake the second it came out of my mouth. Mrs. Holtmeyer lunged at me, her fingernails going for my face. I swung my cast around and connected with her cheek-bone. Her fingers grazed my cheek, but she stumbled and fell at my feet. The movement was too much. I lost my grip on the pipe.

Before I hit the rocks, she was on me, grabbing my hair. "You inter-fering bitch." She twisted my head with my hair and pushed my head into the rocks. I like to think I screamed, but I doubt I did. I didn't have enough air.

"You'll leave my boys alone now, won't you," she said in a low, controlled voice.

I flailed my good arm behind my head and grabbed her wrist. I dug my fingernails into her veins and she screamed. She let go of my hair and grabbed my good wrist. She twisted it behind my back. I heard a pop and a tremendous weight fell on me. My face was driven into the gravel. I forced my head from side to side, trying to make a hollow for air when the weight lifted. I pushed myself over on my side with my cast. Just before I passed out, I saw Aaron looking down at me holding Aunt Miriam's cane in his hand like a mace.

CHAPTER TWENTY-NINE

I woke to a warm hand stroking my forehead and the smell of good cologne in my nose.

"Dad?"

"No, Chuck."

I opened my eyes and saw Chuck bent over me. His white dress shirt had the top two buttons undone, revealing his collarbone and a tangle of chest hair. His shield was at his waist and his face had an expression I'd never seen on it before. Maybe distraught. I tried to move my head, but I was in a neck brace and strapped to a backboard.

"We have to stop meeting like this," he said.

"Stop touching me."

"Not a chance and you called me. Remember?"

"Go away." I tried to yell it, but my lungs and jaw wouldn't let me. If I could've grabbed his hand, I might've bit him.

"Stay still," said Chuck. "And stop trying to bite me."

Someone else knelt beside me and picked up my wrist. I screamed and passed out again. When I woke up, Chuck said, "I guess her lungs are fine."

Several people laughed, and I really wanted to bite him. Cops and EMTs were swarming all over the place. Out of the corner of my eye, I saw another person lying facedown a few feet from me. Chuck saw me looking and said, "That's Holtmeyer. She's still alive, unfortunately."

"They're all crazy," I whispered.

"Not crazy enough and we have the death penalty."

I started to cry, one of those big ugly cries, and I couldn't even cover my face with my hands.

"I didn't know you wear thongs," Chuck said.

"What?" I said.

"Thongs. You wear thongs. I didn't know you were a thong kind of girl."

"How do you know I wear thongs?" Just then a breeze hit my stomach and thighs. The tears dried in my eyes and I was back to biting. "Oh my God. Pull my dress down, you sleazebag."

Chuck tugged on my hem. "I like this dress."

"I'm glad it's ruined then."

Chuck laughed and left me to the EMTs. I watched him walk to the ambulance a few feet away. Aunt Miriam sat on a gurney looking at me with an oxygen mask on her face. Chuck and the ambulance dwarfed her. She looked old and fragile. I wasn't accustomed to seeing her that way, an old woman.

I closed my eyes and watched the spots dance across my vision. The pain was better, but the IV in my arm could've had something to do with that. The EMT told me they were going to transfer me to a gurney for transport to St. John's. Chuck came back and touched my leg. I thought about kicking him, but found I didn't care all that much who touched my leg.

They lifted on three, and there wasn't enough drugs on board to control the pain. I screamed until I panted from the effort then a hand touched my forehead. A kiss brushed my cheek, and I smelled lavender. Aunt Miriam. The oxygen mask was off and her eyes were inches from mine. She whispered in my ear. I wish I could remember what she said. Mostly I remember her eyes. The blueness of them and how much they looked like Dad's.

The next twelve hours alternated between hazy suggestions of events and long periods of nothing. I remember the blinding lights of the ER and the pain they caused. I remember my arm being popped back into its socket. I think Chuck and Nazir tried to ask me questions. I might've told them to shove it or something like. Pete flitted in and out like a hummingbird. I woke up once as he slept with his head on the edge of my bed, snoring and clutching my chart to his chest. I tried to touch his head, but fell asleep before I managed it.

I didn't wake up again until the next day. My IV pump alarm was going ape shit and there were two nurse's aides hitting buttons like a couple of woodpeckers.

"Get the key," I said.

They both turned and stared at me.

"I'm a nurse."

"Do you know how to turn this thing off?" It said Peggy on her tag. She didn't look like a Peggy to me. I wondered if she had the wrong tag.

"You need the key," I said.

Peg and her partner in stupidity asked each other if they had the key. It was a good thing I wasn't coding because that would've been all she wrote. The more I listened to Peg and Glenda the more likely it seemed that they might not have on the right tags. They might, in fact, be janitors.

"Call the desk," I said.

I was on a morphine drip, but the noise was increasing my migraine by the second. Peg tried to call the desk on my intercom, but they couldn't hear her over the alarm and they both went in search of the key. My mother crossed their path, walking in with a tall pink cake box and coffee.

"Unplug it," I yelled.

Mom yanked the plug out of the wall, but the alarm kept going. Mom looked at me and I said, "Push it over here." My formerly good arm was in a sling, but my casted arm was free. I had enough finger mobility to unclip my medication drip from the pump and told Mom to unhook the IV bag. Mom pushed the squealing pump into the hall and closed the door. She took a deep breath and turned around.

"Feeling better, I see," she said.

"I'm okay." I stuck out my lower lip. I wanted sympathy, not a positive assessment.

Mom placed the cake box on my rolling table, lowered it to the height of the chair next to my bed and got a fork out of her purse.

"Hey, I said I'm okay."

"I don't know if okay is good enough for this cake. This is an extreme dessert."

"I think I'll risk it."

Mom kicked off her shoes, a big no-no in public, and cuddled into my bed beside me. She folded down the sides of the cake box and I got all misty. German chocolate. My favorite made by Myrtle and Millicent. I could tell by the huge dark chocolate curls. They made the best curls.

"Don't cry," said Mom, dabbing at my eyes with a tissue.

"It's my cake and I'll cry if I want to."

Then Mom cried a little, although she called it allergies. She has no allergies, the big softy. To distract her, I asked if Ellen had come by. Mom said she had, but I was still out of it and Sophie peed on the floor, so she had to go. Mom didn't approve of Sophie. She said the tiny girl was a hellion. I guess she would know, considering that she'd raised me.

The thought of difficult little blonds dried Mom's eyes, and we ate my unbelievably fabulous cake while we watched Channel 5's coverage of my escapade. I was impressed with myself. Mom wasn't.

"I'll never know why you chose to go into that storage room. What were you thinking?"

"I was trying to call Chuck. It was too loud everywhere else."

"You isolated yourself when you knew a murderer was in the vicinity."

"But I didn't know Darrell knew I knew. Give me a break."

Mom put her head to mine and patted my cheek. "I know, I know. Think before you act next time, honey."

Next time?

"It's a good thing Chuck was there."

"Why? He didn't do anything."

He did get a sweet interview on Channel 5 though. Bastard.

"He arrested the Holtmeyers for double murder."

"After I figured out who did it. Jeez, Mom," I said.

"Oh, Mercy. Everybody knows you did a good job."

Yeah, just not anyone who watches Channel 5.

"If Chuck hadn't been there, they might've gotten away," Mom said.

"No, they wouldn't have. I clobbered Darrell and Aaron clobbered his mom."

Mom gave me a funny look. It did sound stupid. Aaron clobbered her? The only thing Aaron clobbered was food.

"Aaron was there, wasn't he?" I asked.

"Yes, he saved your bacon, so to speak. I'd say you owe him one."

Great. I owed Aaron. The only thing worse would be owing Chuck.

"You owe me, too." Chuck walked into my room, smirking and holding a bag of Krispy Kremes.

"A cop with donuts, imagine that," I said.

"It's a stereotype for a reason, baby."

"Please don't call me baby. It makes me nauseous."

"Whatever you say, baby," he said as he attacked a glazed raised.

"Why are you here? Don't you have some unsuspecting nurse to harass?" I asked.

Chuck smiled so that he looked like Jack Nicholson's Joker, only sleazy, not evil.

"Some *other* nurse. I already suspect you," I said.

"Too bad."

"And what am I supposed to owe you for anyway?"

"How about arresting the people that tried to kill you?"

"Any first year rookie could've done that. Aaron and I did all the hard work," I said.

"So Aaron's your partner now," said Chuck.

"I don't have a partner. I don't need a partner."

"Actually, your father and I have reached a decision," said Mom.

Oh no. The last time I heard that line was when they tried to send me to an all-girls high school.

"Mercy?" asked Mom. "Don't you want to hear what I have to say?"

"No, I'm good."

Chuck laughed and got comfortable.

"This is the second time you've been seriously injured in the course of an investigation and we feel you can't continue helping the family in this manner."

Yes!

"So in future investigations, Aaron will be your partner."

No!

Chuck doubled over.

"Mom, how about we try something else like I'm a nurse and I do nursing. Aaron can help Dad if he wants to. Leave me out of it."

"Don't be ridiculous."

"Yeah, Mercy," said Chuck. "You and Aaron are great partners."

"Please go away," I said.

"He can't. He's here to sit with you," Mom said.

"Oh no," I said.

"Oh yes," Chuck said.

Mom got up and said she had to check on Dad who was about to go stir crazy, but still too weak to go far.

"Plus, I have to interview you," Chuck said.

"Didn't you do that last night?"

"I tried, but you told me to go fuck a duck."

"Oh, is that what I said."

Mom looked at the ceiling and said under her breath, "Give me strength, Lord."

She left us and Chuck pulled up a chair. He put a foot up on my bed and opened his notebook.

"Nice crotch spread. Can't you sit like a gentleman?"

"Are you saying that you, as a lady, deserve such consideration?"

"Drop dead and rot," I said.

"Right. Let's get to it. What happened?"

"What happened when?"

"Mercy!"

I started at the beginning with Dixie's call from the hospital and ended with me lying on a bed of gravel. So I left out a few choice bits like searching Gavin's office. What'd it matter?

"How'd you know Lee was the stalker?"

"How didn't you know?" I said with as much venom as I could muster.

"I knew. We just didn't have enough to pick him up," he said.

"Whatever."

"So how did you know?"

"Uncle Morty told me. He didn't know he told and neither did I, at first," I said.

"Say that again," Chuck said.

"He called me from Lincoln. He told me that Gavin went to the novelty shop and signed the mailing list book. Gavin wrote something down out of it. Morty thought he'd spotted a name in it that made him stay in Lincoln an extra day."

"And?"

"And he said that Lee's name was in the book, but that it wasn't a surprise," I said.

"He brought a present for Sample there."

"Right. But he also read me some of the names and said he had a headache from reading all that bad handwriting." I looked at Chuck, who cocked his chair back on two legs and said, "Shit."

"I didn't put it together until I thought about Lee signing the guest book at Rebecca's memorial. He told me he'd never been to Lincoln, so how did he sign the book? He lied because he was the stalker. Still, I knew Lee didn't kill Gavin because you were interviewing him when it happened. Helen Card said Darrell and his mother treated Lee like he was disabled, so it had to be one of them to kill Rebecca after she found out about Lee. Mrs. Holtmeyer couldn't have overpowered Gavin on her best day, so that left Darrell."

"How'd you know about me interviewing Lee?" asked Chuck.

"Word gets around."

"Not bad. Not bad at all. Care to hear a little info from my side?"

"If you must."

"You were right Lee was in Lincoln. He went to school with Sample for a couple semesters, but he didn't graduate. He had two classes with her. That must've been what Gavin found out at the university. Lee was stalking her even back then."

"How could she not know he was stalking her?"

"She did, sort of. Her roommate said they got a lot of hangups and Sample got flowers with no cards, but it wasn't anything creepy. We think it was pretty casual until she graduated and moved here. He must've taken it as a rejection and stepped it up."

"How in the world did she end up dating him?"

"Dumb luck. He bumped into her in a grocery store."

"People actually meet that way?" I asked.

"I guess so. Her friend Helen was with her. She said he accidentally rammed their cart. Helen knew him from the gym and introduced them properly. The intro made him a known quantity. You can't plan that kind of thing," he said.

"I bet he was stalking her in the store and got turned around. I doubt he ever would've risked face-to-face contact on purpose."

"That's what our shrink says. But if you ask me, he was escalating. He would've done something to her eventually," said Chuck.

"But Gavin wouldn't be dead if it happened that way." I looked past Chuck to the cloudy sky out my window.

Chuck reached forward and touched my hand. "Yeah, Gavin wouldn't be dead."

"So what did Darrell use on Gavin?"

"Epinephrine," Chuck said.

"How'd he get it? I mean, it's not like it's a street drug."

"His mother has a nut allergy. We think he took her EpiPens."

"No way. It would take at least nine to OD somebody. Nobody carries that many pens with them."

"Mrs. Holtmeyer refilled her prescription several times in the week before the wedding. Doctor shopping."

"Why?" I sat up quickly and my vision narrowed to a point for a moment. I grasped the handrail to steady me. "What was she planning?"

"I suspect the epi was meant for Rebecca. Mrs. Holtmeyer was none too fond of her, but when Darrell had to deal with Gavin, she handed them over."

"Sounds good, but Gavin only had one puncture. What'd they do? Milk the pens and combine them into one syringe?"

"Sure, why not?" Chuck stood up and laid me back on my pillows. Behind him Nardo slunk in and shot a round of pictures. Chuck whipped around and shoved Nardo against the wall.

"Mercy," Nardo shouted. "Tell him."

Chuck's hand left Nardo's throat, but he didn't turn around. "Tell me what?"

"It's alright," I said. "He's my official photographer, I guess."

"So that's why the internet traffic slowed down," said Chuck.

Nardo shrugged. "I have connections."

Chuck put his large hand on Nardo's scrawny shoulder and steered him out the door.

"And now you're done." Chuck deleted the pictures over Nardo's protests and closed the door.

"So now you're protecting me?" I asked.

Chuck sat down on my bed, tucking me into an envelope of his fabulous scent. "From everyone but me."

"Please." I rolled my eyes.

"Too much?" asked Chuck.

"Way."

We laughed together, and I forgot how irritating he was until he started going on about his interrogation techniques. I fell asleep as he proclaimed himself brilliant, second only to my dad.

CHAPTER THIRTY

I was discharged on Tuesday after the doctors decided that my severe concussion wasn't going to kill me. Neither were my broken ribs, or dislocated shoulder. Dr. Houtin felt satisfied because I only had a little blood in my urine. Swell. A little kicking goes a long way.

Gavin's funeral happened on Wednesday, and I missed it. I can't say that I minded. I'd had enough of funeral homes. Mom and Dad went, and that was the important thing. Mom said Myrtle and Millicent were there and she talked them in to dumping Mr. Cardiff as their lawyer. She couldn't find out the details of Brooks's case against them. I would've been more curious if I hadn't had so many painkillers on board.

Instead of nosing my way into The Girls's business, I spent the rest of the week lounging on The Oasis, watching baseball with Dad and Merchant Ivory films with Mom and Dixie. We ate popcorn, told stories, and looked through albums. Dad went through two cases of Belgian Trappist beer. It was our own private wake in our own private way. Gavin got a fine send off, and I think he would've liked it with the exception of the Merchant Ivory.

After six hours into my first day home, I begged Mom to stop answering the phone. Every friend and a couple enemies called for a personal account of my ordeal as they put it. Most of them were impressed, but some were disappointed that my face was still intact. All agreed Chuck looked swell on TV. There were more than a couple of inquiries about his marital status. Chuck called to tell me to stop telling people that he had crabs. I promised, but I was on Vicodin, after all.

On Friday, I decided to start weaning myself off the painkillers and celebrated by staying in bed all morning eating Ho Ho's with Aunt Tenne. She left to replenish our supply when Dad peeked in.

"Busy?" he asked.

"Amazingly."

"You've got a phone call."

"Please, no. I can't take it."

"It's some Doreen woman. She wants to talk about her case." Dad's eyebrows were practically touching his hairline, and he was vibrating with excitement. He'd been waiting for me to take a case voluntarily since my birth.

"Get a grip, Dad. It's Gavin's case. I just helped it along."

"When you work on a dead man's case, it's your case, baby girl. Do you need a ride somewhere? I'll drive you."

"Yeah, right. I doubt you could push down the gas pedal."

"So I barfed a few times, get over it. I'm back to full speed. In fact, I'm going out today. Want to ride along?"

I'd rather go to the gynecologist.

"I need to rest," I said.

Dad passed me the phone and paused in case I changed my mind. It was a no-go. I knew there'd be a next time, but I wasn't ready for it to be so soon and with Dad, there was no such thing as just riding along.

"Hello, hello?" a voice said from the phone.

I'd forgotten I was holding it. "Hello. Sorry about that."

"Hi. It's Doreen. You remember me?"

"Of course. How's it going?"

"Great. I got the money," she said.

"Congratulations."

"Could you come by the Crab Shack today? I'd like to thank you properly. Give you all the crab you can stand."

Great. I'd just as soon eat a pile of fingernails.

"Well, you know how it is. I'm not exactly having a good week," I said.

"Come on. You ain't hurt that bad. I got beat up worse by my brother."

"What is with your family?"

"We're pretty normal."

"I don't think so."

"You don't have any siblings, do you? Now get up. I want you to see my boys. I'll make it worth your while," Doreen said.

"Alright. I'll be over in a couple hours."

Doreen said she was thrilled, and I pretended I was. A couple of hours? Who was I kidding? If Mom didn't come home, I'd have to wash my hair with a pasta spoon and rinse it with a ladle. That could take all day.

Mom found me with my ladle an hour later, laughed, and finished up for me. She fastened my bra and picked out a stunning ensemble of sweatpants and one of Dad's button-up shirts. I looked like a shlub, but a comfortable one. As for my face, there was no hope. By some miracle, my nose wasn't broken, but it looked like it was with the black eyes, the bruising and the scratches from my close encounter with gravel.

"We could try some foundation and cover stick," Mom said.

"Got some flesh-toned spackle?"

"It'll be fine." Mom smeared cover stick all over my face.

"That's what you said when I got a huge fever blister an hour before Homecoming," I said.

"It *was* fine. You looked beautiful."

"My nickname was VD for the rest of the year."

"It isn't anymore, so it's fine," Mom said.

You can't argue with that. Mothers. There's no hope for them either.

"Is Dad driving you?"

"No. I want to live," I said.

Mom fussed with my hair. "I think he can do it."

"I have another plan."

After a fifteen-minute argument with Mom, she allowed me to walk to Kronos. By the time I got there, I was exhausted and it felt like I had an elf sitting on top of my head hitting me with a tiny pickax. I'd planned on going in, having a refreshing iced tea and half a Vicodin, but the bar was packed. I'd forgotten the lunch rush, and it was sure to be filled with cops eager to either condemn my lack of vision or congratulate me. I didn't want to hear it. My high school volleyball coach already told me I was an idiot, and that was bad enough.

I circled the block and went in the kitchen entrance. Mario, the head cook, nodded to me and yelled for Rodney. Rodney rushed in through the swinging doors and stopped short when he saw me.

"Man, oh man. You look bad," he said.

"Thanks. I love you, too."

"You wearing makeup?"

"Yes," I said.

"Really?"

"Yes, really, I am wearing makeup. This is what I look like with makeup applied."

"Damn, that's something." Rodney leaned forward to get a closer look.

"Alright, that's enough. Is Aaron here?"

"You know you owe him big."

"So I've been told repeatedly. Is he here?"

Rodney grabbed up a couple orders and went out the door. Aaron came back through with a platter filled with empty dishes and glasses.

"Hey," he said.

"Hey." I watched Aaron shove the dishes into the washer and restock Mario's supply of clean ones. "You busy?"

"Not bad," he said.

"Can you leave?"

"Rod would kill me."

"Doreen at the Crab Shack wants to give me all the crab I can eat," I said.

"Let's go." Aaron took off his apron and nodded to Mario.

"Aren't you going to tell Rodney?" I asked.

"Why?"

"Won't he wonder where you went?"

Aaron looked at me through his smudged lenses. He wasn't following.

"Never mind. You have to drive," I said.

Aaron took the keys for Rodney's 1978 Charger and motioned for me to go out the way I came in. The Charger sat in the alley under a car cover that was made for a minivan. Rodney wasn't taking any chances. It was his high school dream car, and it didn't matter that its rear bumper was rusted off and the paint was three shades of red. It was his baby. I had second and third thoughts about taking the Charger. Rodney memorized every dent and scratch, and he'd tell you about them, if you couldn't get away.

"Maybe you should clean your glasses," I said.

"What for?"

"So you can see the road, other cars, stuff like that."

"I'm cool."

Yeah, real cool. He still had his hairnet on.

I almost told him, but Aaron's hairnet was as much a part of his ensemble as his dirty glasses and stained tees. I settled into the seat, trying not to get pinched by the cracked vinyl. I'd forgotten all the other reasons why driving the Charger was a bad idea. The vinyl for starters, the radio on the floor, and the smell of condoms and cigarette smoke that I'm sure had nothing to do with Rod.

I rolled my jaw, trying to work up enough spit to swallow a Vicodin. No go. Isn't that always the way? Vicodin gave me dry mouth, and I needed spit to take a Vicodin. My headache increased to the point of nausea when Aaron pulled into the Crab Shack parking lot. The smell of crab drifting in through the vents was enough to make my stomach do a Gabby Douglas.

"I can't go in there."

"Huh?" Aaron looked dimmer than usual and my instincts were divided between shaking him and running away from the smell.

"The crab's making me sick. Go in and tell Doreen I'm out here."

I got out, leaned on the hood, and studied the chips and scratches on it. A breeze kicked up and lifted the stink. Doreen trotted out with a big smile. She caught one look at me and stopped dead in her tracks. If our positions were reversed, I'd have stopped dead, too. Doreen was a changed woman. She'd had a makeover that was nothing short of shocking. She'd cut her hair short so that it framed her face and accentuated her eyes. The new hair was colored a true honey blond with intricate highlights and no green. She took a deep breath and started walking again. As she got closer, I could see her makeup was subtle and flattering, no more cakey orange.

"Please tell me that Bart didn't kick the shit out of you."

"He's innocent for once," I said.

"Thank God almighty." Doreen leaned against the Charger and lit a cigarette. "What happened?"

"I guess you haven't watched the news lately."

"Nope, I've been a busy girl. You too, I guess." She stole a sidelong glance at me. "That Aaron didn't mention your face or the cast."

"I doubt he noticed," I said.

"It's hard to miss, if you don't mind me saying so."

I shrugged and said, "I'm not feeling that great and I need to take a Vicodin. Could you get me something to settle my stomach?"

"Vanilla shake, do it?"

I nodded, and Doreen got me a shake. It was excellent, real ice cream, whipped cream and a cherry. I downed my pill and said thanks.

"When your stomach settles, you got to come in and see my boys."

"Why aren't they in school?"

"Teacher work day, so they're here, slinging crab with me. Are you gonna tell me what happened or what?" Doreen wiggled her pedicured toes and admired her gold ankle bracelet.

"I found the guy that killed Gavin, I mean, Mr. Flouder."

"What did he find you with, a bat?"

"Pretty much," I said.

"The cops got him?"

"Yes. Thankfully."

We leaned against the car in silence, and Doreen took a long drag on her cigarette.

"I love the hair, by the way," I said.

"Thanks. A customer told me to go to this Aveda salon, and they gave me the works. Everybody acts like it's a big difference, but I thought I was good before." She looked at me for confirmation.

"I think it makes you look younger," I said.

"Younger than thirty-one?"

Err...

Some guy yelled for Doreen from the door, and I was spared the lie that was sitting on the edge of my swollen lips.

"You better?" Doreen asked.

I said I was, and we went into the Crab Shack. Aaron sat at a table with two young boys sharing an obscene pile of crab legs and fries. Doreen went to the kitchen, and I walked over to the booth. About halfway there I discovered a definite advantage to going facedown in gravel. No one mistook me for Marilyn. I didn't get a single second look. I did get a few grimaces, and I heard one guy say, "Whoa, bad accident," but that was it. I'd finally achieved something I'd been going for since breasts. I was wallpaper and I have to say I dug it.

"Dude, what happened to your face?" one of the boys asked.

"Accident. Always wear a seatbelt," I said.

Both of the boys nodded slowly and went back to the crab.

Aaron slurped the meat out of a leg. "Want some?"

"No, man. It's all for you."

Aaron smiled at me with juice dripping down his chin. He wiped it with his shirt and kept going. Doreen introduced her boys to me. They were more impressed with Aaron's crab-eating abilities than me, but I enjoyed meeting them. The broken wrist was worth it.

We left in an hour after Aaron decimated Doreen's crab leg supply. I was worn out, and the Vicodin had taken full effect. Aaron helped me to the car and belted me in. Doreen told us to come back soon and Aaron drove out of the parking lot, revving the engine until the seats vibrated. My cell starting ringing and ignoring it wasn't going to fly. Whoever it was kept calling back, and Aaron pulled over to answer it.

He handed me the phone. "Tommy."

After a deep breath I said, "Hey Dad."

"Where are you?"

"Eat," I said.

"What?"

"My client's restaurant."

"You finished?" Dad asked.

Hmm. Was I finished? I didn't want to say yes, but my head was too thick to lie.

"I guess," I said.

"Good. I need you to go home and pick up my camera and laptop and bring them to 1109 Shiloh in Chesterfield. You getting this?" I could hear Dad tapping a pencil against the phone.

"Dad. I'm really tired. Can't Mom do it? You have people. What about your people?"

"Everybody's busy. We're backed up since I've been out and Mom's shopping for the cruise," he said.

I guess shopping trumps multiple injuries.

"Mercy, do you have that?"

"Dad, come on. Why do I have to do it?" I asked.

"It's for the family," he said.

Isn't it always?

The End

PREVIEW

Diver Down (Mercy Watts Mysteries Book Two)

Mrs. Lane Sanders was the kind of woman who usually didn't approve of me. Her grey hair flowed back from her widow's peak in thick waves and landed on her white silk blouse that was buttoned as high as possible and, just to make sure, sealed with a heavy amber brooch that weighed a pound at least. No one was getting those buttons undone, by god.

I sat in the walnut-paneled waiting room opposite Mrs. Sanders, very aware that it was her domain, not mine. The room matched her perfectly, cold and dignified. I'd never been accused of being either. She sat behind her oversized desk with arms crossed and refused to say where her boss was. That was nearly the last straw. I'd had enough of lawyers and their critical secretaries. Two days left before vacation and Arlene Cobb, a lawyer my father referred to as the Duchess of Dirt, hadn't even bothered to show up to pelt me with obnoxious questions about my godmothers' sanity in the civil case against them. I had better things to do than be deposed, buy flowered sundresses that I'd never wear again and wax things that really ought not be waxed. In the last month, I'd found myself involved in four high-profile cases, where the lawyers were happy to bill as many hours as humanly possible, wasting my time in cold offices, repeating cold facts. I think they were trying to freeze some sort of confession out of me. Fat chance. All four of the offices were so similar I often forgot which one I was in and which high-priced shark sat across the table. This wasn't going to be one of those days.

I would've walked out and, in retrospect, I should've, but Myrtle and Millicent needed me. Their nephew, Brooks, was trying to get control of their money and their lives. He was using my family to do it. So I sat as far away as possible from Mrs. Sanders, which put me directly across from the stenographer, a spindly redhead that was probably forty but looked twenty. He definitely *did* approve of me and not in a good way. It was all my fault for letting my mother pick out my outfit. She insisted and I'd learned the hard way that it was easier to comply than fight, so I was wearing a wrap dress that was supposed to make me look like I meant business yet be stylish. It did neither job well. Mom's theory that the hideous print of black and yellow daisies would be distract from my chest might've worked if the top would've stopped gapping open and the skirt didn't part to expose my thighs.

Jay the stenographer loved that dress, couldn't take his eyes off it. More to the point, he couldn't stop trying to look up my skirt. So I got to sit there holding my dress together, while listening to my lawyer, Big Steve Warnock, yelling in the hall behind me. Big Steve's voice had been known to go through three feet of concrete and we got to hear every curse word he uttered and there were a lot of them. I say we but Lane and Jay didn't seem to be paying attention. Lane's expression had gone to glaring and Jay had slid down in his seat in an effort to get a better view up my skirt. Why is it when someone's trying to look up your skirt, you get an irresistible urge to cross and recross your legs? Maybe it's just me, but I had to recross my legs. It had to be done. Jay licked his lips and I put my right leg over my left and felt a little pop in the twenty-dollar pantyhose I'd bought for their supposed durability because Mom said I had to wear pantyhose to depositions. I leaned forward and a spidery run raced down my thigh to my knee.

Freaking great.

"I can help you take those off," said Jay, licking his lips.

Just then Big Steve stalked in, still on his cell. "Get her here now!" He tossed me the phone and popped Jay in the head with the back of his hairy hand. "Shut up, fool, or I'll fire you so hard you'll have to sell your equipment for scrap."

Jay blushed as red as his hair. "I'm sorry, sir. It won't happen again."

"Damn straight it won't." Big Steve sat next to me and I scooted over to make room, even though he was in another chair. He was that kind of guy, the kind that took up a lot of space in every room, whether a closet or an auditorium. You just couldn't stop looking at him, even when he was quiet, which was rare.

"We'll give Arlene another fifteen seconds and then we're out of here."

"Thank goodness," I said.

Big Steve looked at his watch. "Ten seconds."

I smiled. Jay the stenographer looked terrified, a normal reaction to Big Steve. Lane sighed and got on the phone.

"Five seconds. Grab your purse, Mercy."

"Got it."

A young man with a receding hairline and watery blue eyes ran through the door, clutching six inches worth of paperwork and a battered laptop. "I'm here. I'm here."

Big Steve pushed past him. "We're out and you're not Arlene. Don't think I don't know the difference, although that is a tie a fifty-year-old woman would wear."

"Please don't leave. Mrs. Cobb will kill me if I don't get this deposition done."

"Where is she? And don't tell me she got caught up in court. She has nothing on any docket today."

"Um..." said the young man and I began to feel sorry for him.

"Um is not an answer." Big Steve gently pushed me out the door.

"Arlene has a new boyfriend!" yelled out the young man behind us.

"Leonard," said Lane, "are you out of your mind?

We turned slowly. Big Steve looked like it was his birthday. "How old is this one?"

Leonard clapped his free hand over his mouth.

"Too late for that, boy. The new cat is out of the bag. I'm truly going to enjoy my next committee meeting with Arlene."

"Please don't tell her I told you," begged Leonard.

"Alright. I'll give you a break."

"Will you please come in the conference room? She'll fire me if I don't get this deposition done."

I crossed my arms. "I thought she was going to kill you."

Leonard barely glanced at me. "Same thing. Please. I'm begging you."

"She's quite the dragon, isn't she?" said Big Steve.

A bead of sweat rolled down Leonard's cheek. Poor guy didn't know Big Steve made dragons look like house cats. He worked sixteen-hour days because he thought the law was good fun and didn't understand that other people needed to do things like, you know, eat and sleep.

"I'll give you fifteen minutes."

Damn. So close.

Leonard led us into the conference room and I sat in a chair designed to be so comfortable that you'd relax and be off your guard. Fat chance. Big Steve touched my hand. "We're in and out. Remember what I told you."

I nodded. How could I forget? He'd told me a dozen times to answer questions briefly and to offer up absolutely nothing. As if I would. I'd been around. This was my tenth deposition in a month, including the murder cases. If this kept up, I'd have to buy stock in pantyhose or paint my legs.

Leonard settled in across from us and spread out his papers like a fan. Jay set up at the end of the room and tried not to look at me. Nice.

"State your name for the record," said Leonard.

Sigh.

"Carolina Watts." I was named after my mother, but my dad had nicknamed me Mercy. I preferred Mercy to Carolina. I was already too much like Mom for comfort.

"Is that the name you're commonly known by?" asked Leonard.

"No."

Leonard looked up and waited. I could see a flicker of a smile on the edge of Big Steve's lips. He loved it when I did as I was told. My parents loved it, too. I didn't get the appeal.

"Let's move it along," said Big Steve.

"Yes, of course. State the name you're commonly called," said Leonard.

"Mercy Watts." I almost said Marilyn, since I was a dead ringer for the late bombshell, Marilyn Monroe, and got called Marilyn as much as I did Mercy.

"Describe your relationship with Myrtle and Millicent Bled."

"I'm their goddaughter."

Defining my relationship to The Girls went on for another five minutes. I don't know what he was looking for and I wasn't sure he did either. Every deposition was the same. Who are you? What's your relationship? Who's decision was it that you attend Whitmore Academy? Who paid for it? Blah. Blah. Blah. But then it got interesting.

"What did your parents pay for the house on Hawthorne Avenue?" asked Leonard without looking up.

"It was a gift," I said.

"A gift from Myrtle and Millicent Bled to your parents whom they barely knew."

"Yes."

"Are you aware of the worth of the Hawthorne house at the time it was signed over?"

"No."

"Would it surprise you if I said that house was worth over seven hundred thousand dollars the year you were born?"

"No."

"You're not surprised that the Bled sisters gave away a seven-hundred-thousand-dollar house to strangers?"

"No."

"I'd be surprised."

"Is that a question?" I asked.

Big Steve's lips twitched. "She's not surprised. Next question."

"Are you aware that the Hawthorne house was signed over to your mother alone? That your father, Tommy Watts, is not in fact on the deed?"

"No."

"You thought it was signed over to both your parents?"

"I've never seen the deed and I never thought about it," I said, stifling a yawn.

"Do you know when exactly your parents met the Bled sisters?"

"No." What in the world was he getting at?

"Would it surprise you that at the time the deed for the Hawthorne house was signed over to your mother, Myrtle and Millicent Bled had never actually met your mother?"

That stopped me cold and I felt Big Steve stiffen beside me.

"Miss Watts, please answer the question," said Leonard with a smile. The goofy lost lawyer act was gone.

"I don't know that's true," I said.

"Did your mother tell you she had met the Bled sisters at the time the deed was signed over?"

"No."

"Why do you think that the Bled sisters gave such an expensive property to a woman they'd never met?"

"I don't know that's true," I said.

"Do you concede that the house was signed over to your mother?"

"No."

"Do you know what cases your father was working on at the time of this supposed gift?"

Supposed?

"No."

"Your father had just become a homicide detective on the St. Louis police force at the time of the signing of the deed. Correct?"

"I guess."

"You don't know?" asked Leonard with such smugness, I wanted to kick him in the shin, but Jay was taking it all down and looking pretty interested, too.

"I don't know the exact dates, since it was before I was born."

"You don't know the events surrounding the giving of this extraordinary house?"

"No."

"What did your parents tell you?"

"Nothing."

"Tommy Watts, a man known for his attention to detail, told you nothing about how your family got entrance into the exclusive world of Hawthorne Avenue?"

"No."

"I find that extraordinary."

Big Steve stood up and his chair flew backwards and hit the wall. "Your fifteen minutes is up." He took my arm and lifted me out of my seat.

"I'm not done," said Leonard.

"Then you should've been on time." Big Steve opened the conference room door and steered me through.

"She'll have to answer these questions."

"She has answered them. My patience is at an end."

We walked through the waiting room and were met by Lane, who handed me two large safety pins.

"For until you get home."

"Thanks," I said, my head still reeling from Leonard's insinuations.

"Did you pick out this dress?" asked Lane.

"My mother did."

"Burn it. It says everything you don't want to say."

"I will. Don't worry. Thank you."

Leonard came charging out of the conference room. "One more question, Miss Watts. How well did your father know Josiah Bled?"

I started to answer that I didn't know, but Lane stepped in front of Leonard. "You're late for court. The Rina case. The clerk has been calling."

Big Steve pushed me through the office door into the warm hall and began yelling into his phone as we walked to the elevator. "Freya, get Bub over to the office now and I want a list of every damn person in the squad when Watts made homicide." He took a breath. "Every person. Right down to the cleaning staff."

I pressed the elevator button and watched Big Steve order poor Freya to pull up his employee list for the same time period. My mom was his legal secretary for years and she would've been in his office when she got the house. He must've thought that someone in their circle had blabbed, but what could they possibly know? Dad always said the house was a thank-you. I gathered there was some kind of favor involved, but I always thought the truth was more special than that. Myrtle and Millicent fell in love with my parents. They adored them and my parents adored them right back. If Leonard thought the house was payment for some kind of illegal act on Dad's part, he was wrong. I'm not saying Dad wasn't above bending the rules or even breaking them. I'd seen him do it and it was always the right thing. My godmothers didn't pay Dad off. There was no way. If they had, it would've been a dirty back-alley deal. They'd never want to see him again. That didn't remotely happen. I was born in the Bled Mansion. The Girls babysat me, while Mom worked. They taught me to garden and bake, against my will but still. Mom was the one they called when they were sick or wanted to shop for ridiculous hats. Dad took care of their security system and fixed faucets for them. Whatever Leonard thought just simply couldn't have happened.

The elevator opened and Big Steve put his phone in his pocket. "I don't want you to worry about this."

"What exactly is this thing I'm not supposed to worry about?" I asked.

"The lawsuit."

"I'm not worried about the lawsuit. Myrtle and Millicent aren't incompetent. What's all this about the house?"

"Nothing to worry about."

Whenever someone says that, I know there's definitely something to worry about.

"Was that dillweed right? Is the house in Mom's name?"

Big Steve looked at the floor numbers slowly counting down.

"You know I can check. It's public record."

"She's on the deed."

"Alone?"

"Yes."

"Had she met The Girls at the time the house was signed over?"

The elevator hit the first floor and the doors started to open. I hit the stop button and an alarm clanged, echoing off the wood paneling.

"Did Mom meet them or not?"

"Mercy, that was twenty-six years ago."

"Don't pretend you don't know."

"Mercy."

"They're my parents, like it or not. I'm not going to tell anyone."

"It's better if you don't know anything. I won't have you lying under oath."

"So that's a no." I let go of the button, the alarm stopped, and the doors jerked open. A crowd stood there, looking as confused as I felt.

"Everything's fine," said Big Steve as he pushed through the crowd. *Yeah, right. I don't think so.*

He walked me to my truck and opened the door for me. "Don't worry. Tommy will dig up something on Brooks and the lawsuit will be a thing of the past."

That was supposed to make me feel better? It didn't. He might as well have said there was something to find out about our house.

I must've looked worried, because he put a heavy hand on my shoulder. "Your parents are good people. The best. Leonard has nothing."

"Come on. Leonard isn't fishing without bait," I said.

"He doesn't even have a hook. Trust me." He moved to close my door, but I blocked it.

"Did Dad know Josiah Bled personally?"

Big Steve grinned. "I have every confidence that you'll be able to figure that out."

He slammed my door and got into his big gold Lexus and squealed the tires on the way out of the parking lot probably yelling into his phone the whole time. Big Steve was right about most things and he was right about me. I'd figure it out eventually, but wouldn't it be nice if my parents would just tell me and save some time. I googled Josiah Bled on my phone and found his Wikipedia page. I'd seen it before, but it still seemed weird that The Girls' uncle had one. Josiah Bled was famous in his own way. First for being a Bled. The Bled Brewery was known all over the world and so was the fabulously rich family. Second for being a WWI flying ace and third being a spy in WWII. He was known to a lesser extent for building our house and The Girls' house. Pictures of both featured prominently on the page below his picture taken in France next to his bi-plane in 1917. He couldn't have been more dashing with his leather flying helmet and white silk scarf. Myrtle and Millicent said their uncle was bad in the best way possible and he looked it as he smiled a rakish smile at the camera, his eyes crinkled like a great joke had just been told.

I scrolled down to his dates. Josiah Aloysius Bled, born July 4, 1900, died unknown. What the heck? How could they not know? He was definitely dead. He'd be over a hundred and ten, if he wasn't. Come to think of it, I'd never seen his grave in the family plot. I wasn't looking for it, but The Girls took me to the family estate Prie-Dieu for picnics and they liked to visit the family. I didn't remember ever visiting Josiah Bled's grave. Maybe he was in Arlington cemetery or someplace like that, but everyone else was in the family plot, no matter where they died or how. Why would the much loved Josiah be any different?

I called Prie-Dieu to ask and got the answering machine. Since their accounts were frozen, The Girls were staying at the old estate to save money. They spent most of their time tending the grounds and giving tours since the mansion was in trust to the Missouri Historical Society. They'd never been so busy.

Then I tried Dad's cell and Mom's. I got voicemail on both. The home office was a lock. Claire, my old high school rival, had taken over after I did a favor for her in exchange for her transcription skills. She practically lived in Dad's office. He was now a private detective and he'd never been so organized. My parents loved Claire. She was the daughter they never had. Obedient, respectful, and quiet. She did absolutely everything they said right down to her dating life. Dad checked out all potential suitors, so Claire hadn't had a date in six months, which was a good thing. If there was a loser con artist in the vicinity, Claire would find him.

"Hey, Claire," I said. "I'm trying to get ahold of my parents, but they're not answering."

"Hi, Mercy. Let me see. That's right. Your dad's chasing a child molester in Jeff City and your mom's testifying in front of the grand jury in Cleveland. Do you want to leave a message in case they get in touch?"

"Will Dad be back tonight?"

"I doubt it. If he gets the guy, he'll follow the arrest through."

"What about Mom? We're supposed to leave in two days."

"She's flying back tomorrow, assuming the indictment goes through. Why? Is something wrong?"

Is something wrong? Not exactly.

"No. Everything's fine. But you've been going through Dad's files reorganizing, right?" I asked.

"Yes. They were a mess."

"Did you perhaps find anything about our house? Maybe some notes?"

Claire got cagey. "What are you looking for?"

"Nothing in particular, just what was going on around the time The Girls gave it to us."

"You'll have to be more specific."

Groan.

"What was Dad working on back then?" I asked.

"He was a police detective."

"I know. He kept every single notebook he used during his career. I just want to know what he was working on."

"I'm afraid I can't tell you," said Claire.

"Why the heck not?"

"I signed a confidentiality agreement."

"I'm his kid. I think you can tell me what cases he was working on before I was born."

"I can't. The agreement was very specific. You're mentioned by name."

"Dad had you sign an agreement not to tell me stuff? Seriously?"

"I can't tell anyone else either, if that makes you feel better," said Claire.

"It doesn't."

"Before you go, I have a message from your mom."

Groan.

"You have to go shopping for appropriate cruise wear today. She's tired of your procrastination. Sheila at Forever Summer is expecting you."

"What in the world is appropriate cruise wear?"

"I have a list for you."

Great. More dresses that fall apart.

"Never mind. I'll figure it out." I hung up and started up my ancient truck. The engine roared in a most satisfying way and the familiar vibrations rumbled through my generous rump, but I didn't know exactly where to go from there. My parents were hiding something and Claire knew what it was. That just sucked.

Read the rest in
Diver Down (Mercy Watts Mysteries Book Two)

A.W. HARTOIN'S NEWSLETTER

To be the first to hear all about the A.W. Hartoin news and new releases click the link or scan the QR code to join the mailing list. Only sales, news, and new releases. No spam. Spam is evil.

Newsletter sign-up

ALSO BY A.W. HARTOIN

Afterlife Issues

Dead Companions (Afterlife Issues Book One)

A Trunk, a Canoe, and all the Barbecue (Afterlife Issues Book Two)

Old Friends and Fedoras (Afterlife Issues Book Three)

Mercy Watts Mysteries

Novels

A Good Man Gone (Mercy Watts Mysteries Book One)

Diver Down (A Mercy Watts Mystery Book Two)

Double Black Diamond (Mercy Watts Mysteries Book Three)

Drop Dead Red (Mercy Watts Mysteries Book Four)

In the Worst Way (Mercy Watts Mysteries Book Five)

The Wife of Riley (Mercy Watts Mysteries Book Six)

My Bad Grandad (Mercy Watts Mysteries Book Seven)

Brain Trust (Mercy Watts Mysteries Book Eight)

Down and Dirty (Mercy Watts Mysteries Book Nine)

Small Time Crime (Mercy Watts Mysteries Book Ten)

Bottle Blonde (Mercy Watts Mysteries Book Eleven)

Mean Evergreen (Mercy Watts Mysteries Book Twelve)

Silver Bells at Hotel Hell (Mercy Watts Mysteries Book Thirteen)

Short stories

Coke with a Twist

Touch and Go

Nowhere Fast

Dry Spell

A Sin and a Shame

Stella Bled Historical Thrillers

The Paris Package (Stella Bled Book One)

Strangers in Venice (Stella Bled Book Two)

One Child in Berlin (Stella Bled Book Three)

Dark Victory (Stella Bled Book Four)

A Quiet Little Place on Rue de Lille (Stella Bled Book Five)

Her London Season (Stella Bled Book Six)

Paranormal

It Started with a Whisper

Young Adult fantasy

Flare-up (Away From Whipplethorn Short)

A Fairy's Guide To Disaster (Away From Whipplethorn Book One)

Fierce Creatures (Away From Whipplethorn Book Two)

A Monster's Paradise (Away From Whipplethorn Book Three)

A Wicked Chill (Away From Whipplethorn Book Four)

To the Eternal (Away From Whipplethorn Book Five)

ABOUT THE AUTHOR

USA Today bestselling author A.W. Hartoin grew up in rural Missouri, but her grandmother lived in the Central West End area of St. Louis. The CWE fascinated her with its enormous houses, every one unique. She was sure there was a story behind each ornate door. Going to Grandma's house was a treat and an adventure. As the only grandchild around for many years, A.W. spent her visits exploring the many rooms with their many secrets. That's how Mercy Watts and the fairies of Whipplethorn came to be.

As an adult, A.W. Hartoin decided she needed a whole lot more life experience if She was going to write good characters so she joined the Air Force. It was the best education she could've hoped for. She met her husband and traveled the world, living in Alaska, Italy, and Germany before settling in Colorado for nearly eleven years. Now A.W. has returned to Germany and lives in picturesque Waldenbuch with her family and two spoiled cats, who absolutely believe they should be allowed to escape and roam the village freely.

Made in the USA
Middletown, DE
20 August 2023

37041758R00179